Nora Roberts is the *New York Times* bestselling author of more than one hundred and ninety novels. A born storyteller, she creates a blend of warmth, humour and poignancy that speaks directly to her readers and has earned her almost every award for excellence in her field. The youngest of five children, Nora Roberts lives in western Maryland. She has two sons.

Visit her website at www.noraroberts.com

D1152619

Nora Roberts

Christmas in the Snow

Containing *Taming Natasha*
& *Considering Kate*

MILLS &
BOON

This edition published in Great Britain 2017
By Mills & Boon, an imprint of HarperCollins*Publishers*
1 London Bridge Street, London, SE1 9GF

CHRISTMAS IN THE SNOW © Harlequin Books S.A. 2017
Taming Natasha © 1990 Nora Roberts
Considering Kate © 2001 Nora Roberts

ISBN: 978-0-263-93139-6

29-1017

MIX
Paper from
responsible sources
FSC® C007454

Printed and bound in Great Britain
by CPI Group (UK) Ltd, Croydon, CR0 4YY

Taming Natasha

For Gayle Link. Welcome to the fold

Chapter 1

"Why is it that all the really great-looking men are married?"

"Is that a trick question?" Natasha arranged a velvet-gowned doll in a child-sized bentwood rocker before she turned to her assistant. "Okay, Annie, what great-looking man are we talking about in particular?"

"The tall, blond and gorgeous one who's standing outside the shop window with his nifty-looking wife and beautiful little girl." Annie tucked a wad of gum into her cheek and heaved a gusty sigh. "They look like an ad for *Perfect Family Digest*."

"Then perhaps they'll come in and buy the perfect toy."

Natasha stepped back from her grouping of Victorian dolls and accessories with a nod of approval. It looked exactly as she wanted—appealing, elegant and old-fashioned. She checked everything down to the tasseled fan in a tiny, china hand.

The toy store wasn't just her business, it was her greatest pleasure. Everything from the smallest rattle to the biggest stuffed bear was chosen by her with the same eye for detail and quality. She insisted on the best for her shop and her customers, whether it was a five-hundred-dollar doll with its own fur wrap or a two-dollar, palm-sized race car. When the match was right, she was pleased to ring up either sale.

In the three years since she had opened her jingling front door, Natasha had made The Fun House one of the most thriving concerns in the small college town on the West Virginia border. It had taken drive and persistence, but her success was more a direct result of her innate understanding of children. She didn't want her clients to walk out with a toy. She wanted them to walk out with the right toy.

Deciding to make a few adjustments, Natasha moved over to a display of miniature cars.

"I think they're going to come in," Annie was saying as she smoothed down her short crop of auburn hair. "The little girl's practically bouncing out of her Mary Janes. Want me to open up?"

Always precise, Natasha glanced at the grinning clown clock overhead. "We have five minutes yet."

"What's five minutes? Tash, I'm telling you this guy is incredible." Wanting a closer look, Annie edged down an aisle to restack board games. "Oh, yes. Six foot two, a hundred and sixty pounds. The best shoulders I've ever seen fill out a suit jacket. Oh Lord, it's tweed. I didn't know a guy in tweed could make me salivate."

"A man in cardboard can make you salivate."

"Most of the guys I know *are* cardboard." A dimple winked at the corner of Annie's mouth. She peeked around the counter of wooden toys to see if he was still at the window. "He must have spent some time at the beach this summer. His hair's sun-streaked and he's got a fabulous tan. Oh, God, he smiled at the little girl. I think I'm in love."

Choreographing a scaled-down traffic jam, Natasha smiled. "You always think you're in love."

"I know." Annie sighed. "I wish I could see the color of his eyes. He's got one of those wonderfully lean and bony faces. I'm sure he's incredibly intelligent and has suffered horribly."

Natasha shot a quick, amused look over her shoulder. Annie, with her tall, skinny build had a heart as soft as marshmallow cream. "I'm sure his wife would be fascinated with your fantasy."

"It's a woman's privilege—no, her obligation—to weave fantasies over men like that."

Though she couldn't have disagreed more, Natasha let Annie have her way. "All right then. Go ahead and open up."

"One doll," Spence said, giving his daughter's ear a tug. "I might have thought twice about moving into that house, if I'd realized there was a toy store a half mile away."

"You'd buy her the bloody toy store if you had your way."

He spared one glance for the woman beside him. "Don't start, Nina."

The slender blonde shrugged her shoulders, rippling the trim, rose linen jacket of her suit, then looked at the little girl. "I just meant your daddy tends to spoil you because he loves you so much. Besides, you deserve a present for being so good about the move."

Little Frederica Kimball's bottom lip pouted. "I like my new house." She slipped her hand into her father's, automatically aligning herself with him and against the world. "I have a yard and a swing set all of my own."

Nina looked them over, the tall, rangy man and the fairy-sized young girl. They had identical stubborn chins. As far as she could remember, she'd never won an argument with either one.

"I suppose I'm the only one who doesn't see that as an advantage over living in New York." Nina's tone warmed slightly as she stroked the girl's hair. "I can't help worrying about you a little bit. I really only want you to be happy, darling. You and your daddy."

"We are." To break the tension, Spence swung Freddie into his arms. "Aren't we, funny face?"

"She's about to be that much happier." Relenting, Nina gave Spence's hand a squeeze. "They're opening."

"Good morning." They were gray, Annie noted, biting back a long, dreamy, "Ahh." A glorious gray. She tucked her little fantasy into the back of her mind and ushered in the first customers of the day. "May I help you?"

"My daughter's interested in a doll." Spence set Freddie on her feet again.

"Well, you've come to the right place." Annie dutifully switched her attention to the child. She really was a cute little thing, with her father's gray eyes and pale, flyaway blond hair. "What kind of doll would you like?"

"A pretty one," Freddie answered immediately. "A pretty one with red hair and blue eyes."

"I'm sure we have just what you want." She offered a hand. "Would you like to look around?"

After a glance at her father for approval, Freddie linked hands with Annie and wandered off.

"Damn it." Spence found himself wincing.

Nina squeezed his hand for the second time. "Spence—"

"I delude myself thinking that it doesn't matter, that she doesn't even remember."

"Just because she wanted a doll with red hair and blue eyes doesn't mean anything."

"Red hair and blue eyes," he repeated; the frustration welled up once more. "Just like Angela's. She remembers, Nina. And it does matter." Stuffing his hands into his pockets he walked away.

Three years, he thought. It had been nearly three years now. Freddie had still been in diapers. But she remembered Angela—beautiful, careless Angela. Not even the most liberal critic would have considered Angela a mother. She had never cuddled or crooned, never rocked or soothed.

He studied a small, porcelain-faced doll dressed in

pale, angelic blue. Tiny, tapering fingers, huge, dreamy eyes. Angela had been like that, he remembered. Ethereally beautiful. And cold as glass.

He had loved her as a man might love a piece of art—distantly admiring the perfection of form, and constantly searching for the meaning beneath it. Between them they had somehow created a warm, gorgeous child who had managed to find her way through the first years of her life almost without help from her parents.

But he would make it up to her. Spence shut his eyes for a moment. He intended to do everything in his power to give his daughter the love, the structure and the security she deserved. The realness. The word seemed trite, but it was the only one he could find that described what he wanted for his daughter—the real, the solid bond of family.

She loved him. He felt some of the tension ease from his shoulders as he thought of the way Freddie's big eyes would shine when he tucked her in at night, at the way her arms would wrap tightly around him when he held her. Perhaps he would never fully forgive himself for being so involved with his own problems, his own life during her infancy, but things had changed. Even this move had been made with her welfare in mind.

He heard her laugh, and the rest of the tension dissolved on a wave of pure pleasure. There was no sweeter music than his little girl's laugh. An entire symphony could be written around it. He wouldn't disturb her yet, Spence thought. Let her indulge herself with the bright and beautiful dolls, before he had to remind her that only one could be hers.

Relaxed again, he began to pay attention to the shop. Like the dolls he'd imagined for his daughter, it was bright and beautiful. Though small, it was packed from wall to wall with everything a child might covet. A big golden giraffe and a sad-eyed purple dog hung from the ceiling. Wooden trains, cars and planes, all painted in bold colors, jockeyed for position on a long display table with elegant miniature furniture. An old-fashioned jack-in-the-box sat beside an intricate scale model of a futuristic space station. There were dolls, some beautiful, some charmingly homely, erector sets and tea sets.

The lack of studied arrangement made the result all the more appealing. This was a place to pretend and to wish, a crowded Aladdin's cave designed to make children's eyes light in wonder. To make them laugh, as his daughter was laughing now. He could already foresee that he'd be hard-pressed to keep Freddie from making regular visits.

That was one of the reasons he'd made the move to a small town. He wanted his daughter to be able to reap the pleasures of local shops, where the merchants would know her name. She would be able to walk from one end of town to the other without those big-city worries about muggings, abductions and drugs. There would be no need for dead bolts and security systems, for "white noise" machines to block out the surge and grind of traffic. Even a girl as little as his Freddie wouldn't be swallowed up here.

And perhaps, without the pace and the pressure, he would make peace with himself.

Idly he picked up a music box. It was of delicately crafted porcelain, graced with a figure of a raven-haired Gypsy woman in a flounced red dress. In her ears were tiny gold loops, and in her hands a tambourine with colored streamers. He was certain he wouldn't have found anything more skillfully made on Fifth Avenue.

He wondered how the owner could leave it out where small, curious fingers might reach and break. Intrigued, he turned the key and watched the figure revolve around the tiny, china campfire.

Tchaikovsky. He recognized the movement instantly, and his skilled ear approved the quality of tone. A moody, even passionate piece, he thought, finding it strange to come across such exquisite workmanship in a toy store. Then he glanced up and saw Natasha.

He stared. He couldn't help it. She was standing a few feet away, her head up, slightly tilted as she watched him. Her hair was as dark as the dancer's and corkscrewed around her face in a wild disarray that flowed beyond her shoulders. Her skin was a dark, rich gold that was set off by the simple red dress she wore.

But this woman was not fragile, he thought. Though she was small, he got the impression of power. Perhaps it was her face, with its full, unpainted mouth and high, slashing cheekbones. Her eyes were almost as dark as her hair, heavy-lidded and thickly lashed. Even from a distance of ten feet he sensed it. Strong, undiluted sex. It surrounded her as other women surrounded themselves with perfumes.

For the first time in years he felt the muscle-numbing heat of pure desire.

Natasha saw it, then recognized and resented it. What kind of man, she wondered, walked into a room with his wife and daughter, then looked at another woman with naked hunger in his eyes?

Not her kind.

Determined to ignore the look as she had ignored it from others in the past, she crossed to him. "Do you need some help?"

Help? Spence thought blankly. He needed oxygen. He hadn't known it was literally possible for a woman to take a man's breath away. "Who are you?"

"Natasha Stanislaski." She offered her coolest smile. "I own the store."

Her voice seemed to hang in the air, husky, vital, with a trace of her Slavic origins adding eroticism as truly as the music still playing behind him. She smelled of soap, nothing more, yet the fragrance completely seduced him.

When he didn't speak, she lifted a brow. It might have been amusing to knock a man off his feet, but she was busy at the moment, and the man was married. "Your daughter has her selection down to three dolls. Perhaps you'd like to help her with her final choice."

"In a minute. Your accent—is it Russian?"

"Yes." She wondered if she should tell him his wife was standing near the front door, bored and impatient.

"How long have you been in America?"

"Since I was six." She aimed a deliberately cold glance. "About the same age as your little girl. Excuse me—"

He had his hand on her arm before he could stop himself. Even though he knew the move was a bad one, the venom in her eyes surprised him. "Sorry. I was going to ask you about this music box."

Natasha shifted her gaze to it as the music began to wind down. "It's one of our best, handcrafted here in the States. Are you interested in buying it?"

"I haven't decided, but I thought you might not have realized it was sitting out on that shelf."

"Why?"

"It's not the kind of merchandise one expects to find in a toy store. It could easily be broken."

Natasha took it and placed it farther back on the shelf. "And it can be mended." She made a quick, clearly habitual movement with her shoulders. It spoke of arrogance rather than carelessness. "I believe children should be allowed the pleasures of music, don't you?"

"Yes." For the first time a smile flickered over his face. It was, as Annie had noted, a particularly effective one, Natasha had to admit. Through her annoyance she felt the trickle of attraction, and strangely, kinship. Then he said, "As a matter of fact, I believe that quite strongly. Perhaps we could discuss it over dinner."

Holding herself rigid, Natasha battled back fury. It was difficult for one with her hot, often turbulent nature, but she reminded herself that the man had not only his wife, but his young daughter in the store.

The angry insults that rose to her throat were swallowed, but not before Spence saw them reflected in her eyes.

"No," was all she said as she turned.

"Miss—" Spence began, then Freddie whirled down the aisle, carrying a big, floppy Raggedy Ann.

"Daddy, isn't she nice?" Eyes shining, she held out the doll for his approval.

It was redheaded, Spence thought. But it was anything but beautiful. Nor, to his relief, was it a symbol of Angela. Because he knew Freddie expected it, he took his time examining her choice. "This is," he said after a moment, "the very best doll I've seen today."

"Really?"

He crouched until he was eye to eye with his daughter. "Absolutely. You have excellent taste, funny face."

Freddie reached out, crushing the doll between them as she hugged her father. "I can have her?"

"I thought she was for me." As Freddie giggled, he picked up the pair of them.

"I'll be happy to wrap her for you." Natasha's tone was warmer, she knew. He might be a jerk, but he loved his daughter.

"I can carry her." Freddie squeezed her new friend close.

"All right. Then I'll just give you a ribbon for her hair. Would you like that?"

"A blue one."

"A blue one it is." Natasha led the way to the cash register.

Nina took one look at the doll and rolled her eyes. "Darling, is that the best you could do?"

"Daddy likes her," Freddie murmured, ducking her head.

"Yes, I do. Very much," he added with a telling look for Nina. Setting Freddie on her feet again, he fished out his wallet.

The mother was certainly no prize, Natasha decided. Though that didn't give the man a right to come on to a clerk in a toy store. She made change and handed over the receipt, then took out a length of blue ribbon.

"Thank you," she said to Freddie. "I think she's going to like her new home with you very much."

"I'll take good care of her," Freddie promised, while she struggled to tie the ribbon through the yarn mop of hair. "Can people come in to look at the toys, or do they have to buy one?"

Natasha smiled, then taking another ribbon, tied a quick, sassy bow in the child's hair. "You can come in and look anytime you like."

"Spence, we really must be going." Nina stood holding the door open.

"Right." He hesitated. It was a small town, he reminded himself. And if Freddie could come in and look, so could he. "It was nice meeting you, Miss Stanislaski."

"Goodbye." She waited until the door jingled and closed, then let out a muttered stream of curses.

Annie peeked around a tower of building blocks. "Excuse me?"

"That man."

"Yes." With a little sigh, Annie waltzed down the aisle. "That man."

"He brings his wife and child into a place like this, then looks at me as if he wants to nibble on my toes."

"Tash." Her expression pained, Annie pressed a hand to her heart. "Please don't excite me."

"I find it insulting." She skirted around the checkout counter and swung a fist at a punching bag. "He asked me to dinner."

"He *what*?" Delight showed in Annie's eyes, before a look from Natasha dampened it. "You're right. It is insulting, seeing as he's a married man—even though his wife seemed like a cold fish."

"His marital problems are no concern of mine."

"No...." Practicality warred with fantasy. "I guess you turned him down."

A choked sound caught in Natasha's throat as she turned. "Of course I turned him down."

"I mean, of course," Annie put in quickly.

"The man has a nerve," Natasha said; her fingers itched to hit something. "Coming into my place of business and propositioning me."

"He didn't!" Scandalized and thrilled, Annie grabbed Natasha's arm. "Tash, he didn't really proposition you? Right here?"

"With his eyes he did. The message was clear." It infuriated her how often men looked at her and only saw the physical. Only wanted to see the physical, she thought in disgust. She had tolerated suggestions, propositions and proposals since before she had fully understood what they meant. But she understood now and tolerated nothing.

"If he hadn't had that sweet little girl with him, I would have slapped his face." Because the image pleased her so much, she let loose on the hapless punching bag again.

Annie had seen her employer's temper fly often enough to know how to cool it. "She was sweet, wasn't she? Her name's Freddie. Isn't that cute?"

Natasha took a long, steadying breath even as she rubbed her fisted hand in her other palm. "Yes."

"She told me they had just moved to Shepherdstown from New York. The doll was going to be her first new friend."

"Poor little thing." Natasha knew too well the fears and anxieties of being a child in a strange place. Forget the father, she told herself with a toss of her head. "She looks to be about the same age as JoBeth Riley." Annoyance forgotten, Natasha went behind the counter again and picked up the phone. It wouldn't hurt to give Mrs. Riley a call.

Spence stood at the music-room window and stared out at a bed of summer flowers. Having flowers outside the window and a bumpy slope of lawn that would need tending was a new experience. He'd never cut grass in his life. Smiling to himself, he wondered how soon he could try his hand at it.

There was a big, spreading maple, its leaves a dark, dark green. In a few weeks, he imagined they would grow red and vibrant before they tumbled from the branches. He had enjoyed the view from his condo on Central Park West, watching the seasons come and go with the changing trees. But not like this, he realized.

Here the grass, the trees, the flowers he saw belonged to him. They were for him to enjoy and to care for. Here he could let Freddie take out her dolls for an afternoon tea party and not have to worry every second she was out of his sight. They would make a good life here, a solid life for both of them. He'd felt it when he'd flown down to discuss his position with the dean—and again when he'd walked through this big, rambling house with the anxious real-estate agent dogging his heels.

She hadn't had to sell it, Spence thought. He'd been sold the moment he'd walked in the front door.

As he watched, a hummingbird swooped to hover at the cup of a bright red petunia. In that instant he was more convinced than ever that his decision to leave the city had been the right one.

Having a brief fling with rural living. Nina's words rolled through his mind as he watched the sun flash on the bird's iridescent wings. It was difficult to blame her for saying it, for believing it when he had always chosen to live in the middle of things. He couldn't deny he had enjoyed those glittery parties that had lasted until dawn, or the elegant midnight suppers after a symphony or ballet.

He had been born into a world of glamour and wealth and prestige. He had lived all of his life in a place where only the best was acceptable. And he had relished it,

Spence admitted. Summering in Monte Carlo, wintering in Nice or Cannes. Weekends in Aruba or Cancun.

He wouldn't wish those experiences away, but he could wish, and did, that he had accepted the responsibilities of his life sooner.

He accepted them now. Spence watched the hummingbird streak away like a sapphire bullet. And as much to his own surprise as to that of people who knew him, he was enjoying those responsibilities. Freddie made the difference. All the difference.

He thought of her and she came running across the back lawn, her new rag doll tucked under her arm. She made a beeline, as he expected, to the swing set. It was so new that the blue and white paint gleamed in the sunlight, and the hard plastic seats were shiny as leather. With the doll in her lap, she pushed off, her face lifted skyward, her tiny mouth moving to some private song.

Love rammed into him with a velvet fist, solid and painful. In all of his life he had never known anything as consuming or as basic as the emotion she brought to him simply by being.

As she glided back and forth, she cuddled the doll, bringing her close to whisper secrets into her ear. It pleased him to see Freddie so taken with the cloth and cotton doll. She could have chosen china or velvet, but had picked something that looked as though it needed love.

She'd spoken of the toy store throughout the morning, and was wishing, Spence knew, for a return trip. Oh, she wouldn't ask for anything, he thought. Not directly. She would use her eyes. It both amused and baffled him that at five, his little girl had already mastered that peculiar and effective feminine trick.

He'd thought of the toy store himself, and its owner. No feminine tricks there, just pure womanly disdain. It made him wince again to remember how clumsy he'd been. Out of practice, he reminded himself with a self-deprecating smile and rubbed a hand over the back of his neck. What was more, he couldn't remember ever experiencing that strong a sexual punch. It was like being hit by lightning, he decided. A man was entitled to fumble a bit after being electrified.

But her reaction... Frowning, Spence replayed the scene in his mind. She'd been furious. She'd damn near been quivering with fury before he'd opened his mouth—and put his foot in it.

She hadn't even attempted to be polite in her refusal. Just no—a single hard syllable crusted with frost at the edges. It wasn't as if he'd asked her to go to bed with him.

But he'd wanted to. From the first instant he had been able to imagine carrying her off to some dark, remote spot in the woods, where the ground was springy with moss and the trees blocked out the sky. There he could take the heat of those full, sulky lips. There he could indulge in the wild passion her face promised. Wild, mindless sex, heedless of time or place, of right or wrong.

Good God. Amazed, he pulled himself back. He was thinking like a teenager. No, Spence admitted, thrusting his hands into his pockets again. He was thinking like a man—one who had gone four years without a woman. He wasn't certain if he wanted to thank Natasha Stanislaski for unlocking all those needs again, or throttle her.

But he was certain he was going to see her again.

"I'm all packed." Nina paused in the doorway. She gave a little sigh; Spence was clearly absorbed in his own thoughts again. "Spencer," she said, raising her voice as she crossed the room. "I said I'm all packed."

"What? Oh." He managed a distracted smile and forced his shoulders to relax. "We'll miss you, Nina."

"You'll be glad to see the back of me," she corrected, then gave him a quick peck on the cheek.

"No." His smile came easier now, she saw, dutifully wiping the faint trace of lipstick from his skin. "I appreciate all you've done to help us settle in. I know how tight your schedule is."

"I could hardly let my brother tackle the wilds of West Virginia alone." She took his hand in a rare show of genuine agitation. "Oh, Spence, are you sure? Forget everything I've said before and think, really think it through. It's such a big change, for both of you. What will you possibly do here in your free time?"

"Cut the grass." Now he grinned at her expression. "Sit on the porch. Maybe I'll even write music again."

"You could write in New York."

"I haven't written two bars in almost four years," he reminded her.

"All right." She walked to the piano and waved a hand. "But if you wanted a change, you could have found a place on Long Island or even in Connecticut."

"I like it here, Nina. Believe me, this is the best thing I could do for Freddie, and myself."

"I hope you're right." Because she loved him, she smiled again. "I still say you'll be back in New York within six months. In the meantime, as that child's only aunt, I expect to be kept apprised of her progress." She glanced down, annoyed to see a chip in her nail polish. "The idea of her attending public school—"

"Nina."

"Never mind." She held up a hand. "There's no use starting this argument when I have a plane to catch. And I'm quite aware she's your child."

"Yes, she is."

Nina tapped a finger on the glossy surface of the baby grand. "Spence, I know you're still carrying around guilt because of Angela. I don't like to see it."

His easy smile vanished. "Some mistakes take a long time to be erased."

"She made you miserable," Nina said flatly. "There were problems within the first year of your marriage. Oh, you weren't forthcoming with information," she added when he didn't respond. "But there were others all too eager to pass it along to me or anyone else who would listen. It was no secret that she didn't want the child."

"And how much better was I, wanting the baby only because I thought it would fill the gaps in my marriage? That's a large burden to hand a child."

"You made mistakes. You recognized them and you rectified them. Angela never suffered a pang of guilt in her life. If she hadn't died, you would have divorced her and taken custody of Freddie. The result's the same. I know that sounds cold. The truth often is. I don't like to think that you're making this move, changing your life this dramatically because you're trying to make up for something that's long over."

"Maybe that's part of it. But there's more." He held out a hand, waiting until Nina came to him. "Look at her." He pointed out the window to where Freddie continued to swing high, free as the hummingbird. "She's happy. And so am I."

Chapter 2

"I'm not scared."

"Of course you're not." Spence looked at his daughter's brave reflection in the mirror while he carefully braided her hair. He didn't need the quaver in her voice to tell him she was terrified. There was a rock in the pit of his own stomach the size of a fist.

"Some of the kids might cry." Her big eyes were already misted. "But I won't."

"You're going to have fun." He wasn't any more certain of that than his nervous daughter. The trouble with being a parent, he thought, was that you were supposed to sound sure of everything. "The first day of school's always a little scary, but once you get there and meet everyone, you'll have a great time."

She fixed him with a steady, owlish stare. "Really?"

"You liked kindergarten, didn't you?" It was evasive,

he admitted to himself, but he couldn't make promises he might not be able to keep.

"Mostly." She lowered her eyes, poking at the yellow, sea horse-shaped comb on her dresser. "But Amy and Pam won't be there."

"You'll make new friends. You've already met Jo-Beth." He thought of the pixieish brunette who had strolled by the house with her mother a couple of days before.

"I guess, and JoBeth is nice, but…" How could she explain that JoBeth already knew all of the other girls? "Maybe I should wait till tomorrow."

Their eyes met in the mirror again; he rested his chin on her shoulder. She smelled of the pale green soap she loved because it was shaped like a dinosaur. Her face was so much like his own, yet softer, finer, and to him infinitely beautiful.

"You could, but then tomorrow would be your first day of school. You'd still have butterflies."

"Butterflies?"

"Right here." He patted her tummy. "Doesn't it feel like butterflies dancing in there?"

That made her giggle. "Kind of."

"I've got them, too."

"Really?" Her eyes opened wide.

"Really. I've got to go to school this morning, just like you."

She fiddled with the pink ribbons he'd tied on the ends of her pigtails. She knew it wasn't the same for him, but didn't say so because she was afraid he'd get that worried look. Freddie had heard him talking to Aunt Nina once, and remembered how impatient he had sounded when she'd complained that he was uprooting *her niece* during her formative years.

Freddie wasn't sure exactly what formative years were, but she knew her daddy had been upset, and that even when Aunt Nina had gone again, he'd still had that worried look. She didn't want to make him worried, or to make him think Aunt Nina was right. If they went back to New York, the only swing sets were in the park.

Besides, she liked the big house and her new room. Even better, her father's new job was so close, he would be home every night long before dinner. Remembering not to pout, Freddie decided that since she wanted to stay, she'd have to go to school.

"Will you be here when I get home?"

"I think so. But if I'm not, Vera will be," he said, thinking of their longtime housekeeper. "You can tell me everything that happened." After kissing the top of her head, he set her on her feet. She looked achingly small in her pink and white playsuit. Her gray eyes were solemn, her bottom lip trembling. He fought back the urge to gather her up and promise that she'd never have to go to school or anywhere else that frightened her. "Let's go see what Vera packed in your new lunch box."

Twenty minutes later he was standing on the curb, holding Freddie's hand in his own. With almost as much dread as his daughter he saw the big yellow school bus lumbering over the hill.

He should have driven her to school, he thought in

sudden panic—at least for the first few days. He should take her himself, instead of putting her onto that bus with strangers. Yet it had seemed better to make the whole event normal, to let her ease into the group and become one of them from the outset.

How could he let her go? She was just a baby. *His baby.* What if he was wrong? This wasn't just a matter of picking out the wrong color dress for her. Simply because it was the designated day and time, he was going to tell his daughter to get onto that bus, then walk away.

What if the driver was careless and drove off a cliff? How could he be sure someone would make certain Freddie got back onto the right bus that afternoon?

The bus rumbled to a halt and his fingers tightened instinctively on hers. When the door clattered open, he was almost ready to make a run for it.

"Hi, there." The driver, a large woman with a wide smile, nodded at him. Behind her, children were yelling and bouncing on the seats. "You must be Professor Kimball."

"Yes." He had excuses for not putting Freddie on the bus on the tip of his tongue.

"I'm Dorothy Mansfield. The kids just call me Miss D. And you must be Frederica."

"Yes, ma'am." She bit her bottom lip to keep from turning away and hiding her face against her father's side. "It's Freddie."

"Whew." Miss D gave another big grin. "I'm glad to hear that. Frederica sure is a mouthful. Well, hop aboard, Freddie girl. This is the big day. John Harman, you give that book back to Mikey, less'n you want to sit behind me in the hot seat the rest of the week."

Eyes swimming, Freddie put one foot onto the first step. Swallowing, she climbed the second.

"Why don't you take a seat with JoBeth and Lisa there?" Miss D suggested kindly. She turned back to Spence with a wink and a wave. "Don't worry about a thing, Professor. We'll take good care of her."

The door closed on a puff of air, then the bus rumbled ahead. Spence could only stand on the curb and watch it take his little girl away.

He wasn't exactly idle. Spence's time was eaten up almost from the moment he walked into the college. He had his own schedule to study, associates to meet, instruments and sheet music to pore over. There was a faculty meeting, a hurried lunch in the lounge, and there were papers, dozens of papers to read and digest. It was a familiar routine, one that he had begun three years before when he'd taken a post at the Juilliard School. But like Freddie, he was the new kid in town, and it was up to him to make the adjustments.

He worried about her. At lunchtime he imagined her sitting in the school cafeteria, a room that smelled of peanut butter and waxy cartons of milk. She would be huddled at the end of a table scattered with crumbs, alone, miserable, while other children laughed and joked with their friends. He could see her at recess, standing apart and looking on longingly, while the others raced and shouted and climbed like spiders on jungle gyms.

The trauma would leave her insecure and unhappy for the rest of her life.

All because he'd put her onto that damn yellow bus.

By the end of the day he was feeling as guilty as a child abuser, certain his little girl would come home in tears, devastated by the rigors of the first day of school. More than once he asked himself if Nina had been right all along. Perhaps he should have left well enough alone and stayed in New York, where at least Freddie had had friends and the familiar.

With his briefcase in one hand and his jacket slung over his shoulder, he started for home. It was hardly more than a mile, and the weather remained unseasonably warm. Until winter hit, he would take advantage of it and walk to and from campus.

He had already fallen in love with the town. There were pretty shops and rambling old houses all along the tree-lined main street. It was a college town and proud of it, but it was equally proud of its age and dignity. The street climbed, and here and there the sidewalk showed cracks where tree roots had undermined it. Though there were cars passing, it was quiet enough to hear the bark of a dog or the music from a radio. A woman weeding marigolds along her walkway looked up and waved at him. Cheered, Spence waved back.

She didn't even know him, he thought. But she had waved. He looked forward to seeing her again, planting bulbs perhaps, or sweeping snow from her porch. He could smell chrysanthemums. For some reason that alone gave him a shot of pleasure.

No, he hadn't made a mistake. He and Freddie belonged here. In less than a week it had become home.

He stopped on the curb to wait for a laboring sedan to pass, and glancing across the street saw the sign for The Fun House. It was perfect, Spence thought. The perfect name. It conjured up laughter and surprises, just as the window display with its building blocks, chubby-cheeked dolls and shiny red cars promised a childhood treasure trove. At the moment he could think of nothing he wanted more than to find something that would bring a smile to his daughter's face.

You spoil her.

He could hear Nina's voice clearly in his ears.

So what? Glancing quickly up and down the street, he crossed to the opposite curb. His little girl had walked onto the school bus as bravely as any soldier marching into battle. There was no harm in buying her a small medal.

The door jingled as he entered. There was a scent, as cheerful as the sound of the bells. Peppermint, he thought and smiled. It delighted him to hear the tinny strains of "The Merry-Go-Round Broke Down," coming from the rear of the shop.

"I'll be right with you."

He had forgotten, Spence realized, how that voice could cruise along the air.

He wouldn't make a fool of himself again. This time he was prepared for what she looked like, sounded like, smelled like. He had come in to buy a present for his daughter, not to flirt with the proprietor. Then he grinned into the face of a forlorn panda. There didn't seem to be any law against doing both.

"I'm sure Bonnie will love it," Natasha said as she carried the miniature carousel for her customer. "It's a beautiful birthday present."

"She saw it in here a few weeks ago and hasn't been able to talk about anything else." Bonnie's grandmother tried not to grimace at the price. "I guess she's old enough to take care of it."

"Bonnie's a very responsible girl," Natasha went on, then spotted Spence at the counter. "I'll be right with you." The temperature of her voice dropped a cool twenty degrees.

"Take your time." It annoyed him that his reaction to her should be so strong, while hers played tug-of-war at the opposite end of the spectrum. It was obvious she'd decided to dislike him. It might be interesting, Spence thought, while he watched her slender, capable hands wrap the carousel, to find out her reasons.

And change her mind.

"That's 55.27, Mrs. Mortimer."

"Oh no, dear, the price tag said 67."

Natasha, who knew Mrs. Mortimer juggled expenses on a fixed income, only smiled. "I'm sorry. Didn't I tell you it was on sale?"

"No." Mrs. Mortimer let out a little breath of relief as she counted out bills. "Well, this must be my lucky day."

"And Bonnie's." Natasha topped the gift with a pretty, celebratory pink bow, remembering it was Bonnie's favorite color. "Be sure to tell her happy birthday."

"I will." The proud grandmother lifted her package. "I can't wait to see her face when she opens this. Bye, Natasha."

Natasha waited until the door closed. "May I help you with something?"

"That was a very nice thing to do."

She lifted a brow. "What do you mean?"

"You know what I mean." He had the absurd urge to take her hand and kiss it. It was incredible, he thought. He was almost thirty-five and tumbling into puppy love with a woman he barely knew. "I'd meant to come in before."

"Oh? Was your daughter dissatisfied with her doll?"

"No, she loves it. It was just that I…" Good God, he was nearly stuttering. Five minutes with her, and he felt as awkward as a teenager at his first dance. He steadied himself with an effort. "I felt we'd gotten off on the wrong foot before. Should I apologize?"

"If you like." Just because he looked appealing and a little awkward was no reason to go easy on him. "Did you come in only for that?"

"No." His eyes darkened, just slightly. Noting it, Natasha wondered if she'd erred in her initial impression. Perhaps he wasn't harmless, after all. There was something deeper in those eyes, stronger and more dangerous. What surprised her further was that she found it exciting.

Disgusted with herself, she gave him a polite smile. "Was there something else?"

"I wanted something for my daughter." The hell with

the gorgeous Russian princess, he thought. He had more important things to tend to.

"What was it you wanted for her?"

"I don't know." That was true enough. Setting down his briefcase, he glanced around the shop.

Unbending a little, Natasha came around the counter. "Is it her birthday?"

"No." Feeling foolish, he shrugged. "It's the first day of school, and she looked so...brave getting on the bus this morning."

This time Natasha's smile was spontaneous and full of warmth. It nearly stopped his heart. "You shouldn't worry. When she comes home, she'll be full of stories about everything and everyone. The first day is much harder, I think, on the parent than on the child."

"It's been the longest day of my life."

She laughed, a rich smoky sound that seemed impossibly erotic in a room full of clowns and stuffed bears. "It sounds like you both deserve a present. You were looking at a music box before. I have another you might like."

So saying, she led the way to the back of the shop. Spence did his best to ignore the subtle sway of her hips and the soft, fresh-scrubbed flavor of her scent. The box she chose was carved of wood, its pedestal topped with a cat and a fiddle, a cow and a quarter moon. As it turned to "Stardust," he saw the laughing dog and the dish with the spoon.

"It's charming."

"It's one of my favorites." She'd decided that any man who adored his daughter so blatantly couldn't be all bad. So she smiled again. "I think it would be a lovely memento, something she could play on her first day of college and remember her father was thinking of her."

"If he survives first grade." He shifted slightly to look at her. "Thank you. It's perfect."

It was the oddest thing—his body had hardly brushed hers, but she'd felt a jolt. For an instant she forgot he was a customer, a father, a husband, and thought of him only as a man. His eyes were the color of the river at dusk. His lips, as they formed the barest hint of a smile, were impossibly attractive, alluring. Involuntarily she wondered what it would be like to feel them against her own—to watch his face as mouth met mouth, and see herself reflected in his eyes.

Appalled, she stepped back and her voice grew colder. "I'll box it for you."

Intrigued by the sudden change in tone, he took his time following her back to the counter. Hadn't he seen something in those fabulous eyes of hers? Or was it wishful thinking? It had gone quickly enough, heat smothered in frost. For the life of him he could find no reason for either.

"Natasha." He laid a hand on hers as she began to pack the music box.

Slowly she lifted her eyes. She was already hating herself for noticing that his hands were beautiful, wide-palmed, long-fingered. There was also a note of patience in his voice that stretched her already frayed nerves.

"Yes?"

"Why do I keep getting the feeling you'd like to boil me in oil?"

"You're mistaken," she said evenly. "I don't think I'd like that."

"You don't sound convinced." He felt her hand flex under his, soft and strong. The image of steel-lined velvet seemed particularly apt. "I'm having some trouble figuring out exactly what I've done to annoy you."

"Then you'll have to think about it. Cash or charge?"

He'd had little practice with rejection. Like a wasp it stung the ego. No matter how beautiful she was, he had no desire to continue to ram his head against the same brick wall.

"Cash." The door jangled open behind them and he released her hand. Three children, fresh from school, came in giggling. A young boy with red hair and a face bursting with freckles stood on his toes in front of the counter.

"I have three dollars," he announced.

Natasha fought back a grin. "You're very rich today, Mr. Jensen."

He flashed her a smile that revealed his latest missing tooth. "I've been saving up. I want the race car."

Natasha only lifted a brow as she counted out Spence's change. "Does your mother know you're here spending your life savings?" Her new customer remained silent. "Scott?"

He shifted from one foot to the other. "She didn't say I couldn't."

"And she didn't say you could," Natasha surmised.

She leaned over to tug at his cowlick. "Go and ask her, then you come back. The race car will still be here."

"But, Tash—"

"You wouldn't want your mother to be mad at me, would you?"

Scott looked thoughtful for a moment, and Natasha could tell it was a tough choice. "I guess not."

"Then go ask her, and I'll hold one for you."

Hope blossomed. "Promise?"

Natasha put a hand on her heart. "Solemnly." She looked back at Spence, and the amusement faded from her eyes. "I hope Freddie enjoys her present."

"I'm sure she will." He walked out, annoyed with himself for wishing he were a ten-year-old boy with a missing tooth.

Natasha locked the shop at six. The sun was still bright, the air still steamy. It made her think of picnics under a shady tree. A nicer fantasy than the microwave meal on her agenda, she mused, but at the moment impractical.

As she walked home, she watched a couple stroll hand in hand into the restaurant across the street. Someone hailed her from a passing car, and she waved in response. She could have stopped in the local pub and whiled away an hour over a glass of wine with any number of people she knew. Finding a dinner companion was as simple as sticking her head through one of a dozen doors and making the suggestion.

She wasn't in the mood for company. Not even her own.

It was the heat, she told herself as she turned the corner, the heat that had hung mercilessly in the air throughout the summer and showed no sign of yielding to autumn. It made her restless. It made her remember.

It had been summer when her life had changed so irrevocably.

Even now, years later, sometimes when she saw the roses in full bloom or heard the drunken buzz of bees she would ache. And wonder what might have happened. What would her life be like now, if…? She detested herself for playing those wishing games.

There were roses now, fragile pink ones that thrived despite the heat and lack of rain. She had planted them herself in the little patch of grass outside her apartment. Tending them brought her pleasure *and* pain. And what was life, she asked herself as she ran a fingertip over a petal, without them both? The warm scent of the roses followed her up the walkway.

Her rooms were quiet. She had thought about getting a kitten or a pup, so that there would be something there to greet her in the evening, something that loved and depended on her. But then she realized how unfair it would be to leave it alone while she was at the shop.

So she turned to music, flicking on the stereo as she stepped out of her shoes. Even that was a test. Tchaikovsky's *Romeo and Juliet*. She could see herself dancing to those haunting, romantic strains, the hot lights surrounding her, the music beating like her blood, her movements fluid, controlled without looking it. A triple pirouette, showing grace without effort.

That was past, Natasha reminded herself. Regrets were for the weak.

She moved out of habit, changing her work clothes for a loose, sleeveless jumpsuit, hanging up her skirt and blouse neatly as she had been taught. It was habit again rather than necessity that had her checking the cotton skirt for wear.

There was iced tea in the refrigerator and one of those packaged meals for the microwave that she both depended on and detested. She laughed at herself as she pushed the buttons to heat it.

She was getting like an old woman, Natasha decided, cranky and cross from the heat. Sighing, she rubbed the cold glass over her forehead.

That man had started her off, she thought. For a few moments in the shop today she had actually started to like him. He'd been so sweet, worrying about his little girl, wanting to reward her for being brave enough to face that momentous first day in school. She'd liked the way his voice had sounded, the way his eyes had smiled. For those few moments he had seemed like someone she could laugh with, talk with.

Then that had changed. A part of it was surely her fault, she admitted. But that didn't diminish his blame. She had felt something she hadn't felt, hadn't chosen to feel in a long, long time. That frisson of excitement. That tug of need. It made her angry and ashamed of herself. It made her furious with him.

The nerve, she thought, as she yanked her dish out

of the microwave. Flirting with her as if she were some naive fool, before he went home to his wife and daughter.

Have dinner with him, indeed. She jammed her fork into the steaming seafood pasta. That kind of man expected payment in full for a meal. The candlelight and wine type, she thought with a sneer. Soft voice, patient eyes, clever hands. And no heart.

Just like Anthony. Impatient, she set the dish aside and picked up the glass that was already dripping with moisture. But she was wiser now than she had been at eighteen. Much wiser. Much stronger. She was no longer a woman who could be lured by charm and smooth words. Not that this man was smooth, she remembered with a quick smile. He—Lord, she didn't even know his name and she already detested him—he was a little clumsy, a little awkward. That was a charm of its own.

But he was, she thought, very much like Anthony. Tall and blond with those oh, so American good looks. Looks that concealed a lack of morals and a carelessly deceitful heart.

What Anthony had cost her could never be tallied. Since that time, Natasha had made very, very certain no man would ever cost her so dearly again.

But she had survived. She lifted her glass in a self-toast. Not only had she survived, but except for times when memories crowded in on her, she was happy. She loved the shop, and the chance it gave her to be around children and make them happy. In her three years there she had watched them grow. She had a wonderful, funny friend in Annie, books that stayed in the black and a home that suited her.

She heard a thump over her head and smiled. The Jorgensons were getting ready for the evening meal. She imagined Don was fussing around Marilyn, who was carrying their first child. Natasha liked knowing they were there, just above her, happy, in love and full of hope.

That was family to her, what she had had in her youth, what she had expected as an adult. She could still see Papa fretting over Mama when she neared her time. Every time, Natasha remembered, thinking of her three younger siblings. How he had wept with happiness when his wife and babies were safe and well. He adored his Nadia. Even now Natasha knew he still brought flowers home to the little house in Brooklyn. When he came home after a day's work, he kissed his wife, not with an absent peck on the cheek, but robustly, joyfully. A man wildly in love after almost thirty years.

It was her father who had kept her from shoveling all men into the pit Anthony had dug for her. Seeing her father and mother together had kept that small, secret hope alight that someday she would find someone who would love her as much and as honestly.

Someday, she thought with a shrug. But for now she had her own business, her own home and her own life. No man, no matter how beautiful his hands or how clear his eyes, was going to rock her boat. Secretly she hoped her newest customer's wife gave him nothing but grief.

* * *

"One more story. Please, Daddy." Freddie, her eyes heavy, her face shiny from her bath, used her most persuasive smile. She was nestled against Spence in her big, white canopy bed.

"You're already asleep."

"No, I'm not." She peeked up at him, fighting to keep her eyes open. It had been the very best day of her life, and she didn't want it to end. "Did I tell you that JoBeth's cat had kittens? Six of them."

"Twice." Spence flicked a finger down her nose. He knew a hint when he heard one, and fell back on the parent's standard. "We'll see."

Sleepy, Freddie smiled. She knew from his tone that her father was already weakening. "Mrs. Patterson's real nice. She's going to let us have Show and Tell every Friday."

"So you said." And he'd been worried, Spence thought. "I get the feeling you like school."

"It's neat." She yawned hugely. "Did you fill out all the forms?"

"They'll be ready for you to take in tomorrow." All five hundred of them, he thought with a sigh. "Time to unplug the batteries, funny face."

"One more story. The made-up kind." She yawned again, comforted by the soft cotton of his shirt beneath her cheek and the familiar scent of his after-shave.

He gave in, knowing she would sleep long before he got to the happy ever after. He wove a story around a beautiful, dark-haired princess from a foreign land, and the knight who tried to rescue her from her ivory tower.

Foolishness, Spence thought even as he added a sorcerer and a two-headed dragon. He knew his thoughts were drifting toward Natasha again. She was certainly beautiful, but he didn't think he'd ever met a woman less in need of rescuing.

It was just his bad luck that he had to pass her shop every day to and from campus.

He'd ignore her. If anything, he should be grateful to her. She'd made him want, made him feel things he hadn't thought he could anymore. Maybe now that he and Freddie were settled, he'd start socializing again. There were plenty of attractive, single women at the college. But the idea of dating didn't fill him with delight.

Socializing, Spence corrected. Dating was for teenagers and conjured up visions of drive-in movies, pizza and sweaty palms. He was a grown man, and it was certainly time he started enjoying female companionship again. Over the age of five, he thought, looking at Freddie's small hand balled in his palm.

Just what would you think, he asked silently, if I brought a woman home to dinner? It made him remember how big and hurt her eyes had been when he and Angela had swept out of the condo for evenings at the theater or the opera.

It won't ever be like that again, he promised as he shifted her from his chest to the pillow. He settled the grinning Raggedy Ann beside her, then tucked the covers under her chin. Resting a hand on the bedpost, he glanced around the room.

It already had Freddie's stamp on it. The dolls lining the shelves with books jumbled beneath them, the fuzzy, pink elephant slippers beside her oldest and most favored sneakers. The room had that little-girl scent of shampoo and crayons. A night-light in the shape of a unicorn assured that she wouldn't wake up in the dark and be afraid.

He stayed a moment longer, finding himself as soothed by the light as she. Quietly he stepped out, leaving her door open a few inches.

Downstairs he found Vera carrying a tray of coffee. The Mexican housekeeper was wide from shoulders to hips, and gave the impression of a small, compact freight train when she moved from room to room. Since Freddie's birth, she had proven not only efficient but indispensable. Spence knew it was often possible to insure an employee's loyalty with a paycheck, but not her love. From the moment Freddie had come home in her silk-trimmed blanket, Vera had been in love.

She cast an eye up the stairs now, and her lined face folded into a smile. "She had one big day, huh?"

"Yes, and one she fought ending to the last gasp. Vera, you didn't have to bother."

She shrugged her shoulders while she carried the coffee into his office. "You said you have to work tonight."

"Yes, for a little while."

"So I make you coffee before I go in and put my feet up to watch TV." She arranged the tray on his desk, fuss-

ing a bit while she talked. "My baby, she's happy with
school and her new friends." She didn't add that she had
wept into her apron when Freddie had stepped onto the
bus. "With the house empty all day, I have plenty of
time to get my work done. You don't stay up too late,
Dr. Kimball."

"No." It was a polite lie. He knew he was too restless
for sleep. "Thank you, Vera."

"¡De nada!" She patted her iron-gray hair. "I wanted
to tell you that I like this place very much. I was afraid
to leave New York, but now I'm happy."

"We couldn't manage without you."

"Sí." She took this as her due. For seven years she had
worked for the *señor*, and basked in the prestige of being
housekeeper for an important man—a respected musician, a doctor of music and a college professor. Since
the birth of his daughter she had been so in love with
her baby that she would have worked for Spence, whatever his station.

She had grumbled about moving from the beautiful
high-rise in New York, to the rambling house in the
small town, but Vera was shrewd enough to know that
the *señor* had been thinking of Freddie. Freddie had
come home from school only hours before, laughing,
excited, with the names of new best friends tumbling
from her lips. So Vera was content.

"You are a good father, Dr. Kimball."

Spence glanced over before he sat down behind his
desk. He was well aware that there had been a time Vera
had considered him a very poor one.

"I'm learning."

"Si." Casually she adjusted a book on the shelf. "In this big house you won't have to worry about disturbing Freddie's sleep if you play your piano at night."

He looked over again, knowing she was encouraging him in her way to concentrate on his music. "No, it shouldn't disturb her. Good night, Vera."

After a quick glance around to be certain there was nothing more for her to tidy, she left him.

Alone, Spence poured the coffee, then studied the papers on his desk. Freddie's school forms were stacked next to his own work. He had a great deal of preparation ahead of him, before his classes began the following week.

He looked forward to it, even as he tried not to regret that the music that had once played so effortlessly inside his head was still silent.

Chapter 3

Natasha scooped the barrette through the hair above her ear and hoped it would stay fixed for more than five minutes. She studied her reflection in the narrow mirror over the sink in the back of the shop before she decided to add a touch of lipstick. It didn't matter that it had been a long and hectic day or that her feet were all but crying with fatigue. Tonight was her treat to herself, her reward for a job well done.

Every semester she signed up for one course at the college. She chose whatever seemed most fun, most intriguing or most unusual. Renaissance Poetry one year, Automotive Maintenance another. This term, two evenings a week, she would be taking Music History. Tonight she would begin an exploration of a new topic. Everything she learned she would store for her own pleasure, as other women stored diamonds and emeralds. It didn't have to be useful. In Natasha's opinion a glittery necklace wasn't particularly useful, either. It was simply exciting to own.

She had her notebook, her pens and pencils and a flood of enthusiasm. To prepare herself, she had raided the library and pored over related books for the last two weeks. Pride wouldn't allow her to go into class ignorant. Curiosity made her wonder if her instructor could take the dry, distant facts and add excitement.

There was little doubt that this particular instructor was adding dashes of excitement in other quarters. Annie had teased her just that morning about the new professor everyone was talking about. Dr. Spencer B. Kimball.

The name sounded very distinguished to Natasha, quite unlike the description of a hunk that Annie had passed along. Annie's information came from her cousin's daughter, who was majoring in Elementary Education with a minor in Music. A sun-god, Annie had relayed and made Natasha laugh.

A very gifted sun-god, Natasha mused while she turned off lights in the shop. She knew Kimball's work well, or the work he had composed before he had suddenly and inexplicably stopped writing music. Why, she had even danced to his Prelude in D Minor when she had been with the corps de ballet in New York.

A million years ago, she thought as she stepped onto the street. Now she would be able to meet the genius, listen to his views and perhaps find new meanings in many of the classics she already loved.

He was probably the temperamental artiste type, she decided, pleased with the way the evening breeze lifted her hair and cooled her neck. Or a pale eccentric with one earring. It didn't matter. She intended to work hard. Each course she took was a matter of pride to her. It still stung to remember how little she had known when she'd been eighteen. How little she had cared to know, Natasha admitted, other than dance. She had of her own choice closed herself off from so many worlds in order to focus everything on one. When that had been taken away, she had been as lost as a child set adrift on the Atlantic.

She had found her way to shore, just as her family had once found its way across the wilds of the Ukraine to the jungles of Manhattan. She liked herself better—the independent, ambitious American woman she had become. As she was now, she could walk into the big, beautiful old building on campus with as much pride as any freshman student.

There were footsteps echoing in the corridors, distant, dislocated. There was a hushed reverence that Natasha always associated with churches and universities. In a way there was religion here—the belief in learning.

She felt somewhat reverent herself as she made her way to her class. As a child of five in her small farming village, she had never even imagined such a building, or the books and beauty it contained.

Several students were already waiting. A mixed bag, she noted, ranging from college to middle age. All of them seemed to buzz with that excitement of beginning. She saw by the clock that it was two minutes shy of eight.

She'd expected Kimball to be there, busily shuffling his papers, peering at them behind glasses, his hair a little wild and streaming to his shoulders.

Absently she smiled at a young man in horn-rims, who was staring at her as if he'd just woken from a dream. Ready to begin, she sat down, then looked up when the same man clumsily maneuvered himself into the desk beside her.

"Hello."

He looked as though she'd struck him with a bat rather than offered a casual greeting. He pushed his glasses nervously up his nose. "Hello. I'm—I'm…Terry Maynard," he finished on a burst as his name apparently came to him at last.

"Natasha." She smiled again. He was on the sunny side of twenty-five and harmless as a puppy.

"I haven't, ah, seen you on campus before."

"No." Though at twenty-seven it amused her to be taken for a coed, she kept her voice sober. "I'm only taking this one class. For fun."

"For fun?" Terry appeared to take music very seriously. "Do you know who Dr. Kimball is?" His obvious awe made him almost whisper the name.

"I've heard of him. You're a Music major?"

"Yes. I hope to, well one day, I hope to play with the New York Symphony." His blunt fingers reached nervously to adjust his glasses. "I'm a violinist."

She smiled again and made his Adam's apple bob. "That's wonderful. I'm sure you're very good."

"What do you play?"

"Five card draw." Then she laughed and settled back in her chair. "I'm sorry. I don't play an instrument. But I love to listen to music and thought I'd enjoy the class." She glanced at the clock on the wall. "If it ever starts, that is. Apparently our esteemed professor is late."

At that moment the esteemed professor was rushing down the corridors, cursing himself for ever agreeing to take on this night class. By the time he had helped Freddie with her homework—how many animals can you find in this picture?—convinced her that brussels sprouts were cute instead of yucky, and changed his shirt because her affectionate hug had transferred some mysterious, sticky substance to his sleeve, he had wanted nothing more than a good book and a warm brandy.

Instead he was going to have to face a roomful of eager faces, all waiting to learn what Beethoven had worn when he'd composed his Ninth Symphony.

In the foulest of moods, he walked into class. "Good evening. I'm Dr. Kimball." The murmurs and rattles quieted. "I must apologize for being late. If you'll all take a seat, we'll dive right in."

As he spoke he scanned the room. And found himself staring into Natasha's astonished face.

"No." She wasn't aware she'd spoken the word aloud, and wouldn't have cared. It was some sort of joke, she thought, and a particularly bad one. This—this *man* in the casually elegant jacket was Spencer Kimball, a musician whose songs she had admired and danced to. The man who, while barely into his twenties had been performing at Carnegie Hall being hailed as a genius. This man who had tried to pick her up in a toy store was the illustrious Dr. Kimball?

It was ludicrous, it was infuriating, it was—

Wonderful, Spence thought as he stared at her. Absolutely wonderful. In fact, it was perfect, as long as he could control the laugh that was bubbling in his throat. So the czarina was one of his students. It was better, much better than a warm brandy and an evening of quiet.

"I'm sure," he said after a long pause, "we'll all find the next few months fascinating."

She should have signed up for Astronomy, Natasha told herself. She could have learned all kinds of interesting things about the planets and stars. Asteroids. She'd have been much better off learning about—what was it?—gravitational pull and inertia. Whatever that was. Surely it was much more important for her to find out how many moons revolved around Jupiter than to study Burgundian composers of the fifteenth century.

She would transfer, Natasha decided. First thing in the morning she would make the arrangements. In fact, she would get up and walk out right now if she wasn't certain Dr. Spencer Kimball would smirk.

Running her pencil between her fingers, she crossed her legs and determined not to listen.

It was a pity his voice was so attractive.

Impatient, Natasha looked at the clock. Nearly an hour to go. She would do what she did when she waited at the dentist's office. Pretend she was someplace else. Struggling to block Spence's voice from her mind she began to swing her foot and doodle on her pad.

She didn't notice when her doodles became notes, or when she began to hang on every word. He made fifteenth-century musicians seem alive and vital—and their music as real as flesh and blood. Rondeaux, vieralais, ballades. She could almost hear the three-part chansons of the dawning Renaissance, the reverent, soaring Kyries and Glorias of the masses.

She was caught up, involved in that ancient rivalry between church and state and music's part in the politics. She could see huge banqueting halls filled with elegantly dressed aristocrats, feasting on music as well as food.

"Next time we'll be discussing the Franco-Flemish school and rhythmic developments." Spence gave his class an easy smile. "And I'll try to be on time."

Was it over? Natasha glanced at the clock again and was shocked to see it was indeed after nine.

"Incredible, isn't he?"

She looked at Terry. His eyes were gleaming behind his lenses. "Yes." It cost her to admit it, but truth was truth.

"You should hear him in theory class." He noticed with envy that several students were grouped around his idol. As yet, Terry hadn't worked up the nerve to approach him. "I'll—see you Thursday."

"What? Oh. Good night, Terry."

"I could, ah, give you a ride home if you want." The fact that he was nearly out of gas and his muffler was currently held on by a coat hanger didn't enter his mind.

She favored him with an absent smile that had his

heart doing a cha-cha. "That's nice of you, but I don't live far."

She hoped to breeze out of the classroom while Spence was still occupied. She should have known better.

He simply put a hand on her arm and stopped her. "I'd like to speak with you a moment, Natasha."

"I'm in a hurry."

"It won't take long." He nodded to the last of his departing students, then eased back against his desk and grinned at her. "I should have paid more attention to my roster, but then again, it's nice to know there are still surprises in the world."

"That depends on your point of view, Dr. Kimball."

"Spence." He continued to grin. "Class is over."

"So it is." Her regal nod made him think again of Russian royalty. "Excuse me."

"Natasha." He waited, almost seeing impatience shimmer around her as she turned. "I can't imagine that someone with your heritage doesn't believe in destiny."

"Destiny?"

"Of all the classrooms in all the universities in all the world, she walks into mine."

She wouldn't laugh. She'd be damned if she would. But her mouth quirked up at the corners before she controlled it. "And here I was thinking it was just bad luck."

"Why Music History?"

She balanced her notebook on her hip. "It was a toss-up between that and Astronomy."

"That sounds like a fascinating story. Why don't we go down the street for a cup of coffee? You can tell me about it." Now he saw it—molten fury that turned her eyes from rich velvet to sharp jet. "Now why does that infuriate you?" he inquired, almost to himself. "Is an offer of a cup of coffee in this town similiar to an illicit proposition?"

"You should know, Dr. Kimball." She turned, but he reached the door before her, slamming it with enough force to make her step back. He was every bit as angry as herself, she noted. Not that it mattered. It was only that he had seemed a mild sort of man. Detestable, but mild. There was nothing mild about him now. Those fascinating bones and angles in his face might have been carved of stone.

"Clarify."

"Open the door."

"Gladly. After you answer my question." He *was* angry. Spence realized he hadn't felt this kind of hot, blood-pumping rage in years. It felt wonderful. "I realize that just because I'm attracted to you doesn't mean you have to return the favor."

She threw up her chin, hating herself for finding the storm-cloud-gray eyes so hypnotic. "I don't."

"Fine." He couldn't strangle her for that, however much he'd like to. "But, damn it, I want to know why you aim and fire every time I'm around you."

"Because men like you deserve to be shot."

"Men like me," he repeated, measuring out the words. "What exactly does that mean?"

He was standing close, all but looming over her. As in the shop when he had brushed up against her, she felt those bubble bursts of excitement, attraction, confusion. It was more than enough to push her over the edge.

"Do you think because you have a nice face and a pretty smile you can do whatever you like? *Yes*," she answered before he could speak and slapped her notebook against his chest. "You think you have only to snap your fingers." She demonstrated dramatically. "And a woman will fall into your arms. Not this woman."

Her accent thickened when she was on a roll, he noted, somewhat baffled by her claim. "I don't recall snapping my fingers."

She let loose one short, explicit Ukrainian oath and grabbed the knob. "You want to have a cup of coffee with me? Good. We'll have your coffee—and we'll call your wife and ask her to join us."

"My what?" He closed his hand over hers so that the door was jerked open, then slammed shut again. "I don't have a wife."

"Really?" The single word dripped with scorn; her eyes flashed at him. "And I suppose the woman who came with you to the shop is your sister."

It should have been funny. But he couldn't quite get the joke. "Nina? As a matter of fact, she is."

Natasha yanked open the door with a sound of disgust. "That is pathetic."

Filled with righteous indignation, she stormed down the corridor and out the main door. In a staccato rhythm that matched her mood, her heels beat on the concrete as she started down the steps. When she was abruptly whirled around, she nearly took the last two in a tumble.

"You've got a hell of a nerve."

"I?" she managed. "I have a nerve?"

"You think you've got it all figured out, don't you?" Having the advantage of height, Spence could stare down at her. Natasha saw shadows move over his face as temper colored his voice. He didn't appear awkward now, but every bit in control. "Or I should say you think you've got me figured."

"It takes very little." The fingers on her arm were very firm. She hated knowing that mixed with her own anger was basic sexual attraction. Fighting it off, she tossed back her hair. "You're really very typical."

"I wonder, can your opinion of me get any lower?" Now fury ground edge to edge with desire.

"Doubtful."

"In that case, I might as well satisfy myself."

The notebook flew out of her hand when he dragged her close. She managed a single, startled sound in her throat before his mouth covered hers. Covered, crushed, then conquered.

Natasha would have fought him. Over and over she told herself she *would* fight him. But it was shock—at least, she prayed it was shock—that had her arms falling limply to her sides.

It was wrong. It was unforgivable. And, oh God, it was wonderful. Instinctively he'd found the key to unlock the passion that had lain dormant in her for so long. Her blood swam hot with it. Her mind hazed. Dimly she heard someone laugh as they strolled down the sidewalk below. A beep of a car horn, a shout of greeting, then silence once more.

She murmured, a pitiful protest that shamed her and was easily ignored as his tongue glided over her own. His taste was a banquet after a long fast. Though she kept her hands balled at her sides, she leaned into the kiss.

Kissing her was like walking through a mine field. Any moment he expected the bomb to go off and blow him to pieces. He should have stopped after the first shock, but danger had a thrill of its own.

And she was dangerous. As his fingers dived into her hair, he could feel the ground quiver and quake. It was her—the promise, the threat of titanic passion. He could taste it on her lips, even as she fought to hold it back. He could feel it in her taut, terrified stance. If she released it, she could make him a slave.

Needs such as he'd never known battered his system with heavy fists. Images, all fire and smoke, danced in his brain. Something struggled to break free, like a bird beating at the bars of a cage. He could feel it straining. Then Natasha was pulling away from him, standing apart and staring at him with wide, eloquent eyes.

She couldn't breathe. For an instant she was genuinely afraid she would die on the spot with this unwanted, shameful desire on her conscience. In defiance she took a huge gulp of air.

"I could never hate anyone as much as I hate you."

He shook his head to clear it. She had left him dizzy, dazed and utterly defenseless. For his own sake he waited until he was sure he could speak. "That's a lofty position you put me in, Natasha." He stepped down until they were at eye level. There were tears on her lashes, but they were offset by the condemnation in her eyes. "Let's just be sure you've put me there for the right reasons. Is it because I kissed you, or because you liked it?"

She swung her hand out. He could have avoided the blow easily enough, but thought she deserved a hit. As the crack of the slap echoed, he decided they were even.

"Don't come near me again," she said, breathing hard. "I warn you, if you do, I won't care what I say or who hears me. If it wasn't for your little girl—" She broke off and bent to gather her things. Her pride was shattered, along with her self-esteem. "You don't deserve such a beautiful child."

He caught her arm again, but this time the expression on his face made her blood go cold. "You're right. I never have and probably never will deserve Freddie, but I'm all she has. Her mother—my wife—died three years ago."

He strode off, was caught in the beam of a street lamp, then disappeared into the dark beyond. Her notebook pressed against her chest, Natasha sank weakly onto the bottom step.

What in hell was she going to do now?

There was no choice. No matter how much she hated it, there was really only one course to take. Natasha rubbed the palms of her hands on the thighs of her khakis, then started up the freshly painted wooden steps.

It was a nice house, she thought, stalling. Of course

she'd seen it so often that she rarely noticed it anymore. It was one of those sturdy old brick places tucked back from the street and shielded by trees and box hedges.

The summer flowers had yet to fade, but the fall blooms were already staking their claim. Showy delphiniums vied with spicy scented mums, vivid dahlias with starry asters. Someone was caring for them. She could see fresh mulch on the flower beds, damp with watering.

Wanting a little more time, she studied the house. There were curtains at the windows, thin ivory sheers that would let in the light. Higher up she caught a glimpse of a fanciful pattern of unicorns that identified a little girl's room.

She gathered her courage and crossed the porch to the front door. It would be quick, she promised herself. Not painless, but quick. She rapped, released her breath and waited.

The woman who answered was short and wide with a face as brown and wrinkled as a raisin. Natasha found herself fixed by a pair of small, dark eyes while the housekeeper dried her hands on the skirt of a stained apron.

"May I help you?"

"I'd like to see Dr. Kimball if he's in." She smiled, pretending she didn't feel as though she were stepping into the pillory. "I'm Natasha Stanislaski." She saw the housekeeper's little eyes narrow, so that they nearly disappeared into the folds of her face.

Vera had at first taken Natasha for one of the *señor*'s

students, and had been prepared to nudge her on her way. "You own the toy store in town."

"That's right."

"Ah." With a nod, she opened the door wider to let Natasha in. "Freddie says you are a very nice lady, who gave her a blue ribbon for her doll. I promised to take her back, but just to look." She gestured for Natasha to follow.

As they made their way down the hall, Natasha caught the hesitant notes of a piano. When she saw her reflection in an old oval mirror, it surprised her that she was smiling.

He was sitting at the piano with the child on his lap, looking over her head while she slowly tapped out "Mary Had a Little Lamb." The sun streamed in through the windows behind them. At that moment she wished she could paint. How else could it be captured?

It was perfect. The light, the shadows, the pale pastels of the room all combined to make the perfect backdrop. The alignment of their heads, their bodies, was too natural and eloquent ever to be posed. The girl was in pink and white, the laces of one sneaker untied. He had taken off his jacket and tie, then rolled up the sleeves of the pale dress shirt to the elbows like a workman.

There was the fragile shine of the child's hair, the deeper glow of his. The child leaned back against her father, her head resting just under his collarbone; the faintest smile of pleasure lighted her face. Over it all was the simple nursery rhyme music she was playing.

He had his hands on the knees of her jeans, his long,

beautiful fingers tapping the time in tandem with the tick of the antique metronome. She could see it all, the love, the patience, the pride.

"No, please," Natasha whispered, holding out a hand to Vera. "Don't disturb them."

"You play now, Daddy." Freddie tilted her head toward his. Her hair wisped around her face where it had escaped from its clips. "Play something pretty."

"Für Elise." Natasha recognized it instantly, that soft, romantic, somehow lonely music. It went straight to her heart as she watched his fingers stroke, caress, seduce the keys.

What was he thinking? She could see that his thoughts had turned inward—to the music, to himself. There was an effortlessness in the way his fingers flowed over the keys, and yet she knew that kind of beauty was never achieved without the greatest effort.

The song swelled, note after note, unbearably sad, impossibly beautiful, like the vase of waxy calla lilies that rested on the glossy surface of the piano.

Too much emotion, Natasha thought. Too much pain, though the sun was still shining through the gauzy curtains and the child on his lap continued to smile. The urge to go to him, to put a comforting hand onto his shoulder, to hold them both against her heart, was so strong that she had to curl her fingers into her palms.

Then the music drifted away, the last note lingering like a sigh.

"I like that one," Freddie told him. "Did you make it up?"

"No." He looked at his fingers, spreading them, flexing them, then letting them rest on hers. "Beethoven did." Then he was smiling again, pressing his lips to the soft curve of his daughter's neck. "Had enough for today, funny face?"

"Can I play outside until dinner?"

"Well… What'll you give me?"

It was an old game and a favorite one. Giggling, she swiveled on his lap and gave him a hard, smacking kiss. Still squealing from the bear hug, she spotted Natasha. "Hi!"

"Miss Stanislaski would like to see you, Dr. Kimball." At his nod, Vera walked back to the kitchen.

"Hello." Natasha managed to smile, even when Spence lifted his daughter and turned. She wasn't over the music yet. It was still pouring through her like tears. "I hope I haven't come at a bad time."

"No." After a last squeeze, he set Freddie down, and she immediately bounded to Natasha.

"We're all finished with my lesson. Did you come to play?"

"No, not this time." Unable to resist, Natasha bent to stroke Freddie's cheek. "Actually I came to talk to your father." But she was a coward, Natasha thought in disgust. Rather than look at him, she continued to address Freddie. "How do you like school? You have Mrs. Patterson, don't you?"

"She's nice. She didn't even yell when Mikey Towers's icky bug collection got loose in the classroom. And I can read all of *Go, Dog, Go.*"

Natasha crouched so that they were eye to eye. "Do you like my hat?"

Freddie laughed, recognizing the line from the Dr. Seuss classic. "I like the dog party part the best."

"So do I." Automatically she tied Freddie's loose laces. "Will you come to the store and visit me soon?"

"Okay." Delighted with herself, Freddie raced for the door. "Bye Miss Stanof—Stanif—"

"Tash." She sent Freddie a wink. "All the kids call me Tash."

"Tash." Freddie grinned at the sound of the name, then streaked away.

She listened to Freddie's sneakers squeak down the hall, then took a long breath. "I'm sorry to disturb you at home, but I felt it would be more…" What was the word? Appropriate, comfortable? "It would be better."

"All right." His eyes were very cool, not like those of the man who had played such sad and passionate music. "Would you like to sit down?"

"No." She said it too quickly, then reminded herself that it was better if they were both stiffly polite. "It won't take long. I only want to apologize."

"Oh? For something specific?"

Fire blazed in her eyes. He enjoyed seeing it, particularly since he'd spent most of the night cursing her. "When I make a mistake, I make a point of admitting it. But since you behaved so—" Oh, why did she always lose her English when she was angry?

"Unconscionably?" he suggested.

Her brow shot up into her fall of hair. "So you admit it."

"I thought you were the one who was here to admit something." Enjoying himself, he sat on the arm of a wing chair in pale blue damask. "Don't let me interrupt."

She was tempted, very tempted, to turn on her heel and stalk out. Pride was equally as strong as temper. She would do what she had come to do, then forget it.

"What I said about you—about you and your daughter was unfair and untrue. Even when I was...mistaken about other things, I knew it was untrue. And I'm very sorry I said it."

"I can see that." Out of the corner of his eye he caught a movement. He turned his head in time to see Freddie make her sprinter's rush for the swings. "We'll forget it."

Natasha followed his gaze and softened. "She really is a beautiful child. I hope you let her come into the shop from time to time."

The tone of her voice had him studying Natasha more carefully. Was it longing, sorrow? "I doubt I could keep her away. You're very fond of children."

Natasha brought her emotions under control with a quick jerk. "Yes, of course. In my business it's a requirement. I won't keep you, Dr. Kimball."

He rose to accept the hand she had formally held out. "Spence," he corrected, gently tightening his fingers on hers. "What else was it you were mistaken about?"

So it wasn't going to be easy. Then again, Natasha thought she deserved a dose of humiliation. "I thought you were married, and was very angry and insulted when you asked me out."

"You're taking my word now that I'm not married."

"No. I looked it up in the library in *Who's Who*."

He stared at her for a moment longer, then threw back his head and laughed. "God, what a trusting soul. Find anything else that interested you?"

"Only things that would fill your ego. You still have my hand."

"I know. Tell me, Natasha, did you dislike me on general principles, or only because you thought I was a married man and had no business flirting with you?"

"Flirting?" She nearly choked on the word. "There was nothing so innocent in the way you looked at me. As if…"

"As if—?" he prompted.

As if we were already lovers, she thought, and felt her skin heat. "I didn't like it," she said shortly.

"Because you thought I was married?"

"Yes. No," she said, correcting herself when she realized where that could lead. "I just didn't like it." He brought her hand to his lips. "Don't," she managed.

"How would you like me to look at you?"

"It isn't necessary for you to look at all."

"But it is." He could feel it again, that high-strung passion, just waiting to burst free from whatever cell she had locked it in. "You'll be sitting right in front of me tomorrow night in class."

"I'm going to transfer."

"No, you won't." He brushed a finger over the small gold hoop in her ear. "You enjoyed it too much. I could see the wheels turning in that fabulous head of yours. And if you did," he continued before she could sputter out a response, "I'd just make a nuisance of myself in your shop."

"Why?"

"Because you're the first woman I've wanted in longer than I can remember."

Excitement rippled up her spine like chain lightning. Before she could prevent it, the memory of that stormy kiss curved back to weaken her. Yes, that had been a man who had wanted. And had, no matter how she had resisted, made her want, too.

But that had only been one kiss, fueled by lust despite the moonlight and soft air. She knew heartbreakingly well where such desires could lead.

"That's nonsense."

"Simple honesty," he murmured, fascinated by the emotions that came and went in her dark eyes. "I thought it best, since we'd gotten off to such a shaky beginning. Since you've determined for yourself that I'm not married, knowing I'm attracted to you shouldn't insult you."

"I'm not insulted," she said carefully. "I'm just not interested."

"Do you always kiss men you're not interested in?"

"I didn't kiss you." She jerked her hand free. "You kissed me."

"We can fix that." He gathered her close. "This time kiss me back."

She could have pulled away. His arms weren't banding her as they had before, but were wrapped loosely, coaxingly around her. His lips were soft this time, soft, persuasive, patient. She could feel the warmth seep into her bloodstream like a drug. With a little moan, she slipped her hands up his back and held on.

It was like holding a candle and feeling the wax slowly melt as the fire burned at its center. He could feel her yield degree by degree until her lips parted for his own, accepting, inviting. But even as she gave, he could sense some strong, hard core that resisted, held back. She didn't want to feel whatever he was making her feel.

Impatient, he dragged her closer. Though her body molded itself to his and her head fell back in erotic surrender, there was still a part of her standing just out of his reach. What she gave him only stirred his appetite for more.

She was breathless when he released her. It took an effort, too much of an effort, Natasha thought, to level herself. But once she had, her voice was steady.

"I don't want to be involved."

"With me, or with anyone?"

"With anyone."

"Good." He brushed a hand over her hair. "It'll be simpler to change your mind."

"I'm very stubborn," she muttered.

"Yes, I've noticed. Why don't you stay for dinner?"

"No."

"All right. I'll take you to dinner Saturday night."

"No."

"Seven-thirty. I'll pick you up."

"No."

"You wouldn't want me to come by the shop Saturday afternoon and embarrass you."

Out of patience, she stalked to the door. "I can't understand how a man that could play music with such sensitivity could be such a clod."

Just lucky, I guess, he thought when the door slammed. Alone again, he caught himself whistling.

Chapter 4

Saturdays in a toy store were noisy, crowded and chaotic. They were supposed to be. To a child even the word Saturday was magic—it meant a magic twenty-four hours when school was too faraway to be a problem. There were bikes to be ridden, games to be played, races to be won. For as long as Natasha had been running The Fun House, she had enjoyed Saturdays as much as her pint-size clientele.

It was one more black mark against Spence that he was the reason she couldn't enjoy this one.

She'd told him no, she reminded herself as she rang up sales on a set of jacks, three plastic dinosaurs and a pint of blowing bubbles. And she'd meant no.

The man didn't seem to understand plain English.

Why else would he have sent her the single red rose? And to the shop, of all places? she thought now, trying to scowl at it. Annie's romantic enthusiasm had been impossible to hold off. Even when Natasha had ignored the flower, Annie had rescued it, running across the street to buy a plastic bud vase so that it could have a place of honor on the checkout counter.

Natasha did her best not to look at it, not to stroke the tightly closed petals, but it wasn't as easy to ignore the fragile scent that wafted toward her every time she rang up a sale.

Why did men think they could soften up a woman with a flower?

Because they could, Natasha admitted, biting off a sigh as she glanced toward it.

That didn't mean she was going out to dinner with him. Tossing back her hair, Natasha counted out the pile of sweaty pennies and nickels the young Hampston boy passed her for his monthly comic-book purchase. Life should be so simple, she thought as the boy rushed out with the latest adventures of Commander Zark. Damn it, it was that simple. On a deep breath she steeled her determination. Her life was exactly that simple, no matter how Spence tried to complicate it. To prove it, she intended to go home, soak in a hot tub, then spend the rest of her evening stretched out on the sofa, watching an old movie and eating popcorn.

He'd been clever. She left the counter to go into the next aisle to referee a huffy disagreement between the Freedmont brothers about how they should spend their pooled resources. She wondered if the esteemed professor looked at their relationship—their nonrelationship, she corrected—as a chess match. She'd always been too reckless to succeed at that particular game, but she had a feeling Spence would play it patiently and well. All the same, if he thought she would be easily checkmated, he had a surprise coming.

Spence had led her second class brilliantly, never looking at her any longer than he had looked at any of his other students, answering her questions in the same tone he used with others. Yes, a very patient player.

Then, just when she'd relaxed, he'd passed her that first red rose as she walked out of class. A very smart move to endanger her queen.

If she'd had any spine at all, Natasha thought now, she would have dropped it onto the floor and ground it under her heel. But she hadn't, and now had to scramble to keep one play ahead of him. Because it had caught her off guard, Natasha told herself. Just like the one that had been delivered to the shop this morning.

If he kept it up, people were going to begin to talk. In a town this size, news items like red roses bounced from shop to pub, from pub to front stoop and from front stoop to backyard gossip sessions. She needed to find a way to stop it. At the moment, she couldn't come up with anything better than ignoring it. Ignoring Spence, she added. How she wished she could.

Bringing herself back to the problem at hand, Natasha hooked an arm around each of the squabbling Freedmont boys in a mock headlock.

"Enough. If you keep calling each other names like nerd and…what was the other?"

"Dork," the taller of the boys told her with relish.

"Yes, dork." She couldn't resist committing it to memory. "That's a good one. If you keep it up, I'll tell your mother not to let you come in for two weeks."

"Aw, Tash."

"That means everyone else will see all the creepy things I get in for Halloween before either of you." She let that threat hang, giving the two little necks a quick squeeze. "So, I'll make a suggestion. Flip a coin and decide whether to buy the football or the magic set. Whatever you don't get now, you ask for for Christmas. Good idea?"

The boys grimaced at each other from either side of her. "Pretty good."

"No, you have to say it's very good, or I'll knock your heads together."

She left them arguing over which coin to use for the fatal flip.

"You missed your calling," Annie commented when the brothers raced off with the football.

"How's that?"

"You should be working for the UN." She nodded out the front window; the boys were practicing passing on their way down the street. "There aren't many tougher nuts than the Freedmont brothers."

"I make them afraid of me first, then offer them a dignified way out."

"See? Definitely UN material."

With a laugh, Natasha shook her head. "Other people's problems are the easiest to solve." Weakening, she glanced toward the rose again. If she had one wish at the moment, it would be for someone to come along and solve her own.

An hour later she felt a tug on the hem of her skirt.

"Hi."

"Freddie, hello." She flicked her finger over a bow that was trying to hold back Freddie's flyaway hair. It was tied from the blue ribbon Natasha had given her on her first visit. "Don't you look pretty today."

Freddie beamed, female to female. "Do you like my outfit?"

Natasha surveyed the obviously new blue denim overalls, parade stiff with sizing. "I like it very much. I have a pair just like them."

"You do?" Nothing, since Freddie had decided to make Natasha her newest heroine, could have pleased her more. "My daddy got them for me."

"That's nice." Despite her better judgment, Natasha scanned the shop for him. "Did he, ah, bring you in today?"

"No, Vera did. You said it was all right just to look."

"Sure it is. I'm glad you came in." And she was, Natasha realized. Just as she was stupidly disappointed that Freddie hadn't brought her daddy.

"I'm not supposed to touch anything." Freddie tucked her itchy fingers into her pockets. "Vera said I should look with my eyes and not with my hands."

"That's very good advice." And some Natasha wouldn't have minded others passing along to nimble-fingered children. "But some things are okay to touch. You just ask me."

"Okay. I'm going to join the Brownies and get a uniform and everything."

"That's wonderful. You'll come in and show it to me?"

Delight nearly split Freddie's face in two. "Okay. It has a hat, and I'm going to learn how to make pillows and candle holders and all kinds of things. I'll make you something."

"I'd like that." She tidied Freddie's lopsided bow.

"Daddy said you were going to eat dinner with him in a restaurant tonight."

"Well, I—"

"I don't like restaurants very much, except for pizza, so I'm going to stay home, and Vera's going to fix tortillas for me and JoBeth. We get to eat in the kitchen."

"That sounds nice."

"If you don't like the restaurant, you can come back and have some. Vera always makes a lot."

Uttering a helpless little sigh, Natasha bent to tie Freddie's left shoelace. "Thank you."

"Your hair smells pretty."

Half in love, Natasha leaned closer to sniff Freddie's. "So does yours."

Fascinated by Natasha's tangle of curls, Freddie reached out to touch. "I wish my hair was like yours," she said. "It's straight as a pin," she added, quoting her Aunt Nina.

Smiling, Natasha brushed at the fragile wisps over Freddie's brow. "When I was a little girl, we put an angel on top of the Christmas tree every year. She was very beautiful, and she had hair just like yours."

Pleasure came flushing into Freddie's cheeks.

"Ah, there you are." Vera shuffled down the crowded aisle, straw carryall on one arm, a canvas bag on the other. "Come, come, we must get back home before your father thinks we are lost." She held out a hand for Freddie and nodded to Natasha. "Good afternoon, miss."

"Good afternoon." Curious, Natasha raised a brow. She was being summed up again by the little dark eyes, and definitely being found wanting, Natasha thought. "I hope you'll bring Freddie back to visit soon."

"We will see. It is as hard for a child to resist a toy store as it is for a man to resist a beautiful woman."

Vera led Freddie down the aisle, not looking back when the girl waved and grinned over her shoulder.

"Well," Annie murmured as she stuck her head around the corner. "What brought that on?"

With a humorless smile, Natasha shoved a pin back into her hair. "At a guess, I would say the woman believes I have designs on her employer."

Annie gave an unladylike snort. "If anything, the employer has designs on you. I should be so lucky." Her sigh was only a little envious. "Now that we know the new hunk on the block isn't married, all's right with the world. Why didn't you tell me you were going out with him?"

"Because I wasn't."

"But I heard Freddie say—"

"He asked me out," Natasha clarified. "I said no."

"I see." After a brief pause, Annie tilted her head. "When did you have the accident?"

"Accident?"

"Yes, the one where you suffered brain damage."

Natasha's face cleared with a laugh, and she started toward the front of the shop.

"I'm serious," Annie said as soon as they had five free minutes. "Dr. Spencer Kimball is gorgeous, unattached and…" She leaned over the counter to sniff at the rose. "Charming. Why aren't you taking off early to work on real problems, like what to wear tonight?"

"I know what I'm wearing tonight. My bathrobe."

Annie couldn't resist the grin. "Aren't you rushing things just a tad? I don't think you should wear your robe until at least your third date."

"There's not going to be a first one." Natasha smiled at her next customer and rang up a sale.

It took Annie forty minutes to work back to the subject at hand. "Just what are you afraid of?"

"The IRS."

"Tash, I'm serious."

"So am I." When her pins worked loose again, she gave up and yanked them out. "Every American businessperson is afraid of the IRS."

"We're talking about Spence Kimball."

"No," Natasha corrected. "You're talking about Spence Kimball."

"I thought we were friends."

Surprised by Annie's tone, Natasha stopped tidying

the racetrack display her Saturday visitors had wrecked. "We are. You know we are."

"Friends talk to each other, Tash, confide in each other, ask advice." Puffing out a breath, Annie stuffed her hands into the pockets of her baggy jeans. "Look, I know that things happened to you before you came here, things you're still carrying around but never talk about. I figured I was being a better friend by not asking you about it."

Had she been so obvious? Natasha wondered. All this time she'd been certain she had buried the past and all that went with it—deeply. Feeling a little helpless, she reached out to touch Annie's hand. "Thank you."

With a dismissive shrug, Annie turned to flick the lock on the front door. The shop was empty now, the bustle of the afternoon only an echo. "Remember when you let me cry on your shoulder after Don Newman dumped me?"

Natasha pressed her lips into a thin line. "He wasn't worth crying over."

"I enjoyed crying over him," Annie returned with a quick, amused smile. "I needed to cry and yell and moan and get a little drunk. You were right there for me, saying all those great, nasty things about him."

"That was the easy part," Natasha remembered. "He was a dork." It pleased her tremendously to use the young Freedmont boy's insult.

"Yeah, but he was a terrific-looking dork." Annie allowed herself a brief reminiscence. "Anyway, you helped me over that rough spot until I convinced myself I was better off without him. You've never needed my shoulder, Tash, because you've never let a guy get past this." She lifted a hand, pressing her palm against empty air.

Amused, Natasha leaned back against the counter. "And what is that?"

"The Great Stanislaski Force Field," Annie told her. "Guaranteed to repel all males from the age of twenty-five to fifty."

Natasha lifted a brow, not quite sure if she was amused any longer. "I'm not certain if you're trying to flatter or insult me."

"Neither. Just listen to me a minute, okay?" Annie took a deep breath to keep herself from rushing through something she thought should be taken step-by-step. "Tash, I've seen you brush off guys with less effort than you'd swat away a gnat. And just as automatically," she added when Natasha remained silent. "You're very pleasant about it, and also very definite. I've never seen you give any man a second's thought once you've politely shown him the door. I've even admired you for it, for being so sure of yourself, so comfortable with yourself that you didn't need a date on Saturday night to keep your ego out of the dirt."

"Not sure of myself," Natasha murmured. "Just apathetic about relationships."

"All right." Annie nodded slowly. "I'll accept that. But this time it's different."

"What is?" Natasha skirted the counter and began to tally the day's sales.

"You see? You know I'm going to mention his name, and you're nervous."

"I'm not nervous," Natasha lied.

"You've been nervous, moody and distracted since Kimball walked into the shop a couple of weeks ago. In over three years, I've never seen you give a man more than five minutes' thought. Until now."

"That's only because this one is more annoying than most." At Annie's shrewd look, Natasha gave up. "All right, there is…something," she admitted. "But I'm not interested."

"You're afraid to be interested."

Natasha didn't like the sound of that, but forced herself to shrug it off. "It's the same thing."

"No, it's not." Annie put a hand over Natasha's and squeezed. "Look, I'm not pushing you toward this guy. For all I know, he could have murdered his wife and buried her in the rose garden. All I'm saying is, you're not going to be comfortable with yourself until you stop being afraid."

Annie was right, Natasha thought later as she sat on her bed with her chin on her hand. She was moody, she was distracted. And she was afraid. Not of Spence, Natasha assured herself. No man would ever frighten her again. But she was afraid of the feelings he stirred up. Forgotten, unwanted feelings.

Did that mean she was no longer in charge of her emotions? No. Did that mean she would act irrationally, impulsively, just because needs and desires had pried their way back into her life? No. Did that mean she would hide in her room, afraid to face a man? A most definite no.

She was only afraid because she had yet to test herself, Natasha thought, moving toward her closet. So tonight she would have dinner with the persistent Dr. Kimball, prove to herself that she was strong and perfectly capable of resisting a fleeting attraction, then get back to normal.

Natasha frowned at her wardrobe. With a restless move of her shoulders she pulled out a deep blue cocktail dress with a jeweled belt. Not that she was dressing for him. He was really irrelevant. It was one of her favorite dresses, Natasha thought as she stripped off her robe, and she rarely had the opportunity to wear anything but work clothes.

He knocked at precisely seven twenty-eight. Natasha detested herself for anxiously watching the clock. She had reapplied her lipstick twice, checked and rechecked the contents of her purse and fervently wished that she had delayed taking her stand.

She was acting like a teenager, Natasha told herself as she walked to the door. It was only dinner, the first and last dinner she intended to share with him. And he was only a man, she added, pulling the door open.

An outrageously attractive man.

He looked wonderful, was all she could think, with his hair swept back from his face, and that half smile in his eyes. It had never occurred to her that a man could be gut-wrenchingly sexy in a suit and a tie.

"Hi." He held out another red rose.

Natasha nearly sighed. It was a pity the smoke-gray

suit didn't make him seem more professorial. Giving in a little, she tapped the blossom against her cheek. "It wasn't the roses that changed my mind."

"About what?"

"About having dinner with you." She stepped back, deciding that she had no choice but to let him in while she put the flower into water.

He smiled then, fully, and exasperated her by looking charming and cocky at the same time. "What did?"

"I'm hungry." She set her short velvet jacket on the arm of the sofa. "I'll put this in water. You can sit if you like."

She wasn't going to give him an inch, Spence thought as he watched her walk away. Oddly enough, that only made her more interesting. He took a deep breath, shaking his head. Incredible. Just when he was convinced that nothing smelled sexier than soap, she put something on that made him think of midnight and weeping violins.

Deciding that he was safer thinking of something else, he studied the room. She preferred vivid colors, he mused, noting the emerald and teal slashes of the pillows on a sapphire-blue couch. There was a huge brass urn beside it, stuffed with silky peacock feathers. Candles of varying sizes and shades were set around the room so that it smelled, romantically, of vanilla and jasmine and gardenia. A shelf in the corner was crammed with books that ran the gamut from popular fiction to classic literature by way of home improvements for the novice.

The table surfaces were crowded with mementos, framed pictures, dried bouquets, fanciful statuettes inspired by fairy tales. There was a gingerbread house no bigger than his palm, a girl dressed as Red Riding Hood, a pig peeking out of the window of a tiny straw house, a beautiful woman holding a single glass slipper.

Practical tips on plumbing, passionate colors and fairy tales, he mused, touching a fingertip to the tiny crystal slipper. It was as curious and as intriguing a combination as the woman herself.

Hearing her come back into the room, Spence turned. "These are beautiful," he said, gesturing to one of the figures. "Freddie's eyes would pop out."

"Thank you. My brother makes them."

"Makes them?" Fascinated, Spence picked up the gingerbread house to study it more closely. It was carved from polished wood, then intricately painted so that each licorice whip and lollipop looked good enough to eat. "It's incredible. You rarely see workmanship like this."

Whatever her reservations, she warmed toward him and crossed the room to join him. "He's been carving and sculpting since he was a child. One day his art will be in galleries and museums."

"It should be already."

The sincerity in his voice hit her most vulnerable spot, her love of family. "It's not so easy. He's young and hardheaded and proud, so he keeps his job, hammering wood, instead of carving it to bring in money for the family. But one day..." She smiled at the collection. "He makes these for me, because I struggled so hard to learn to read English from this book of fairy tales I found in the boxes of things the church gave us when we came to

New York. The pictures were so pretty, and I wanted so badly to know the stories that went with them."

She caught herself, embarrassed to have said anything. "We should go."

He only nodded, having already decided to pry gently until she told him more. "You should wear your jacket." He lifted it from the sofa. "It's getting chilly."

The restaurant he'd chosen was only a short drive away and sat on one of the wooded hills that overlooked the Potomac. If Natasha had been given a guess, she would have been on target with his preference for a quiet, elegant backdrop and discreetly speedy service. Over her first glass of wine, she told herself to relax and enjoy.

"Freddie was in the shop today."

"So I heard." Amused, Spence lifted his own glass. "She wants her hair curled."

Natasha's puzzled look became a smile; she lifted a hand to her own. "Oh. That's sweet."

"Easy for you to say. I've just gotten the hang of pigtails."

To her surprise, Natasha could easily picture him patiently braiding the soft, flaxen tresses. "She's beautiful." The image of him holding the girl on his lap at the piano slipped back into her mind. "She has your eyes."

"Don't look now," Spence murmured, "but I believe you've given me a compliment."

Feeling awkward, Natasha lifted the menu. "To soften the blow," she told him. "I'm about to make up for skipping lunch this afternoon."

True to her word, she ordered generously. As long as

she was eating, Natasha figured, the interlude would go smoothly. Over appetizers she was careful to steer the conversation toward subjects they had touched on in class. Comfortably they discussed late fifteenth-century music with its four-part harmonies and traveling musicians. Spence appreciated her genuine curiosity and interest, but was equally determined to explore more personal areas.

"Tell me about your family."

Natasha slipped a hot, butter-drenched morsel of lobster into her mouth, enjoying the delicate, almost decadent flavor. "I'm the oldest of four," she began, then became abruptly aware that his fingertips were playing casually with hers on the tablecloth. She slid her hand out of reach.

Her maneuver had him lifting his glass to hide a smile. "Are you all spies?"

A flicker of temper joined the lights that the candle brought to her eyes. "Certainly not."

"I wondered, since you seem so reluctant to talk about them." His face sober, he leaned toward her. "Say 'Get moose and squirrel.'"

Her mouth quivered before she gave up and laughed. "No." She dipped her lobster in melted butter again, coating it slowly, enjoying the scent, then the taste and texture. "I have two brothers and a sister. My parents still live in Brooklyn."

"Why did you move here, to West Virginia?"

"I wanted a change." She lifted a shoulder. "Didn't you?"

"Yes." A faint line appeared between his brows as he studied her. "You said you were about Freddie's age when you came to the States. Do you remember much about your life before that?"

"Of course." For some reason she sensed he was thinking more of his daughter than of her own memories of the Ukraine. "I've always believed impressions made on us in those first few years stay the longest. Good or bad, they help form what we are." Concerned, she leaned closer, smiling. "Tell me, when you think about being five, what do you remember?"

"Sitting at the piano, doing scales." It came so clearly that he nearly laughed. "Smelling hothouse roses and watching the snow outside the window. Being torn between finishing my practice and getting to the park to throw snowballs at my nanny."

"Your nanny," Natasha repeated, but with a chuckle rather than a sneer he noted. She cupped her chin in her hands, leaning closer, alluring him with the play of light and shadow over her face. "And what did you do?"

"Both."

"A responsible child."

He ran a fingertip down her wrist and surprised a shiver out of her. Before she moved her hand away, he felt her pulse scramble. "What do you remember about being five?"

Because her reaction annoyed her, she was determined to show him nothing. She only shrugged. "My father bringing in wood for the fire, his hair and coat all covered with snow. The baby crying—my youngest brother. The smell of the bread my mother had baked. Pretending to be asleep while I listened to Papa talk to her about escape."

"Were you afraid?"

"Yes." Her eyes blurred with the memory. She didn't often look back, didn't often need to. But when she did, it came not with the watery look of old dreams, but clear as glass. "Oh, yes. Very afraid. More than I will ever be again."

"Will you tell me?"

"Why?"

His eyes were dark, and fixed on her face. "Because I'd like to understand."

She started to pass it off, even had the words in her mind. But the memory remained too vivid. "We waited until spring and took only what we could carry. We told no one, no one at all, and set off in the wagon. Papa said we were going to visit my mother's sister who lived in the west. But I think there were some who knew, who watched us go with tired faces and big eyes. Papa had papers, badly forged, but he had a map and hoped we would avoid the border guards."

"And you were only five?"

"Nearly six by then." Thinking, she ran a fingertip around and around the rim of her glass. "Mikhail was between four and five, Alex just two. At night, if we could risk a fire, we would sit around it and Papa would tell stories. Those were good nights. We would fall asleep listening to his voice and smelling the smoke from the fire. We went over the mountains and into Hungary. It took us ninety-three days."

He couldn't imagine it, not even when he could see it reflected so clearly in her eyes. Her voice was low, but the emotions were all there, bringing it richness. Thinking of the little girl, he took her hand and waited for her to go on.

"My father had planned for years. Perhaps he had dreamed it all of his life. He had names, people who would help defectors. There was war, the cold one, but I was too young to understand. I understood the fear, in my parents, in the others who helped us. We were smuggled out of Hungary into Austria. The church sponsored us, brought us to America. It was a long time before I stopped waiting for the police to come and take my father away."

She brought herself back, embarrassed to have spoken of it, surprised to find her hand caught firmly in his.

"That's a lot for a child to deal with."

"I also remember eating my first hot dog." She smiled and picked up her wine again. She never spoke of that time, never. Not even with family. Now that she had, with him, she felt a desperate need to change the subject. "And the day my father brought home our first television. No childhood, even one with nannies, is ever completely secure. But we grow up. I'm a businesswoman, and you're a respected composer. Why don't you write?" She felt his fingers tense on hers. "I'm sorry," she said quickly. "I had no business asking that."

"It's all right." His fingers relaxed again. "I don't write because I can't."

She hesitated, then went on impulse. "I know your music. Something that intense doesn't fade."

"It hasn't mattered a great deal in the past couple of years. Just lately it's begun to matter again."

"Don't be patient."

When he smiled, she shook her head, at once impatient and regal. Her hand was gripping his now, hard and strong.

"No, I mean it. People always say when the time is right, when the mood is right, when the place is right. Years are wasted that way. If my father had waited until we were older, until the trip was safer, we might still be in the Ukraine. There are some things that should be grabbed with both hands and taken. Life can be very, very short."

He could feel the urgency in the way her hands gripped his. And he could see the shadow of regret in her eyes. The reason for both intrigued him as much as her words.

"You may be right," he said slowly, then brought the palm of her hand to his lips. "Waiting isn't always the best answer."

"It's getting late." Natasha pulled her hand free, then balled it into a fist on her lap. But that didn't stop the heat from spearing her arm. "We should go."

She was relaxed again when he walked her to her door. During the short drive home he had made her laugh with stories of Freddie's ploys to interest him in a kitten.

"I think cutting pictures of cats from a magazine to make you a poster was very clever." She turned to lean back against her front door. "You are going to let her have one?"

"I'm trying not to be a pushover."

Natasha only smiled. "Big old houses like yours tend to get mice in the winter. In fact, in a house of that size, you'd be wise to take two of JoBeth's kittens."

"If Freddie pulls that one on me, I'll know exactly where she got it." He twirled one of Natasha's curls around his fingers. "And you have a quiz coming up next week."

Natasha lifted both brows. "Blackmail, Dr. Kimball?"

"You bet."

"I intend to ace your quiz, and I have a strong feeling that Freddie could talk you into taking the entire litter all by herself, if she put her mind to it."

"Just the little gray one."

"You've already been to see them."

"A couple of times. You're not going to ask me in?"

"No."

"All right." He slipped his arms around her waist.

"Spence—"

"I'm just taking your advice," he murmured as he skimmed his lips over her jaw. "Not being patient." He brought her closer; his mouth brushed her earlobe. "Taking what I want." His teeth scraped over her bottom lip. "Not wasting time."

Then he was crushing his mouth against hers. He could taste the faintest tang of wine on her lips and knew he could get drunk on that alone. Her flavors were rich, exotic, intoxicating. Like the hint of autumn in the air, she made him think of smoking fires, drifting fog. And her body was already pressed eagerly against his in an instantaneous acknowledgment.

Passion didn't bloom, it didn't whisper. It exploded so that even the air around them seemed to shudder with it.

She made him feel reckless. Unaware of what he murmured to her, he raced his lips over her face, coming back, always coming back to her heated, hungry mouth. In one rough stroke he took his hands over her.

Her head was spinning. If only she could believe it was the wine. But she knew it was he, only he who made her dizzy and dazed and desperate. She wanted to be touched. By him. On a breathless moan, she let her head fall back, and the urgent trail of his lips streaked down her throat.

Feeling this way had to be wrong. Old fears and doubts swirled inside her, leaving empty holes that begged to be filled. And when they were filled, with liquid, shimmering pleasure, the fear only grew.

"Spence." Her fingers dug into his shoulders; she fought a war between the need to stop him and the impossible desire to go on. "Please."

He was as shaken as she and took a moment, burying his face in her hair. "Something happens to me every time I'm with you. I can't explain it."

She wanted badly to hold him against herself, but forced her arms to drop to her sides. "It can't continue to happen."

He drew away, just far enough to be able to take her face into both hands. The chill of the evening and the heat of passion had brought color to her cheeks. "If I wanted to stop it, which I don't, I couldn't."

She kept her eyes level with his and tried not to be moved by the gentle way he cradled her face. "You want to go to bed with me."

"Yes." He wasn't certain if he wanted to laugh or curse her for being so matter-of-fact. "But it's not quite that simple."

"Sex is never simple."

His eyes narrowed. "I'm not interested in having sex with you."

"You just said—"

"I want to make love with you. There's a difference."

"I don't choose to romanticize it."

The annoyance in his eyes vanished as quickly as it had appeared. "Then I'm sorry I'll have to disappoint you. When we make love, whenever, wherever, it's going to be very romantic." Before she could evade, he closed his mouth over hers. "That's a promise I intend to keep."

Chapter 5

"Natasha! Hey, ah, Natasha!"

Broken out of thoughts that weren't particularly productive, Natasha glanced over and spied Terry. He was wearing a long yellow-and-white-striped scarf in defense against a sudden plunge in temperature that had sprinkled frost on the ground. As he raced after her, it flapped awkwardly behind him. By the time he reached her, his glasses had slipped crookedly down to the tip of his reddening nose.

"Hi, Terry."

The hundred-yard dash had winded him. He dearly hoped it wouldn't aggravate his asthma. "Hi. I was—I saw you heading in." He'd been waiting hopefully for her for twenty minutes.

Feeling a bit like a mother with a clumsy child, she straightened his glasses, then wrapped the scarf more securely around his skinny neck. His rapid breathing fogged his lenses. "You should be wearing gloves," she told him, then patting his chilled hand, led him up the steps.

Overwhelmed, he tried to speak and only made a strangled sound in his throat.

"Are you catching a cold?" Searching through her purse, she found a tissue and offered it.

He cleared his throat loudly. "No." But he took the tissue and vowed to keep it until the day he died. "I was just wondering if tonight—after class—you know, if you don't have anything to do… You've probably got plans, but if you don't, then maybe…we could have a cup of coffee. Two cups," he amended desperately. "I mean you could have your own cup, and I'd have one." So saying, he turned a thin shade of green.

The poor boy was lonely, Natasha thought, giving him an absent smile. "Sure." It wouldn't hurt to keep him company for an hour or so, she decided as she walked into class. And it would help her keep her mind off…

Off the man standing in front of the class, Natasha reflected with a scowl; the man who had kissed the breath out of her two weeks before and who was currently laughing with a sassy little blonde who couldn't have been a day over twenty.

Her mood grim, she plopped down at her desk and poked her nose into a textbook.

Spence knew the moment she walked into the room. He was more than a little gratified to have seen the huffy jealousy on her face before she stuck a book in front of it. Apparently fate hadn't been dealing him such a bad hand when it kept him up to his ears in professional and personal problems for the last couple of weeks. Between leaky plumbing, PTA and Brownie meetings and a faculty conference, he hadn't had an hour free. But now things were running smoothly again. He studied the top of Natasha's head. He intended to make up for lost time.

Sitting on the edge of his desk, he opened a discussion of the distinctions between sacred and secular music during the baroque period.

She didn't want to be interested. Natasha was sure he knew it. Why else would he deliberately call on her for an opinion—twice?

Oh, he was clever, she thought. Not by a flicker, not by the slightest intonation did he reveal a more personal relationship with her. No one in class would possibly suspect that this smooth, even brilliant lecturer had kissed her senseless, not once, not twice, but three times. Now he calmly talked of early seventeenth-century operatic developments.

In his black turtleneck and gray tweed jacket he looked casually elegant and totally in charge. And of course, as always, he had the class in the palms of those beautiful hands he eloquently used to make a point. When he smiled over a student's comment, Natasha heard the little blonde two seats behind her sigh. Because she'd nearly done so herself, Natasha stiffened her spine.

He probably had a whole string of eager women. A man who looked like him, talked like him, kissed like him was bound to. He was the type that made promises to one woman at midnight and snuggled up to another over breakfast in bed.

Wasn't it fortunate she no longer believed in promises?

Something was going on inside that fabulous head of hers, Spence mused. One moment she was listening to him as if he had the answers to the mysteries of the universe on the tip of his tongue. The next, she was sitting rigidly and staring off into space, as though she wished herself somewhere else. He would swear that she was angry, and that the anger was directed squarely at him. Why was an entirely different matter.

Whenever he'd tried to have a word with her after class over the last couple of weeks, she'd been out of the building like a bullet. Tonight he would have to outmaneuver her.

She stood the moment class was over. Spence watched her smile at the man sitting across from her. Then she bent down to pick up the books and pencils the man scattered as he rose.

What was his name? Spence wondered. Maynard. That was it. Mr. Maynard was in several of his classes, and managed to fade into the background in each one. Yet at the moment the unobtrusive Mr. Maynard was crouched knee to knee with Natasha.

"I think we've got them all." Natasha gave Terry's glasses a friendly shove back up his nose.

"Thanks."

"Don't forget your scarf—" she began, then looked up. A hand closed over her arm and helped her to her feet. "Thank you, Dr. Kimball."

"I'd like to talk to you, Natasha."

"Would you?" She gave the hand on her arm a brief look, then snatched up her coat and books. Feeling as though she were on a chessboard again, she decided to aggressively counter his move. "I'm sorry, it'll have to wait. I have a date."

"A date?" he managed, getting an immediate picture of someone dark, dashing and muscle-bound.

"Yes. Excuse me." She shook off his hand and stuck an arm into the sleeve of her coat. Since the men on either side of her seemed equally paralyzed, she shifted the books to her other arm and struggled to find the second sleeve. "Are you ready, Terry?"

"Well, yeah, sure. Yeah." He was staring at Spence with a mixture of awe and trepidation. "But I can wait if you want to talk to Dr. Kimball first."

"There's no need." She scooped up his arm and pulled him to the door.

Women, Spence thought as he sat down at a desk. He'd already accepted the fact that he had never understood them. Apparently he never would.

"Jeez, Tash, don't you think you should have seen what Dr. Kimball wanted?"

"I know what he wanted," she said between her teeth as she pushed open the main doors. The rush of autumn air cooled her cheeks. "I wasn't in the mood to discuss it tonight." When Terry tripped over the uneven sidewalk, she realized she was still dragging him and slowed her pace. "Besides, I thought we were going to have some coffee."

"Right." When she smiled at him, he tugged on his scarf as if to keep from strangling.

They walked into a small lounge where half the little square tables were empty. At the antique bar two men were muttering over their beers. A couple in the corner were all but sitting on each other's laps and ignoring their drinks.

She'd always liked this room with its dim lighting and old black-and-white posters of James Dean and Marilyn Monroe. It smelled of cigarettes and jug wine. There was a big portable stereo on a shelf above the bar that played an old Chuck Berry number loudly enough to make up for the lack of patrons. Natasha felt the bass vibrate through her chair as she sat down.

"Just coffee, Joe," she called to the man behind the bar before she leaned her elbows on the table. "So," she said to Terry, "how's everything going?"

"Okay." He couldn't believe it. He was here, sitting with her. On a date. She'd called it a date herself.

It would take a little prodding. Patient, she shrugged out of her coat. The overheated room had her pushing the sleeves of her sweater past her elbows. "It must be different for you here. Did you ever tell me where you were going to college before?"

"I graduated from Michigan State." Because his lenses were fogged again, Natasha seemed to be shrouded by a thin, mysterious mist. "When I, ah, heard that Dr. Kimball would be teaching here, I decided to take a couple years of graduate study."

"You came here because of Spence—Dr. Kimball?"

"I didn't want to miss the opportunity. I went to New York last year to hear him lecture." Terry lifted a hand and nearly knocked over a bowl of sugar. "He's incredible."

"I suppose," she murmured as their coffee was served.

"Where you been hiding?" the bartender asked, giving her shoulder a casual squeeze. "I haven't seen you in here all month."

"Business is good. How's Darla?"

"History." Joe gave her a quick, friendly wink. "I'm all yours, Tash."

"I'll keep it in mind." With a laugh, she turned back to Terry. "Is something wrong?" she asked when she saw him dragging at his collar.

"Yes. No. That is… Is he your boyfriend?"

"My…" To keep herself from laughing in Terry's face, she took a sip of coffee. "You mean Joe? No." She cleared her throat and sipped again. "No, he's not. We're just…" She searched for a word. "Pals."

"Oh." Relief and insecurity warred. "I just thought, since he… Well."

"He was only joking." Wanting to put Terry at ease again, she squeezed his hand. "What about you? Do you have a girl back in Michigan?"

"No. There's nobody. Nobody at all." He turned his hand over, gripping hers.

Oh, my God. As realization hit, Natasha felt her mouth drop open. Only a fool would have missed it, she thought as she stared into Terry's adoring, myopic eyes. A fool, she added, who was so tied up with her own problems that she missed what was happening under her nose. She was going to have to be careful, Natasha decided. Very careful.

"Terry," she began. "You're very sweet—"

That was all it took to make his hand shake. Coffee spilled down his shirt. Moving quickly, Natasha shifted chairs so that she was beside him. Snatching paper napkins from the dispenser, she began to blot the stain.

"It's a good thing they never serve it hot in this place. If you soak this in cold water right away, you should be all right."

Overcome, Terry grabbed both of her hands. Her head was bent close, and the scent of her hair was making him dizzy. "I love you," he blurted, and took aim with his mouth; his glasses slid down his nose.

Natasha felt his lips hit her cheekbone, cold and trembly. Because her heart went out to him, she decided that being careful wasn't the right approach. Firmness was called for, quickly.

"No, you don't." Her voice was brisk, she pulled back far enough to dab at the spill on the table.

"I don't?" Her response threw him off. It was nothing like any of the fantasies he'd woven. There was the one where he'd saved her from a runaway truck. And another where he'd played the song he was writing for her and she had collapsed in a passionate, weeping puddle into his arms. His imagination hadn't stretched far enough to see her wiping up coffee and calmly telling him he wasn't in love at all.

"Yes, I do." He snatched at her hand again.

"That's ridiculous," she said, and smiled to take the sting out of the words. "You like me, and I like you, too."

"No, it's more than that. I—"

"All right. Why do you love me?"

"Because you're beautiful," he managed, losing his grip as he stared into her face again. "You're the most beautiful woman I've ever seen."

"And that's enough?" Disengaging her hand from his, she linked her fingers to rest her chin on them. "What if I told you I was a thief—or that I liked to run down small, furry animals with my car? Maybe I've been married three times and have murdered all my husbands in their sleep."

"Tash—"

She laughed, but resisted the temptation to pet his cheek. "I mean, you don't know me enough to love me. If you did, what I looked like wouldn't matter."

"But—but I think about you all the time."

"Because you've told yourself it would be nice to be in love with me." He looked so forlorn that she took a chance and laid one hand upon his. "I'm very flattered."

"Does this mean you won't go out with me?"

"I'm out with you now." She pushed her cup of coffee in front of him. "As friends," she said before the light could dawn again in his eyes. "I'm too old to be anything but your friend."

"No, you're not."

"Oh, yes." Suddenly she felt a hundred. "Yes, I am."

"You think I'm stupid," he muttered. In place of confused excitement came a crushing wave of humiliation. He could feel his cheeks sting with it.

"No, I don't." Her voice softened, and she reached once more for his hands. "Terry, listen—"

Before she could stop him, he pushed back his chair. "I've got to go."

Cursing herself, Natasha picked up his striped scarf. There was no use in following him now. He needed time, she decided. And she needed air.

The leaves were beginning to turn, and a few that had fallen early scraped along the sidewalk ahead of the wind. It was the kind of evening Natasha liked best, but now she barely noticed it. She'd left her coffee untouched to take a long, circular walk through town.

Heading home, she thought of a dozen ways she could have handled Terry's infatuation better. Through her clumsiness she had wounded a sensitive, vulnerable boy. It could have been avoided, all of it, if she had been paying attention to what was happening in front of her face.

Instead she'd been blinded by her own unwelcome feelings for someone else.

She knew too well what it was to believe yourself in love, desperately, hopelessly in love. And she knew how it hurt to discover that the one you loved didn't return those feelings. Cruel or kind, the rejection of love left the heart bruised.

Uttering a sigh, she ran a hand over the scarf in her pocket. Had she ever been so trusting and defenseless? Yes, she answered herself. That and much, much more.

* * *

It was about damn time, Spence thought as he watched her start up the walk. Obviously her mind was a million miles away. On her date, he decided and tried not to grind his teeth. Well, he was going to see to it that she had a lot more to think about in very short order.

"Didn't he walk you home?"

Natasha stopped dead with an involuntary gasp. In the beam of her porch light she saw Spence sitting on her stoop. That was all she needed, she thought while she dragged a hand through her hair. With Terry she'd felt as though she'd kicked a puppy. Now she was going to have to face down a large, hungry wolf.

"What are you doing here?"

"Freezing."

She nearly laughed. His breath was puffing out in white steam. With the windchill, she imagined that the effective temperature was hovering around twenty-five degrees Fahrenheit. After a moment, Natasha decided she must be a very poor sport to be amused at the thought of Spence sitting on cold concrete for the past hour.

He rose as she continued down the walk. How could she have forgotten how tall he was? "Didn't you invite your friend back for a drink?"

"No." She reached out and twisted the knob. Like most of the doors in town, it was unlocked. "If I had, you'd be very embarrassed."

"That's not the word for it."

"I suppose I'm lucky I didn't find you waiting up for me inside."

"You would have," he muttered, "if it had occurred to me to try the door."

"Good night."

"Wait a damn minute." He slapped his palm on the door before she could close it in his face. "I didn't sit out here in the cold for my health. I want to talk to you."

There was something satisfying in the brief, fruitless push-push they played with the door. "It's late."

"And getting later by the second. If you close the door, I'm just going to beat on it until all your neighbors poke their heads out their windows."

"Five minutes," she said graciously, because she had planned to grant him that in any case. "I'll give you a brandy, then you'll go."

"You're all heart, Natasha."

"No." She laid her coat over the back of the couch. "I'm not."

She disappeared into the kitchen without another word. When she returned with two snifters of brandy, he was standing in the center of the room, running Terry's scarf through his fingers.

"What kind of game are you playing?"

She set down his brandy, then sipped calmly at her own. "I don't know what you mean."

"What are you doing, going out on dates with some college kid who's still wet behind the ears?"

Both her back and her voice stiffened. "It's none of your business whom I go out with."

"It is now," Spence replied, realizing it now mattered to him.

"No, it's not. And Terry's a very nice young man."

"Young's the operative word." Spence tossed the scarf aside. "He's certainly too young for you."

"Is that so?" It was one thing for her to say it, and quite another to have Spence throw it at her like an accusation. "I believe that's for me to decide."

"Hit a nerve that time," Spence muttered to himself. There had been a time—hadn't there?—when he had been considered fairly smooth with women. "Maybe I should have said you're too old for him."

"Oh, yes." Despite herself, she began to see the humor of it. "That's a great deal better. Would you like to drink this brandy or wear it?"

"I'll drink it, thanks." He lifted the glass, but instead of bringing it to his lips, took another turn around the room. He was jealous, Spence realized. It was rather pathetic, but he was jealous of an awkward, tongue-tied grad student. And while he was about it, he was making a very big fool of himself. "Listen, maybe I should start over."

"I don't know why you would want to start something over you should never have begun."

But like a dog with a bone, he couldn't stop gnawing. "It's just that he's obviously not your type."

Fire blazed again. "Oh, and you'd know about my type?"

Spence held up his free hand. "All right, one straight question before my foot is permanently lodged in my mouth. Are you interested in him?"

"Of course I am." Then she cursed herself; it was

impossible to use Terry and his feelings as a barricade against Spence. "He's a very nice boy."

Spence almost relaxed, then spotted the scarf again, still spread over the back of her couch. "What are you doing with that?"

"I picked it up for him." The sight of it, bright and a little foolish on the jewel colors of her couch, made her feel like the most vicious kind of femme fatale. "He left it behind after I broke his heart. He thinks he's in love with me." Miserable, she dropped into a chair. "Oh, go away. I don't know why I'm talking to you."

The look on her face made him want to smile and stroke her hair. He thought better of it and kept his tone brisk. "Because you're upset, and I'm the only one here."

"I guess that'll do." She didn't object when Spence sat down across from her. "He was very sweet and nervous, and I had no idea what he was feeling—or what he thought he was feeling. I should have realized, but I didn't until he spilled his coffee all over his shirt, and... Don't laugh at him."

Spence continued to smile as he shook his head. "I'm not. Believe me, I know exactly how he must have felt. There are some women who make you clumsy."

Their eyes met and held. "Don't flirt with me."

"I'm past flirting with you, Natasha."

Restless, she rose to pace the room. "You're changing the subject."

"Am I?"

She waved an impatient hand as she paced. "I hurt his feelings. If I had known what was happening, I might have stopped it. There is nothing," she said passionately, "nothing worse than loving someone and being turned away."

"No." He understood that. And he could see by the shadows haunting her eyes that she did, too. "But you don't really believe he's in love with you."

"He believes it. I ask him why he thinks it, and do you know what he says?" She whirled back, her hair swirling around her shoulders with the movement. "He says because he thinks I'm beautiful. That's it." She threw up her hands and started to pace again. Spence only watched, caught up in her movements and by the musical cadence that agitation brought to her voice. "When he says it, I want to slap him and say—what's wrong with you? A face is nothing but a face. You don't know my mind or my heart. But he has big, sad eyes, so I can't yell at him."

"You never had a problem yelling at me."

"You don't have big, sad eyes, and you're not a boy who thinks he's in love."

"I'm not a boy," he agreed, catching her by the shoulders from behind. Even as she stiffened, he turned her around. "And I like more than your face, Natasha. Though I like that very much."

"You don't know anything about me, either."

"Yes, I do. I know you lived through experiences I can hardly imagine. I know you love and miss your family, that you understand children and have a natural affection for them. You're organized, stubborn and passionate." He ran his hands down her arms, then back to her shoulders. "I know you've been in love before." He tightened his grip before she could pull away. "And you're not ready to talk about it. You have a sharp, curious mind and caring heart, and you wish you weren't attracted to me. But you are."

She lowered her lashes briefly to veil her eyes. "Then it would seem you know more of me than I of you."

"That's easy to fix."

"I don't know if I want to. Or why I should."

His lips brushed hers, then retreated before she could respond or reject. "There's something there," he murmured. "That's reason enough."

"Maybe there is," she began. "No." She drew back when he would have kissed her again. "Don't. I'm not very strong tonight."

"A good way to make me feel guilty if I press my advantage."

She felt twin rushes of disappointment and relief when he released her. "I'll make you dinner," she said on impulse.

"Now?"

"Tomorrow. Just dinner," she added, wondering if she should already be regretting the invitation. "If you bring Freddie."

"She'd like that. So would I."

"Good. Seven o'clock." Natasha picked up his coat and held it out. "Now you have to go."

"You should learn to say what's on your mind." With a half laugh, Spence took the coat from her. "One more thing."

"Only one?"

"Yeah." He swung her back into his arms for one long, hard, mind-numbing kiss. He had the satisfaction of seeing her sink weakly onto the arm of the sofa when he released her.

"Good night," he said, then stepping outside, gulped in a deep breath of cold air.

It was the first time Freddie had been asked out to a grown-up dinner, and she waited impatiently while her father shaved. Usually she enjoyed watching him slide the razor through the white foam on his face. There were even times when she secretly wished she were a boy, so that she could look forward to the ritual. But tonight she thought her father was awfully slow.

"Can we go now?"

Standing in his bathrobe, Spence rinsed off the traces of lather. "It might be a better idea if I put some pants on."

Freddie only rolled her eyes. "When are you going to?"

Spence scooped her up to bite gently at her neck. "As soon as you beat it."

Taking him at his word, she raced downstairs to prowl the foyer and count to sixty. Around the fifth round, she sat on the bottom step to play with the buckle of her left shoe.

Freddie had it all figured out. Her father was going to marry either Tash or Mrs. Patterson, because they were both pretty and had nice smiles. Afterward, the one he married would come and live in their new house. Soon she would have a new baby sister. A baby brother would do in a pinch, but it was definitely a second choice. Everybody would be happy, because everybody would like each other a lot. And her daddy would play his music late at night again.

When she heard Spence start down, Freddie jumped up and whirled around to face him. "Daddy, I counted to sixty a jillion times."

"I bet you left out the thirties again." He took her coat from the hall closet and helped bundle her into it.

"No, I didn't." At least she didn't think she had. "You took forever." With a sigh, she pulled him to the door.

"We're still going to be early."

"She won't mind."

At that moment, Natasha was pulling a sweater over her head and wondering why she had invited anyone to dinner, particularly a man every instinct told her to avoid. She'd been distracted all day, worrying if the food would be right, if she'd chosen the most complementary wine. And now she was changing for the third time.

Totally out of character, she told herself as she frowned at her reflection in the mirror. The casual blue sweater and leggings calmed her. If she looked at ease, Natasha decided she would be at ease. She fastened long silver columns at her ears, gave her hair a quick toss, then hurried back to the kitchen. She had hardly checked her sauce when she heard the knock.

They were early, she thought, allowing herself one mild oath before going to the door.

They looked wonderful. Agitation vanished in a smile. The sight of the little girl with her hand caught firmly in her father's went straight to her heart. Because it came naturally, she bent to kiss Freddie on both cheeks. "Hello."

"Thank you for asking me to dinner." Freddie recited the sentence, then looked at her father for approval.

"You're welcome."

"Aren't you going to kiss Daddy, too?"

Natasha hesitated, then caught Spence's quick, challenging grin. "Of course." She brushed her lips formally against his cheeks. "That is a traditional Ukrainian greeting."

"I'm very grateful for *glasnost*." Still smiling, he took her hand and brought it to his lips.

"Are we going to have borscht?" Freddie wanted to know.

"Borscht?" Natasha lifted a brow as she helped Freddie out of her coat.

"When I told Mrs. Patterson that me and Daddy were going to have dinner at your house, she said that borscht was Russian for beet soup." Freddie managed not to say she thought it sounded gross, but Natasha got the idea.

"I'm sorry I didn't make any," she said, straight faced. "I made another traditional dish instead. Spaghetti and meatballs."

It was easy, surprisingly so. They ate at the old gateleg table by the window, and their talk ranged from Freddie's struggles with arithmetic to Neapolitan opera. It took only a little prodding for Natasha to talk of her family. Freddie wanted to know everything there was about being a big sister.

"We didn't fight very much," Natasha reflected as she drank after-dinner coffee and balanced Freddie on her knee. "But when we did, I won, because I was the oldest. And the meanest."

"You're not mean."

"Sometimes when I'm angry I am." She looked at Spence, remembering—and regretting—telling him he didn't deserve Freddie. "Then I'm sorry."

"When people fight, it doesn't always mean they don't like each other," Spence murmured. He was doing his best not to think how perfect, how perfectly right his daughter looked cuddled on Natasha's lap. Too far, too fast, he warned himself. For everyone involved.

Freddie wasn't sure she understood, but she was only five. Then she remembered happily that she would soon be six. "I'm going to have a birthday."

"Are you?" Natasha looked appropriately impressed. "When?"

"In two weeks. Will you come to my party?"

"I'd love to." Natasha looked at Spence as Freddie recited all the wonderful treats that were in store.

It wasn't wise to get so involved with the little girl, she warned herself. Not when the little girl was attached so securely to a man who made Natasha long for things she had put behind her. Spence smiled at her. No, it wasn't wise, she thought again. But it was irresistible.

Chapter 6

"Chicken pox." Spence said the two words again. He stood in the doorway and watched his little girl sleep. "It's a hell of a birthday present, sweetie."

In two days his daughter would be six, and by then, according to the doctor, she'd be covered with the itchy rash that was now confined to her belly and chest.

It was going around, the pediatrician had said. It would run its course. Easy for him to say, Spence thought. It wasn't his daughter whose eyes were teary. It wasn't his baby with a hundred-and-one-degree temperature.

She'd never been sick before, Spence realized as he rubbed his tired eyes. Oh, the sniffles now and again, but nothing a little TLC and baby aspirin hadn't put right. He dragged a hand through his hair; Freddie moaned in her sleep and tried to find a cool spot on her pillow.

The call from Nina hadn't helped. He'd had to come

down hard to prevent her from catching the shuttle and arriving on his doorstep. That hadn't stopped her telling him that Freddie had undoubtedly caught chicken pox because she was attending public school. That was nonsense, of course, but when he looked at his little girl, tossing in her bed, her face flushed with fever, the guilt was almost unbearable.

Logic told him that chicken pox was a normal part of childhood. His heart told him that he should be able to find a way to make it go away.

For the first time he realized how much he wanted someone beside him. Not to take things over, not to smooth over the downside of parenting. Just to be there. To understand what it felt like when your child was sick or hurt or unhappy. Someone to talk to in the middle of the night, when worries or pleasures kept you awake.

When he thought of that someone, he thought only of Natasha.

A big leap, he reminded himself and walked back to the bedside. One he wasn't sure he could make again and land on both feet.

He cooled Freddie's forehead with the damp cloth Vera had brought in. Her eyes opened.

"Daddy."

"Yes, funny face. I'm right here."

Her lower lip trembled. "I'm thirsty."

"I'll go get you a cold drink."

Sick or not, she knew how to maneuver. "Can I have Kool Aid?"

He pressed a kiss on her cheek. "Sure. What kind?"

"The blue kind."

"The blue kind." He kissed her again. "I'll be right back." He was halfway down the stairs when the phone rang simultaneously with a knock on the door. "Damn it. Vera, get the phone, will you?" Out of patience, he yanked open the front door.

The smile Natasha had practiced all evening faded. "I'm sorry. I've come at a bad time."

"Yeah." But he reached out to pull her inside. "Hang on a minute. Vera—oh good," he added when he saw the housekeeper hovering. "Freddie wants some Kool Aid, the blue kind."

"I will make it." Vera folded her hands in front of her apron. "Mrs. Barklay is on the phone."

"Tell her—" Spence broke off, swearing as Vera's mouth pruned. She didn't like to tell Nina anything. "All right, I'll get it."

"I should go," Natasha put in, feeling foolish. "I only came by because you weren't at class tonight, and I wondered if you were well."

"It's Freddie." Spence glanced at the phone and wondered if he could strangle his sister over it. "She has the chicken pox."

"Oh. Poor thing." She had to smother the automatic urge to go up and look in on the child herself. Not your child, Natasha reminded herself. Not your place. "I'll get out of your way."

"I'm sorry. Things are a little confused."

"Don't be. I hope she's well soon. Let me know if I can do anything."

At that moment Freddie called for her father in a voice that was half sniffle and half croak.

It was Spence's quick helpless glance up the stairs that had Natasha ignoring what she thought was her better judgment. "Would you like me to go up for a minute? I could sit with her until you have things under control again."

"No. Yes." Spence blew out a long breath. If he didn't deal with Nina now, she'd only call back. "I'd appreciate it." Reaching the end of his rope, he yanked up the phone receiver. "Nina."

Natasha followed the glow of the night-light into Freddie's room. She found her sitting up in bed, surrounded by dolls. Two big tears were sliding down her cheeks. "I want my daddy," she said obviously miserable.

"He'll be right here." Her heart lost, Natasha sat down on the bed and drew Freddie into her arms.

"I don't feel good."

"I know. Here, blow your nose."

Freddie complied, then settled her head on Natasha's breast. She sighed, finding it pleasantly different from her father's hard chest or Vera's cushy one. "I went to the doctor and got medicine, so I can't go to my Brownie meeting tomorrow."

"There'll be other meetings, as soon as the medicine makes you well."

"I have chicken pox," Freddie announced, torn between discomfort and pride. "And I'm hot and itchy."

"It's a silly thing, the chicken pox," Natasha said

soothingly. She tucked Freddie's tousled hair behind one ear. "I don't think chickens get it at all."

Freddie's lips turned up, just a little. "JoBeth had it last week, and so did Mikey. Now I can't have a birthday party."

"You'll have a party later, when everyone's well again."

"That's what Daddy said." A fresh tear trailed down her cheek. "It's not the same."

"No, but sometimes not the same is even better."

Curious, Freddie watched the light glint off the gold hoop in Natasha's ear. "How?"

"It gives you more time to think about how much fun you'll have. Would you like to rock?"

"I'm too big to rock."

"I'm not." Wrapping Freddie in a blanket, Natasha carried her to the white wicker rocker. She cleared it of stuffed animals, then tucked one particularly worn rabbit in Freddie's arms. "When I was a little girl and I was sick, my mother would always rock me in this big, squeaky chair we had by the window. She would sing me songs. No matter how bad I felt, when she rocked me I felt better."

"My mother didn't rock me." Freddie's head was aching, and she wanted badly to pop a comforting thumb into her mouth. She knew she was too old for that. "She didn't like me."

"That's not true." Natasha instinctively tightened her arms around the child. "I'm sure she loved you very much."

"She wanted my daddy to send me away."

At a loss, Natasha lowered her cheek to the top of Freddie's head. What could she say now? Freddie's words had been too matter-of-fact to dismiss as a fantasy. "People sometimes say things they don't mean, and that they regret very much. Did your daddy send you away?"

"No."

"There, you see?"

"Do you like me?"

"Of course I do." She rocked gently, to and fro. "I like you very much."

The movement, the soft female scent and voice lulled Freddie. "Why don't you have a little girl?"

The pain was there, deep and dull. Natasha closed her eyes against it. "Perhaps one day I will."

Freddie tangled her fingers in Natasha's hair, comforted. "Will you sing, like your mother did?"

"Yes. And you try to sleep."

"Don't go."

"No, I'll stay awhile."

Spence watched them from the doorway. In the shadowed light they looked achingly beautiful, the tiny, flaxen-haired child in the arms of the dark, golden-skinned woman. The rocker whispered as it moved back and forth while Natasha sang some old Ukrainian folk song from her own childhood.

It moved him as completely, as uniquely as holding the woman in his own arms had moved him. And yet so differently, so quietly that he wanted to stand just as he was, watching through the night.

Natasha looked up and saw him. He looked so frazzled that she had to smile.

"She's sleeping now."

If his legs were weak, he hoped it was because he'd climbed up and down the stairs countless times in the last twenty-four hours. Giving in to them, he sat down on the edge of the bed.

He studied his daughter's flushed face, nestled peacefully in the crook of Natasha's arm. "It's supposed to get worse before it gets better."

"Yes, it does." She stroked a hand down Freddie's hair. "We all had it when we were children. Amazingly, we all survived."

He blew out a long breath. "I guess I'm being an idiot."

"No, you're very sweet." She watched him as she continued to rock, wondering how difficult it had been for him to raise a baby without a mother's love. Difficult enough, she decided, that he deserved credit for seeing that his daughter was happy, secure and unafraid to love. She smiled again.

"Whenever one of us was sick as children, and still today, my father would badger the doctor, then he would go to church to light candles. After that he would say this old gypsy chant he'd learned from his grandmother. It's covering all the bases."

"So far I've badgered the doctor." Spence managed a smile of his own. "You wouldn't happen to remember that chant?"

"I'll say it for you." Carefully she rose, lifting Freddie in her arms. "Should I lay her down?"

"Thanks." Together they tucked in the blankets. "I mean it."

"You're welcome." She looked over the sleeping child, and though her smile was easy, she was beginning to feel awkward. "I should go. Parents of sick children need their rest."

"At least I can offer you a drink." He held up the glass. "How about some Kool Aid? It's the blue kind."

"I think I'll pass." She moved around the bed toward the door. "When the fever breaks, she'll be bored. Then you'll really have your work cut out for you."

"How about some pointers?" He took Natasha's hand as they started down the steps.

"Crayons. New ones. The best is usually the simplest."

"How is it someone like you doesn't have a horde of children of her own?" He didn't have to feel her stiffen to know he'd said the wrong thing. He could see the sorrow come and go in her eyes. "I'm sorry."

"No need." Recovered, she picked up her coat from where she'd laid it on the newel post. "I'd like to come and see Freddie again, if it's all right."

He took her coat and set it down again. "If you won't take the blue stuff, how about some tea? I could use the company."

"All right."

"I'll just—" He turned and nearly collided with Vera.

"I will fix the tea," she said after a last look at Natasha.

"Your housekeeper thinks I have designs on you."

"I hope you won't disappoint her," Spence said as he led Natasha into the music room.

"I'm afraid I must disappoint both of you." Then she laughed and wandered to the piano. "But you should be very busy. All the young women in college talk about Dr. Kimball." She tucked her tongue into her cheek. "You're a hunk, Spence. Popular opinion is equally divided between you and the captain of the football team."

"Very funny."

"I'm not joking. But it's fun to embarrass you." She sat and ran her fingers over the keys. "Do you compose here?"

"I did once."

"It's wrong of you not to write." She played a series of chords. "Art's more than a privilege. It's a responsibility." She searched for the melody, then with a sound of impatience shook her head. "I can't play. I was too old when I tried to learn."

He liked the way she looked sitting there, her hair falling over her shoulders, half curtaining her face, her fingers resting lightly on the keys of the piano he had played since childhood.

"If you want to learn, I'll teach you."

"I'd rather you write a song." It was more than impulse, she thought. Tonight he looked as though he needed a friend. She smiled and held out a hand. "Here, with me."

He glanced up as Vera carried in a tray. "Just set it there, Vera. Thank you."

"You will want something else?"

He looked back at Natasha. Yes, he would want something else. He wanted it very much. "No. Good night." He listened to the housekeeper's shuffling steps. "Why are you doing this?"

"Because you need to laugh. Come, write a song for me. It doesn't have to be good."

He did laugh. "You want me to write a bad song for you?"

"It can be a terrible song. When you play it for Freddie, she'll hold her ears and giggle."

"A bad song's about all I can do these days." But he was amused enough to sit down beside her. "If I do this, I have to have your solemn oath that it won't be repeated for any of my students."

"Cross my heart."

He began to noodle with the keys, Natasha breaking in now and then to add her inspiration. It wasn't as bad as it might have been, Spence considered as he ran through some chords. No one would call it brilliant, but it had a certain primitive charm.

"Let me try." Tossing back her hair, Natasha struggled to repeat the notes.

"Here." As he sometimes did with his daughter, he put his hands over Natasha's to guide them. The feeling, he realized, was entirely different. "Relax." His murmur whispered beside her ear.

She only wished she could. "I hate to do poorly at anything," she managed. With his palms firmly over her hands, she struggled to concentrate on the music.

"You're doing fine." Her hair, soft and fragrant, brushed his cheek.

As they bent over the keys, it didn't occur to him that he hadn't played with the piano in years. Oh, he had played—Beethoven, Gershwin, Mozart and Bernstein, but hardly for fun.... It had been much too long since he had sat before the keys for entertainment.

"No, no, an A minor maybe."

Natasha stubbornly hit a B major again. "I like this better."

"It throws it off."

"That's the point."

He grinned at her. "Want to collaborate?"

"You do better without me."

"I don't think so." His grin faded; he cupped her face in one hand. "I really don't think so."

This wasn't what she had intended. She had wanted to lighten his mood, to be his friend. She hadn't wanted to stir these feelings in both of them, feelings they would be wiser to ignore. But they were there, pulsing. No matter how strong her will, she couldn't deny them. Even the light touch of his fingers on her face made her ache, made her yearn, made her remember.

"The tea's getting cold." But she didn't pull away, didn't try to stand. When he leaned over to touch his mouth to hers, she only shut her eyes. "This can't go anywhere," she murmured.

"It already has." His hand moved up her back, strong, possessive, in contrast with the light play of his lips. "I think about you all the time, about being with you, touching you. I've never wanted anyone the way I want you." Slowly he ran a hand down her throat, over her shoulder, along her arm until their fingers linked over the piano keys. "It's like a thirst, Natasha, a constant thirst. And when I'm with you like this, I know it's the same for you."

She wanted to deny it, but his mouth was roaming hungrily over her face, taunting hers to tremble with need. And she did need, to be held like this, wanted like this. It had been easy in the past to pretend that being desired wasn't necessary. No, she hadn't had to pretend. Until now, until him, it had been true.

Now, suddenly, like a door opening, like a light being switched on, everything had changed. She yearned for him, and her blood swam faster, just knowing he wanted her. Even for a moment, she told herself as her hands clutched at his hair to pull his mouth to hers. Even for this moment.

It was there again, that whirlwind of sensation that erupted the instant they came together. Too fast, too hot, too real to be borne. Too stunning to be resisted.

It was as though he were the first, though he was not. It was as though he were the only one, though that could never be. As she poured herself into the kiss, she wished desperately that her life could begin again in that moment, with him.

There was more than passion here. The emotions that swirled inside her nearly swallowed him. There was desperation, fear and a bottomless generosity that left him dazed. Nothing would ever be simple again. Knowing it, a part of him tried to pull back, to think, to reason. But the taste of her, hot, potent, only drew him closer to the flame.

"Wait." For the first time she admitted her own weakness and let her head rest against his shoulder. "This is too fast."

"No." He combed his fingers through her hair. "It's taken years already."

"Spence." Struggling for balance, she straightened. "I don't know what to do," she said slowly, watching him. "It's important for me to know what to do."

"I think we can figure it out." But when he reached for her again, she rose quickly and stepped away.

"This isn't simple for me." Unnerved, she pushed back her hair with both hands. "I know it might seem so, because of the way I respond to you. I know that it's easier for men, less personal somehow."

He rose very carefully, very deliberately. "Why don't you explain that?"

"I only mean that I know that men find things like this less difficult to justify."

"Justify," he repeated, rocking back on his heels. How could he be angry so quickly, after being so bewitched? "You make this sound like some kind of crime."

"I don't always find the right words," she snapped. "I'm not a college professor. I didn't speak English until I was eight, couldn't read it for longer than that."

He checked his temper as he studied her. Her eyes were dark with something more than anger. She was standing stiffly, head up, but he couldn't tell if her stand was one of pride or self-defense. "What does that have to do with anything?"

"Nothing. And everything." Frustrated, she whirled back into the hallway to snatch up her coat. "I hate feeling stupid—hate being stupid. I don't belong here. I shouldn't have come."

"But you did." He grabbed her by her shoulders, so that her coat flew out to fall onto the bottom step. "Why did you?"

"I don't know. It doesn't matter why."

He gave her an impatient squeeze. "Why do I feel as if I'm having two conversations at the same time? What's going on in that head of yours, Natasha?"

"I want you," she said passionately. "And I don't want to."

"You want me." Before she could jerk away, he pulled her against himself. There was no patience in this kiss, no persuasion. It took and took, until she was certain she could have nothing left to give. "Why does that bother you?" he murmured against her lips.

Unable to resist, she ran her hands over his face, memorizing the shape. "There are reasons."

"Tell me about them."

She shook her head, and this time when she pulled back, he released her. "I don't want my life to change. If something happened between us, yours would not, but mine might. I want to be sure it doesn't."

"Does this lead back to that business about men and women thinking differently?"

"Yes."

That made him wonder who had broken her heart, and he didn't smile. "You look more intelligent than that. What I feel for you has already changed my life."

That frightened her, because it made her want to believe it. "Feelings come and go."

"Yes, they do. Some of them. What if I told you I was falling in love with you?"

"I wouldn't believe you." Her voice shook, and she bent to pick up her coat. "And I would be angry with you for saying it."

Maybe it was best to wait until he could make her believe. "And if I told you that until I met you, I didn't know I was lonely?"

She lowered her eyes, much more moved by this than she would have been by any words of love. "I would have to think."

He touched her again, just a hand to her hair. "Do you think everything through?"

Her eyes were eloquent when she looked at him. "Yes."

"Then think about this. It wasn't my intention to seduce you—not that I haven't given that a great deal of thought on my own, but I didn't see it happening with my daughter sick upstairs."

"You didn't seduce me."

"Now she's taking potshots at my ego."

That made her smile. "There was no seduction. That implies planned persuasion. I don't want to be seduced."

"I'll keep that in mind. All the same, I don't think I want to dissect all this like a Music major with a

Beethoven concerto. It ruins the romance in much the same way."

She smiled again. "I don't want romance."

"That's a pity." And a lie, he thought, remembering the way she'd looked when he'd given her a rose. "Since chicken pox is going to be keeping me busy for the next week or two, you'll have some time. Will you come back?"

"To see Freddie." She shrugged into her coat, then relented. "And to see you."

She did. What began as just a quick call to bring Freddie a get-well present turned into the better part of an evening, soothing a miserable, rash-ridden child and an exhausted, frantic father. Surprisingly she enjoyed it, and made a habit over the next ten days of dropping in over her lunch break to spell a still-suspicious Vera, or after work to give Spence a much-needed hour of peace and quiet.

As far as romance went, bathing an itchy girl in corn starch left a lot to be desired. Despite it, Natasha found herself only more attracted to Spence and more in love with his daughter.

She watched him do his best to cheer the miserably uncomfortable patient on her birthday, then helped him deal with the pair of kittens that were Freddie's favored birthday gift. As the rash faded and boredom set in, Natasha pumped up Spence's rapidly fading imagination with stories of her own.

"Just one more story."

Natasha smoothed Freddie's covers under her chin. "That's what you said three stories ago."

"You tell good ones."

"Flattery will get you nowhere. It's past my bedtime." Natasha lifted a brow at the big red alarm clock. "And yours."

"The doctor said I could go back to school on Monday. I'm not 'fectious."

"Infectious," Natasha corrected. "You'll be glad to see your friends again."

"Mostly." Stalling, Freddie played with the edge of her blanket. "Will you come and see me when I'm not sick?"

"I think I might." She leaned over to make a grab and came up with a mewing kitten. "And to see Lucy and Desi."

"And Daddy."

Cautious, Natasha scratched the kitten's ears. "Yes, I suppose."

"You like him, don't you?"

"Yes. He's a very good teacher."

"He likes you, too." Freddie didn't add that she had seen her father kiss Natasha at the foot of her bed just the night before, when they'd thought she was asleep. Watching them had given her a funny feeling in her stomach. But after a minute it had been a good funny feeling. "Will you marry him and come and live with us?"

"Well, is that a proposal?" Natasha managed to smile. "I think it's nice that you'd want me to, but I'm only friends with your daddy. Like I'm friends with you."

"If you came to live with us, we'd still be friends."

The child, Natasha reflected, was as clever as her father. "Won't we be friends if I live in my own house?"

"I guess." The pouty lower lip poked out. "But I'd like it better if you lived here, like JoBeth's mom does. She makes cookies."

Natasha leaned toward her, nose to nose. "So, you want me for my cookies."

"I love you." Freddie threw her arms around Natasha's neck and clung. "I'd be a good girl if you came."

Stunned, Natasha hugged the girl tight and rocked. "Oh, baby, I love you, too."

"So you'll marry us."

Put like that, Natasha wasn't sure whether to laugh or cry. "I don't think getting married right now is the answer for any of us. But I'll still be your friend, and come visit and tell you stories."

Freddie gave a long sigh. She knew when an adult was evading, and realized that it would be smart to retreat a step. Particularly when she had already made up her mind. Natasha was exactly what she wanted for a mother. And there was the added bonus that Natasha made her daddy laugh. Freddie decided then and there that her most secret and solemn Christmas wish would be for Natasha to marry her father and bring home a baby sister.

"Promise?" Freddie demanded.

"Cross my heart." Natasha gave her a kiss on each cheek. "Now you go to sleep. I'll find your daddy so he can come up and kiss you good-night."

Freddie closed her eyes, her lips curved with her own secret smile.

Carrying the kitten, Natasha made her way downstairs. She'd put off her monthly books and an inventory to visit tonight. More than a little midnight oil would be burned, she decided, rubbing the kitten against her cheek.

She would have to be careful with Freddie now, and with herself. It was one thing for her to have fallen in love with the youngster, but quite another for the girl to love her enough to want her for a mother. How could she expect a child of six to understand that adults often had problems and fears that made it impossible for them to take the simple route?

The house was quiet, but a light was shining from the music room. She set down the kitten, knowing he would unerringly race to the kitchen.

She found Spence in the music room, spread on the two-cushion sofa so that his legs hung over one end. In sloppy sweats and bare feet he looked very little like the brilliant composer and full professor of music. Nor had he shaved. Natasha was forced to admit that the shadow of stubble only made him more attractive, especially when combined with tousled hair a week or two late for the barber.

He was sleeping deeply, a throw pillow crunched under his head. Natasha knew, because Vera had unbent long enough to tell her that Spence had stayed up throughout two nights during the worst of his daughter's fever and discomfort.

She was aware, too, that he had juggled his schedule at the college with trips home during the day. More than once during her visits she'd found him up to his ears in paperwork.

Once she had thought him pampered, a man who'd come by his talents and his position almost by birth. Perhaps he had been born with his talent, she thought now, but he worked hard, for himself and for his child. There was nothing she could admire more in a man.

I'm falling in love with him, she admitted. With his smile and his temper, his devotion and his drive. Perhaps, just perhaps they could give something to each other. Cautiously, carefully, with no promises between them.

She wanted to be his lover. She had never wanted such a thing before. With Anthony it had just happened, overwhelming her, sweeping her up and away, then leaving her shattered. It wouldn't be that way with Spence. Nothing would ever hurt her that deeply again. And with him there was a chance, just a chance of happiness.

Shouldn't she take it? Moving quietly, she unfolded the throw of soft blue wool that was draped along the back of the couch to spread it over him. It had been a long time since she'd taken a risk. Perhaps the time was here. She bent to brush her lips over his brow. And the man.

Chapter 7

The black cat screeched a warning. A rushing gust of wind blew open the door with an echoing slam and maniacal laughter rolled in. What sounded like ooze dripped down the walls, plunking dully onto the bare concrete floor as the prisoners rattled their chains. There was a piercing scream followed by a long, desperate moan.

"Great tunes," Annie commented and popped a gum ball into her mouth.

"I should have ordered more of those records." Natasha took an orange fright wig and turned a harmless stuffed bear into a Halloween ghoul. "That's the last one."

"After tonight you'll have to start thinking Christmas, anyway." Annie pushed back her pointed black hat, then grinned, showing blackened teeth. "Here come the Freedmont boys." She rubbed her hands together and tried out a cackle. "If this costume's worth anything, I should be able to turn them into frogs."

She didn't quite manage that, but sold them fake blood and latex scars.

"I wonder what those little dears have in store for the neighborhood tonight," Natasha mused.

"Nothing good." Annie ducked under a hanging bat. "Shouldn't you get going?"

"Yes, in a minute." Stalling, Natasha fiddled with her dwindling supply of masks and fake noses. "The pig snouts sold better than I'd imagined. I didn't realize so many people would want to dress up as livestock." She picked one up to hold it over her nose. "Maybe we should keep them out year round."

Recognizing her friend's tactics, Annie ran her tongue over her teeth to keep from grinning. "It was awfully nice of you to volunteer to help decorate for Freddie's party tonight."

"It's a little thing," Natasha said and hated herself for being nervous. She replaced the snout, then ran her finger over a wrinkled elephant trunk attached to over-size glasses. "Since I suggested the idea of her having a Halloween party to make up for her missed birthday, I thought I should help."

"Uh-huh. I wonder if her daddy's going to come as Prince Charming."

"He is not Prince Charming."

"The Big Bad Wolf?" On a laugh, Annie held up her hands in a gesture of peace. "Sorry. It's just such a kick to see you unnerved."

"I'm not unnerved." That was a big lie, Natasha admitted while she packed up some of her contributions to the party. "You know, you're welcome to come."

"And I appreciate it. I'd rather stay home and guard my house from preadolescent felons. And don't worry," she added before Natasha could speak again. "I'll lock up."

"All right. Maybe I'll just—" Natasha broke off as the door jingled open. Another customer, she thought, would give her a little more time. When she spotted Terry, there was no way of saying who was more surprised. "Hello."

He swallowed over the huge lump in his throat and tried to look beyond her costume. "Tash?"

"Yes." Hoping he'd forgiven her by now, she smiled and held out a hand. He'd changed his seat in class, and every time she had tried to approach him, he'd darted off. Now he stood trapped, embarrassed and uncertain. He touched her outstretched hand, then stuck his own into his pocket.

"I didn't expect to see you here."

"No?" She tilted her head. "This is my shop." She wondered if it would strike him that she had been right when she'd said how little he knew her, and her voice softened. "I own it."

"You own it?" He looked around, unable to hide the impression it made on him. "Wow. That's something."

"Thank you. Did you come to buy something or just to look?"

Instantly he colored. It was one thing to go into a

store, and another to go into one where the owner was a woman he'd professed to love. "I just…ah…"

"Something for Halloween?" she prompted. "They have parties at the college."

"Yeah, well, I kind of thought I might slip into a couple. I guess it's silly really, but…"

"Halloween is very serious business here at The Fun House," Natasha told him solemnly. As she spoke, another scream ripped from the speakers. "You see?"

Embarrassed that he'd jumped, Terry managed a weak smile. "Yeah. Well, I was thinking, maybe a mask or something. You know." His big, bony hands waved in space, then retreated to his pockets.

"Would you like to be scary or funny?"

"I don't, ah, I haven't thought about it."

Understanding, Natasha resisted the urge to pat his cheek. "You might get some ideas when you look at what we have left. Annie, this is my friend, Terry Maynard. He's a violinist."

"Hi." Annie watched his glasses slide down his nose after his nervous nod of greeting and thought him adorable. "We're running low, but we've still got some pretty good stuff. Why don't you come over and take a look? I'll help you pick one out."

"I have to run." Natasha began gathering up her two shopping bags, hoping that the visit had put them back on more solid ground. "Have a good time at your party, Terry."

"Thanks."

"Annie, I'll see you in the morning."

"Right. Don't bob for too many apples." Pushing her pointed hat out of her eyes again, Annie grinned at Terry. "So, you're a violinist."

"Yeah." He gave Natasha's retreating back one last look. When the door closed behind her he felt a pang, but only a small one. "I'm taking some graduate classes at the college."

"Great. Hey, can you play 'Turkey in the Straw'?"

Outside Natasha debated running home to get her car. The cool, clear air changed her mind. The trees had turned. The patchwork glory of a week before, with its scarlets and vivid oranges and yellows, had blended into a dull russet. Dry, curling leaves spun from the branches to crowd against the curbs and scatter on the sidewalks. They crackled under her feet as she began the short walk.

The hardiest flowers remained, adding a spicy scent so different from the heavy fragrances of summer. Cooler, cleaner, crisper, Natasha thought as she drew it in.

She turned off the main street to where hedges and big trees shielded the houses. Jack-o'-lanterns sat on stoops and porches, grinning as they waited to be lighted at dusk. Here and there effigies in flannel shirts and torn jeans hung from denuded branches. Witches and ghosts stuffed with straw sat on steps, waiting to scare and delight the wandering trick-or-treaters.

If anyone had asked her why she had chosen a small town in which to settle, this would have been one of her answers. People here took the time—the time to carve a pumpkin, the time to take a bundle of old clothes and fashion it into a headless horseman. Tonight, before the moon rose, children could race along the streets, dressed as fairies or goblins. Their goody bags would swell with store-bought candy and homemade cookies, while adults pretended not to recognize the miniature hoboes, clowns and demons. The only thing the children would have to fear was make-believe.

Her child would have been seven.

Natasha paused for a moment, pressing a hand to her stomach until the grief and the memory could be blocked. How many times had she told herself the past was past? And how many times would that past sneak up and slice at her?

True, it came less often now, but still so sharply and always unexpectedly. Days could go by, even months, then it surfaced, crashing over her, leaving her a little dazed, a little tender, like a woman who had walked into a wall.

A car engine was gunned. A horn blasted. "Hey, Tash."

She blinked and managed to lift a hand in passing salute, though she couldn't identify the driver, who continued on his way.

This was now, she told herself, blinking to focus again on the swirl of leaves. This was here. There was never any going back. Years before she had convinced herself that the only direction was forward. Deliberately she took a long, deep breath, relieved when she felt her system level. Tonight wasn't the time for sorrows. She had promised another child a party, and she intended to deliver.

She had to smile when she started up the steps of Spence's home. He had already been working, she noted. Two enormous jack-o'-lanterns flanked the porch. Like Comedy and Tragedy, one grinned and the other scowled. Across the railing a white sheet had been shaped and spread so that the ghost it became seemed to be in full flight. Cardboard bats with red eyes swooped down from the eaves. In an old rocker beside the door sat a hideous monster who held his laughing head in his hand. On the door was a full-size cutout of a witch stirring a steaming cauldron.

Natasha knocked under the hag's warty nose. She was laughing when Spence opened the door. "Trick or treat," she said.

He couldn't speak at all. For a moment he thought he was imagining things, had to be. The music-box gypsy was standing before him, gold dripping from her ears and her wrists. Her wild mane of hair was banded by a sapphire scarf that flowed almost to her waist with the corkscrew curls. More gold hung around her neck, thick, ornate chains that only accented her slenderness. The red dress was snug, scooped at the bodice and full in the skirt, with richly colored scarfs tied at the waist.

Her eyes were huge and dark, made mysterious by some womanly art. Her lips were full and red, turned up now as she spun in a saucy circle. It took him only seconds to see it all, down to the hints of black lace at the hem. He felt as though he'd been standing in the doorway for hours.

"I have a crystal ball," she told him, reaching into her

pocket to pull out a small, clear orb. "If you cross my palm with silver, I'll gaze into it for you."

"My God," he managed. "You're beautiful."

She only laughed and stepped inside. "Illusions. Tonight is meant for them." With a quick glance around, she slipped the crystal back into her pocket. But the image of the gypsy and the mystery remained. "Where's Freddie?"

His hand had gone damp on the knob. "She's…" It took a moment for his brain to kick back into gear. "She's at JoBeth's. I wanted to put things together when she wasn't around."

"A good idea." She studied his gray sweats and dusty sneakers. "Is this your costume?"

"No. I've been hanging cobwebs."

"I'll give you a hand." Smiling, she held up her bags. "I have some tricks and I have some treats. Which would you like first?"

"You have to ask?" he said quietly, then hooking an arm around her waist, brought her up hard against himself. She threw her head back, words of anger and defiance in her eyes and on the tip of her tongue. Then his mouth found hers. The bags slipped out of her hands. Freed, her fingers dived into his hair.

This wasn't what she wanted. But it was what she needed. Without hesitation her lips parted, inviting intimacy. She heard his quiet moan of pleasure merge with her own. It seemed right, somehow it seemed perfectly right to be holding him like this, just inside his front door, with the scents of fall flowers and fresh polish in the air, and the sharp-edged breeze of autumn rushing over them.

It was right. He could taste and feel the rightness with her body pressed against his own, her lips warm and agile. No illusion this. No fantasy was she, despite the colorful scarfs and glittering gold. She was real, she was here, and she was his. Before the night was over, he would prove it to both of them.

"I hear violins," he murmured as he trailed his lips down her throat.

"Spence." She could only hear her heartbeat, like thunder in her head. Struggling for sanity, she pushed away. "You make me do things I tell myself I won't." After a deep breath she gave him a steady look. "I came to help you with Freddie's party."

"And I appreciate it." Quietly he closed the door. "Just like I appreciate the way you look, the way you taste, the way you feel."

She shouldn't have been so aroused by only a look. Couldn't be, not when the look told her that whatever the crystal in her pocket promised, he already knew their destiny. "This is a very inappropriate time."

He loved the way her voice could take on that regal tone, czarina to peasant. "Then we'll find a better one."

Exasperated, she hefted the bags again. "I'll help you hang your cobwebs, if you promise to be Freddie's father—and only Freddie's father while we do."

"Okay." He didn't see any other way he'd survive an evening with twenty costumed first-graders. And the party, he thought, wouldn't last forever. "We'll be pals for the duration."

She liked the sound of it. Choosing a bag, she reached inside. She held up a rubber mask of a bruised, bloodied and scarred face. Competently she slipped it over Spence's head. "There. You look wonderful."

He adjusted it until he could see her through both eyeholes, and had a foolish and irresistible urge to look at himself in the hall mirror. Behind the mask he grinned. "I'll suffocate."

"Not for a couple of hours yet." She handed him the second bag. "Come on. It takes time to build a haunted house."

It took them two hours to transform Spence's elegantly decorated living room into a spooky dungeon, fit for rats and screams of torture. Black and orange crepe paper hung on the walls and ceiling. Angel-hair cobwebs draped the corners. A mummy, arms folded across its chest leaned in a corner. A black-caped witch hung in the air, suspended on her broom. Thirsty and waiting for dusk, an evil-eyed Dracula lurked in the shadows, ready to pounce.

"You don't think it's too scary?" Spence asked as he hung up a Pin-the-Nose-on-the-Pumpkin game. "They're first-graders."

Natasha flicked a finger over a rubber spider that hung by a thread and sent him spinning. "Very mild. My brothers made a haunted house once. They blindfolded Rachel and me to take us through. Mikhail put my hand in a bowl of grapes and told me it was eyes."

"Now that's disgusting," Spence decided.

"Yes." It delighted her to remember it. "Then there was this spaghetti—"

"Never mind," he interrupted. "I get the idea."

She laughed, adjusting her earring. "In any case, I had a wonderful time and have always wished I'd thought of it first. The children tonight would be very disappointed if we didn't have some monsters waiting for them. After they've been spooked, which they desperately want to be, you turn on the lights, so they see it's all pretend."

"Too bad we're out of grapes."

"It's all right. When Freddie's older, I'll show you how to make a bloodied severed hand out of a rubber glove."

"I can't wait."

"What about food?"

"Vera's been a Trojan." With his mask on top of his head, Spence stood back to study the whole room. It felt good, really good to look at the results, and to know that he and Natasha had produced them together. "She's made everything from deviled eggs to witch's brew punch. You know what would have been great? A fog machine."

"That's the spirit." His grin made her laugh and long to kiss him. "Next year."

He liked the sound of that, he realized. Next year, and

the year after. A little dazed at the speed with which his thoughts were racing, he only studied her.

"Is something wrong?"

"No." He smiled. "Everything's just fine."

"I have the prizes here." Wanting to rest her legs, Natasha sat on the arm of a chair beside a lounging ghoul. "For the games and costumes."

"You didn't have to do that."

"I told you I wanted to. This is my favorite." She pulled out a skull, then flicking a switch, set it on the floor where it skimmed along, disemboded, its empty eyes blinking.

"Your favorite." Tongue in cheek, Spence picked it up where it vibrated in his hand.

"Yes. Very gruesome." She tilted her head. "Say 'Alas, poor Yorick!'"

He only laughed and switched it off. Then he pulled down his mask. "'O, that this too, too solid flesh would melt.'" She was chuckling when he came over and lifted her to her feet. "Give us a kiss."

"No," she decided after a moment. "You're ugly."

"Okay." Obligingly he pushed the mask up again. "How about it?"

"Much worse." Solemnly she slid the mask down again.

"Very funny."

"No, but it seemed necessary." Linking her arm with his, she studied the room. "I think you'll have a hit."

"We'll have a hit," he corrected. "You know Freddie's crazy about you."

"Yes." Natasha gave him an easy smile. "It's mutual."

They heard the front door slam and a shout. "Speaking of Freddie."

Children arrived first in trickles, then in a flood. When the clock struck six, the room was full of ballerinas and pirates, monsters and superheroes. The haunted house brought gasps and shrieks and shudders. No one was brave enough to make the tour alone, though many made it twice, then a third time. Occasionally a stalwart soul was courageous enough to poke a finger into the mummy or touch the vampire's cape.

When the lights were switched on there were moans of disappointment and a few relieved sighs. Freddie, a life-size Raggedy Ann, tore open her belated birthday presents with abandon.

"You're a very good father," Natasha murmured.

"Thanks." He linked his fingers with hers, no longer questioning why it should be so right for them to stand together and watch over his daughter's party. "Why?"

"Because you haven't once retreated for aspirin, and you hardly winced when Mikey spilled punch on your rug."

"That's because I have to save my strength for when Vera sees it." Spence dodged, in time to avoid collision with a fairy princess being chased by a goblin. There were squeals from every corner of the room, punctuated by the crashing and moaning of the novelty record on the stereo. "As for the aspirin… How long can they keep this up?"

"Oh, a lot longer than we can."

"You're such a comfort."

"We'll have them play games now. You'll be surprised how quickly two hours can pass."

She was right. By the time the numbered noses had all been stuck in the vicinity of the pumpkin head, when musical chairs was only a fond memory, after the costume parade and judging, when the last apple bobbed alone and the final clothespin had clunked into a mason jar, parents began to trail in to gather up their reluctant Frankensteins and ghoulies. But the fun wasn't over.

In groups and clutches, trick-or-treaters canvassed the neighborhood for candy bars and caramel apples. The wind-rushed night and crackling leaves were things they would remember long after the last chocolate drop had been consumed.

It was nearly ten before Spence managed to tuck an exhausted and thrilled Freddie into bed. "It was the best birthday I ever had," she told him. "I'm glad I got the chicken pox."

Spence rubbed a finger over a smeared orange freckle the cold cream had missed. "I don't know if I'd go that far, but I'm glad you had fun."

"Can I have—?"

"No." He kissed her nose. "If you eat one more piece of candy you'll blow up."

She giggled, and because she was too tired to try any strategy, snuggled into her pillow. Memories were already swirling in her head. "Next year I want to be a gypsy like Tash. Okay?"

"Sure. Go to sleep now. I'm going to take Natasha home, but Vera's here."

"Are you going to marry Tash soon, so she can stay with us?"

Spence opened his mouth, then closed it again as Freddie yawned hugely. "Where do you get these ideas?" he muttered.

"How long does it take to get a baby sister?" she asked as she drifted off.

Spence rubbed a hand over his face, grateful that she had fallen asleep and saved him from answering.

Downstairs he found Natasha cleaning up the worst of the mess. She flicked back her hair as he came in. "When it looks as bad as this, you know you've had a successful party." Something in his expression had her narrowing her eyes. "Is something wrong?"

"No. No, it's Freddie."

"She has a tummy ache," Natasha said, instantly sympathetic.

"Not yet." He shrugged it off with a half laugh. "She always manages to surprise me. Don't," he said and took the trash bag from her. "You've done enough."

"I don't mind."

"I know."

Before he could take her hand, she linked her own. "I should be going. Tomorrow's Saturday—our busiest day."

He wondered what it would be like if they could simply walk upstairs together, into his bedroom. Into his bed. "I'll take you home."

"That's all right. You don't have to."

"I'd like to." The tension was back. Their eyes met, and he understood that she felt it as well. "Are you tired?"

"No." It was time for some truths, she knew. He had done what she'd asked and been only Freddie's father during the party. Now the party was over. But not the night.

"Would you like to walk?"

The corners of her lips turned up, then she put her hand into his. "Yes. I would."

It was colder now, with a bite in the air warning of winter. Above, the moon was full and chillingly white. Clouds danced over it, sending shadows shifting. Over the rustle of leaves they heard the echoing shouts and laughter of lingering trick-or-treaters. Inevitably the big oak on the corner had been wrapped in bathroom tissue by teenagers.

"I love this time," Natasha murmured. "Especially at night when there's a little wind. You can smell smoke from the chimneys."

On the main street, older children and college students still stalked in fright masks and painted faces. A poor imitation of a wolf howl bounced along the storefronts, followed by a feminine squeal and laughter. A car full of ghouls paused long enough for them to lean out the windows and screech.

Spence watched the car turn a corner, its passengers still howling. "I can't remember being anywhere that Halloween was taken so seriously."

"Wait until you see what happens at Christmas."

Natasha's own pumpkin was glowing on her stoop

beside a bowl half-filled with candy bars. There was a sign on her door. Take Only One. Or Else.

Spence shook his head at it. "That really does it?"

Natasha merely glanced at the sign. "They know me."

Leaning over, Spence plucked one. "Can I have a brandy to go with it?"

She hesitated. If she let him come in, it was inevitable that they would pick up where the earlier kiss had left off. It had been two months, she thought, two months of wondering, of stalling, of pretending. They both knew it had to stop sooner or later.

"Of course." She opened the door and let him in.

Wound tight, she went into the kitchen to pour drinks. It was yes or it was no, she told herself. She had known the answer long before this night, even prepared for it. But what would it be like with him? What would she be like? And how, when she had shared herself with him in that most private way, would she be able to pretend she didn't need more?

Couldn't need more, Natasha reminded herself. Whatever her feelings for him, and they were deeper, much deeper than she dared admit, life had to continue as it was. No promises, no vows. No broken hearts.

He turned when she came back into the room, but didn't speak. His own thoughts were mixed and confused. What did he want? Her, certainly. But how much, how little could he accept? He'd been sure he'd never feel this way again. More than sure that he would never want to. Yet it seemed so easy to feel, every time he looked at her.

"Thanks." He took the brandy, watching her as he sipped. "You know, the first time I lectured, I stood at the podium and my mind went completely blank. For one terrible moment I couldn't think of anything I'd planned to say. I'm having exactly the same problem now."

"You don't have to say anything."

"It's not as easy as I thought it would be." He took her hand, surprised to find it cold and unsteady. Instinctively he lifted it to press his lips to the palm. It helped, knowing she was as nervous as he. "I don't want to frighten you."

"This frightens me." She could feel sensation spear her. "Sometimes people say I think too much. Maybe it's true. If it is, it's because I feel too much. There was a time…." She took her hand from his, wanting to be strong on her own. "There was a time," she repeated, "when I let what I felt decide for me. There are some mistakes that you pay for until you die."

"This isn't a mistake." He set down the brandy to take her face between his hands.

Her fingers curled around his wrists. "I don't want it to be. There can't be any promises, Spence, because I'd rather not have them than have them broken. I don't need or want pretty words. They're too easily said." Her grip tightened. "I want to be your lover, but I need respect, not poetry."

"Are you finished?"

"I need for you to understand," she insisted.

"I'm beginning to. You must have loved him a great deal."

She dropped her hands, but steadied herself before she answered. "Yes."

It hurt, surprising him. He could hardly be threatened by someone from her past. He had a past, as well. But he *was* threatened, and he *was* hurt. "I don't care who he was, and I don't give a damn what happened." That was a lie, he realized, and one he'd have to deal with sooner or later. "But I don't want you thinking of him when you're with me."

"I don't, not the way you mean."

"Not in any way."

She raised a brow. "You can't control my thoughts or anything else about me."

"You're wrong." Fueled by impotent jealousy, he pulled her into his arms. The kiss was angry, demanding, possessive. And tempting. Tempting her so close to submission that she struggled away.

"I won't be taken." Her voice was only more defiant because she was afraid she was wrong.

"Your rules, Natasha?"

"Yes. If they're fair."

"To whom?"

"Both of us." She pressed her fingers against her temples for a moment. "We shouldn't be angry," she said more quietly. "I'm sorry." She offered a shrug and a quick smile. "I'm afraid. It's been a long time since I've been with anyone—since I've wanted to be."

He picked up his brandy, staring into it as it swirled. "You make it hard for me to stay mad."

"I'd like to think we were friends. I've never been friends with a lover."

And he'd never been in love with a friend. It was a huge and frightening admission, and one he was certain he couldn't make out loud. Perhaps, if he stopped being clumsy, he could show her.

"We are friends." He held out a hand, then curled his fingers around hers. "Friends trust each other, Natasha."

"Yes."

He looked at their joined hands. "Why don't we—?" A noise at the window had him breaking off and glancing over. Before he could move, Natasha tightened her hold. It took only a moment to see that she wasn't frightened, but amused. She brought a finger from her free hand to her lips.

"I think it's a good idea to be friends with my professor," she said, lifting her voice and making a go-ahead gesture to Spence.

"I, ah, I'm glad Freddie and I have found so many nice people since we've moved." Puzzled, he watched Natasha root through a drawer.

"It's a nice town. Of course, sometimes there are problems. You haven't heard about the woman who escaped from the asylum."

"What asylum?" At her impatient glance, he covered himself. "No, I guess not."

"The police are keeping very quiet about it. They know she's in the area and don't want people to panic." Natasha flicked on the flashlight she'd uncovered and nodded in approval as the batteries proved strong. "She's quite insane, you know, and likes to kidnap small children. Especially young boys. Then she tortures them, hideously. On a night with a full moon she creeps up on them, so silently, so evilly. Then before they can scream, she grabs them around the throat."

So saying, she whipped up the shade on the window. With the flashlight held under her chin, she pressed her face against the glass and grinned.

Twin screams echoed. There was a crash, a shout, then the scramble of feet.

Weak from laughter, Natasha leaned against the windowsill. "The Freedmont boys," she explained when she'd caught her breath. "Last year they hung a dead rat outside Annie's door." She pressed a hand to her heart as Spence came over to peer out the window. All he could see was two shadows racing across the lawn.

"I think the tables are well-turned."

"Oh, you should have seen their faces." She dabbed a tear from her lashes. "I don't think their hearts will start beating again until they pull the covers over their heads."

"This should be a Halloween they don't forget."

"Every child should have one good scare they remember always." Still smiling, she stuck the light under her chin again. "What do you think?"

"It's too late to scare me away." He took the flashlight and set it aside. Closing his hand over hers, he drew her to her feet. "It's time to find out how much is illusion, how much is reality." Slowly he pulled the shade down.

Chapter 8

It was very real. Painfully real. The feel of his mouth against hers left no doubt that she was alive and needy. The time, the place, meant nothing. Those could have been illusions. But he was not. Desire was not. She felt it spring crazily inside her at only a meeting of lips.

No, it wasn't simple. She had known since she had first tasted him, since she had first allowed herself to touch him that whatever happened between them would never be simple. Yet that was what she had been so certain she'd wanted. Simplicity, a smooth road, an easy path.

Not with him. And not ever again.

Accepting, she twined her arms around him. Tonight there would be no past, no future. Only one moment taken in both hands, gripped hard and enjoyed.

Answer for answer, need for need, they clung together.

The low light near the door cast their silhouettes onto the wall, one shadow. It shifted when they did, then stilled.

When he swept her into his arms, she murmured a protest. She had said she wouldn't be taken and had meant it. Yet cradled there she didn't feel weak. She felt loved. In gratitude and in acceptance she pressed her lips to his throat. As he carried her toward the bedroom, she allowed herself to yield.

Then there was only moonlight. It crept through the thin curtain, softly, quietly, as a lover might creep through the window to find his woman. Her lover said nothing as he set her on her feet by the bed. His silence told her everything.

He'd imagined her like this. It seemed impossible, yet he had. The image had been clear and vivid. He had seen her with her hair in wild tangles around her face, with her eyes dark and steady, her skin gleaming like the gold she wore. And in his imaginings, he'd seen much, much more.

Slowly he reached up to slip the scarf from her hair, to let it float soundlessly to the floor. She waited. With his eyes on hers he loosened another and another of the slashes of color—sapphire, emerald, amber—until they lay like jewels at her feet. She smiled. With his finger-tips he drew the dress off her shoulders, then pressed his lips to the skin he'd bared.

A sigh and a shudder. Then she reached for him, struggling to breathe while she pulled his shirt over his head. His skin was taut and smooth under her palms. She could feel the quiver of muscle at the passage of her hands. As her eyes stayed on his, she could see the flash and fury of passion that darkened them.

He had to fight every instinct to prevent himself from tearing the dress from her, ripping aside the barriers and taking what she was offering. She wouldn't stop him. He could see it in her eyes, part challenge, part acknowledgment and all desire.

But he had promised her something. Though she claimed she wanted no promises, he intended to keep it. She would have romance, as much as he was capable of giving her.

Fighting for patience, he undid the range of buttons down her back. Her lips were curved when she pressed them to his chest. Her hands were smooth when she slipped his pants over his hips. As the dress slid to the floor, he brought her close for a long, luxurious kiss.

She swayed. It seemed foolish to her, but she was dizzy. Colors seemed to dance in her head to some frantic symphony she couldn't place. Her bracelets jingled when he lifted her hand to press a small circle of kisses upon her wrist. Material rustled, more notes to the song, when he slipped petticoat after colorful petticoat over her hips.

He hadn't believed she could be so beautiful. But now, standing before him in only a thin red chemise and the glitter of gold, she was almost more than a man could bear. Her eyes were nearly closed, but her head was up—a habit of pride that suited her well. Moonlight swam around her.

Slowly she lifted her arms, crossing them in front of

her to push the slender straps from her shoulders. The material trembled over her breasts, then clung for a fleeting instant before it slithered to the floor at their feet. Now there was only the glitter of gold against her skin. Exciting, erotic, exotic. She waited, then lifted her arms again—to him.

"I want you," she said.

Flesh met flesh, drawing twin moans from each of them. Mouth met mouth, sending shock waves of pleasure and pain through both. Desire met desire, driving out reason.

Inevitable. It was the only thought that filtered through the chaos in her mind as her hands raced over him. No force this strong, no need this deep could be anything but inevitable. So she met that force, met that need, with all of her heart.

Patience was forgotten. She was a hunger in him already too long denied. He wanted all, everything she was, everything she had. Before he could demand, she was giving. When they tumbled onto the bed, his hands were already greedily searching to give and to take pleasure.

Could he have known it would be so huge, so consuming? Everything about her was vivid and honed sharp. Her taste an intoxicating mix of honey and whiskey, both heated. Her skin as lush as a rose petal drenched in evening dew. Her scent as dark as his own passion. Her need as sharp as a freshly whetted blade.

She arched against him, offering, challenging, crying out when he sought and found each secret. Pleasure arrowed into him as her small, agile body pressed against his. Strong, willful, she rolled over him to exploit and explore until his breath was a fire in his lungs and his body a mass of sensation. Half-mad, he tumbled with her over the bed and spread a tangle of sheets around them. When he lifted himself over her, he could see the wild curtain of her hair like a dark cloud, the deep, rich glow of her eyes as they clung to his. Her breathing was as hurried as his own, her body as willing.

Never before, he realized, and never again would he find anyone who matched him so perfectly. Whatever he needed, she needed, whatever he wanted, she wanted. Before he could ask, she was answering. For the first time in his life, he knew what it was to make love with mind and heart and soul as well as body.

She thought of no one and of nothing but him. When he touched her, it was as though she'd never been touched before. When he said her name, it was the first time she'd heard it. When his mouth sought hers, it was a first kiss, the one she'd been waiting for, wishing for all of her life.

Palm to palm their hands met, fingers gripping hard like one soul grasping another. They watched each other as he filled her. And there was a promise, felt by both. In a moment of panic she shook her head. Then he was moving in her, and she with him.

"Again," was all he said as he pulled her against him. "Spence."

"Again." His mouth covered hers, waking her out of a half dream and into fresh passion.

He wanted her just as much, now that he knew what they could make between them, but with a fire that held steady on slow burn. This time, though desire was still keen, the madness was less intense. He could appreciate the subtle curves, the soft angles, the lazy sighs he could draw out of her with only a touch. It was like making love to some primitive goddess, naked but for the gold draped over her skin. After so long a thirst he quenched himself slowly, leisurely after that first, greedy gulp.

How had she ever imagined she had known what it was to love a man, or to be loved by one? There were pleasures here that as a woman she knew she had never tasted before. This was what it was to be steeped, to be drowned, to be sated. She ran her hands over him, absorbing the erotic sensations of the flick of his tongue, the scrape of his teeth, the play of those clever fingertips. No, these were new pleasures, very new. And their taste was freedom.

As the moon soared high into the night, so did she.

"I thought I had imagined what it would be like to be with you." Her head resting on his shoulder, Spence trailed his fingers up and down her arm. "I didn't even come close."

"I thought I would never be here with you." She smiled into the dark. "I was very wrong."

"Thank God. Natasha—"

With a quick shake of her head, she put a finger to his

lips. "Don't say too much. It's easy to say too much in the moonlight." And easy to believe it, she added silently.

Though impatient, he bit back the words he wanted to say. He had made a mistake once before by wanting too much, too quickly. He was determined not to make mistakes with Natasha. "Can I tell you that I'll never look at gold chains in quite the same way again?"

With a little chuckle she pressed a kiss to his shoulder. "Yes, you can tell me that."

He toyed with her bracelets. "Can I tell you I'm happy?"

"Yes."

"Are you?"

She tilted her head to look at him. "Yes. Happier than I thought I could be. You make me feel…" She smiled, making a quick movement with her shoulders. "Like magic."

"Tonight was magic."

"I was afraid," she murmured. "Of you, of this. Of myself," she admitted. "It's been a very long time for me."

"It's been a long time for me, too." At her restless movement, he caught her chin in his hand. "I haven't been with anyone since before my wife died."

"Did you love her very much? I'm sorry," she said quickly and closed her eyes tight. "I have no business asking that."

"Yes, you do." He kept his fingers firm. "I loved her once, or I loved the idea of her. That idea was gone long before she died."

"Please. Tonight isn't the time to talk about things that were."

When she sat up, he went with her, cupping her forearms in his hands. "Maybe not. But there are things I need to tell you, things we will talk about."

"Is what happened before so important?"

He heard the trace of desperation in her voice and wished he could find the reason. "I think it could be."

"This is now." She closed her hands over his. It was as close to a promise as she dared make. "Now I want to be your friend and your lover."

"Then be both."

She calmed herself with a deliberate effort.

"Perhaps I don't want to talk about other women while I'm in bed with you."

He could feel that she was braced and ready to argue. In a move that threw her off, he leaned closer to touch his lips to her brow. "We'll let you use that one for now."

"Thank you." She brushed a hand through his hair. "I'd like to spend this night with you, all night." With a half smile, she shook her head. "You can't stay."

"I know." He caught her hand to bring it to his lips. "Freddie would have some very awkward questions for me if I wasn't around for breakfast in the morning."

"She's a very lucky girl."

"I don't like leaving this way."

She smiled and kissed him. "I understand, as long as the other woman is only six."

"I'll see you tomorrow." Bending closer, he deepened the kiss.

"Yes." On a sigh she wrapped her arms around him. "Once more," she murmured, drawing him down to the bed. "Just once more."

In her cramped office at the back of the shop, Natasha sat at her desk. She had come in early to catch up on the practical side of business. Her ledger was up-to-date, her invoices had been filled. With Christmas less than two months away, she had completed her orders. Early merchandise was already stacked wherever room could be found. It made her feel good to be surrounded by the wishes of children, and to know that on Christmas morning what was now stored in boxes would cause cries of delight and wonder.

But there were practicalities as well. She had only begun to think of displays, decorations and discounts. She would have to decide soon whether she wanted to hire part-time help for the seasonal rush.

Now, at midmorning, with Annie in charge of the shop, she had textbooks and notes spread out. Before business there were studies, and she took both very seriously.

There was to be a test on the baroque era, and she intended to show her teacher—her lover—that she could hold her own.

Perhaps it shouldn't have been so important to prove she could learn and retain. But there had been times in her life, times she was certain Spence could never understand, when she had been made to feel inadequate, even stupid. The little girl with broken English, the thin teenager who'd thought more about dance than school-books, the dancer who'd fought so hard to make her body bear the insults of training, the young woman who had listened to her heart, not her head.

She was none of those people any longer, and yet she was all of them. She needed Spence to respect her in-telligence, to see her as an equal, not just as the woman he desired.

She was being foolish. On a sigh, Natasha leaned back in her chair to toy with the petals of the red rose that stood at her elbow. Even more than foolish, she was wrong. Spence was nothing like Anthony. Except for the vaguest of physical similarities, those two men were almost opposites. True, one was a brilliant dancer, the other a brilliant musician, but Anthony had been self-ish, dishonest, and in the end cowardly.

She had never known a man more generous, a man kinder than Spence. He was compassionate and hon-est. Or was that her heart talking? To be sure. But the heart, she thought, didn't come with a guarantee like a mechanical toy. Every day she was with him, she fell deeper and deeper in love. So much in love, she thought, that there were moments, terrifying moments, when she wanted to toss aside everything and tell him.

She had offered her heart to a man before, a heart pure and fragile. When it had been given back to her, it had been scarred.

No, there were no guarantees.

How could she dare risk that again? Even knowing that what was happening to her now was different, very different from what had happened to the young girl of seventeen, how could she possibly take the chance of leaving herself open again to that kind of pain and humiliation?

Things were better as they were, she assured herself. They were two adults, enjoying each other. And they were friends.

Taking the rose out of its vase, she stroked it along her cheek. It was a pity that she and her friend could only find a few scattered hours to be alone. There was a child to consider, then there were schedules and responsibilities. But in those hours when her friend became her lover, she knew the true meaning of bliss.

Bringing herself back, she slipped the flower into the vase and shifted her concentration to her studies. Within five minutes the phone rang.

"Good morning, Fun House."

"Good morning, businessperson."

"Mama!"

"So, you are busy or you have a moment to talk to your mother?"

Natasha cradled the phone in both hands, loving the sound of her mother's voice. "Of course I have a moment. All the moments you like."

"I wondered, since you have not called me in two weeks."

"I'm sorry." For two weeks a man had been the center of her life. But she could hardly tell that to her mother. "How are you and Papa and everyone?"

"Papa and me and everyone are good. Papa gets a raise."

"Wonderful."

"Mikhail doesn't see the Italian girl anymore." Nadia gave thanks in Ukrainian and made Natasha laugh. "Alex, he sees all the girls. Smart boy, my Alex. And Rachel has time for nothing but her studies. What of Natasha?"

"Natasha is fine. I'm eating well and getting plenty of sleep," she added before Nadia could ask.

"Good. And your store?"

"We're about to get ready for Christmas, and I expect a better year than last."

"I want you to stop sending your money."

"I want you to stop worrying about your children."

Nadia's sigh made Natasha smile. It was an old argument. "You are a very stubborn woman."

"Like my mama."

That was true enough, and Nadia clearly didn't intend to concede. "We will talk about this when you come for Thanksgiving."

Thanksgiving, Natasha thought. How could she have forgotten? Clamping the receiver between ear and shoulder, she flipped through her calendar. It was less than two weeks away. "I can't argue with my mother on Thanksgiving." Natasha made a note for herself to call the train station. "I'll be up late Wednesday evening. I'll bring the wine."

"You bring yourself."

"Myself and the wine." Natasha scribbled another note

to herself. It was a difficult time to take off, but she had never missed—and would never miss—a holiday at home. "I'll be so glad to see all of you again."

"Maybe you bring a friend."

It was another old routine, but this time, for the first time, Natasha hesitated. No, she told herself with a shake of her head. Why would Spence want to spend Thanksgiving in Brooklyn?

"Natasha?" Nadia's well-honed instincts had obviously picked up her daughter's mental debate. "You have friend?"

"Of course. I have a lot of friends."

"Don't be smart with your mama. Who is he?"

"He's no one." Then she rolled her eyes as Nadia began tossing out questions. "All right, all right. He's a professor at the college, a widower," she added. "With a little girl. I was just thinking they might like company for the holiday, that's all."

"Ah."

"Don't give me that significant ah, Mama. He's a friend, and I'm very fond of the little girl."

"How long you know him?"

"They just moved here late this summer. I'm taking one of his courses, and the little girl comes in the shop sometimes." It was all true, she thought. Not all the truth, but all true. She hoped her tone was careless. "If I get around to it, I might ask him if he'd like to come up."

"The little girl, she can sleep with you and Rachel."

"Yes, if—"

"The professor, he can take Alex's room. Alex can sleep on the couch."

"He may already have plans."

"You ask."

"All right. If it comes up."

"You ask," Nadia repeated. "Now go back to work."

"Yes, Mama. I love you."

Now she'd done it, Natasha thought as she hung up. She could almost see her mother standing beside the rickety telephone table and rubbing her hands together.

What would he think of her family, and they of him? Would he enjoy a big, rowdy meal? She thought of the first dinner they had shared, the elegant table, the quiet, discreet service. He probably has plans anyway, Natasha decided. It just wasn't something she was going to worry about.

Twenty minutes later the phone ran again. It was probably her mother, Natasha thought, calling with a dozen questions about this "friend." Braced, Natasha picked up the receiver. "Good morning, Fun House."

"Natasha."

"Spence?" Automatically she checked her watch. "Why aren't you at the university? Are you sick?"

"No. No. I came home between classes. I've got about an hour. I need you to come."

"To your house?" There was an urgency in his voice, but it had nothing to do with disaster and everything to do with excitement. "Why? What is it?"

"Just come, will you? It's nothing I can explain. I have to show you. Please."

"Yes, all right. Are you sure you're not sick?"

"No." She heard his laugh and relaxed. "No, I'm not sick. I've never felt better. Hurry up, will you?"

"Ten minutes." Natasha snatched up her coat. He'd sounded different. Happy? No, elated, ecstatic. What did a man have to be ecstatic about in the middle of the morning? Perhaps he was sick. Pulling on her gloves, she dashed into the shop.

"Annie, I have to—" She stopped, blinked, then stared at the image of Annie being kissed, soundly, by Terry Maynard. "I…excuse me."

"Oh, Tash, Terry just… Well, he…" Annie blew the hair out of her eyes and grinned foolishly. "Are you going out?"

"Yes, I have to see someone." She bit her lip to keep from grinning back. "I won't be more than an hour. Can you manage?"

"Sure." Annie smoothed down her hair, while Terry stood beside her, turning various shades of red. "It has been a quiet morning. Take your time."

Perhaps the world had decided to go crazy today, Natasha thought as she rushed down the street. First her mother calling, already preparing to kick Alex out of his bed for a stranger. Spence demanding she come to his house and see…something in the middle of the day. And now Annie and Terry, kissing each other beside the cash register. Well, she could only deal with one at a time. It looked as though Spence was first on the list.

She took his steps two at time, convinced he was suffering from some sort of fever. When he pulled open the door before she reached it, she was certain of it. His eyes were bright, his color up. His sweater was rumpled and his tie unknotted.

"Spence, are you—?"

Before she could get the words out, he was snatching her up, crushing his mouth to hers as he swung her around and around. "I thought you'd never get here."

"I came as quickly as I could." Instinctively she put a hand to his cheek. Then the look in his eyes had her narrowing her own. No, it wasn't a fever, she decided. At least it wasn't the kind that required medical attention. "If you had me run all the way over here for that, I'm going to hit you very hard."

"For—no," he answered on a laugh. "Though it's a wonderful idea. A really wonderful idea." He kissed her again until she thoroughly agreed with him. "I feel like I could make love with you for hours, days, weeks."

"They might miss you in class," she murmured. Steadying herself, she stepped back. "You sounded excited. Did you win the lottery?"

"Better. Come here." Remembering the door, he slammed it shut, then pulled her into the music room. "Don't say anything. Just sit."

She obliged, but when he went to the piano, she started to stand again. "Spence, I'd enjoy a concert, but—"

"Don't talk," he said impatiently. "Just listen."

And he began to play.

It took only moments for her to realize it was nothing she'd heard before. Nothing that had been written before. A tremor ran through her body. She clasped her hands tightly in her lap.

Passion. Each note swelled with it, soared with it, wept with it. She could only stare, seeing the intensity in his eyes and the fluid grace of his fingers on the keys. The beauty of it ripped at her, digging deep into heart and into soul. How could it be that her feelings, her most intimate feelings could be put to music?

As the tempo built, her pulse beat thickly. She couldn't have spoken, could hardly breathe. Then the music flowed into something sad and strong. And alive. She closed her eyes as it crashed over her, unaware that tears had begun to spill onto her cheeks.

When it ended, she sat very still.

"I don't have to ask you what you think," Spence murmured. "I can see it."

She only shook her head. She didn't have the words to tell him. There were no words. "When?"

"Over the last few days." The emotion the song had wrenched from him came flooding back. Rising, he went to her to take her hands and pulled her to her feet. As their fingers met, she could feel the intensity he'd poured into his music. "It came back." He pressed her hands to his lips. "At first it was terrifying. I could hear it in my head, the way I used to. It's like being plugged into heaven, Natasha. I can't explain it."

"No. You don't have to. I heard it."

She understood, he thought. Somehow he'd been sure she would. "I thought it was just wishful thinking, or that when I sat down there…" He looked back at the piano.

"That it would vanish. But it didn't. It flowed. God, it's like being given back your hands or your eyes."

"It was always there." She lifted her hands to his face. "It was just resting."

"No, *you* brought it back. I told you once, my life had changed when I met you. I didn't know how much. It's for you, Natasha."

"No, it's for you. Very much for you." Wrapping her arms around him, she pressed her mouth to his. "It's just the beginning."

"Yes." He dragged his hands through her hair so that her face was tilted to his. "It is." His grip only tightened when she would have pulled away. "If you heard that, if you understood that, you know what I mean. And you know what I feel."

"Spence, it would be wrong for you to say anything now. Your emotions are all on the surface. What you feel about your music is easily confused with other things."

"That's nonsense. You don't want to hear me tell you that I love you."

"No." Panic skidded up her spine. "No, I don't. If you care for me at all, you won't."

"It's a hell of a position you put me in."

"I'm sorry. I want you to be happy. As long as things go on as they are—"

"And how long can things go on as they are?"

"I don't know. I can't give you back the words you want to give to me. Even feeling them, I can't." Her eyes lifted again to meet his. "I wish I could."

"Am I still competing against someone else?"

"No." Quickly she reached out to take his hands. "No. What I felt for—before," she corrected, "was a fantasy. A girl's make-believe. This is real. I'm just not strong enough to hold on to it."

Or too strong to give in to it, he thought. And it was hurting her. Perhaps because he wanted her so badly, his impatience was adding pressure that would break them apart instead of bring them together.

"Then I won't tell you that I love you." He kissed her brow. "And that I need you in my life." He kissed her lips, lightly. "Not yet." His fingers curled tightly over hers. "But there'll come a time, Natasha, when I will tell you. When you'll listen. When you'll answer me."

"You make it sound like a threat."

"No, it's one of those promises you don't want to hear." He kissed her on both cheeks, casually enough to confuse her. "I have to get back."

"Yes, so do I." She picked up her gloves, only to run them restlessly through her hands. "Spence, it meant a very great deal that you wanted to share this with me. I know what it's like to lose part of yourself. I'm very proud of you and for you. And I'm glad that you celebrated this with me."

"Come back, have dinner with me. I haven't begun to celebrate."

She smiled again. "I'd like that."

She didn't often buy champagne, but it seemed appropriate. Even necessary. A bottle of wine was little enough to offer for what he had given her that morning.

The music itself was a gift she would always treasure. With it, he'd given her time and a glimpse of hope.

Perhaps he did love her. If she believed it, she could allow herself time to let it strengthen. If she believed it, she would have to tell him everything. It was that, even more than her own fears that still held her back.

She needed time for that, as he did.

But tonight was for celebrating.

She knocked and tried a sober smile for Vera. "Good evening."

"Miss." With this noncommital greeting, Vera opened the door wider. She kept her thoughts on Natasha very much to herself. True, the woman made the *señor* happy and seemed very fond of Freddie. But after more than three years of having them to herself, Vera was very cautious of sharing. "Dr. Kimball is in the music room with Freddie."

"Thank you. I brought some wine."

"I will take it."

With only a little sigh, Natasha watched Vera walk away. The more the housekeeper held firm, the more determined Natasha was to win her over.

She heard Freddie's giggles as she approached the music room. And others, she realized. When she reached the door, she spotted Freddie and JoBeth clinging to each other and squealing. And why not? Natasha thought with a grin. Spence was wearing a ridiculous helmet and aiming a cardboard spool like a weapon.

"Stowaways aboard my ship are fed to the Beta Monster," he warned them. "He has six-foot teeth and bad breath."

"No!" Eyes wide, heart pounding with delight and dread, Freddie scrambled for cover. "Not the Beta Monster."

"He likes little girls best." With an evil laugh, he scooped the squealing JoBeth under one arm. "He swallows little boys whole, but he chews and chews and chews when I feed him girls."

"That's gross." JoBeth covered her mouth with both hands.

"You bet." So saying, Spence made a dive and came up with a squirming Freddie. "Say your prayers, you're about to be the main course." Then with a muffled "Oomph," he tumbled onto the couch with both of them.

"We vanquished you!" Freddie announced, climbing over him. "The Wonder Sisters vanquished you."

"This time, but next time it's the Beta Monster." As he blew the hair out of his eyes, he spotted Natasha in the doorway. "Hi." She thought his smile was adorably sheepish. "I'm a space pirate."

"Oh. Well, that explains it." Before she could step into the room, both girls deserted the space pirate to launch themselves at her.

"We always beat him," Freddie told her. "Always, always."

"I'm glad to hear it. I wouldn't want anyone I know to be eaten by the Beta Monster."

"He just made it up," JoBeth said wisely. "Dr. Kimball makes things up real good."

"Yes, I know."

"JoBeth's going to stay for dinner, too. You're going to be Daddy's guest and she's going to be mine. You get to have seconds first."

"That's very polite." She bent to kiss Freddie's cheeks, then JoBeth's. "How is your mama?"

"She's going to have a baby." JoBeth screwed up her face and shrugged her shoulders.

"I heard." Natasha smoothed JoBeth's hair. "Are you taking care of her?"

"She doesn't get sick in the mornings anymore, but Daddy says she'll be fat soon."

Miserably envious, Freddie shifted from one foot to the other. "Let's go up to my room," she told JoBeth. "We can play with the kittens."

"You will wash your hands and faces," Vera told them as she came in with the ice bucket and glasses. "Then you will come down to dinner, walking like ladies, not running like elephants." She nodded to Spence. "Miss Stanislaski brought champagne."

"Thank you, Vera." Belatedly he remembered to remove his helmet.

"Dinner in fifteen minutes," she stated, then went out.

"Now she knows I have designs on you," Natasha muttered. "And is certain I'm after your great wealth."

With a laugh, he pried the cork free. "That's all right, I know you're only after my body." Wine frothed to the lip of the glasses, then receded.

"I like it very much. Your body." With a smile she accepted the flute of champagne.

"Then maybe you'd like to enjoy it later." He touched the rim of his glass to hers. "Freddie twisted my arm and got me to agree to a sleep-over at the Rileys'. So I don't feel left out, maybe I can stay with you tonight. All night."

Natasha took her first sip of wine, letting the taste explode on her tongue. "Yes," she said, and smiled at him.

Chapter 9

Natasha watched the shadows dancing from the lights the candles tossed around the room. Soothing, they played over the curtains, the top rung of the old ladder-back chair in the corner, over the coxcomb she had impulsively slipped into an empty milk bottle and set on her dresser. Her room, she thought. It had always been very much hers. Until…

With a half sigh she let her hand rest on Spence's heart.

It was no longer quiet; the wind had risen to toss a late, cold rain against the panes. Outside it was a chilled, gusty night that promised a chilled, frosty morning. Winter often came early to the little town snuggled in the foothills of the Blue Ridge. But she was warm, beautifully warm, in Spence's arms.

The silence between them was easy, as the loving

had been. Curled close, they lay still, content to let the hours pass, one lazy second at a time. Each of them quietly celebrated the knowledge that in the morning they wouldn't wake alone. His hand skimmed over her thigh, her hip, until it linked with hers.

There was music playing inside her head—the song he had given her that morning. She knew she would remember each note, each chord, for the rest of her life. And it was only the beginning for him, or a new beginning. The idea of that delighted her. In the years to come she would hear his music and remember the time they had had together. On hearing it she would celebrate again, even if his music took him away.

Still, she had to ask.

"Will you go back to New York?"

He brushed his lips through her hair. "Why?"

"You're composing again." She could imagine him there, in evening dress, attending the opening of his own symphony.

"I don't need to be in New York to compose. And if I did, there are more reasons to stay here."

"Freddie."

"Yes, there's Freddie. And there's you."

Her restless movement rustled the sheets. She could see him after the symphony at some small intimate party, the Rainbow Room perhaps, or a private club. He would be dancing with a beautiful woman.

"The New York you lived in is different from mine."

"I imagine." He wondered why that should matter to her. "Do you ever think of going back?"

"To live, no. But to visit." It was silly, she thought, to be nervous about asking such a simple thing. "My mother called me today."

"Is everything all right?"

"Yes. She only called to remind me about Thanksgiving. I'd almost forgotten. Every year we have a big dinner and eat too much. Do you go home for the holiday?"

"I am home."

"I mean to your family." She shifted to watch his face.

"I only have Freddie. And Nina," he added. "She always goes out to the Waldorf."

"Your parents. I've never asked you if you still have them, or where they live."

"They're in Cannes." Or was it Monte Carlo? It occurred to him suddenly that he didn't know for certain. The ties there were loose, comfortably so for everyone involved.

"Won't they come back for the holidays?"

"They never come to New York in the winter."

"Oh." Try as she might, she couldn't picture the holidays without family.

"We never ate at home on Thanksgiving. We always went out, were usually traveling." His memories of his childhood were more of places than people, more of music than words. "When I was married to Angela, we usually met friends at a restaurant and went to the theater."

"But—" She caught herself and fell silent.

"But what?"

"Once you had Freddie."

"Nothing changed." He shifted onto his back to stare at the ceiling. He'd wanted to tell her about his marriage, about himself—the man he had been—but had put it off. For too long, he reflected. How could he expect to build, when he had yet to clear away the emotional rubble of his past? "I've never explained to you about Angela."

"It's not necessary." She took his hand again. She'd wanted to invite him to a meal, not dredge up old ghosts.

"It is for me." Sitting up, he reached for the bottle of champagne they had brought back with them. Filling both glasses, he handed her one.

"I don't need explanations, Spence."

"But you'll listen?"

"Yes, if it's important to you."

He took a moment to gather his thoughts. "I was twenty-five when I met her. On top of the world as far as my music went, and to be honest, at twenty-five, very little else mattered to me. I had spent my life traveling, doing exactly what I pleased and being successful in what was most important to me. I don't believe anyone had ever told me, 'No, you can't have that. No, you can't do that.' When I saw her, I wanted her."

He paused to sip, to look back. Beside him Natasha stared into her glass, watching bubbles rise. "And she wanted you."

"In her way. The pity was that her attraction for me was as shallow as mine for her. And in the end just as destructive. I loved beautiful things." With a half laugh he tilted his glass again. "And I was used to having them. She was exquisite, like a delicate porcelain doll.

We moved in the same circles, attended the same parties, preferred the same literature and music."

Natasha shifted her glass from one hand to the other, wishing his words didn't make her feel so miserable. "It's important to have things in common."

"Oh, we had plenty in common. She was as spoiled and as pampered as I, as self-absorbed and as ambitious. I don't think we shared any particularly admirable qualities."

"You're too hard on yourself."

"You didn't know me then." He found himself profoundly grateful for that. "I was a very rich young man who took everything I had for granted, because I had always had it. Things change," he murmured.

"Only people who are born with money can consider it a disadvantage."

He glanced over to see her sitting cross-legged, the glass cupped in both hands. Her eyes were solemn and direct, and made him smile at himself. "Yes, you're right. I wonder what might have happened if I had met you when I was twenty-five." He touched her hair, but didn't dwell on the point. "In any case, Angela and I were married within a year and bored with each other only months after the ink had dried on the marriage certificate."

"Why?"

"Because at that time we were so much alike. When it started to fall apart, I wanted badly to fix it. I'd never failed at anything. The worst of it was, I wanted the marriage to work more for my own ego than because of my feelings for her. I was in love with the image of her and the image we made together."

"Yes." She thought of herself and her feelings for Anthony. "I understand."

"Do you?" The question was only a murmur. "It took me years to understand it. In any case, once I did, there were other considerations."

"Freddie," Natasha said again.

"Yes, Freddie. Though we still lived together and went through the motions of marriage, Angela and I had drifted apart. But in public and in private we were… civilized. I can't tell you how demeaning and destructive a civilized marriage can be. It's a cheat, Natasha, to both parties. And we were equally to blame. Then one day she came home furious, livid. I remember how she stalked over to the bar, tossing her mink aside so that it fell on the floor. She poured a drink, drank it down, then threw the glass against the wall. And told me she was pregnant."

Her throat dry, Natasha drank. "How did you feel?"

"Stunned. Rocked. We'd never planned on having children. We were much too much children, spoiled children ourselves. Angela had had a little more time to think it all through and had her answer. She wanted to go to Europe to a private clinic and have an abortion."

Something tightened inside Natasha. "Is that what you wanted?"

He wished, how he wished he could have answered unequivocably no. "At first I didn't know. My marriage was falling apart, I'd never given a thought to having children. It seemed sensible. And then, I'm not sure why, but I was furious. I guess it was because it was the easy way again, the easy way out for both of us. She wanted me to snap my fingers and get rid of this...inconvenience."

Natasha stared down at her own balled fist. His words were hitting much too close to home. "What did you do?"

"I made a bargain with her. She would have the baby, and we would give the marriage another shot. She would have the abortion and I would divorce her, and make certain that she didn't get what she considered her share of the Kimball money."

"Because you wanted the child."

"No." It was a painful admission, one that still cost him. "Because I wanted my life to run the way I'd imagined it would. I knew if she had an abortion, we would never put the pieces back. I thought perhaps if we shared this, we'd pull it all together again."

Natasha remained silent for a moment, absorbing his words and seeing them reflected in her own memories. "People sometimes think a baby will fix what's broken."

"And it doesn't," he finished. "Nor should it have to. By the time Freddie was born, I was already losing my grip on my music. I couldn't write. Angela had delivered Freddie, then passed her over to Vera, as though she were no more than a litter of kittens. I was little better."

"No." She reached out to take his wrist. "I've seen you with her. I know how you love her."

"Now. What you said to me that night on the steps of the college, about not deserving her. It hurt because it was true." He saw Natasha shake her head but went on. "I'd made a bargain with Angela, and for more than a year I kept it. I barely saw the child, because I was so busy escorting Angela to the ballet or the theater. I'd stopped working completely. I did nothing. I never fed her or bathed her or cuddled her at night. Sometimes I'd hear her crying in the other room and wonder—what is that noise? Then I'd remember."

He picked up the bottle to top off his glass. "Sometime before Freddie was two I stepped back and looked at what I'd done with my life. And what I hadn't done. It made me sick. I had a child. It took more than a year for it to sink in. I had no marriage, no wife, no music, but I had a child. I decided I had an obligation, a responsibility, and it was time to pull myself up and deal with it. That's how I thought of Freddie at first, when I finally began to think of her. An obligation." He drank again, then shook his head. "That was little better than ignoring her. Finally I looked, really looked at that beautiful little girl and fell in love. I picked her up out of her crib, scared to death, and just held her. She screamed for Vera."

He laughed at that, then stared once more into his wine. "It took months before she was comfortable around me. By that time I'd asked Angela for a divorce. She'd snapped up my offer without a blink. When I told her I was keeping the child, she wished me luck and walked out. She never came back to see Freddie, not once in all the months the lawyers were battling over a settlement. Then I heard that she'd been killed. A boating accident in the Mediterranean. Sometimes I'm afraid Freddie remembers what her mother was like. More, I'm afraid she'll remember what I was like."

Natasha remembered how Freddie had spoken of her mother when they had rocked. Setting aside her glass, she took Spence's face in her hand. "Children forgive," she told him. "Forgiveness is easy when you're loved. It's harder, so much harder to forgive yourself. But you must."

"I think I've begun to."

Natasha took his glass and set it aside. "Let me love you," she said simply, and enfolded him.

It was different now that passion had mellowed. Slower, smoother, richer. As they knelt on the bed, their mouths met dreamily—a long, lazy exploration of tastes that had become hauntingly familiar. She wanted to show him what he meant to her, and that what they had together, tonight, was worlds apart from what had been. She wanted to comfort, excite and cleanse.

A sigh, then a murmur, then a low, liquid moan. The sounds were followed by a light, breezy touch. Fingertips trailing on flesh. She knew his body now as well as her own, every angle, every plane, every vulnerability. When his breath caught on a tremble, her laughter came quietly. Watching him in the shifting candlelight, she brushed kisses at his temple, his cheek, the corner of his mouth, his throat. There a pulse beat for her, heavy and fast.

She was as erotic as any fantasy, her body swaying first to, then away from his. Her eyes stayed on him, glowing, aware, and her hair fell in a torrent of dark silk over her naked shoulders.

When he touched her, skimming his hands up and over, her head fell back. But there was nothing of submission in the gesture. It was a demand. Pleasure me.

On a groan he lowered his mouth to her throat and felt the need punch like a fist through his gut. His open mouth growing greedy, he trailed down her, pausing to linger at the firm swell of her breast. He could feel her heart, almost taste it, as its beat grew fast and hard against his lips. Her hands came to his hair, gripping tight while she arched like a bow.

Before he could think he reached for her and sent her spiraling over the first crest.

Breathless, shuddering, she clung, managing only a confused murmur as he laid her back on the bed. She struggled for inner balance, but he was already destroying will and mind and control.

This was seduction. She hadn't asked for it, hadn't wanted it. Now she welcomed it. She couldn't move, couldn't object. Helpless, drowning in her own pleasure, she let him take her where he willed. His mouth roamed freely over her damp skin. His hands played her as skillfully as they might a fine-tuned instrument. Her muscles went lax.

Her breath began to rush through her lips. She heard music. Symphonies, cantatas, preludes. Weakness became strength and she reached for him, wanting only to feel his body fit against her own.

Slowly, tormentingly, he slid up her, leaving trails

of heat and ice, of pleasure and pain. His own body throbbed as she moved under him. He found her mouth, diving deep, holding back even when her fingers dug into his hips.

Again and again he brought them both shivering to the edge, only to retreat, prolonging dozens of smaller pleasures. Her throat was a long white column he could feast on as she rose to him. Her arms wrapped themselves fast around him like taut silk. Her breath rushed along his cheek, then into his mouth, where it formed his own name like a prayer against his lips.

When he slipped into her, even pleasure was shattered.

Natasha awoke to the scent of coffee and soap, and the enjoyable sensation of having her neck nuzzled.

"If you don't wake up," Spence murmured into her ear, "I'm going to have to crawl back into bed with you."

"All right," she said on a sigh and snuggled closer.

Spence took a long, reluctant look at her shoulders, which the shifting sheets had bared. "It's tempting, but I should be home in an hour."

"Why?" Her eyes still closed, she reached out. "It's early."

"It's nearly nine."

"Nine? In the morning?" Her eyes flew open. She shot up in bed, and he wisely moved the cup of coffee out of harm's way. "How can it be nine?"

"It comes after eight."

"But I never sleep so late." She pushed back her

hair with both hands, then managed to focus. "You're dressed."

"Unfortunately," he agreed, even more reluctantly when the sheets pooled around her waist. "Freddie's due home at ten. I had a shower." Reaching out, he began to toy with her hair. "I was going to wake you, see if you wanted to join me, but you looked so terrific sleeping I didn't have the heart." He leaned over to nip at her bottom lip. "I've never watched you sleep before."

The very idea of it had the blood rushing warm under her skin. "You should have gotten me up."

"Yes." With a half smile he offered her the coffee. "I can see I made a mistake. Easy with the coffee," he warned. "It's really terrible. I've never made it before."

Eyeing him, she took a sip, then grimaced. "You really should have wakened me." But she valiantly took another sip, thinking how sweet it was of him to bring it to her. "Do you have time for breakfast? I'll make you some."

"I'd like that. I was going to grab a doughnut from the bakery down the street."

"I can't make pastries like Ye Old Sweet Shoppe, but I can fix you eggs." Laughing, she set the cup aside. "And coffee."

In ten minutes she was wrapped in a short red robe, frying thin slices of ham. He liked watching her like this, her hair tousled, eyes still heavy with sleep. She moved competently from stove to counter, like a woman who had grown up doing such chores as a matter of course.

Outside a thin November rain was falling from a pewter sky. He heard the muffled sound of footsteps from the apartment above, then the faint sound of music. Jazz from the neighbor's radio. And there was the sizzle of meat grilling, the hum of the baseboard heater under the window. Morning music, Spence thought.

"I could get used to this," he said, thinking aloud.

"To what?" Natasha popped two slices of bread into the toaster.

"To waking up with you, having breakfast with you."

Her hands fluttered once, as if her thoughts had suddenly taken a sharp turn. Then, very deliberately they began to work again. And she said nothing at all.

"That's the wrong thing to say again, isn't it?"

"It isn't right or wrong." Her movements brisk, she brought him a cup of coffee. She would have turned away once more, but he caught her wrist. When she forced herself to look at him, she saw that the expression in his eyes was very intense. "You don't want me to fall in love with you, Natasha, but neither one of us have a choice about it."

"There's always a choice," she said carefully. "It's sometimes hard to make the right one, or to know the right one."

"Then it's already been made. I am in love with you."

He saw the change in her face, a softening, a yielding, and something in her eyes, something deep and shadowed and incredibly beautiful. Then it was gone. "The eggs are going to burn."

His hand balled into a fist as she walked back to the stove. Slowly, carefully he flexed his fingers. "I said I love you, and you're worried about eggs burning."

"I'm a practical woman, Spence. I've had to be." But it was hard to think, very hard, when her mind and heart were dragging her in opposing directions. She fixed the plates with the care she might have given to a state dinner. Going over and over the words in her head, she set the plates on the table, then sat down across from him.

"We've only known each other a short time."

"Long enough."

She moistened her lips. What she heard in his voice was more hurt than anger. She wanted nothing less than to hurt him. "There are things about me you don't know. Things I'm not ready to tell you."

"They don't matter."

"They do." She took a deep breath. "We have something. It would be ridiculous to try to deny it. But love— there is no bigger word in the world. If we share that word, things will change."

"Yes."

"I can't let them. From the beginning I told you there could be no promises, no plans. I don't want to move my life beyond what I have now."

"Is it because I have a child?"

"Yes, and no." For the first time since he'd met her, nerves showed in the way she linked and unlinked her fingers. "I would love Freddie even if I hated you. For herself. Because I care for you, I only love her more. But for you and me to take what we have and make something more from this would change even that. I'm not ready to take on the responsibilities of a child." Under the table she pressed her hand hard against her stomach.

"But with or without Freddie, I don't want to take the next step with you. I'm sorry, and I understand if you don't want to see me again."

Torn between frustration and fury, he rose to pace to the window. The rain was still falling thinly, coldly upon the dying flowers outside. She was leaving something out, something big and vital. She didn't trust him yet, Spence realized. After everything they'd shared, she didn't yet trust him. Not enough.

"You know I can't stop seeing you, any more than I can stop loving you."

You could stop being in love, she thought, but found herself afraid to tell him. It was selfish, hideously so, but she wanted him to love her. "Spence, three months ago I didn't even know you."

"So I'm rushing things."

She moved her shoulder and began to poke at her eggs.

He studied her from behind, the way she held herself, how her fingers moved restlessly from her fork to her cup, then back again. He wasn't rushing a damn thing, and they both knew it. She was afraid. He leaned against the window, thinking it through. Some jerk had broken her heart, and she was afraid to have it broken again.

All right, he thought. He could get around that. A little time and the most subtle kind of pressure. He would get around it, he promised himself. For the first part of his life, he'd thought nothing would ever be as important to him as his music. In the last few years he'd learned differently. A child was infinitely more important, more precious and more beautiful. Now he'd been taught in a matter of weeks that a woman could be as important, in a different way, but just as important.

Freddie had waited for him, bless her. He would wait for Natasha.

"Want to go to a matinee?"

She'd been braced for anger, so only looked blankly over her shoulder. "What?"

"I said would you like to go to a matinee? The movies." Casually he walked back to the table to join her. "I promised Freddie I'd take her to the movies this afternoon."

"I—yes." A cautious smile bloomed. "I'd like to go with you. You're not angry with me?"

"Yes, I am." But he returned her smile as he began to eat. "I figured if you came along, you'd buy the popcorn."

"Okay."

"The jumbo size."

"Ah, now I begin to see the strategy. You make me feel guilty, so I spend all my money."

"That's right, and when you're broke, you'll have to marry me. Great eggs," he added when her mouth dropped open. "You should eat yours before they get cold."

"Yes." She cleared her throat. "Since you've offered me an invitation, I have one for you. I was going to mention it last night, but you kept distracting me."

"I remember." He rubbed his foot over hers. "You're easily distracted, Natasha."

"Perhaps. It was about my mother's phone call and

Thanksgiving. She asked me if I wanted to bring someone along." She frowned at her eggs. "I imagine you have plans."

His smile was slow and satisfied. Perhaps the wait wouldn't be as long as he'd thought. "Are you asking me to Thanksgiving dinner at your mother's?"

"My mother asked," Natasha said precisely. "She always makes too much food, and she and Papa enjoy company. When it came up, I thought about you and Freddie."

"I'm glad to know that you think about us."

"It's nothing," she said, annoyed with herself for stringing out what should have been a simple invitation. "I always take the train up on Wednesday after work and come back Friday evening. Since there is no school, it occurred to me that you both might enjoy the trip."

"Do we get borscht?"

The corners of her lips curved. "I could ask." She pushed her plate aside when she saw the gleam in his eyes. He wasn't laughing, she thought, as much as planning. "I don't want you to get the wrong idea. It's simply an invitation from friend to friend."

"Right."

She frowned at him. "I think Freddie would enjoy a big family meal."

"Right again."

His easy agreement had her blowing out a frustrated breath. "Just because it's at my parents' home doesn't mean I'm taking you there for..." She waved her hand as she searched for an appropriate phrase. "For approval, or to show you off."

"You mean your father won't take me into the den and ask me my intentions?"

"We don't have a den," she muttered. "And no. I'm a grown woman." Because Spence was grinning, she lifted a brow. "He will, perhaps, study you discreetly."

"I'll be on my best behavior."

"Then you'll come?"

He sat back, sipping his coffee and smiling to himself. "I wouldn't miss it."

Chapter 10

Freddie sat in the backseat with a blanket tucked up to her chin and clutched her Raggedy Ann. Because she wanted to drift with her own daydreams she pretended to sleep, and pretended so well that she actually dozed from time to time. It was a long drive from West Virginia to New York, but she was much too excited to be bored.

There was soft music on the car radio. She was enough of her father's daughter to recognize Mozart, and child enough to wish there were words to sing along to. Vera had already been dropped off at her sister's in Manhattan, where the housekeeper would holiday until Sunday. Now Spence was directing the big, quiet car through the traffic toward Brooklyn.

Freddie was only a little disappointed that they hadn't taken the train, but liked snuggling up and listening to her father and Natasha talk. She didn't pay much attention to what they said. Their voices were enough.

She was almost sick with excitement at the idea of meeting Natasha's family and sharing a big turkey dinner. Though she didn't like turkey very much, Natasha had told her that there would be plenty of cranberry sauce and succotash. Freddie had never eaten succotash, but the name was so funny, she knew it would be good. Even if it wasn't, even if it was disgusting, she was determined to be polite and clean her plate. JoBeth had told her that her grandmother got upset if JoBeth didn't eat all her vegetables, so Freddie wasn't taking any chances.

Lights flickered over her closed lids. Her lips curved a little as she heard Natasha's laugh merging with her father's. In her imaginings they were already a family. Instead of Raggedy Ann, Freddie was carefully tending to her baby sister as they all drove through the night to her grandparents' house. It was just like the song, she thought, but she didn't know if they were going over any rivers. And she didn't think they would pass through the woods.

Her baby sister's name was Katie, and she had black, curly hair like Natasha. Whenever Katie cried, Freddie was the only one who could make her happy again. Katie slept in a white crib in Freddie's room, and Freddie always made sure she was covered with a pink blanket. Babies caught colds, Freddie knew. When they did, you had to give them medicine out of a little dropper. They couldn't blow their noses themselves. Everyone said that Katie took her medicine best from Freddie.

Delighted with herself, Freddie snuggled the doll closer. "We're going to Grandmother's," she whispered, and began to build a whole new fantasy around the visit.

The trouble was, Freddie wasn't sure that the people she was pretending were her grandparents would like her. Not everyone liked kids, she thought. Maybe they wished she wasn't coming to visit. When she got there, they would want her to sit in a chair with her hands folded on her lap. That was the way Aunt Nina told her young ladies sat. Freddie hated being a young lady. But she would have to sit for just hours, not interrupting, not talking too loud, and never, never running in the house.

They would get mad and frown at her if she spilled something on the floor. Maybe they would yell. She'd heard JoBeth's father yell, especially when JoBeth's big brother, who was in third grade already and was supposed to know better, had taken one of his father's golf clubs to hit at rocks in the backyard. One of the rocks had crashed right through the kitchen window.

Maybe she would break a window. Then Natasha wouldn't marry her daddy and come to stay with them. She wouldn't have a mother or a baby sister, and Daddy would stop playing his music at night again.

Almost paralyzed by her thoughts, Freddie shrank against the seat as the car slowed.

"Yes, turn right here." At the sight of her old neighborhood, Natasha's spirits rose even higher. "It's about halfway down, on the left. You might be able to find a space…yes, there." She spotted a parking space behind her father's ancient pickup. Obviously the Stanislaskis had put out the word that their daughter and friends were coming, and the neighbors had cooperated.

It was like that here, she thought. The Poffenbergers had lived on one side, the Andersons on the other for as long as Natasha could remember. One family would bring food when there was illness, another would mind a child after school. Joys and sorrows were shared. And gossip abounded.

Mikhail had dated the pretty Anderson girl, then had ended up as best man at her wedding, when she'd married one of his friends. Natasha's parents had stood as godparents for one of the Poffenberger babies. Perhaps that was why, when Natasha had found she'd needed a new place and a new start, she had picked a town that had reminded her of home. Not in looks, but in ties.

"What are you thinking?" Spence asked her.

"Just remembering." She turned her head to smile at him. "It's good to be back." She stepped onto the curb, shivered once in the frosty air, then opened the back door for Freddie while Spence popped the trunk. "Freddie, are you asleep?"

Freddie kept herself balled tight, but squeezed her eyes open. "No."

"We're here. It's time to get out."

Freddie swallowed, clutching the doll to her chest. "What if they don't like me?"

"What's this?" Crouching, Natasha brushed the hair from Freddie's cheeks. "Have you been dreaming?"

"They might not like me and wish I wasn't here. They might think I'm a pest. Lots of people think kids're pests."

"Lots of people are stupid then," Natasha said briskly, buttoning up Freddie's coat.

"Maybe. But they might not like me, anyway."

"What if you don't like them?"

That was something that hadn't occurred to her. Mulling it over, Freddie wiped her nose with the back of her hand before Natasha could come up with a tissue. "Are they nice?"

"I think so. After you meet them, you can decide. Okay?"

"Okay."

"Ladies, maybe you could pick another time to have a conference." Spence stood a few feet away, loaded down with luggage. "What was that all about?" he asked when they joined him on the sidewalk.

"Girl talk," Natasha answered with a wink that made Freddie giggle.

"Great." He started up the worn concrete steps behind Natasha. "Nothing I like better than to stand in the brisk wind holding three hundred pounds of luggage. What did you pack in here? Bricks?"

"Only a few, along with some essentials." Delighted with him, she turned and kissed his cheek—just as Nadia opened the door.

"Well." Pleased, Nadia folded her arms across her chest. "I told Papa you would come before Johnny Carson was over."

"Mama." Natasha rushed up the final steps to be enfolded in Nadia's arms. There was the scent she always remembered. Talc and nutmeg. And, as always, there was the strong, sturdy feel of her mother's body. Nadia's dark and sultry looks were just as strong, more so, perhaps, with the lines etched by worry, laughter and time.

Nadia murmured an endearment, then drew Natasha back to kiss her cheeks. She could see herself as she had been twenty years before. "Come on, you leave our guests standing in the cold."

Natasha's father bounded into the hall to pluck her off the floor and toss her into the air. He wasn't a tall man, but the arms beneath his work shirt were thick as cinder blocks from his years in the construction trade. He gave a robust laugh as he kissed her.

"No manners," Nadia declared as she shut the door. "Yuri, Natasha brings guests."

"Hello." Yuri thrust out a callused hand and pumped Spence's. "Welcome."

"This is Spence and Freddie Kimball." As she made introductions, Natasha noticed Freddie slip her hand into her father's.

"We are happy to meet you." Because warmth was her way, Nadia greeted them both with kisses. "I will take your coats, and you please come in and sit. You will be tired."

"We appreciate you having us," Spence began. Then, sensing that Freddie was nervous, he picked her up and carried her into the living room.

It was small, the wallpaper old and the furniture worn. But there were lace doilies on the arms of the chairs, the woodwork gleamed in the yellow lamplight from vigorous polishing, and here and there were exquisitely worked pillows. Framed family pictures fought for space among the potted plants and knicknacks.

A husky wheeze had Spence glancing down. There was an old gray dog in the corner. His tail began to thump when he saw Natasha. With obvious effort he rose and waddled to her.

"Sasha." She crouched to bury her face in the dog's fur. She laughed as he sat down again and leaned against her. "Sasha is a very old man," she explained to Freddie. "He likes best now to sleep and eat."

"And drink vodka," Yuri put in. "We will all have some. Except you," he added and flicked a finger down Freddie's nose. "You would have some champagne, huh?"

Freddie giggled, then bit her lip. Natasha's father didn't look exactly like she'd imagined a grandfather. He didn't have snow-white hair and a big belly. Instead his hair was black and white at the same time, and he had no belly at all. He talked funny, with a deep, rumbly kind of voice. But he smelled good, like cherries. And his smile was nice.

"What's vodka?"

"Russian tradition," Yuri answered her. "A drink we make from grain."

Freddie wrinkled her nose. "That sounds yucky," she said, then immediately bit her lip again. But at Yuri's burst of laughter she managed a shy smile.

"Natasha will tell you that her papa always teases little girls." Nadia poked an elbow into Yuri's ribs. "It's because he is really just little boy at heart. You would like hot chocolate?"

Freddie was torn between the comfort of her father's hand and one of her favorite treats. And Nadia was smiling at her, not with that goofy look grown-ups sometimes put on when they had to talk to kids. It was a warm smile, just like Natasha's.

"Yes, ma'am."

Nadia gave a nod of approval at the child's manners. "Maybe you would like to come with me. I show you how to make it with big, fat marshmallows."

Forgetting shyness, Freddie took her hand from Spence's and put it into Nadia's. "I have two cats," she told Nadia proudly as they walked into the kitchen. "And I had chicken pox on my birthday."

"Sit, sit," Yuri ordered, gesturing toward the couch. "We have a drink."

"Where are Alex and Rachel?" With a contented sigh, Natasha sank into the worn cushions.

"Alex takes his new girlfriend to the movies. Very pretty," Yuri said, rolling his bright, brown eyes. "Rachel is at lecture. Big-time lawyer from Washington, D.C. comes to college."

"And how is Mikhail?"

"Very busy. They remodel apartment in Soho." He passed out glasses, tapping each before he drank. "So," he said to Spence as he settled in his favorite chair, "you teach music."

"Yes. Natasha's one of my best students in Music History."

"Smart girl, my Natasha." He settled back in his chair and studied Spence. But not, as Natasha had hoped, discreetly. "You are good friends."

"Yes," Natasha put in, uneasy about the gleam in her father's eyes. "We are. Spence just moved into town this summer. He and Freddie used to live in New York."

"So. This is interesting. Like fate."

"I like to think so," Spence agreed, enjoying himself. "It was especially fortunate that I have a little girl and Natasha owns a very tempting toy store. Added to that, she signed up for one of my classes. It made it difficult for her to avoid me when she was being stubborn."

"She is stubborn," Yuri agreed sadly. "Her mother is stubborn. Me, I am very agreeable."

Natasha gave a quick snort.

"Stubborn and disrespectful women run in my family." Yuri took another healthy drink. "It is my curse."

"Perhaps one day I'll be fortunate enough to say the same." Spence smiled over the rim of his glass. "When I convince Natasha to marry me."

Natasha sprang up, ignoring her father's grin. "Since the vodka's gone to your head so quickly, I'll see if Mama has any extra hot chocolate."

Yuri pushed himself out of his chair to reach for the bottle as Natasha disappeared. "We'll leave the chocolate to the women."

Natasha awoke at first light with Freddie curled in her arms. She was in the bed of her childhood, in a room where she and her sister had spent countless hours talking, laughing, arguing. The wallpaper was the same. Faded roses. Whenever her mother had threatened to paint it, both she and Rachel had objected. There was something comforting about waking up to the same walls from childhood through adolescence to adulthood.

Turning her head, she could see her sister's dark hair against the pillow of the next bed. The sheets and blankets were in tangles. Typical, Natasha thought with a smile. Rachel had more energy asleep than most people had fully awake. She had come in the night before after midnight, bursting with enthusiasm over the lecture she had attended, full of hugs and kisses and questions.

Natasha brushed a kiss over Freddie's hair, then carefully shifted her. The child snuggled into the pillow without making a sound. Quietly Natasha rose. She took a moment to steady herself when the floor tilted. Four hours' sleep, she decided, was bound to make anyone light-headed. Gathering her clothes, she went off to shower and dress.

Arriving downstairs, she caught the scent of coffee brewing. It didn't seem to appeal to her, but she followed it into the kitchen.

"Mama." Nadia was already at the counter, busily rolling out piecrusts. "It's too early to cook."

"On Thanksgiving it's never too early." She lifted her cheek for a kiss. "You want coffee?"

Natasha pressed a hand to her uneasy stomach. "No. I don't think so. I assume that bundle of blankets on the couch is Alex."

"He gets in very late." Nadia pursed her lips briefly in disapproval, then shrugged. "He's not a boy anymore."

"No. You'll just have to face it, Mama, you have grown children—and you raised them very well."

"Not so well that Alex learns to pick up his socks." But she smiled, hoping her youngest son wouldn't deprive her of that last vestige of motherhood too soon.

"Did Papa and Spence stay up very late?"

"Papa likes talking to your friend. He's a nice man." Nadia laid a circle of dough on a pie plate, then took up another chunk to roll out. "Very handsome."

"Yes," Natasha agreed, but cautiously.

"He has good job, is responsible, loves his daughter."

"Yes," Natasha said again.

"Why don't you marry him when he wants you to?"

She'd figured on this. Biting back a sigh, Natasha leaned on the kitchen table. "There are a lot of nice, responsible and handsome men, Mama. Should I marry them all?"

"Not so many as you think." Smiling to herself, Nadia started on a third crust. "You don't love him?" When Natasha didn't answer, Nadia's smile widened. "Ah."

"Don't start. Spence and I have only known each other for a few months. There's a lot he doesn't know about me."

"So tell him."

"I don't seem to be able to."

Nadia put down her rolling pin to cup her daughter's face in two floury hands. "He is not like the other one."

"No, he's not. But—"

Impatient, Nadia shook her head. "Holding on to something that's gone only makes a sickness inside. You have a good heart, Tash. Trust it."

"I want to." She wrapped her arms around her mother and held tight. "I do love him, Mama, but it still scares me. And it still hurts." On a long breath she drew back. "I want to borrow Papa's truck."

Nadia didn't ask where she was going. Didn't need to. "Yes. I can go with you."

Natasha only kissed her mother's cheek and shook her head.

She'd been gone an hour before Spence made his bleary-eyed way downstairs. He and the gray dog exchanged glances of sympathy. Yuri had been generous with the vodka the night before, to guests and pets. At the moment, Spence felt as though a chain gang were chipping rock in his head. Operating on automatic, he found the kitchen, following the scents of baking, and blissfully, coffee.

Nadia took one look, laughed broadly and gestured to the table. "Sit." She poured a cup of coffee, strong and black. "Drink. I fix you breakfast."

Like a dying man, Spence clutched the cup in both hands. "Thanks. I don't want to put you out."

Nadia merely waved a hand as she reached for a cast-iron skillet. "I know a man with a hangover. Yuri poured you too much vodka."

"No. I took care of that all on my own." He opened

the aspirin bottle she set on the table. "Bless you, Mrs. Stanislaski."

"Nadia. You call me Nadia when you get drunk in my house."

"I don't remember feeling like this since college." So saying he downed three aspirins. "I can't imagine why I thought it was fun at the time." He managed a weak smile. "Something smells wonderful."

"You will like my pies." She pushed fat sausages around in the skillet. "You met Alex last night."

"Yes." Spence didn't object when she filled his cup a second time. "That was cause enough for one more drink. You have a beautiful family, Nadia."

"They make me proud." She laughed as the sausage sizzled. "They make me worry. You know, you have daughter."

"Yes." He smiled at her, picturing what Natasha would look like in a quarter of a century.

"Natasha is the only one who moves far away. I worry most for her."

"She's very strong."

Nadia only nodded as she added eggs to the pan. "Are you patient, Spence?"

"I think so."

Nadia glanced over her shoulder. "Don't be too patient."

"Funny. Natasha once told me the same thing."

Pleased, Nadia popped bread into the toaster. "Smart girl."

The kitchen door swung open. Alex, dark, rumpled and heavy-eyed, grinned. "I smelled breakfast."

The first snow was falling, small, thin flakes that swirled in the wind and vanished before they hit the ground. There were some things, Natasha knew, that were beautiful and very precious, and here for only such a short time.

She stood alone, bundled against the cold she didn't feel. Except inside. The light was pale gray, but not dreary, not with the tiny, dancing snowflakes. She hadn't brought flowers. She never did. They would look much too sad on such a tiny grave.

Lily. Closing her eyes, she let herself remember how it had felt to hold that small, delicate life in her arms. Her baby. *Milaya*. Her little girl. Those beautiful blue eyes, Natasha remembered, those exquisite miniature hands.

Like the flower she had been named for, Lily had been so lovely, and had lived such a brief, brief time. She could see Lily, small and red and wrinkled, her little hands fisted when the nurse had first laid her in Natasha's arms. She could feel even now that sweet ache that tugged when Lily had nursed at her breast. She remembered the feel of that soft, soft skin and the smell of powder and lotion, the comfort of rocking late at night with her own baby girl on her shoulder.

So quickly gone, Natasha thought. A few precious weeks. No amount of time, no amount of prayer would ever make her understand it. Accept, perhaps, but never understand.

"I love you, Lily. Always." She bent to press her palm against the cold grass. Rising again, she turned and walked away through the lightly dancing snow.

Where had she gone? There could be a dozen places, Spence assured himself. It was foolish to be worried. But he couldn't help it. Some instinct was at work here, heightened by the certainty that Natasha's family knew exactly where she was, but refused to say.

The house was already filled with noise, laughter, and the smells of the celebrational meal to come. He tried to shake off the feeling that wherever Natasha was, she needed him.

There was so much she hadn't told him. That had become crystal clear when he saw the pictures in the living room. Natasha in tights and dance shoes, in ballet skirts and toe shoes. Natasha with her hair streaming behind her, caught at the apex of a grand jeté.

She'd been a dancer, quite obviously a professional, but had never mentioned it.

Why had she given it up? Why had she kept something that had been an important part of her life a secret from him?

Coming out of the kitchen, Rachel saw him with one of the photographs in his hand. She kept silent for a moment, studying him. Like her mother, she approved of what she saw. There was a strength here and a gentleness. Her sister needed and deserved both.

"It's a beautiful picture."

He turned. Rachel was taller than Natasha, more willowy. Her dark hair was cut short in a sleek cap around her face. Her eyes, more gold than brown, dominated. "How old was she?"

Rachel dipped her hands into the pockets of her trousers as she crossed the room. "Sixteen, I think. She was in the corps de ballet then. Very dedicated. I always envied Tash her grace. I was a klutz." She smiled and gently changed the subject. "Always taller and skinnier than the boys, knocking things over with my elbows. Where's Freddie?"

Spence set down the picture. Without saying it, Rachel had told him that if he had questions, they were for Natasha. "She's upstairs, watching the Macy's parade with Yuri."

"He never misses it. Nothing disappointed him more than when we grew too old to want to sit in his lap and watch the floats."

A laughing squeal from the second floor had them both turning toward the stairs. Feet clomped. A pink whirlwind in her jumpsuit, Freddie came dashing down to launch herself at Spence. "Daddy, Papa makes bear noises. *Big* bear noises."

"Did he rub his beard on your cheek?" Rachel wanted to know.

"It's scratchy." She giggled, then wriggled down to run upstairs once more, hoping he'd do it again.

"She's having the time of her life," Spence decided.

"So's Papa. How's your head?"

"Better, thanks." He heard the sound of the truck pulling up outside, and glanced toward the window.

"Mama needs my help." Rachel slipped back into the kitchen.

He was at the door waiting for her. Natasha looked very pale, very tired, but she smiled when she saw him. "Good morning." Because she needed him, she slipped her arms around his waist and held tight.

"Are you all right?"

"Yes." She was now, she realized, when he was holding her like this. Stronger, she pulled back. "I thought you might sleep late."

"No, I've been up awhile. Where have you been?"

She unwound her scarf. "There was something I needed to do." After peeling off her coat, she hung it in the narrow closet. "Where is everyone?"

"Your mother and Rachel are in the kitchen. The last time I looked, Alex was on the phone."

This time the smile came easily. "Sweet-talking a girl."

"Apparently. Freddie's up with your father, watching the parade."

"And putting him in heaven." She touched her fingertips to Spence's cheek. "Will you kiss me?"

There was some need here, he thought as he bent toward her. Some deep, private need she still refused to share. Her lips were cold when his met them, but they softened, then warmed. At last they curved.

"You're very good for me, Spence."

"I was hoping you'd catch on to that." He gave her bottom lip a playful nip. "Better?"

"Much. I'm glad you're here." She squeezed his hand. "How do you feel about some of Mama's hot chocolate?"

Before he could answer, Freddie came sprinting down the steps again, one shoelace trailing, to throw her arms around Natasha's waist. "You're back!"

"So I am." Natasha bent to kiss the top of Freddie's head. "What have you been up to?"

"I'm watching the parade with Papa. He can talk just like Donald Duck, and he lets me sit on his lap."

"I see." Leaning closer, Natasha took a sniff. There was the telltale fragrance of gumdrops lingering on Freddie's breath. "Does he still hog all the yellow ones?"

Freddie giggled, casting a quick, cautious look at her father. Spence had a much different view of gumdrops than Yuri. "It's okay. I like the red ones best."

"How many red ones?" Spence asked her.

Freddie lifted her shoulders and let them fall. It was, Spence noted with some amusement, almost a mirror image of Natasha's habitual gesture. "Not too many. Will you come up and watch with us?" She tugged at Natasha's hand. "It's almost time for Santa Claus."

"In a little while." Out of habit, Natasha crouched to tie Freddie's shoelace. "Tell Papa that I won't mention the gumdrops to Mama. If he saves me some."

"Okay." She dashed up the stairs.

"He's made quite an impression on her," Spence observed.

"Papa makes impressions on everyone." She started to rise, and felt the room spin. Before she could sink to the floor again, Spence had her arms.

"What is it?"

"Nothing." She pressed a hand to her head, waiting for the dizziness to pass. "I stood up too fast, that's all."

"You're pale. Come sit down." He had an arm hooked around her waist, but she shook her head.

"No, I'm fine, really. Just a little tired." Relieved that the room had steadied, she smiled at him. "Blame it on Rachel. She would have talked through the night if I hadn't fallen asleep on her in self-defense."

"Have you eaten anything?"

"I thought you were a doctor of music." She smiled again and patted his cheek. "Don't worry, the minute I go into the kitchen, Mama will start feeding me."

Just then the front door opened. Spence watched Natasha's face light up. "Mikhail!" With a laugh, she threw herself into the arms of her brother.

He had the dark, blinding good looks that ran in the family. The tallest of the brood, he had to bend to gather Natasha close. His hair curled over his ears and collar. His coat was worn, his boots were scarred. His hands, as they stroked Natasha's hair, were wide-palmed and beautiful.

It took Spence only seconds to see that while Natasha loved all of her family deeply, there was a separate and special bond here.

"I've missed you." She drew back just far enough to kiss his cheeks, then hugged him close again. "I've really missed you."

"Then why don't you come more often?" He pushed her away, wanting a good long look. He didn't care for the pallor in her cheeks, but since her hands were still cold, he realized she'd been out. And he knew where she'd spent that morning. He murmured something in Ukrainian, but she only shook her head and squeezed his hands tight. With a shrug very like her own, he put the subject aside.

"Mikhail, I want you to meet Spence."

As he took off his coat, Mikhail turned to study Spence. Unlike Alex's friendly acceptance or Rachel's subtle measuring, this was an intense and prolonged stare that left Spence in no doubt that if Mikhail didn't approve, he wouldn't hesitate to say so.

"I know your work," he said at length. "It's excellent."

"Thank you." Spence met look for look. "I can say the same about yours." When Mikhail lifted one dark brow, Spence continued. "I've seen the figures you carved for Natasha."

"Ah." A glimmer of a smile curved Mikhail's mouth. "My sister always was fond of fairy tales." There was a squeal from upstairs, followed by rumbling laughter.

"That's Freddie," Natasha explained. "Spence's daughter. She's making Papa's day."

Mikhail slipped a thumb through one belt loop. "You are a widower."

"That's right."

"And now you teach at college."

"Yes."

"Mikhail," Natasha interrupted. "Don't play big brother. I'm older than you."

"But I'm bigger." Then with a quick, flashing grin, he tossed an arm around her shoulder. "So what's to eat?"

Too much, Spence decided as the family gathered around the table late that afternoon. The huge turkey in the center of the hand-crocheted tablecloth was only the beginning. Faithful to her adopted country's holiday, Nadia had prepared a meal that was an American tradition from the chestnut dressing to the pumpkin pies.

Wide-eyed, Freddie gawked, staring at platter after platter. The room was full of noise as everyone talked over and around everyone else. The china was mismatched. Old Sasha lay sprawled under the table near her feet, hoping for a few unobtrusive handouts. She was sitting on a wobbly chair and the New York Yellow Pages. As far as she was concerned, it was the best day of her life.

Alex and Rachel began to argue over some childhood infraction. Mikhail joined in to tell them they were both wrong. When her opinion was sought, Natasha just laughed and shook her head, then turned to Spence and murmured something into his ear that made him chuckle.

Nadia, her cheeks rosy with the pleasure of having her family together, slipped a hand into Yuri's as he lifted his glass.

"Enough," he said, and effectively silenced the table. "You can argue later about who let white mice loose in science lab. Now we toast. We are thankful for this food that Nadia and my girls have fixed for us. And more thankful for the friends and family who are here together to enjoy it. We give thanks, as we did on our first Thanksgiving in our country, that we are free."

"To freedom," Mikhail said as he lifted his glass.

"To freedom," Yuri agreed. His eyes misted and he looked around the table. "And to family."

Chapter 11

That evening, with Freddie dozing in his lap, Spence listened to Yuri tell stories of the old country. While the meal had been a noisy competition for conversation, this hour was one of quiet and content. Across the room Rachel and Alex played a trivia game. They argued often, but without heat.

In the corner, Natasha and Mikhail sat close, dark heads together. Spence could hear their murmurs and noted that one often reached to touch the other's hand, to touch a cheek. Nadia sat smiling, interrupting Yuri occasionally to correct or comment as she worked another pillow cover.

"Woman." Yuri pointed at his wife with the stem of his after-dinner pipe. "I remember like yesterday."

"You remember as you like to remember."

"Tak." He stuck the pipe back into his mouth. "And what I remember makes better story."

When Freddie stirred, Spence shifted her. "I'd better put her to bed."

"I will do it." Nadia set her needlework aside and rose. "I would like to." Making soothing noises, she lifted Freddie. Sleepy and agreeable, Freddie snuggled into her neck.

"Will you rock me?"

"Yes." Touched, Nadia kissed her hair as she started toward the steps. "I will rock you in the chair where I rocked all my babies."

"And sing?"

"I will sing you a song my mother sang to me. You would like that?"

Freddie gave a yawn and a drowsy nod.

"You have a beautiful daughter." Like Spence, Yuri watched them turn up the steps. "You must bring her back often."

"I think I'll have a hard time keeping her away."

"She is always welcome, as you are." Yuri took a puff on his pipe. "Even if you don't marry my daughter."

That statement brought on ten seconds of humming silence until Alex and Rachel bent back over their game, smothering grins. Spence didn't bother to smother his own as Natasha rose.

"There isn't enough milk for the morning," she decided on the spot. "Spence, why don't you walk with me to get some?"

"Sure."

A few moments later they stepped outside, wrapped in coats and scarves. The air had a bite that Natasha welcomed. Overhead the sky was clear as black glass and icy with stars.

"He didn't mean to embarrass you," Spence began.

"Yes, he did."

Spence didn't bother to hold back the chuckle, and draped an arm over her shoulders. "I suppose he did. I like your family."

"So do I. Most of the time."

"You're lucky to have them. Watching Freddie here has made me realize how important family is. I don't suppose I've really tried to get closer to Nina or my parents."

"They're still family. Perhaps we're as close as we are, because when we came here we only had each other."

"It's true my family never crossed the mountains into Hungary in a wagon."

That made her laugh. "Rachel was always jealous that she hadn't been born yet. When she was little, she would get back by saying she was more American, because she'd been born in New York. Then not long ago, someone said to her that if she wanted to be a lawyer, she should think of changing or shortening her name." With a new laugh, Natasha looked up at him. "She became very insulted and very Ukrainian."

"It's a good name. You could always keep it professionally after you marry me."

"Don't start."

"Must be your father's influence." He glanced at the

dark shop, where a Closed sign hung on the door. "The store's closed."

"I know." She turned into his arms. "I just wanted to walk. Now that we're standing here in a dark doorway, alone, I can kiss you."

"Good point." Spence lowered his mouth to hers.

Natasha was annoyed with herself for dozing off and on during the drive home. She felt as though she'd spent a week mountain climbing, rather than less than forty-eight hours in her family home. By the time she shook herself awake for the last time, they were crossing the Maryland border into West Virginia.

"Already." She straightened in her seat and cast an apologetic glance at Spence. "I didn't help you drive."

"It's all right. You looked like you needed the rest."

"Too much food, too little sleep." She looked back at Freddie, who was sleeping soundly. "We've been poor company for you."

"You can make up for it. Come home with me for a while."

"All right." It was the least she could do, Natasha thought. With Vera away until Sunday, she could help him tuck Freddie into bed and fix him a light meal.

When they pulled up in front of the house, they managed the suitcases and the sleeping child between them. "I'll take her up," he murmured. "It won't take long."

Natasha waited in the kitchen, brewing tea and making sandwiches. It was ridiculous, she thought. She not only was exhausted but starving. By the time Spence came down again, she had Vera's worktable set.

"She's sleeping like a rock." He scanned the table. "You read my mind."

"With two unconscious passengers you couldn't stop and eat."

"What have we got?"

"Old Ukrainian tradition." She pulled back her chair. "Tuna fish."

"Wonderful," Spence decided after the first bite.

It was more than the sandwich. He liked having her there, sitting across from him in the glare of the kitchen light with the house quiet around them. "I guess you'll open the shop tomorrow."

"Absolutely. It'll be a madhouse from now until Christmas. I've hired a college student part-time, and he starts tomorrow." She lifted her cup and grinned at him over the rim. "Guess who it is."

"Melony Trainor," he said, naming one of his most attractive students and earning a punch on the shoulder.

"No. She's too busy flirting with men to work. Terry Maynard."

"Maynard? Really?"

"Yes. He can use the money to buy a new muffler for his car. And…" She paused dramatically. "He and Annie are an item."

"No kidding?" He was grinning as he sat back. "Well, he certainly got over having his life shattered quickly."

Natasha lifted a brow. "It wasn't shattered, only

shaken. They've been seeing each other almost every night for three weeks."

"Sounds serious."

"I think it is. But Annie's worried she's too old for him."

"How much older is she?"

Natasha leaned forward and lowered her voice. "Oh, very much older. Nearly an entire year."

"Cradle robber."

With a laugh she leaned back again. "It's nice to see them together. I only hope they don't forget to wait on customers because they're mooning at each other." She shrugged, and went back to her tea. "I think I'll go in early and start on the decorations."

"You'll be tired at the end of the day. Why don't you come here for dinner?"

Curious, she tilted her head. "You cook?"

"No." He grinned and polished off his sandwich. "But I do great takeout. You can get a whole box of chicken or pizza with the works. I've even been known to come up with oriental seafood."

"I'll leave the menu to you." She rose to clear the table, but he took her hand.

"Natasha." He stood, using his free hand to stroke her hair. "I want to thank you for sharing the last couple of days with me. It meant a lot."

"To me too."

"Still, I've missed being alone with you." He bent to brush his lips over hers. "Come upstairs with me. I want very much to make love with you in my bed."

She didn't answer. Nor did she hesitate. Slipping an arm around his waist, she went with him.

He left the bedside light on low. She could just see the dark, masculine colors he'd chosen for his room. Midnight blue, forest green. An oil painting in a heavy, ornate frame dominated one wall. She could see the silhouettes of exquisite antiques. The bed was big, a generous private space covered by a thick, soft quilt. A special space, Natasha realized, knowing he had never brought another woman to this bed, to this room.

In the mirror over the bureau she caught their reflections as they stood side by side and saw herself smile when he touched a hand to her cheek.

There was time, time to savor. The fatigue she had felt earlier had vanished. Now she felt only the glow that came from loving and being loved. Words were too difficult, but when she kissed him, her heart spoke for her.

Slowly they undressed each other.

She slipped his sweater over his head. He undid the buttons of her cardigan, then pushed it from her shoulders. Keeping her eyes on his, she unfastened his shirt. He slid up the cotton sweater, letting his fingers trail until she was free of it. She unhooked his trousers. He flipped the three snaps that held her slacks at the waist. Keeping his hands light, he drew the teddy down her body as she tugged away the last barrier between them.

Quietly they moved together, her palms pressing against his back, his skimming up her sides. Heads tilting first this way, then that, they experimented with long, lingering kisses. Enjoyment. Their bodies warming, their mouths seeking, it seemed so easy here.

They drew back in unspoken agreement. Spence pulled down the quilt. They slipped under it together.

Intimacy had no rival, Natasha thought. There was nothing to compare with this. Their bodies rubbed against each other, so that the sheets whispered with each movement. Her sigh answered his murmurs. The flavor and fragrance of his skin was familiar, personal. His touch, gentle, then persuasive, then demanding, was everything she wanted.

She was simply beautiful. Not just her body, not just that exquisite face, but her spirit. When she moved with him, there was a harmony more intense than any he could create with music. She was his music—her laugh, her voice, her gestures. He knew of no way to tell her. Only to show her.

He made love with her as though it were the first and the only time. Never had she felt so elegant, so graceful. Never had she felt so strong or so sure.

When he rose over her, when she rose to meet him, it was perfect.

"I'd like you to stay."

Natasha turned her face into his throat. "I can't. Freddie would ask questions in the morning I don't know how to answer."

"I have a very simple answer. I'll tell her the truth. I'm in love with you."

"That's not simple."

"It is the truth." He shifted so that he could look at her. Her eyes were shadowed in the dim light. "I do love you, Natasha."

"Spence—"

"No. No logic or excuses. We're past that. Tell me if you believe me."

She looked into his eyes and saw what she already knew. "Yes, I believe you."

"Then tell me what you feel. I need to know."

He had a right to know, she thought, though she could all but taste the panic on her tongue. "I love you. And I'm afraid."

He brought her hand to his lips to press a kiss firmly against her fingers. "Why?"

"Because I was in love before, and nothing, nothing could have ended as badly."

There was that shadow again, he thought impatiently. The shadow from her past that he could neither fight nor conquer because it was nameless.

"Neither of us have come into this without a few bruises, Natasha. But we have a chance to make something new, something important."

She knew he was right, felt he was right, yet still held back. "I wish I were so sure. Spence, there are things you don't know about me."

"That you were a dancer."

She shifted then, to gather the sheets to her breast and sit up. "Yes. Once."

"Why haven't you mentioned it?"

"Because it was over."

He drew the hair away from her face. "Why did you stop?"

"I had a choice to make." The ache came back, but briefly. She turned to him and smiled. "I was not so good. Oh, I was adequate, and perhaps in time I would have been good enough to have been a principal dancer. Perhaps... It was something I wanted very badly once. But wanting something doesn't always make it happen."

"Will you tell me about it?"

It was a beginning, one she knew she had to make. "It's not very exciting." She lifted her hands, then let them fall onto the sheet. "I started late, after we came here. Through the church my parents met Martina Latovia. Many years ago she was an important Soviet dancer who defected. She became friends with my mother and offered to give me classes. It was good for me, the dance. I didn't speak English well, so it was hard to make friends. Everything was so different here, you see."

"Yes, I can imagine."

"I was nearly eight by that time. It becomes difficult to teach the body, the joints, to move as they weren't meant to move. But I worked very hard. *Madame* was kind and encouraging. My parents were so proud." She laughed a little, but warmly. "Papa was sure I would be the next Pavlova. The first time I danced *en pointe*, Mama cried. Dance is obsession and pain and joy. It's a different world, Spence. I can't explain. You have to know it, be a part of it."

"You don't have to explain."

She looked over at him. "No, not to you," she murmured. "Because of the music. I joined the corps de ballet when I was almost sixteen. It was wonderful. Perhaps I didn't know there were other worlds, but I was happy."

"What happened?"

"There was another dancer." She shut her eyes. It was important to take this slowly, carefully. "You've heard of him, I imagine. Anthony Marshall."

"Yes." Spence had an immediate picture of a tall, blond man with a slender build and incredible grace. "I've seen him dance many times."

"He was magnificent. Is," she corrected. "Though it's been years since I've seen him dance. We became involved. I was young. Too young. And it was a very big mistake."

Now the shadow had a name. "You loved him."

"Oh yes. In a naive and idealistic kind of way. The only way a girl can love at seventeen. More, I thought he loved me. He told me he did, in words, in actions. He was very charming, romantic…and I wanted to believe him. He promised me marriage, a future, a partnership in dance, all the things I wanted to hear. He broke all those promises, and my heart."

"So now you don't want to hear promises from me."

"You're not Anthony," she murmured, then lifted a hand to his cheek. Her eyes were dark and beautiful, her voice only more exotic as emotions crowded. "Believe me, I know that. And I don't compare, not now. I'm not the same woman who built dreams on a few careless words."

"What I've said to you hasn't been careless."

"No." She leaned closer to rest her cheek against his. "Over the past months I've come to see that, and to understand that what I feel for you is different from anything I've felt before." There was more she wanted to tell him, but the words clogged her throat. "Please, let that be enough for now."

"For now. It won't be enough forever."

She turned her mouth to his. "Just for now."

How could it be? Natasha asked herself. How could it be that when she was just beginning to trust herself, to trust her heart, that this should happen? How could she face it again?

It was like a play run backward and started again, when her life had changed so drastically and completely. She sat back on her bed, no longer concerned about dressing for work, about starting a normal day. How could things be normal now? How could she expect them to be normal ever again?

She held the little vial in her hand. She had followed the instructions exactly. Just a precaution, she had told herself. But she'd known in her heart. Since the visit to her parents two weeks before she'd known. And had avoided facing the reality.

It was not the flu that made her queasy in the mornings. It was not overwork or stress that caused her to be so tired, or that brought on the occasional dizzy spells. The simple test that she'd bought over the counter in the drugstore had told her what she'd already known and feared.

She was carrying a child. Once again she was carrying a child. The rush of joy and wonder was totally eclipsed by the bone-deep fear that froze her.

How could it be? She was no longer a foolish girl and had taken precautions. Romance aside, she had been practical enough, responsible enough to visit her doctor and begin taking those tiny little pills, when she had realized where her relationship with Spence was bound to go. Yet she was pregnant. There was no denying it.

How could she tell him? Covering her face with her hands, Natasha rocked back and forth to give herself some small comfort. How could she go through all of it again, when that time years before was still so painfully etched on her memory?

She had known Anthony no longer loved her, if he had ever. But when she'd learned she was carrying his child, she had been thrilled. And so certain that he would share her delight. When she'd gone to him, almost bubbling over, glowing with the joy of it, his cruelty had all but cut her in two.

How grudgingly he'd let her into his apartment, Natasha remembered. How difficult it had been for her to continue to smile when she'd seen his table set for two, the candles lighted, the wine chilling—as he'd so often prepared the stage when he'd loved her. Now he'd set that stage for someone else. But she'd persuaded herself that it didn't matter. Once she'd told him, everything would change.

Everything had.

"What the hell are you talking about?" She remembered the fury in his eyes as he'd stared at her.

"I went to the doctor this afternoon. I'm pregnant, almost two months." She reached out for him. "Anthony—"

"That's an old game, Tash." He'd said it casually, but perhaps he'd been shaken. He'd stalked to the table to pour a glass of wine.

"It's not a game."

"No? Then how could you be so stupid?" He'd grabbed her arm and given her a quick shake, his magnificent mane of hair flying. "If you've gotten yourself in trouble, don't expect to come running to me to fix it."

Dazed, she'd lifted a hand to rub her arm where his fingers had bit in. It was only that he didn't understand, she'd told herself. "I'm having a child. Your child. The doctor says the baby will come in July."

"Maybe you're pregnant." He'd shrugged as he'd downed the wine. "It doesn't concern me."

"It must."

He'd looked at her then, his glass held aloft, his eyes cool. "How do I know it's mine?"

At that she'd paled. As she'd stood there, she'd remembered how it had felt when she'd almost stepped in front of a bus on her first trip to New York City. "You know. You have to know."

"I don't have to know anything. Now, if you'll excuse me, I'm expecting someone."

In desperation she'd reached out for him. "Anthony, don't you understand? I'm carrying our baby."

"Your baby," he corrected. "Your problem. If you want some advice, get rid of it."

"Get—" She hadn't been so young or so naive that she hadn't understood his meaning. "You can't mean it."

"You want to dance, Tash? Try picking classes back up after taking off nine months to give birth to some brat you're going to end up giving away in any case. Grow up."

"I have grown up." She'd laid a hand on her stomach, in protection and defense. "And I will have this child."

"Your choice." He'd gestured with his wineglass. "Don't expect to pull me into it. I've got a career to think of. You're probably better off," he decided. "Talk some loser into marrying you and set up housekeeping. You'd never be any better than mediocre at dance anyway."

So she had had the child and loved it—for a brief, brief time. Now there was another. She couldn't bear to love it, couldn't bear to want it. Not when she knew what it was like to lose.

Frantic, she threw the vial across the room and began pulling clothes out of her closet. She had to get away. She had to think. She would get away, Natasha promised herself, then pressed her fingers against her eyes until she calmed. But she had to tell him.

This time she drove to his house, struggling for calm as the car brought her closer. Because it was Saturday, children were playing in yards and on the sidewalk. Some called out to her as she passed, and she managed to lift a hand in a wave. She spotted Freddie wrestling with her kittens on the grass.

"Tash! Tash!" Lucy and Desi darted for cover, but Freddie raced to the car. "Did you come to play?"

"Not today." Summoning a smile, Natasha kissed her cheeks. "Is your daddy home?"

"He's playing music. He plays music a lot since we came here. I drew a picture. I'm going to send it to Papa and Nana."

Natasha struggled to keep the smile in place at Freddie's names for her parents. "They will like that very much."

"Come on, I'll show you."

"In a little while. I need to speak to your father first. By myself."

Freddie's bottom lip threatened. "Are you mad at him?"

"No." She pressed a finger to Freddie's nose. "Go find your kittens. I'll talk to you before I go."

"Okay." Reassured, Freddie raced off, sending out whoops that would have the kittens cowering in the bushes, Natasha reflected.

It was better to keep her mind a blank, she decided as she knocked on the front door. Then she would take it slowly, logically, like an adult.

"Miss." Vera opened the door, her expression less remote than usual. Freddie's description of the Thanksgiving holiday in Brooklyn had done a great deal to win her over.

"I'd like to see Dr. Kimball if he's not busy."

"Come in." She found herself frowning a bit as she studied Natasha. "Are you all right, miss? You're very pale."

"Yes, I'm fine. Thank you."

"Would you like tea?"

"No—no, I can't stay long."

Though Vera privately thought Natasha looked like a cornered rabbit, she nodded. "You'll find him in the music room. He's been up half the night working."

"Thank you." Clutching her bag, Natasha started down the hall. She could hear the music he was playing, something weepy. Or perhaps it was her own mood, she thought; she blinked back tears.

When she saw him, she remembered the first time she had walked into that room. Perhaps she had started to fall in love with him that day, when he had sat there with a child on his lap, surrounded by sunlight.

She pulled off her gloves, running them through her nervous hands as she watched him. He was lost in it, both captor and captive of the music. Now she would change his life. He hadn't asked for this, and they both knew that loving wasn't always enough.

"Spence." She murmured his name when the music stopped, but he didn't hear. She could see the intensity was still on him as he scribbled on staff paper. He hadn't shaved. It made her want to smile, but instead her eyes filled. His shirt was rumpled and open at the collar. His hair was tousled. As she watched, he ran a hand through it. "Spence," she repeated.

He looked up—annoyed at first. Then he focused and smiled at her. "Hi. I didn't expect to see you today."

"Annie's watching the shop." She knit her hands. "I needed to see you."

"I'm glad you did." He rose, though the music was still filling his head. "What time is it anyway?" Absently he glanced at his watch. "Too early to ask you for lunch. How about some coffee?"

"No." Even the thought of coffee made her stomach roll. "I don't want anything. I needed to tell you…." Her fingers knotted. "I don't know how. I want you to know I never intended—this isn't intended to put you under obligation…."

The words trailed off again, he shook his head and started toward her. "If something's wrong, why don't you tell me?"

"I'm trying to."

He took her hand to lead her to the couch. "The best way's often straight out."

"Yes." She put her hand to her spinning head. "You see, I…" She saw the concern in his eyes, then everything went black….

She was lying on the sofa, and Spence was kneeling beside her, chafing her wrists. "Take it easy," he murmured. "Just lie still. I'll call a doctor."

"No. There's no need." Carefully she pushed herself up. "I'm all right."

"The hell you are." Her skin was clammy under his hand. "You're like ice, and pale as a ghost. Damn it, Natasha, why didn't you tell me you weren't well? I'll take you to the hospital."

"I don't need the hospital or the doctor." Hysteria was bubbling under her heart. She fought it back and forced herself to speak. "I'm not sick, Spence. I'm pregnant."

Chapter 12

"What?" It was the best he could do; he sank back onto his heels and stared at her. "What did you say?"

She wanted to be strong, had to be. He looked as though she'd hit him with a blunt instrument. "I'm pregnant," she repeated, then made a helpless gesture. "I'm sorry."

He only shook his head, waiting for it to sink in. "Are you sure?"

"Yes." It was best to be matter-of-fact, Natasha told herself. He was a civilized man. There would be no accusations, no cruelty. "This morning I took a test. I suspected before, for a couple of weeks, but..."

"Suspected." His hand curled into a fist on the cushion. She didn't look furious, as Angela had. She looked destroyed. "And you didn't mention it."

"I saw no need until I knew. There was no point in upsetting you."

"I see. Is that what you are, Natasha? Upset?"

"What I am is pregnant," she said briskly. "And I felt it was only right to tell you. I'm going away for a few days." Though she still felt shaky, she managed to stand.

"Away?" Confused, afraid she would faint again, furious, he caught her. "Now just a damn minute. You drop in, tell me you're pregnant, and now you calmly tell me you're going away?" He felt something sharp punch into his gut. Its name was fear. "Where?"

"Just away." She heard her own voice, snappish and rude, and pressed a hand to her head. "I'm sorry, I'm not handling this well. I need some time. I need to go away."

"What you need to do is sit down until we talk this out."

"I can't talk about it." She felt the pressure inside her build like floodwaters against a dam. "Not yet—not until I...I only wanted to tell you before I left."

"You're not going anywhere." He grabbed her arm to pull her back. "And you damn well will talk about it. What do you want from me? Am I supposed to say, 'Well, that's interesting news, Natasha. See you when you get back'?"

"I don't want anything." When her voice rose this time, she couldn't control it. Passions, griefs, fears, poured out even as the tears began. "I never wanted anything from you. I didn't want to fall in love with you, I didn't want to need you in my life. I didn't want your child inside me."

"That's clear enough." His grip tightened, and he let his own temper free. "That's crystal clear. But you do have my child inside you, and now we're going to sit down and talk about what we're going to do about it."

"I tell you I need time."

"I've already given you more than enough time, Natasha. Apparently fate's taken a hand again, and you're going to have to face it."

"I can't go through this again. I won't."

"Again? What are you talking about?"

"I had a child." She jerked away to cover her face with her hands. Her whole body began to quake. "I had a child. Oh, God."

Stunned, he put a gentle hand upon her shoulder. "You have a child?"

"Had." The tears seemed to be shooting up, hot and painful, from the center of her body. "She's gone."

"Come sit down, Natasha. Talk to me."

"I can't. You don't understand. I lost her. My baby. I can't bear the thought of going through it all again." She tore herself away. "You don't know, you can't know, how much it hurts."

"No, but I can see it." He reached for her again. "I want you to tell me about this, so I can understand."

"What would that change?"

"We'll have to see. It isn't good for you to get so upset now."

"No." She swiped a hand over her cheek. "It doesn't do any good to be upset. I'm sorry I'm behaving like this."

"Don't apologize. Sit down. I'll get you some tea.

We'll talk." He led her to a chair and she went unresistingly. "I'll only be a minute."

He was away for less than that, he was sure, but when he came back, she was gone.

Mikhail carved from a block of cherrywood and listened to the blast of rock and roll through his earphones. It suited the mood he could feel from the wood. Whatever was inside—and he wasn't sure just what that was yet—was young and full of energy. Whenever he carved, he listened, whether it was to blues or Bach or simply the rush and whoosh of traffic four floors below his window. It left his mind free to explore whatever medium his hands were working in.

Tonight his mind was too cluttered, and he knew he was stalling. He glanced over his worktable and across his cramped and cluttered two-room apartment. Natasha was curled in the overstuffed, badly sprung chair he'd salvaged off the street the previous summer. She had a book in her hands, but Mikhail didn't think she'd turned a page in more than twenty minutes. She, too, was stalling.

As annoyed with himself as with her, he pulled off the headphones. He only had to turn to be in the kitchen. Saying nothing, he put a pot onto one of the two temperamental gas burners and brewed tea. Natasha made no comment. When he brought over two cups, setting hers on the scarred surface of a nearby table, she glanced up blankly.

"Oh. *Dyakuyu.*"

"It's time to tell me what's going on."

"Mikhail—"

"I mean it." He dropped onto the mismatched hassock at her feet. "You've been here nearly a week, Tash."

She managed a small smile. "Ready to kick me out?"

"Maybe." But he put a hand over hers, rubbing lightly. "I haven't asked any questions, because that was what you wanted. I haven't told Mama and Papa that you arrived at my door one evening, looking pale and frightened, because you asked me to say nothing."

"And I appreciate it."

"Well, stop appreciating it." He made one of his characteristically abrupt gestures. "Talk to me."

"I told you I needed to get away for a little while, and I didn't want Mama and Papa to fuss over me." She moved her shoulders, then reached for her tea. "You don't fuss."

"I'm about to. Tell me what's wrong." He leaned over and cupped her chin in one hand. "Tash, tell me."

"I'm pregnant," she blurted out, then shakily set the tea down again.

He opened his mouth, but when the words didn't come, he simply wrapped his arms around her. Taking a long, labored breath, she held on.

"You're all right? You're well?"

"Yes. I went to the doctor a couple days ago. He says I'm fine. We're fine."

He drew back to study her face. "The college professor?"

"Yes. There hasn't been anyone but Spence."

Mikhail's dark eyes kindled. "If the bastard's treated you badly—"

"No." She found it odd that she was able to smile and caught Mikhail's fisted hands in hers. "No, he's never treated me badly."

"So he doesn't want the child." When Natasha merely looked down at their joined hands, Mikhail narrowed his eyes. "Natasha?"

"I don't know." She pulled away to stand and pace through Mikhail's collection of beat-up furniture and blocks of wood and stone.

"You haven't told him?"

"Of course I told him." As she moved, her hands clasped and unclasped. To calm herself, she stopped by Mikhail's Christmas tree—a one-foot evergreen in a pot that she'd decorated with bits of colored paper. "I just didn't give him much of a chance to say anything when I did. I was too upset."

"You don't want the child."

She turned at that, her eyes wide. "How can you say that? How could you think that?"

"Because you're here, instead of working things out with the college professor."

"I needed time to think."

"You think too much."

It wasn't anything he hadn't said before. Natasha's jaw set. "This isn't a matter of deciding between a blue dress and a red one. I'm having a child."

"*Tak*. Why don't you sit down and relax before you give it wrinkles."

"I don't want to sit down." She began to prowl again, shoving a box out of her way with one foot. "I didn't want to get involved with him in the first place. Even when I did, when he made it impossible for me to do otherwise, I knew it was important to keep some distance. I wanted to make sure I didn't make the same mistakes again. And now…" She made a helpless gesture.

"He isn't Anthony. This baby isn't Lily." When she turned around, her eyes were so drenched with emotion that he rose to go to her. "I loved her, too."

"I know."

"You can't judge by what's gone, Tash." Gently he kissed her cheeks. "It isn't fair to you, your professor or the child."

"I don't know what to do."

"Do you love him?"

"Yes, I love him."

"Does he love you?"

"He says—"

He caught her restless hands in his own. "Don't tell me what he says, tell me what you know."

"Yes, he loves me."

"Then stop hiding and go home. You should be having this conversation with him, not with your brother."

He was slowly going out of his mind. Every day Spence went by Natasha's apartment, certain that this time she would answer the door. When she didn't, he stalked over to harass Annie in the shop. He barely noticed the Christmas decorations in shop windows, the fat, cheerful Santas, the glittery angels, the colored lights strung around the houses. When he did, it was to scowl at them.

It had taken all of his efforts to make a show of holiday spirit for Freddie. He'd taken her to pick out a tree, spent hours decorating it with her and complimenting her crumbling popcorn strings. Dutifully he'd listened to her ever-growing Christmas list, and had taken her to the mall to sit in Santa's lap. But his heart wasn't in it.

It had to stop, he told himself and he stared out the window at the first snowfall. Whatever crisis he was facing, whatever chaos his life was in, he wouldn't see Freddie's Christmas spoiled.

She asked about Natasha every day. It only made it more difficult because he had no answers. He'd watched Freddie play an angel in her school's Christmas pageant and wished Natasha had been with him.

And what of their child? He could hardly think of anything else. Even now Natasha might be carrying the baby sister Freddie so coveted. The baby, Spence had already realized, that he desperately wanted. Unless... He didn't want to think of where she had gone, what she had done. How could he think of anything else?

There had to be a way to find her. When he did, he would beg, plead, browbeat and threaten until she came back to him.

She'd had a child. The fact left him dazed. A child she had lost, Spence remembered. But how, and when? Questions that needed answering crowded his mind. She had said she loved him, and he knew that saying it had been difficult for her. Even so, she had yet to trust him.

"Daddy." Freddie bounced into the room, her mind full of the Christmas that was only six days away. "We're making cookies."

He glanced over his shoulder to see Freddie grinning, her mouth smeared with red and green sugar. Spence swooped her up to hold her close. "I love you, Freddie."

She giggled, then kissed him. "I love you, too. Can you come make cookies with us?"

"In a little while. I have to go out first." He was going to go to the shop, corner Annie and find out where Natasha had gone. No matter what the redhead said, Spence didn't believe that Natasha would have left her assistant without a number where she could be reached.

Freddie's lip poked out while she fiddled with Spence's top button. "When will you come back?"

"Soon." He kissed her again before he set her down. "When I come back, I'll help you bake cookies. I promise."

Content, Freddie rushed back to Vera. She knew her father always kept his promises.

Natasha stood outside the front door as the snow fell. There were lights strung along the roof and around the posts. She wondered how they would look when they were lighted. There was a full-size Santa on the door, his load of presents making him bend from the waist. She remembered the witch that had stood there on Halloween. On that first night she and Spence had made love. On that night, she was certain, their child had been conceived.

For a moment she almost turned back, telling herself she should go to her apartment, unpack, catch her breath. But that would only be hiding again. She'd hidden long enough. Gathering her courage, she knocked.

The moment Freddie opened the door, the little girl's eyes shone. She let out a squeal and all but jumped into Natasha's arms. "You're back, you're back! I've been waiting for you forever."

Natasha held her close, swaying back and forth. This was what she wanted, needed, she realized as she buried her face in Freddie's hair. How could she have been such a fool? "It's only been a little while."

"It's been days and days. We got a tree and lights, and I already wrapped your present. I bought it myself at the mall. Don't go away again."

"No," Natasha murmured. "I won't." She set Freddie down to step inside and close out the cold and snow.

"You missed my play. I was an angel."

"I'm sorry."

"We made the halos in school and got to keep them, so I can show you how I looked."

"I'd like that."

Certain everything was back to normal, Freddie took her hand. "I tripped once, but I remembered all my lines. Mikey forgot his. I said 'A child is born in Bethlehem,' and 'Peace on Earth,' and sang 'Gloria in selfish Deo.'"

Natasha laughed for the first time in days. "I wish I had heard that. You will sing it for me later?"

"Okay. We're baking cookies." Still holding Natasha's hand, she began to drag her toward the kitchen.

"Is your daddy helping you?"

"No, he had to go out. He said he'd come back soon and bake some. He promised."

Torn between relief and disappointment, Natasha followed Freddie into the kitchen.

"Vera, Tash is back."

"I see." Vera pursed her lips. Just when she'd thought Natasha *might* be good enough for the *señor* and her baby, the woman had gone off without a word. Still, she knew her duty. "Would you like some coffee or tea, miss?"

"No, thank you. I don't want to be in your way."

"You have to stay." Freddie tugged at Natasha's hand again. "Look, I've made snowmen and reindeers and Santas." She plucked what she considered one of her best creations from the counter. "You can have one."

"It's beautiful." Natasha looked down at the snowman with red sugar clumped on his face and the brim of his hat broken off.

"Are you going to cry?" Freddie asked.

"No." She managed to blink back the mist of tears. "I'm just glad to be home."

As she spoke, the kitchen door opened. Natasha held her breath when Spence stepped into the room. He didn't speak. His hand still on the door, he stopped to stare. It was as if he'd conjured her up out of his own chaotic thoughts. There was snow melting in her hair and on the shoulders of her coat. Her eyes were bright, teary.

"Daddy, Tash is home," Freddie announced, running to him. "She's going to bake cookies with us."

Vera briskly untied her apron. Whatever doubts she'd had about Natasha were eclipsed by the look on her face. Vera knew a woman in love when she saw her. "We need more flour. Come, Freddie, we will go buy some."

"But I want to—"

"You want to bake, we need flour to bake. Come, we'll get your coat." Businesslike, Vera bustled Freddie out of the room.

Alone, Spence and Natasha stood where they were; the moment stretched out. The heat in the kitchen was making her dizzy. Natasha stripped off her coat and laid it over the back of a chair. She wanted to talk to him, reasonably. That couldn't be done if she fainted at his feet.

"Spence." The word seemed to echo off the walls, and she took a deep breath. "I was hoping we could talk."

"I see. Now you've decided talking's a good idea."

She started to speak, then changed her mind. When the oven timer went off behind her, she turned automatically to take up the hot mitt and remove the latest batch of cookies from the oven. She took her time setting them on the cooling rack.

"You're right to be angry with me. I behaved very badly toward you. Now I have to ask you to listen to me, and hope you can forgive me."

He studied her for one long, silent moment. "You certainly know how to defuse an argument."

"I didn't come to argue with you. I've had time to think, and I realize that I chose a very poor way to tell you about the baby, then to leave as I did." She looked down at her hands, her tightly laced fingers. "To just run away was inexcusable. I can only tell you that I was afraid and confused and too emotional to think clearly."

"One question," he interjected, then waited until she lifted her head. He needed to see her face. "Is there still a baby?"

"Yes." The blank puzzlement in her eyes became awareness. Awareness became regret. "Oh, Spence, I'm sorry, so sorry to have caused you to think that I might have…" She blinked away tears, knowing her emotions were still too close to the surface. "I'm sorry. I went to Mikhail's to stay with him a few days." She let out a shaky breath. "May I sit?"

He only nodded, then moved to the window as she slid behind the table. Laying his palms upon the counter, he looked out at the snow. "I've been going out of my mind, wondering where you were, how you were. The state you were in when you left, I was terrified you'd do something rash before we could talk it through."

"I could never do what you thought, Spence. This is our baby."

"You said you didn't want it." He turned again. "You said you wouldn't go through it again."

"I was afraid," Natasha admitted. "And it's true I hadn't wanted to get pregnant, not now. Not ever. I'd like to tell you everything."

He wanted badly, much too badly, just to reach out to her, to hold her and tell her that nothing mattered.

Because he knew it did matter, he busied himself at the stove. "Do you want some coffee?"

"No. It makes me sick now." She smiled a little when he fumbled with the pot. "Please, would you sit down?"

"All right." He sat down across from her, then spread his hands. "Go ahead."

"I told you that I had been in love with Anthony while I was with the corps de ballet. I was just seventeen when we became lovers. He was the first for me. There's been no one for me until you."

"Why?"

The answer was much easier than she'd believed. "I'd never loved again until you. The love I feel for you is much different from the fantasies I had for Anthony. With you it isn't dreams and knights and princes. With you it's real and solid. Day-to-day. Ordinary—ordinary in the most beautiful way. Can you understand?"

He looked at her. The room was quiet, insulated by the snow. It smelled of warm cookies and cinnamon. "Yes."

"I was afraid to feel this strongly for you, for anyone, because what happened between Anthony and me..." She waited a moment, surprised that there was no pain now, only sadness. "I had believed him, everything he said, everything he promised me. When I discovered he made many of the same promises to other women, I was crushed. We argued, and he sent me away like a child who had displeased him. A few weeks later I discovered I was pregnant. I was thrilled. I could only think that I was carrying Anthony's child and that when I told him, he would see that we belonged together. Then I told him."

Spence reached for her hand without a word.

"It was not as I had imagined. He was angry. The things he said…. It doesn't matter," she went on. "He didn't want me, he didn't want the child. In those few moments I grew up years. He wasn't the man I had wanted him to be, but I had the child. I wanted that baby." Her fingers tightened on his. "I so desperately wanted that baby."

"What did you do?"

"The only thing I could. There could be no dancing now. I left the company and went home. I know it was a burden for my parents, but they stood by me. I got a job in a department store. Selling toys." She smiled at that.

"It must have been difficult for you." He tried to imagine her, a teenager, pregnant, deserted by the father of her child, struggling to hold it all together.

"Yes, it was. It was also a wonderful time. My body changed. After the first month or two when I felt so fragile, I began to feel strong. So strong. I would sit in bed at night and read books on babies and birthing. I would ask Mama dozens of questions. I knit—badly," she said with a quiet laugh. "Papa built a bassinet, and Mama sewed a white skirt with pink and blue ribbons. It was beautiful." She felt the tears well up and shook her head. "Could I have some water?"

He rose, and filling a glass from the tap, set it beside her. "Take your time, Natasha." Because he knew they both needed it, he stroked her hair. "You don't have to tell me everything at once."

"I need to." She sipped slowly, waiting for him to sit down again. "I called her Lily," she murmured. "She was so lovely, so tiny and soft. I had no idea it was possible to love anything, anyone, the way you love a child. I would watch her sleep for hours, so thrilled, so awed that she had come from me."

The tears were falling now, soundlessly. One fell onto the back of her hand. "It was hot that summer, and I would take her out in this little carriage to get air and sunshine. People would stop to look at her. She hardly cried, and when I nursed her, she would put a hand on my breast and watch me with those big eyes. You know what it is. You have Freddie."

"I know. There's nothing like having a child."

"Or losing one," Natasha said softly. "It was so quick. She was only five weeks old. I woke up in the morning, surprised that she had slept through the night. My breasts were full of milk. The bassinet was by my bed. I reached down for her, picked her up. At first I didn't understand, didn't believe…." She broke off to press her hands to her eyes. "I remember screaming and screaming—Rachel rushing up out of the next bed, the rest of the family running in—Mama taking her from me." The silent tears turned to weeping. Her face now covered by her hands, she let go in a way she usually only allowed herself in private.

There was nothing he could say, nothing to be said. Instead of searching for meaningless words, he rose to crouch beside her and gather her into his arms. The passion of her grief held sway. Then on a half sob, she turned and clung to him, accepting comfort.

Her hands were fisted against his back. Gradually they relaxed as he kept her close. The hot tears slowed, and the pain, now shared, eased.

"I'm all right," she managed at length. Pulling away, she began to fumble in her bag for a tissue. Spence took it from her to dry her cheeks himself. "The doctor called it crib death. No reason," she said as she closed her eyes once more. "That was somehow worse. Not knowing why, not being sure if I could have stopped it."

"No." He took both her hands and she opened her eyes. "Don't do that. Listen to me. I can only imagine what it would be like to go through what you went through, but I know that when truly horrible things happen, it's usually out of our control."

"It took me a long time to accept what I can never understand." She turned over her hands in his. "A long time to start living again, going back to work, finally moving here, starting my business. I think I would have died without my family." She gave herself a moment, sipping the water to cool her dry throat. "I didn't want to love anyone again. Then there was you. And Freddie."

"We need you, Natasha. And you need us."

"Yes." She took his hand to press it to her lips. "I want you to understand. Spence, when I learned I was pregnant, it all came flying back at me. I tell you, I don't think I could survive going through that again. I'm so afraid to love this child. And I already do."

"Come here." He lifted her to her feet, keeping her hands locked tight in his. "I know that you loved Lily, and that you'll always love her and grieve for her. So will I now. What happened before can't be changed, but this is a different place, a different time. A different child. I want you to understand that we're going to go through this pregnancy, the birth and the rearing together. Whether you want me or not."

"I'm afraid."

"Then we'll be afraid together. And when this baby is eight and rides a two-wheeler for the first time, we'll be afraid together."

Her lips trembled into a smile. "When you say it, I can almost believe it."

"Believe it." He bent to kiss her. "Because it's a promise."

"Yes, it's time for promises." Her smile grew. "I love you." It was so easy to say it now. So easy to feel it. "Will you hold me?"

"On one condition." He rubbed away a drying tear with his thumb. "I want to tell Freddie she's expecting a baby brother or sister. I think it would make a great Christmas present for her."

"Yes." She felt stronger, surer. "I want us to tell her."

"All right, you've got five days."

"Five days for what?"

"To make whatever plans you want to make, to arrange to have your family come down, buy a dress, whatever you need to do to get ready for the wedding."

"But—"

"No buts." He framed her face with his hands and silenced her. "I love you, I want you. You're the best thing to come into my life since Freddie, and I don't intend to lose you. We've made a child, Natasha." Watching her, he laid a hand on her stomach, gently possessive. "A child I want. A child I already love."

In a gesture of trust, she placed her hand on his. "I won't be afraid if you're with me."

"We have a date here Christmas Eve. I'm going to wake up Christmas morning with my wife."

She steadied herself by putting her hands on his forearms. "Just like that?"

"Just like that."

With a laugh, she threw her arms around his neck and said one word. "Yes."

Epilogue

Christmas Eve was the most beautiful day in the year as far as Natasha was concerned. It was a time to celebrate life and love and family.

The house was quiet when she came in. She was drawn to the tree and the light. She sent an angel spinning on one branch, then turned to study the room.

On the table there was a papier-mâché reindeer with only one ear. Compliments of Freddie's second-grade art class. Beside it stood a pudgy snowman holding a lantern. An exquisite porcelain crèche was displayed on the mantel. Beneath it hung four stockings. A fire crackled in the grate.

A year before she had stood before the fire and promised to love, honor and cherish. They had been the easiest promises she had ever had to keep. Now this was her home.

Home. She took a deep breath to draw in the scents of pine and candles. It was so good to be home. Last-minute shoppers had crowded The Fun House until late in the afternoon. Now there was only family.

"Mama." Freddie raced in, trailing a bright red ribbon. "You're home."

"I'm home." Laughing, Natasha scooped her up to spin her around.

"We took Vera to the airport so she can spend Christmas with her sister, then we watched the planes. Daddy said when you got home we'd have dinner, then sing Christmas carols."

"Daddy's absolutely right." Natasha draped the ribbon over Freddie's shoulder. "What's this?"

"I'm wrapping a present, all by myself. It's for you."

"For me? What is it?"

"I can't tell you."

"Yes, you can. Watch." She dropped onto the couch to run her fingers along Freddie's ribs. "It'll be easy," she said as Freddie squealed and squirmed.

"Torturing the child again," Spence commented from the doorway.

"Daddy!" Springing up, Freddie raced to him. "I didn't tell."

"I knew I could count on you, funny face. Look who woke up." He bounced a baby on his hip.

"Here, Brandon." Madly in love, Freddie passed up the ribbon so that he could play with it. "It's pretty, just like you."

At six months, young Brandon Kimball was chubby,

rosy-cheeked and delighted with the world in general. He clutched the ribbon in one hand and reached for Freddie's hair with the other.

Walking over, Natasha held out her arms. "Such a big boy," she murmured as her son reached for her. Gathering him close, she pressed a kiss to his throat. "So beautiful."

"He looks just like his mother." Spence stroked a hand over Brandon's thick, black curls. As if he approved of the statement, Brandon let out a gurgling laugh. When he wriggled, Natasha set him down to crawl on the rug.

"It's his first Christmas." Natasha watched him scoot over to torment one of the cats and saw Lucy dart under the sofa. She's no fool, Natasha thought happily.

"And our second." He turned Natasha into his arms. "Happy anniversary."

Natasha kissed him once, then twice. "Have I told you today that I love you?"

"Not since I called you this afternoon."

"Much too long ago." She slipped her arms around his waist. "I love you. Thank you for the most wonderful year of my life."

"You're very welcome." He glanced over her head only long enough to see that Freddie had prevented Brandon from pulling an ornament from a low branch. "But it's only going to get better."

"Do you promise?"

He smiled and lowered his mouth to hers again. "Absolutely."

Freddie stopped crawling with Brandon to watch

them. A baby brother had turned out to be nice, after all, but she was still holding out for that baby sister. She smiled as she saw her parents embrace.

Maybe next Christmas.

* * * * *

Considering Kate

To my guys.

Chapter 1

It was going to be perfect. She was going to see to it. Every step, every stage, every detail would be done precisely as she wanted, as she envisioned, until her dream became her reality.

Settling for less than what was exactly right was a waste of time after all.

And Kate Kimball was not a woman to waste anything.

At twenty-five, she had seen and experienced more than a great many people did in a lifetime. When other young girls had been giggling over boys or worrying about fashion, she'd been traveling to Paris or Bonne, wearing glamorous costumes and doing extraordinary things.

She had danced for queens, and dined with princes.

She had sipped champagne at the White House, and wept with triumph and fatigue at the Bolshoi.

She would always be grateful to her parents, to the big, sprawling family who'd given her the opportunities to do so. Everything she had she owed to them.

Now it was time to start earning it herself.

Dance had been her dream for as long as she could remember. Her obsession, her brother, Brandon, would have said. And not, Kate acknowledged, inaccurately. There was nothing wrong with an obsession—as long as it was the *right* obsession and you worked for it.

God knew she'd worked for the dance.

Twenty years of practice, of study, of joy and pain. Of sweat and toe shoes. Of sacrifices, she thought. Hers, and her parents. She understood how difficult it had been for them to let her, the baby of the family, go to New York to study when she'd been only seventeen. But they'd never offered her anything but support and encouragement.

Of course, they'd known that though she was leaving the pretty little town in West Virginia for the big city, she'd be surrounded—watched over—by family. Just as she knew they had loved and trusted—believed in her enough—to let her go in any case.

She'd practiced and worked, and had danced, as much for them as for herself. And when she'd joined the Company and had appeared on stage the first time, they'd been there. When she'd earned a spot as principal dancer, they'd been there.

She'd danced professionally for six years, had known the spotlight, and the thrill of *feeling* the music inside her body. She'd traveled all over the world, had become

Giselle, Aurora, Juliet, dozens of characters both tragic and triumphant. She had prized every moment of it.

No one was more surprised than Kate herself when she'd decided to step out of that spotlight and walk off that stage. There was only one way to explain it.

She'd wanted to come home.

She wanted a life, a real one. As much as she loved the dance, she'd begun to realize it had nearly absorbed and devoured every other aspect of her. Classes, rehearsals, performances, travel, media. The dancer's career was far more than slipping on toe shoes and gliding into the spotlight—or it certainly had been for Kate.

So she wanted a life, and she wanted home. And, she'd discovered, she wanted to give something back for all the joy she'd reaped. She could accomplish all of that with her school.

They would come, she told herself. They would come because her name was Kimball, and that meant something solid in the area. They would come because her name was *Kate Kimball,* and that meant something in the world of dance.

Before long, she promised herself, they would come because the school itself meant something.

Time for a new dream, she reminded herself as she turned around the huge, echoing room. The Kimball School of Dance was her new obsession. She intended it to be just as fulfilling, just as intricate, and just as perfect as her old one.

And it would, no doubt, entail as much work, effort, skill and determination to bring to life.

With her hands fisted on her hips, she studied the grime-gray walls that had once been white. They'd be white again. A clean surface for displaying framed posters of the greats. Nuryev, Fontayne, Baryshnikov, Davidov, Bannion.

And the two long side walls would be mirrored behind their *barres*. This professional vanity was as necessary as breathing. A dancer must see each tiny movement, each arch, each flex, even as the body felt it, to perfect the positioning.

It was really more window than mirror, Kate thought. Where the dancer looked through the glass to see the dance.

The old ceiling would be repaired or replaced—whatever was necessary. The furnace…she rubbed her chilly arms. Definitely replaced. The floors sanded and sealed until they were a smooth and perfect surface. Then there was the lighting, the plumbing, probably some electrical business to see to.

Well, her grandfather had been a carpenter before he'd retired—or semiretired, she thought with affection. She wasn't totally ignorant of what went on in a rehab situation. And she'd study more, ask questions, until she understood the process and could direct the contractor she hired appropriately.

Imagining what would be, she closed her eyes, dipped into a deep plié. Her body, long and wand-slim, simply flowed into the movement until her crotch rested on her heels, rose up again, lowered again.

She'd bundled her hair up, impatient to get out and

take another look at what would soon be hers. With her movements, pins loosened and a few locks of glossy black curls spilled out. Freed, they would fall to her waist—a wildly romantic look that suited her image on stage.

Smiling, a bit dreamy, her face took on a quiet glow. She had her mother's dusky skin and high, slashing cheekbones, her father's smoky eyes and stubborn chin.

It made an arresting combination, again a romantic one. The gypsy, the mermaid, the faerie queen. There had been men who'd looked at her, taken in the delicacy of her form, and had assumed a romanticism and fragility—and never anticipated the steel.

It was, always, a mistake.

"One of these days you're going to get stuck like that, then you'll have to hop around like a frog."

Kate sprang up, eyes popping open. "Brandon!" With a full-throated war whoop, she leaped across the room and into his arms.

"What are you doing here? When did you get in? I thought you were playing winter ball in Puerto Rico. How long are you staying?"

He was barely two years her senior—an accident of birth he'd used to torment her when they'd been children, unlike her half sister, Frederica, who was older than both of them and had never lorded it over them. Despite it, he was the love of her life.

"Which question do you want me to answer first?" Laughing, he held her away from him, taking a quick study of her out of tawny and amused eyes. "Still scrawny."

"And you're still full of it. Hi." She kissed him smackingly on the lips. "Mom and Dad didn't say you were coming home."

"They didn't know. I heard you were settling in and figured I'd better check things out, keep an eye on you." He glanced around the big, filthy room, rolled his eyes. "I guess I'm too late."

"It's going to be wonderful."

"Gonna be. Maybe. Right now it's a dump." Still, he slung his arm around her shoulders. "So, the ballet queen's going to be a teacher."

"I'm going to be a wonderful teacher. Why aren't you in Puerto Rico?"

"Hey, a guy can't play ball twelve months a year."

"Brandon." Her eyebrow arched up.

"Bad slide into second. Pulled a few tendons."

"Oh, how bad? Have you seen a doctor? Will you—"

"Jeez, Katie. It's no big deal. I'm on the Disabled List for a couple of months. I'll be back in action for spring training. And it gives me lots of time to hang around here and make your life a living hell."

"Well, that's some compensation. Come on, I'll show you around." And get a look at the way he moved. "My apartment's upstairs."

"From the looks of that ceiling, your apartment may be downstairs any minute."

"It's perfectly sound," she said with a wave of the hand. "Just ugly at the moment. But I have plans."

"You've always had plans."

But he walked with her, favoring his right leg, through the room and into a nasty little hallway with cracked plaster and exposed brick. Up a creaking set of stairs and into a sprawling space that appeared to be occupied by mice, spiders and assorted vermin he didn't want to think about.

"Kate, this place—"

"Has potential," she said firmly. "And history. It's pre-Civil War."

"It's pre-Stone Age." He was a man who preferred things already ordered, and in an understandable pattern. Like a ballpark. "Have you any clue what it's going to cost you to make this place livable?"

"I have a clue. And I'll firm that up when I talk to the contractor. It's mine, Brand. Do you remember when we were kids and you and Freddie and I would walk by this old place?"

"Sure, used to be a bar, then it was a craft shop or something, then—"

"It used to be a lot of things," Kate interrupted. "Started out as a tavern in the 1800s. Nobody's really made a go of it. But I used to look at it when we were kids and think how much I'd like to live here, and look out these tall windows, and rattle around in all the rooms."

The faintest flush bloomed on her cheeks, and her eyes went deep and dark. A sure sign, Brandon thought, that she had dug in.

"Thinking like that when you're eight's a lot different than buying a heap of a building when you're a grown-up."

"Yes, it is. It is different. Last spring, when I came home to visit, it was up for sale. Again. I couldn't stop thinking about it."

She circled the room. She could see it, as it would be. Wood gleaming, walls sturdy and clean. "I went back to New York, went back to work, but I couldn't stop thinking about this old place."

"You get the screwiest things in your head."

She shrugged that off. "It's mine. I was sure of it the minute I came inside. Haven't you ever felt that?"

He had, the first time he'd walked into a ballpark. He supposed, when it came down to it, most sensible people would have told him that playing ball for a living was a kid's dream. His family never had, he remembered. Any more than they'd discouraged Kate from her dreams of ballet.

"Yeah, I guess I have. It just seems so fast. I'm used to you doing things in deliberate steps."

"That hasn't changed," she told him with a grin. "When I decided to retire from performing, I knew I wanted to teach dance. I knew I wanted to make this place a school. My school. Most of all, I wanted to be home."

"Okay." He put his arm around her again, pressed a kiss to her temple. "Then we'll make it happen. But right now, let's get out of here. This place is freezing."

"New heating system's first on my list."

Brandon took one last glance around. "It's going to be a really long list."

* * *

They walked together through the brisk December wind, as they had since childhood. Along cracked and uneven sidewalks, under trees that spread branches stripped of leaves under a heavy gray sky.

She could smell snow in the air, the teasing hint of it.

Storefronts were already decorated for the holidays, with red-cheeked Santas and strings of lights, flying reindeer and overweight snowpeople.

But the best of them, always the best of them, was The Fun House. The toy store's front window was crowded with delights. Miniature sleighs, enormous stuffed bears in stocking caps, dolls both elegant and homely, shiny red trucks, castles made of wooden blocks.

The look was delightfully jumbled and…fun, Kate thought. One might think the toys had simply been dropped wherever they fit. But she knew that great care, and a deep, affectionate knowledge of children, had gone into the design of the display.

Bells chimed cheerfully as they stepped inside.

Customers wandered. A toddler banged madly on a xylophone in the play corner. Behind the counter, Annie Maynard boxed a flop-eared stuffed dog. "He's one of my favorites," she said to the waiting customer. "Your niece is going to love him."

Her glasses slid down her nose as she tied the fuzzy red yarn around the box. Then she glanced up over them, blinked and squealed.

"Brandon! Tash! Come see who's here. Oh, come give me a kiss, you gorgeous thing."

When he came around the counter and obliged, she patted her heart. "Been married twenty-five years," she said to her customer. "And this boy can make me feel like a co-ed again. Happy holidays. Let me go get your mother."

"No, I'll get her." Kate grinned and shook her head. "Brandon can stay here and flirt with you."

"Well, then." Annie winked. "Take your time."

Her brother, Kate mused, had been leaving females puddled at his feet since he'd been five. No, since he'd been born, she corrected as she wandered through the aisles.

It was more than looks, though his were stellar. Even more than charm, though he could pump out plenty when he was in the mood. She'd long ago decided it was simply pheromones.

Some men just stood there and made women drool. Susceptible women, of course. Which she had never been. A man had to have more than looks, charm and sex appeal to catch her interest. She'd known entirely too many who were pretty to look at, but empty once you opened the package.

Then she turned the corner by the toy cars and very nearly turned into a puddle.

He was gorgeous. No, no, that was too female a term. Handsome was too fussily male. He was just...

Man.

Six-two if he was an inch, and all of it brilliantly packaged. As a dancer she appreciated a well-toned body. The specimen currently studying rows of miniature vehicles had his packed into snug and faded jeans, a flannel shirt and a denim jacket that was scarred and too light for the weather.

His work boots looked ancient and solid. Who would have thought work boots could be so sexy?

Then there was all that hair; dark, streaky blond masses of it waving around a lean, sharp-angled face. Not rugged, not classic, not anything she could label. His mouth was full, and appeared to be the only soft thing about him. His nose was long and straight, his chin, well, chiseled. And his eyes...

She couldn't quite see his eyes, not the color, with all those wonderful lashes in the way. But they were heavy-lidded, so she imagined them a deep, slumberous blue.

She shifted her gaze to his hands as he reached for one of the toys. Big, wide-palmed, blunt-fingered. Strong.

Holy cow.

And while indulging in a moment's fantasy—a perfectly harmless moment's fantasy—she leaned and knocked over a small traffic jam of cars.

The resulting clatter slapped her out of her daydream, and turned the man's eyes—his surprising and intense green eyes—in her direction.

"Oops," she said. And grinning at him, laughing at herself, crouched down to pick up the cars. "I hope there were no casualties."

"We've got an ambulance right here, if necessary." He tapped the shiny red-and-white emergency vehicle, then hunkered down to help her.

"Thanks. If we can get these back before the cops

get here, I may just get off with a warning." He smelled as good as he looked, she decided. Wood shavings and man. She shifted, deliberately, and their knees bumped. "Come here often?"

"Yeah, actually." He glanced up at her, took a good long look. She recognized the stirring of interest in his eyes. "Guys never outgrow their toys."

"So I've heard. What do you like to play with?"

His eyebrows shot up. A man didn't often come across a beautiful—provocative—woman in a toy store on a Wednesday afternoon. He very nearly stuttered, then did something he hadn't done in years—spoke without thinking first.

"Depends on the game. What's yours?"

She laughed, pushed back a tendril of hair that tickled her cheek. "Oh, I like all kinds of games—especially if I win."

She started to rise, but he beat her to it, straightening those yard-long legs and holding out a hand. She gripped it, discovered to her pleasure it was as hard as she'd imagined, and as strong.

"Thanks again. I'm Kate."

"Brody." He offered the tiny blue convertible he was still holding. "In the market for a car?"

"No, not today. I'm more or less browsing, until I see what I want...." Her lips curved again, amused, flirtatious.

Brody had to order himself not to whistle out a breath. He'd had women come on to him from time to time, but never quite like this. And he'd been in a self-imposed female drought for... For what was beginning to seem entirely too long.

"Kate." He leaned on a shelf, angled his body toward her. Funny, how the moves came back, how the system could pick up the dance as if it had never sat one out. "Why don't we—"

"Katie. I didn't know you'd come in." Natasha Kimball hurried across the shop, carting an enormous toy cement mixer.

"I brought you a surprise."

"I love surprises. But first here you are, Brody, as promised. Just came in Monday, and I put it aside for you."

"It's great." The cool-eyed, flirtatious expression had vanished into a delighted grin. "It's perfect. Jack'll flip."

"The manufacturer makes its toys to last. This is something he'll enjoy for years, not just for a week after Christmas. Have you met my daughter?" Natasha asked, sliding an arm around Kate's waist.

Brody's eyes flicked up from the truck in its open-fronted box. "Daughter?"

So this is the ballerina, he thought. Doesn't it just figure?

"We just met—over a slight vehicular accident." Kate kept the smile on her face. Surely she had imagined the sudden chill. "Is Jack your nephew?"

"Jack's my son."

"Oh." She took a long step back in her mind. The nerve of the man! The nerve of the *married* man flirting with her. It hardly mattered who had flirted first after all. *She* wasn't married. "I'm sure he'll love it," she said, coolly now and turned to her mother.

"Mama—"

"Kate, I was just telling Brody about your plans. I thought you might like him to look at your building."

"Whatever for?"

"Brody's a contractor. And a wonderful carpenter. He remodeled your father's studio last year. And has promised to take a look at my kitchen. My daughter insists on the best," Natasha added, her dark gold eyes laughing. "So naturally, I thought of you."

"I appreciate it."

"No, I do, because I know you do quality work at a fair price." She gave his arm a little squeeze. "Spence and I would be grateful if you looked the building over."

"I don't even settle for two days, Mama. Let's not rush things. But I did run into something annoying in the building just a bit ago. It's up in the front charming Annie."

"What...Brandon? Oh, why didn't you say so!" As Natasha rushed off, Kate turned to Brody. "Nice to have met you."

"Likewise. Give me a call if you want me to look at your place."

"Of course." She placed the little car he'd handed her neatly back on the shelf. "I'm sure your son will love his truck. Is he your only child?"

"Yes. There's just Jack."

"I'm sure he keeps you and your wife busy. Now if you'll excuse me—"

"Jack's mother died four years ago. But he keeps me plenty busy. Watch those intersections, Kate," he suggested, and tucking the truck under his arm, walked away.

"Nice going." She hissed under her breath. "Really nice going."

Now maybe she could run out and see if there were any puppies she could kick, just to finish off the afternoon.

One of the best things about running your own business, in Brody's opinion, was being able to prioritize your time. There were plenty of headaches—responsibilities, paperwork, juggling jobs—not to mention making damn sure there were jobs to juggle. But that one element made up for any and all of the downside.

For the last six years he'd had one priority.

His name was Jack.

After he'd hidden the cement truck under a tarp in the back of his pickup, had run by a job site to check on progress, called on a supplier to put a bug in their ear about a special order and stopped at yet another site to give a potential client an estimate on a bathroom rehab, he headed home.

Mondays, Wednesdays and Fridays, he made a point to be home before the school bus grumbled to the end of the lane. The other two school days—and in the case of any unavoidable delay—Jack was delivered to the Skully house, where he could spend an hour or two with his best pal Rod under the watchful eye of Beth Skully.

He owed Beth and Jerry Skully a great deal, and most of it was for giving Jack a safe and happy place to be when he couldn't be home. In the ten months Brody had been back in Shepherdstown he was reminded, on an almost daily basis, just how comforting small towns could be.

Now, at thirty, he was amazed at the young man who had shaken that town off his shoes as fast as he could manage a little more than ten years before.

All for the best, he decided as he rounded the curve toward home. If he hadn't left home, hadn't been so hardheadedly determined to make his mark elsewhere, he wouldn't have lived and learned. He wouldn't have met Connie.

He wouldn't have Jack.

He'd come nearly full circle. If he hadn't completely closed the rift with his parents, he was making progress. Or Jack was, Brody corrected. His father might still hold a grudge against his son, but he couldn't resist his grandson.

He'd been right to come home. Brody looked at the woods, growing thick on either side of the road. A few thin flakes of snow were beginning to drift out of the leaden sky. Hills, rocky and rough, rose and fell as they pleased.

It was a good place to raise a boy. Better for them both to be out of the city, to start fresh together in a place Jack had family.

Family who could and would accept him for what

he was, instead of seeing him as a reminder of what was lost.

He turned into the lane, stopped and turned off the truck. The bus would be along in minutes, and Jack would leap out, race over and climb in, filling the cab of the truck with the thrills and spills of the day.

It was too bad, Brody mused, he couldn't share the spills and thrills of his own with a six-year-old.

He could hardly tell his son that he'd felt his blood move for a woman again. Not just a mild stir, but a full leap. He couldn't share that for a moment, a bit longer than a moment, he'd contemplated acting on that leap of blood.

It had been so damn long.

And what harm would it have done, really? An attractive woman, and one who obviously had no problem making the first move. A little mating dance, a couple of civilized dates, then some not-so-civilized sex. Everybody got what they wanted, and nobody got hurt.

He cursed under his breath, rubbed at the tension that had settled into the back of his neck.

Someone always got hurt.

Still, it might have been worth the risk…if she hadn't been Natasha and Spencer Kimball's pampered and perfect daughter.

He'd gone that route once before, and had no intention of navigating those pitfalls a second time.

He knew plenty about Kate Kimball. Prima ballerina, society darling and toast of the arty set. Over and above the fact that he'd rather have his teeth pulled—one at a time—than sit through a ballet, he'd had his fill of the cultured class during his all-too-brief marriage.

Connie had been one in a million. A natural in a sea of pretense and pomp. And even then, it had been a hard road. He'd never know if they'd have continued to bump their way over it together, but he liked to believe they would have.

As much as he'd loved her, his marriage to Connie had taught him life was easier if you stuck with your own. And easier yet if a man just avoided any serious entanglements with a woman.

It was a good thing he'd been interrupted before he'd followed impulse and asked Kate Kimball out. A good thing he'd learned who she was before that flirtation had shifted into high gear.

A very good thing he'd had the time to remember his priority. Fatherhood had kicked the stuffing out of the arrogant, careless and often reckless boy. And had made a man out of him.

He heard the rumble of the bus, and sat up grinning. There was no place in the world Brody O'Connell would rather be than right here, right now.

The big yellow bus groaned to a stop, its safety lights flashing. The driver waved, a cheerful little salute. Brody waved back and watched his lightning bolt shoot out the door.

Jack was a compact boy, except for his feet. It would take some years for him to grow into them. At the end of the lane, he tipped back his head and tried to catch one of those thin snowflakes on his tongue. His face was round and cheerful, his eyes green like his father's, his mouth still the innocent bow of youth.

Brody knew when Jack stripped off his red ski cap— as he would at the first opportunity—his pale blond hair would shoot up in sunflower spikes.

Watching his son, Brody felt love swarm him, fill him so fast it was a flood of the heart.

Then the door of the truck opened, and the little boy clambered in, an eager puppy with oversize paws.

"Hey, Dad! It's snowing. Maybe it'll snow eight feet and there won't be any school and we can build a million snowmen in the yard and go sledding." He bounced on the seat. "Can we?"

"The minute it snows eight feet, we start the first of a million snowmen."

"Promise?"

Promises, Brody knew, were always a solemn business. "Absolutely promise."

"Okay! Guess what?"

Brody started the engine and drove up the lane. "What?"

"It's only fifteen days till Christmas, and Miss Hawkins says tomorrow it'll be fourteen and that's just two weeks."

"I guess that means one from fifteen is fourteen."

"Yeah?" Jack's eyes went wide. "Okay. So it's Christmas in two weeks, and Grandma says that time flies, so it's practically Christmas *now.*"

"Practically." Brody stopped the truck in front of the old three-story farmhouse. Eventually he'd have the whole thing rehabbed. Maybe by the time he was eligible for social security.

"So okay, if it's almost practically Christmas, can I have a present?"

"Hmm." Brody pursed his lips, wrinkled his brow and appeared to give this due consideration. "You know, Jacks, that was good. That was a really good one. No."

"Aw."

"Aw," Brody echoed in the same sorrowful tone. Then he laughed and snatched his son off the seat. "But if you give me a hug, I'll make O'Connell's Amazing Magic Pizza for dinner."

"Okay!" Jack wrapped his arms around his father's neck.

And Brody was home.

Chapter 2

"Nervous?" Spencer Kimball watched his daughter pour a cup of coffee. She looked flawless, he thought. Her mass of curling hair was tied neatly into a tail that streamed down her back. Her stone-gray jacket and trousers were trim and tailored in an understated chic he sometimes thought she'd been born with. Her face— Lord, she looked like her mother—was composed.

Yes, she looked flawless, and lovely. And grown up. Why was it so hard to see his babies grown?

"Why should I be nervous? More coffee?"

"Yeah, thanks. It's D-Day," he added when she topped off his cup. "Deed Day. In a couple hours, you'll be a property owner, with all the joys and frustrations that entails."

"I'm looking forward to it." She sat to nibble on the

half bagel she'd toasted for breakfast. "I've thought it all through very carefully."

"You always do."

"Mmm. I know it's a risk using so much of my savings, and a good portion of my trust fund in this investment. But I'm financially sound and I know I can handle the projected expenses over the next five years."

He nodded, watching her face. "You have your mother's business sense."

"I like to think so. I also like to think I'll have your skill for teaching. After all, I'm an artist, who comes from two people who are artists. And the little bit of teaching I did in New York gave me a taste for it." She picked up the cream, added a little more to her coffee. "I'm establishing my business in my hometown, where I have solid contacts with the community."

"Absolutely true."

She set the bagel aside and picked up her coffee. "The Kimball name is respected here, and my name is respected in dance circles. I've studied dance for twenty years, sweated and ached my way through thousands of hours of instructions. I should have learned more than how to execute a clean *tour jeté*."

"Without question."

She sighed. There was no fooling her father. He knew her inside and out. He was all that was solid, she thought, all that was steady. "Okay. You know how you get butterflies in your stomach?"

"Yeah."

"Mine are frogs. Big, fat, hopping frogs. I wasn't this nervous before my first professional solo."

"Because you never doubted your talent. This is new ground, honey." He laid a hand over hers. "You're entitled to the frogs. Fact is, I'd worry about you if you didn't have the jumps."

"You're also worried I'm making a big mistake."

"No, not a mistake." He gave her hand a squeeze. "I've got some concerns—and a father's entitled to the jumps, too—that in a few months you might miss performing. Miss the company and the life you built. Part of me wishes you'd waited a bit longer before making such a big commitment. And the other part's just happy to have you home again."

"Well, tell your frogs to settle down. Once I make a commitment, I keep it."

"I know."

That was one of the things that concerned him, but he wasn't going to say that.

She picked up her bagel again, grinning a little. She knew just how to distract him. "So, tell me about the plans to remodel the kitchen."

He winced, his handsome face looking pained. "I'm not getting into it." As he glanced around the room he raked a hand through his hair so the gold and silver of it tangled. "Your mother's got this bug over a full redo here. New this, new that, and Brody O'Connell's aiding and abetting. What's wrong with the kitchen?"

"Maybe it has something to do with the fact it hasn't been remodeled in twenty-odd years?"

"So what's your point?" Spencer gestured with his coffee cup. "It's great. It's perfectly comfortable. But then he had to go and show her sample books."

Her lips twitched at the betrayal in her father's voice, but she spoke with sober sympathy. "The dog."

"And they're talking about bow and bay windows. We've got a window." He gestured to the one over the sink. "It's fine. You can look through it all you want. I tell you, that boy has seduced my wife with promises of solid surface countertops and oak trim."

"Oak trim, hmm. Very sexy." Laughing, she propped an elbow on the table. "Tell me about O'Connell."

"He does good work. But that doesn't mean he should come tear up my kitchen."

"Has he lived in the area long?"

"Grew up not far from here. His father's Ace Plumbing. Brody left when he was about twenty. Went down to D.C. Worked construction."

All right, Kate thought. She'd have to pry if that was all she could shake loose. "I heard he has a little boy."

"Yeah, Jack. A real pistol. Brody's wife died several years ago. Cancer of some kind, I think. My impression is he wanted to raise his son closer to family. Been back about a year, I guess. He's established a nice business, with a reputation for quality work. He'll do a good job for you."

"If I decide to hire him."

She wondered what he looked like in a tool belt, then reminded herself that was not only *not* the kind of question a woman should ask her doting father, but also one that had nothing to do with establishing a business relationship.

But she bet he looked just fine.

It was done. The frogs in her stomach were still pretty lively, but she was now the owner of a big, beautiful, dilapidated building in the pretty college town of Shepherdstown, West Virginia.

A building that was a short walk from the house where she'd grown up, from her mother's toy shop, from the university where her father taught.

She was surrounded by family, friends and neighbors.

Oh, God.

Everyone knew her—and everyone would be watching to see if she pulled it off, stuck it out, or fell flat on her face. Why hadn't she opened her school in Utah or New Mexico or someplace she was anonymous, somewhere with no expectations hovering over her?

And that, she reminded herself, was just stupid. She was establishing her school here because it was home. Home, Kate thought, was exactly where she wanted to be.

There would be no falling, flat or otherwise, Kate promised herself as she parked her car. She would succeed because she would personally oversee every detail. She would take each upcoming step the way she'd taken all the others that had led here. Carefully, meticulously. And she would work like a Trojan to see it through.

She wouldn't disappoint her parents.

The important thing was that the property was now

hers—and the bank's—and that those next steps could be taken.

She walked up the steps—her steps—crossed the short, slightly sagging porch and unlocked the door to her future.

It smelled of dust and cobwebs.

That would change. Oh, yes, she told herself as she set her bag and keys aside. That would begin to change very soon. In short order, the air would smell of sawdust and fresh paint and the sweat of a working crew.

She just had to hire the crew.

She started to cross the floor, just to hear her footsteps echo, and saw the little portable stereo in the center of the room. Baffled, she hurried to it, picked up the card set on top of the machine and grinned at her mother's handwriting.

She ripped open the envelope and took out the card fronted with a lovely painting of a ballerina at the *barre*.

Congratulations, Katie!
Here's a small housewarming gift so you'll always have music.
Love, Mom, Dad and Brandon

"Oh, you guys. You just never let me down." A little teary-eyed, she crouched and turned the stereo on.

It was one of her father's compositions, and one of her favorites. She remembered how thrilled, and how proud she had been, when she had danced to it the first time on stage in New York.

Kimball dancing to Kimball, she thought, and shrugged out of her coat, kicked off her shoes.

Slow at first—a long extension. The muscles tremble, but hold, and hold. A bend at the knee to change the line. Turning, beat by beat.

Lower. A gentle series of pirouettes, fluid rather than sharp.

She moved around the dingy room, sliding into the well-remembered steps. Music swelled into the space, into her mind, into her body.

Building now, from romance toward passion. *Arabesque,* quick, light triple pirouette and into *ballottes*.

The joy of it rushed into her. The confining band flew out of her hair. *Grande jeté*. And again. Again. Feel like you could fly forever. Look like you can.

End it with flair, with joy, in a fast rush of *fouetté* turns. Then set! Snap like a statue, one arm up, one back.

"I guess I'm supposed to throw roses, but I don't have any on me."

Her breath was already coming fast, and she nearly lost it completely as the statement shoved her out of dance mode. She pressed a hand to her speeding heart, and panting lightly, stared at Brody.

He stood just inside the door, hands in his pockets and a toolbox at his feet.

"You can owe me," she managed to say. "I like red ones. God, you scared the life out of me."

"Sorry. Your door wasn't locked, and you didn't hear me knock." Or wouldn't have, he decided, if he'd thought to knock.

But when he'd seen her through the window, he hadn't thought at all. He'd just walked in, dazzled. A woman who looked like that, who moved like that, was bound to dazzle a man. He imagined she knew it.

"It's all right." She turned and walked over to turn down the music. "I was initiating the place. Though the dance looks better with the costumes and lights. So." She pushed at her tumbled hair, willing her speeding heart to settle. "What can I do for you, Mr. O'Connell?"

He walked toward her, stopping to pick up her hair band. "You lost this during a spin."

"Thanks." She tucked it into her pocket.

He wished she'd pulled her hair back into it. He didn't care for his reaction to the way she looked just now, flushed and tousled and…available. "I get the feeling you weren't expecting me."

"No, but I don't mind the unexpected." Especially, she thought, when it comes with fabulous green eyes and a sexy little scowl.

"Your mother asked me to come by, take a look at the place."

"Ah. You're another housewarming present."

"I beg your pardon?"

"Nothing." She angled her head. Dancers, she mused, knew as much about body language as a psychiatrist. His was stiff, just a little defensive. And he was certainly careful to keep a good, safe distance between them. "Do I make you nervous, O'Connell, or just annoy you?"

"I don't know you well enough to be nervous or annoyed."

"Want to?"

His belly muscles quivered. "Look, Ms. Kimball—"

"All right, don't get huffy." She waved him off. A pity, she thought. She preferred being direct, and he, obviously, didn't. "I find you attractive, and I got the impression you were interested, initially. My mistake."

"You make a habit of coming on to strange men in your mother's toy store?"

She blinked, a quick flicker of temper and hurt. Then she shrugged. "Oh, well. Ouch."

"Sorry." Disgusted with himself, he held up both hands. "Way out of line. Maybe you do annoy me after all. Not your fault. I'm out of practice when it comes to… aggressive women. Let's just say I'm not in the market for any entanglements right now."

"This is a blow—I'd already picked the band for the wedding, but I expect I'll recover."

His lips curved. "Oh, well. Ouch."

He had a great smile when he used it, Kate thought. It was a damn shame he was so stingy with it where she was concerned. "Now that we have all that out of the way. What do you think?" She spread her arms to encompass the room.

Since here he was on solid ground, Brody relaxed. "It's a great old place. Lots of atmosphere and potential. Solid foundation. Built to last."

The little prickle of annoyance that still chilled her skin faded away. Warmth radiated. "That's it. Now I love you."

It was his turn to blink. He'd already taken a defensive step in retreat when Kate laughed. "Boy, you *are* out of practice. I'm not going to throw myself into your arms, Brody—though it's tempting. It's just that you're the first person who's agreed with me on this. Everyone else thinks I'm crazy to sink so much time and money into this building."

He couldn't remember having a woman make him feel like an idiot so often in such a short space of time. He shoved his hands into his pockets again. "It's a good investment—if you do it right and you're in for the long haul."

"Oh, I'm in. Why don't you tell me how you'd do it right?"

"First thing I'd do is have the heating system looked at. It's freezing in here."

She grinned at him. "We may just get along after all. The furnace is in the basement. Want to take a look?"

She came down with him—which he didn't expect. She didn't bolt when they came across a startled mouse—or the old shedded skin of a snake that had likely dined on the rodent's relatives. And that he had expected.

In his experience, women—well, intensely female women types—generally made a quick retreat when they came across anything that slithered or skittered. But Kate just wrinkled her nose and took a little notebook out of her jacket pocket to jot something down.

The light was poor, the air thick and stale, and the ancient furnace that squatted on the original dirt floor, a lost cause.

He gave her that bad news, then explained her options, the pros and cons of electric heat pumps, gas, oil. BTU's, efficiency, initial cost outlay and probable monthly expenses.

He imagined he'd do just as well speaking in Greek and offered to send brochures and information to her father.

"My father's a composer and a college professor," she said with cool politeness. "Do you assume he'd understand all of this better than I would because we have different chromosomes?"

Brody considered for a moment. "Yeah."

"You assume incorrectly. You can send me your information, but at this point I'm more inclined to the steam heat. It seems simpler and more efficient as the pipes and radiators are already in place. I want to keep as much of the building's character as possible, while making it more livable and attractive. Also, I'll have secondary heat sources, if and when I need them, when the chimneys are checked—repaired if necessary."

He didn't much care for the icy tone, even if he did agree with the content. "You're the boss."

"There, you're absolutely correct."

"You have cobwebs in your hair. Boss."

"So do you. I'll need this basement area cleaned, and however authentic the dirt floor might be, I'll want cement poured. And an exterminator. Better lighting. As it is, it's virtually wasted space. It can be put to use for storage."

"Fine." He took a notepad and pencil out of his breast pocket and began scribbling notes.

She walked to the stairs, jiggling the banister as she started up. "The stairs don't have to be pretty, but they have to be safe."

"You'll get safe. All the work will be up to code. I don't work any other way."

"Good to know. Now, let me show you what I want on the main level."

She knew what she wanted. Maybe a little too precisely for his taste. Still, he had to give her points for not intending to simply gut the building, but to make use of its eccentricities and charm.

He couldn't see a ballet school, but she apparently could. Right down to the bench she envisioned built in under the front windows, and the canned ceiling lights.

She wanted the kitchen redone, turning it into a smaller, more efficient room and using the extra space for an office.

Spaces that had metamorphosed over the years from bedrooms to storage rooms to display rooms would become dressing areas with counters and wardrobes built in.

"It seems a little elaborate for a small-town dance school."

She merely lifted an eyebrow. "It's not elaborate. It's correct. Now these two bathrooms." She stopped in the hall beside two doors that were side by side.

"If you want to enlarge and remodel, I can open the wall between them."

"Dancers have to forgo a great deal of modesty along the way, but let's draw the line at coed bathrooms."

"Coed." He lowered the notebook, stared at her. "You're planning on having boys?" His grin came fast. "You think you're going to get boys in here doing what's it? Pirouettes? Get out."

"Ever hear of Baryshnikov? Davidov?" She was too used to the knee-jerk reaction to be particularly offended. "I'd put a well-trained dancer in his prime up against any other athlete you name in a test of strength and endurance."

"Who wears the tutu?"

She sighed, only because she was perfectly aware this was the sort of bias she'd be facing in a rural town. "For your information, male dancers are real men. In fact, my first lover was a *premier danseur* who drove a Harley and could execute a *grande jeté* with more height than Michael Jordan can pull off for a slam dunk. But then Jordan doesn't wear tights, does he? Just those cute little boxers."

"Trunks," Brody muttered. "Basketball trunks."

"Ah, well, it's all perception, isn't it? The bathrooms stay separate. New stalls, new sinks, new floors. One sink in each low enough for a child to reach. White fixtures. I want clean and streamlined."

"I got that picture."

"Then moving right along." She gestured toward the stairs at the back end of the corridor. "Third floor, my apartment."

"You're going to live here—over the school?"

"I'm going to live, breathe, eat and work here. That's how you turn a concept into reality. And I have very specific ideas about my living quarters."

"I bet you do."

Specific ideas, Brody thought an hour later, and good ones. He might have disagreed with some of the details she wanted on the main level, but he couldn't fault her vision for the third floor.

She wanted the original moldings and woodwork restored—and added that she'd like whoever had painted all that gorgeous oak white caught, dragged into the street and horsewhipped.

Brody could only agree.

Portions of the woodwork were damaged. He liked the prospect of crafting the replacement sections himself, blending them in with the old. She wanted the floors sanded down, and coated with a clear seal. He'd have done precisely the same.

As he toured the top rooms with her, he felt the old anticipation building. To make his mark on something that had stood for generations, and to preserve it as it was meant to be preserved.

There had been a time when he'd done no more than put in his hours—do the job, pick up the pay. Pride and responsibility had come later. And the simple pleasure they gave him had pushed him to better himself, to hone his craft—to build something more than rooms.

To build a life.

He could make a difference here, Brody thought. And

he wanted, badly, to get his hands on this place and make that difference. Even if it meant dealing with Kate Kimball, and his irritating reaction to her.

He hoped—if he got the job—she wouldn't be one of those clients who hovered. At least not while she was wearing that damn perfume.

Then they were back to bathrooms. The old cast iron tub stayed. The beige wall hung sink went, and Brody was directed to find a suitable white pedestal sink to replace it.

The boss also wanted ceramic tile—navy and white—though she agreed to look at product samples before making the final decision.

She was just as decisive in the kitchen, but there he stopped her.

"Look, are you actually going to cook in here, or just heat up takeout?"

"Cook. I do know how."

"Then you want solid work space there, instead of breaking it up." Brody gestured. "You want efficient traffic flow, so you work from the window. You want your sink under the window instead of on that wall. You move the refrigerator there, the stove there. See, then you've got flow instead of zigzagging back and forth. Wasted effort, wasted space."

"Yes, but there—"

"That's for your pantry," he interrupted, the room clear in his mind. "It gives you a nice line of counter. You angle it out here..." He pulled out his measuring tape. "Yeah, angle it out and you've got room for a couple of stools, so you get work space and seating space instead of dead space."

"I was thinking of putting a table—"

"Then you'll always be walking around it, and crowding yourself in."

"Maybe." She thought of the kitchen table where she'd sat with her father only that morning. And had sat with her family on countless mornings. Sentimental, she decided. And in this case probably impractical.

"Let me get the measurements, and I'll draw it up for you in the next few days. You can think about it."

"All right. Plenty of time. The main level's my priority."

"It'll take me some time to work it up and get you a bid. But I can tell you now, you're cruising toward six figures and a good four months work for the complete rehab."

She'd come to that conclusion herself, but hearing it was still a jolt. "Work it up, draw it up, whatever it is you do. If I decide to hire you for the job, when would you be able to start?"

"I can get the permits pretty quick. And put in a materials and supply order right off. Probably start work first of the year."

"Those are magic words. If I go with you, I want to get started right away. Get me a bid, Mr. O'Connell, and we'll see if we can do business."

She left him to measure and calculate, and went down to stand on her little front porch.

She could hear the light traffic from the main street,

only a half block over. And smell the smoke from someone's fireplace or woodstove. Her bumpy little front lawn was a disgrace of dead and dying weeds and a sad and ugly stump of what had once been a regal maple.

Across the narrow side street was another brick building that had been converted into apartments. It was old, tidy and utterly quiet at this midday hour.

Another hundred thousand, she thought. Well, it could be done. Fortunately she hadn't lived extravagantly over the past few years. And she did, indeed, have her mother's head for business. Her savings had been carefully invested—and the trust fund was there as a cushion.

If she felt too much was going out, while nothing was coming in, she could agree to do a few guest appearances with the company. That door had been left open.

The fact was, with all the weeks of construction ahead, it would make sense to do so—and not only for financial reasons.

She was used to working, used to being busy. Once the work began on the building there would be nothing for her to do but wait until each stage was complete.

It was an easy trip to New York, and the simplest thing in the world to stay with family there. Rehearse, train, perform, come home again. Yes, that might be the best solution all around.

But not yet. Not quite yet. She wanted to see her plans get off the ground first.

"Kate?" Brody stepped out, her coat in his hand. "It's cold out here."

"A bit. I was hoping it would snow. We got teased the other day."

"As long as it's not eight feet."

"Hmm?"

"Nothing." He laid her coat over her shoulders, automatically lifting her hair out of the collar. There was so damn much of it, he thought. Soft, curling miles of it.

His hands were still caught in it when she turned, when she looked up, met his eyes. Interested after all, she realized with a lovely liquid tug in the belly. "Why don't we walk around the corner. You can buy me a cup of coffee." She moved in, a deliberate test for both of them. "We can discuss…counter space."

She clogged his brain, his lungs, and did a hell of a job on his loins. "You're coming on to me again."

Her smile was slow, devastatingly female. "I certainly am."

"You're probably the most beautiful woman I've ever seen."

"That's the good fortune of birth, but since I look a great deal like my mother, thank you. I particularly like your mouth." She shifted her gaze to it, lingered. "I just keep coming back to it."

His throat was dry as the Sahara. What had happened with women since he'd been out of the game? he wondered. When had they started seducing men on the front porch in the middle of the afternoon?

He could feel the chill December wind whipping against his face. And the heat swarming into his blood. "Look." In self-defense, he took her by the arms. Her coat slid off her shoulders, and he felt the taut sculpted muscle beneath her suit jacket.

"I've been looking." Her gaze flicked up to his again. So male, she thought. So frustrated. "I just happen to like what I see."

Her eyes were pure gray, he thought. Mysterious as smoke. He had only to lower his head, or better, yes better, to yank her to her toes. Then his mouth would be on those sultry, self-satisfied lips of hers.

He had a feeling, a bad one, it would be like bare-handing a live wire. Thrilling, and potentially deadly.

"I told you I wasn't interested."

"Yes, you did. But you lied." To prove it, she rose up to her toes and took a quick, hard nip into his bottom lip. His hands tightened like vises on her arms. "See?" she whispered when he held her there, only a breath away. "You're very interested."

Amused at both of them, she lowered to the flats of her feet, eased back. "You just don't want to be."

"It comes down to the same thing." He let her go, bent to pick up his toolbox. Damn it, his hands weren't even close to steady.

"I don't agree, but I won't push it. I'd like to see you socially, if and when that suits you. Meanwhile, since we have similar views on this building, and I liked most of your ideas, I hope we'll be able to work together."

He hissed out a breath. Cool as January, he noted. While he was flustered, heated up and churning. "You're a real piece of work, Kate."

"I am, that's true. I won't apologize for being what I

am. I'll look forward to getting the brochures and in-formation we discussed, and your bid on the job. If you need to get back in for more measurements or whatever, you know how to reach me."

"Yeah, I know how to reach you."

She stayed where she was, watched him stride down to the curb, climb into his truck. He'd have been sur-prised if he'd heard the long shaky breath she expelled as he drove away.

Surprised as well if he'd seen her slowly lower her-self to the top step.

She was nowhere near as cool as January. She sat in the brisk breeze waiting to cool off. And for the frogs in her belly to settle down again.

Brody O'Connell, she thought. Wasn't it strange and fascinating that a man she'd only met twice should have such a strong effect on her? It wasn't that she was shy around men—far from it. But she was selective. The lover she'd tossed in Brody's face had been one of the three men—all of whom she'd cared for deeply—that she'd allowed into her life, and into her bed.

Yet, after two meetings—no, she thought, ordering herself to be brutally honest—after *one* meeting, she'd wanted Brody in her bed. The second meeting had only sharpened that want into a keen-edged desire she wasn't prepared for.

So she would do the logical and practical thing. She'd settle herself down, clear her mind. Then she'd begin to plan the best way to get him there.

Chapter 3

Jack sat at the partner's desk in what he and his dad called their office and carefully printed out the alphabet. It was his job. Just like Dad was doing his job, on his side of the desk.

The drafting paper and rulers and stuff looked like a lot more fun than the alphabet. But Dad had said, if he got it all done, he could have some paper to draw with, too.

He thought he would draw a big, giant house, just like their house, with the old barn that was Dad's workshop. And there would be lots of snow, too. Eight whole feet of snow and millions and billions of snowmen.

And a dog.

Grandpa and Grandma had a dog, and even though Buddy was sort of old, he was fun. But he had to stay at Grandma's. One day he'd have a dog all of his own and its name would be Mike and he'd chase balls and sleep in the bed at night.

He could have one as soon as he was old enough to be responsible. Which could even be tomorrow.

Jack peeked up to study his father's face and see if it was maybe time to ask if he was responsible yet.

But his dad had that look where he was kind of frowning but not mad. His working look. If you interrupted the working look, the answer was almost always: Not now.

But the alphabet was boring. He wanted to draw the house or play with his trucks or with the computer. Or maybe just look outside and see if it was snowing yet.

He butted his foot against the desk. Squirmed. Butted his foot.

"Jack, don't kick the desk."

"Do I have to write the *whole* alphabet?"

"Yep."

"How come?"

"Because."

"But I got all the way up to the *P*."

"If you don't do the rest, you can't say any words that have the letters in them you left out."

"But—"

"Can't say 'but.' *B-U-T*."

Jack heaved the heavy sigh of a six-year-old. He wrote the next three letters, then peeked up again. "Dad."

"Hmm."

"Dad, Dad, Dad, Dad. *D-A-D*."

Brody glanced up, saw his son grinning at him. "Smart aleck."

"I know how to spell Dad and Jack."

Brody narrowed his eyes, lifted a fist. "Do you know how to spell knuckle sandwich?"

"Nuh-uh. Does it have mustard?"

The kid, Brody thought, was sharp as a bucket of tacks. "How'd you get to be such a wise guy?"

"Grandma says I got it from you. Can I see what you're drawing? You said it's for the dancing lady. Are you drawing her, too?"

"Yes, it's for the dancing lady, and no, you can't see it until you're finished your job." However much he wanted to set his own work aside and just *be* with his son, the only way to teach responsibility was to be responsible.

That was one of those sneaky circles of parenthood.

"What happens when you don't finish what you start?"

Jack rolled his eyes. "Nothing."

"Exactly."

Jack heaved another sigh and applied his pencil. He didn't see his father's lips twitch.

God, what a kid. Brody wanted to toss his own pencil down, snatch Jack up and do whatever this major miracle of his life wanted to do for the rest of the evening. The hell with work, with responsibility, with what needed to be done.

There was only one thing he wanted more than that. To finish what he started. There was no job more vital than Jack O'Connell.

Had his own father ever looked at him and wondered, and worried? Probably, Brody thought. It had never showed, but probably. Still, Bob O'Connell hadn't been one for wrestling on the rug or foolish conversations. He'd gone to work. He'd come home from work. He'd expected dinner on the table at six.

He'd expected his son to do his chores, stay out of trouble, and to—above all—do what he was told without question. One of those expectations had been to follow, precisely, in his father's footsteps.

Brody figured he'd disappointed his father in every possible area. And had been disappointed by him.

He wasn't going to put those same demands and expectations on his own son.

"Zee! Zee, Zee, Zee!" Jack picked up the paper, waved it madly. "I finished."

"Hold it still, hotshot, so I can see." A long way from neat, Brody noted when Jack held the paper up. But it was done. "Good job. You want some graph paper?"

"Can I come over there and help work on yours?"

"Sure." So he'd stay up an extra hour and work, Brody thought as Jack scrambled down from his stool. It would be worth it to have this time with his son. He reached down, hauled Jack up on his lap. "Okay, so what we've got here is the apartment above the school."

"How come they wear those funny clothes when they dance?"

"I have no idea. How do you know they wear funny clothes?"

"I saw a cartoon, and there were elephants in funny skirts. They were dancing on their toes. Do elephants really have toes?"

"Yeah." Didn't they? "We'll look it up later so you can

see. Here, take the pencil. You can draw this line here, right against the straight edge."

"Okay!"

Father and son worked, heads close together, with the big hand guiding the small.

When Jack began to yawn, Brody shifted him, laying Jack over his shoulder as he rose.

"I'm not tired," Jack claimed even as his head drooped.

"When you wake up, it'll only be five days till Christmas."

"Can I have a present?"

Brody smiled. His son's voice was thick, his body already going limp. He paused in the living room, by the tree, swaying slightly as he had when Jack had been an infant, and fretful in the night. As Christmas trees went, Brody mused, this one wasn't pretty. But it was festive. The mix of ornaments covered every available inch. Wads of tinsel shone in the multicolored lights Jack had wanted.

Rather than an angel or a star, there was a grinning Santa at the top. Jack still believed in Santa Claus. Brody wondered if he would this time the following year.

Thinking of that, of the years passed and passing still, he turned his face into his son's hair. And just breathed him in.

After he'd carried Jack up to bed, he came down and brewed a fresh pot of coffee. Probably a mistake, Brody thought even as he poured the first cup. It would very likely keep him awake.

Still he stood, looking out the dark window, sipping it black. The house was too quiet with Jack asleep. There were times, God knew, when the boy made so much noise, caused so much chaos, it seemed there would never be a moment of peace and quiet.

Then when he got it, Brody wanted the noise.

Parenting, he thought, had to be the damnedest business going.

But the problem now was restlessness. It was a feeling he hadn't experienced for quite some time. With parenting, establishing a business, making a home, soliciting jobs, he hadn't had much excess time.

Still don't, he thought, and began to pace the kitchen while he drank his coffee.

There was enough work to be done on the house to keep him busy for...probably the rest of his life. Should have bought something smaller, he thought, and less needy. Something more practical—and he'd heard variations on those thoughts from his father since he'd dug up the down payment.

Trouble was, he'd fallen head over heels for the old place, and so had Jack. And it was working, he reminded himself, glancing around the completed kitchen with its glass-fronted cabinets and granite counters.

Still, work was the bottom line, and he really had to carve out the time to deal with the rooms he'd put off.

Hard to find time when there were only days left until Christmas.

Then, there was the job due to be completed the next afternoon. And on the heels of that came the school holiday. He should have lined up a babysitter—he'd meant to. But Jack disliked them so much, and the guilt was a slow burn.

He knew Beth Skully would take Jack at least part of the time. But after a while, it felt like imposing. In an emergency, he could call on his mother. But that was a tricky business. Whenever he passed Jack off in that direction, he felt like a failure.

He'd make it work. Jack could come along with him some of the time, go to his pal Rod's some of the time. And in a pinch, he'd visit his grandmother.

And that wasn't the problem at all, Brody admitted. That wasn't the distraction, lodged like a splinter in his mind.

The splinter was Kate Kimball.

He didn't have the time nor the inclination for her.

All right, damn it, he didn't have the time. Whatever he did have for her was a hell of a ways up from inclination. He dragged a hand through his mass of sun-streaked hair and tried to ignore the sheer sexual frustration eating at his gut.

Had he ever felt this much pure physical hunger for a woman before? He must have. He just didn't remember clearly, that was all. Didn't remember being churned up this way.

And it really ticked him off.

It was only because it had been a long time. Because she was so openly provocative. So unbelievably beautiful.

But he wasn't a kid anymore who could grab pretty

toys without considering the consequences. He was no longer free to do whatever he liked, when he liked. And he wouldn't want it any other way.

Not that taking her up on her obvious invitation had to have consequences. In the long run. Even in the short. They were both adults, they both knew the ropes.

And that kind of thinking, he decided, would only get him in trouble.

Do your job, he told himself. Take her money. Keep your distance.

And stop thinking about that amazing, streamlined body of hers.

He poured a second cup of coffee—knowing he was damning himself to a sleepless night—then went back to work.

The next afternoon, Kate opened the door to find Brody on her doorstep. Her pleasure at that was side-tracked by the bright-eyed little boy at his side.

"Well, hello, handsome."

"I'm Jack."

"Handsome Jack. I'm Kate. Come in."

"I'm just dropping off the drawings, and the bid." Brody held them out, kept a hand firm on Jack's shoulder. "My card's in there. If you have any questions or want to discuss the drawings or the figures, just get in touch."

"Let's save time and look them over now. What's your hurry?" She barely looked at him, but beamed smiles at

Jack. "*Brr.* It's cold out there. Cold enough for cookies and hot chocolate."

"With marshmallows?"

"In this house, it's illegal to serve hot chocolate without marshmallows." She held out a hand. Jack's was already in it as he bolted inside.

"Listen—"

"Oh, come on, O'Connell. Be a sport. So, what grade are you in, Handsome Jack?" She crouched down to unzip his coat. "Eighth, ninth?"

"No." He giggled. "First."

"You're kidding. This is such a coincidence. We happen to be running a special today for blond-haired boys in first grade. Your choice of sugar, chocolate chip or peanut butter cookies."

"Can I have one of each?"

"Jack—"

"Ah, a man after my own heart," Kate said, ignoring Brody. She straightened, handed Brody Jack's coat and cap and muffler, then took the boy's hand.

"Are you the dancing lady?"

She laughed as she started back with him toward the kitchen. "Yes, I am." With that sultry smile on her lips, she glanced back over her shoulder at Brody. Gotcha, she thought. "Kitchen's this way."

"I know where the damn kitchen is."

"Dad said damn," Jack announced.

"So I hear. Maybe he shouldn't get any cookies."

"It's okay for grown-ups to say damn. But they're not supposed to say sh—"

"Jack!"

"But sometimes he says that, too," Jack finished in a conspirator's whisper. "And once when he banged his hand, he said *all* the curse words."

"Really?" Absolutely charmed, she pulled a chair out for the boy. "In a row, or all mixed up?"

"All mixed up. He said some of them lots of times." He gave her a bright smile. "Can I have three marsh-mallows?"

"Absolutely. You can hang those coats on the pegs there, Brody." She sent him a sunny smile, then got out the makings for the hot chocolate.

And not a little paper pack, Brody noted. But a big hunk of chocolate, milk. "We don't want to take up your time," he began.

"I have time. I put in a few hours at the store this morning. My mother's swamped. But Brandon's taking the afternoon shift. That's my brother's ball mitt," she told Jack, who instantly snatched his hand away from it.

"I was only looking."

"It's okay. You can touch, he doesn't mind. Do you like baseball?"

"I played T-ball last year, and I'm going to play Little League when I'm old enough."

"Brand played T-ball, too, and Little League. And now he plays for a real major league team. He plays third base for the L.A. Kings."

Jack's eyes rounded—little green gems. "For real?"

"For real." She crossed over, slipped the glove onto

the delighted Jack's hand. "Maybe when your hand's big enough to fit, you'll play, too."

"Holy cow, Dad. It's a real baseball guy's mitt."

"Yeah." He gave up. He couldn't block anyone who gave his son such a thrill. "Very cool." He ruffled Jack's hair, smiled over at Kate. "Can I have three marshmallows, too?"

"Absolutely."

The boy was a jewel, Kate thought as she prepared the hot chocolate, set out cookies. She had a weakness for kids, and this one was, as her father had said, a pistol.

Even more interesting, she noted, was the obvious link between father and son. Strong as steel and sweet as candy. It made her want to cuddle both of them.

"Lady?"

"Kate," she said and put his mug of chocolate in front of him. "Careful now, it's hot."

"Okay. Kate, how come you wear funny clothes when you dance? Dad has no idea."

Brody made a small sound—it might have been a groan—then took an avid interest in the selection of cookies.

Kate arched her eyebrows, set the other mugs on the table, then sat. "We like to call them costumes. They help us tell whatever story we want through the dance."

"How can you tell stories with dancing? I like stories with talking."

"It's like talking, but with movement and music. What do you think of when you hear 'Jingle Bells,' without the words?"

"Christmas. It's only five days till Christmas."

"That's right, and if you were going to dance to Jingle Bells, the movements would be happy and fast and fun. They'd make you think of sleigh rides and snow. But if it was 'Silent Night,' it would be slow and reverent."

"Like in church."

Oh, aren't you quick, she thought. "Exactly. You come by my school sometime, and I'll show you how to tell a story with dancing."

"Dad's maybe going to build your school."

"Yes, maybe he is."

She opened the folder. Interesting, Brody thought, how she set the bid aside and went straight to the drawings. Possibilities rather than the bottom line.

Jack got down to business with the hot chocolate, his eyes huge with anticipation as he blew on the frothy surface to cool it. Kate ignored hers, and the cookies. When she began to ask questions, Brody scooted his chair over so they bent over the drawings together.

She smelled better than the cookies, and that was saying something.

"What is this?"

"A pocket door—it slides instead of swings. Saves space. That corridor's narrow. I put one here, too, on your office. You need privacy, but you don't have to sacrifice space."

"I like it." She turned her head. Faces close, eyes locked. "I like it very much."

"I drew some of the lines," Jack announced.

"You did a fine job," Kate told him, then went back to

studying the drawings while Brody dealt with the tangle of knots in his belly.

She looked at each one carefully, considering changes, rejecting them, or putting them aside for future possibilities. She could see it all quite clearly—the lines, the angles, the flow. And noted the details Brody had added or altered. She couldn't find fault with them. At the moment.

More, she was impressed with his thoroughness. The drawings were clean and professional. She doubted she'd have gotten better with an architect.

When she was done, she picked up the bid—meticulously clear—ran down the figures. And swallowed the lump of it.

"Well, Handsome Jack." She set the paperwork down again. "You and your dad are hired."

Jack let out a cheer, and since nobody told him not to, took another cookie.

Brody didn't realize he'd been holding his breath, not until it wanted to expel in one great whoosh. He controlled it, eased back. It was the biggest job he'd taken on since moving back to West Virginia.

The work would keep him and his crew busy all through the winter—when building work was often slow. There'd be no need to cut back on his men, or their hours.

And the income would give him a whole lot of breathing room.

Over and above the vital practicalities, he'd wanted to get his hands on that building. The trick would be to keep them there, and off Kate.

"I appreciate the business."

"Remember that when I drive you crazy."

"You started out doing that. Got a pen?"

She smiled, rose to get one out of the drawer. Leaning over the table, she signed her name to the contract, dated it. "Your turn," she said, handing him the pen.

When he was done, she took the pen back, looked over at Jack. "Jack?"

"Huh?" Crumbs dribbled from the corner of his mouth. Catching his father's narrow stare, he swallowed. "I mean, yes, ma'am."

"Can you write your name?"

"I can print it. I know all the alphabet, and how to spell Jack and Dad and some stuff."

"Good. Well, come on over here and make it official." She tilted her head at his blank look. "You drew some of the lines, didn't you? You want to be hired, or not?"

Pure delight exploded on his face. "Okay!"

He scrambled down, scattering more crumbs. Taking the pen, he locked his tongue between his teeth and with painful care printed his name under his father's signature.

"Look, Dad! That's me."

"Yeah, it sure is."

Stupefied by emotion, Brody looked up, met Kate's eyes. What the hell was he going to do now? She'd hit him at his weakest point.

"Jack, go wash your hands."

"They're not dirty."

"Wash them anyway."

"Right down the hall, Jack," Kate said quietly. "Count one door, then two, on the side of the hand you write your name with."

Jack made little grumbling sounds, but he skipped out of the room.

Brody got to his feet. She didn't back off. No, she wouldn't have, he thought. So their bodies bumped a little, and his went on full alert.

"That was nice. What you did, making him feel part of it."

"He is part of it. That is clear." And so was something else that needled into her heart. "It wasn't a strategy, Brody."

"I said it was nice."

"Yes, but you're also thinking—at least wondering if—it was also clever of me. A slick little ploy to get to you. I want to sleep with you, and I'm very goal oriented, but I draw the line at using your son to achieve the desired end."

She snatched up his empty mug, started to turn. Brody laid a hand on her arm. "Okay, maybe I wondered. Now I'll apologize for it."

"Fine."

He shifted, gripped her arm until she turned to face him. "Sincerely apologize, Kate."

She relaxed. "All right. Sincerely accepted. He's beautiful, and he's great. It's tough not to get stuck on him right off the bat."

"I'm pretty stuck on him myself."

"Yes, and he on you. It shows. I happen to like children, and admire loving parents. It only makes you more attractive."

"I'm not going to sleep with you." He wasn't gripping her arm now, but sliding his hands down the length.

She smiled. "So you say."

"I'm not going to mess up this job, complicate it and my life. I can't afford…"

He'd had something definite to say. Decisive. But she slid her hands up his chest, over his shoulders.

"You're not on the clock yet," she murmured and lifted her mouth to his.

He closed the gap and lights exploded inside his head. Eruptions blasted inside his body. Her mouth was warm, tart, persuasive. The sensations simply took control of the two of them. Of him.

He meant to take her by the shoulders, pull her back. He meant to. He could hold her at arm's length. And would.

In a little while.

But for now, for right now, he wanted to just lose himself in the sheer sensation. He wanted to have to hold her to keep his balance. She smelled dark. And dangerous.

It was irresistible. He was irresistible. He kissed like a dream, she thought, letting out a throaty little purr. As if it was all he'd ever done, all he ever wanted to do.

His mouth was soft, and hot. His hands hard, and strong. Was there anything sexier in a man than strength? The strength that came from muscles and from the heart.

He made her mind spin a dozen lazy pirouettes, with her pulse throbbing thick to keep the beat.

She wanted to send that rhythm speeding. Wanted it more than she'd anticipated. And floating on that lovely mix of anticipation, sensation and desire, she let her head fall back.

"That was nice." Her fingers slid up into his hair. "Why don't we do that again?"

He wanted to—to start and finish in one huge gulp. And his six-year-old son was splashing in the sink down the hall. "I can't do this."

"I think we just proved you could."

"I'm not going to do this." Now he did hold her at arm's length. Her eyes were dark, her mouth soft. "Damn, you muddle a man's brain."

"Apparently not enough. But it's a beginning."

He let her go. It was the safest move. And stepped back. "You know, it's been a long time since I…played this game."

"It'll come back to you. You may have been on the bench for a while, but it'll come back. Why don't we go out to dinner and start your training?"

"I washed both sides," Jack announced as he hopped back into the room. "Can I have another cookie?"

"No." He couldn't take his eyes off hers. Couldn't seem to do anything but stare and want. And wonder. "We have to go. Say thank you to Kate."

"Thanks, Kate."

"You're welcome, Jack. Come back and see me, okay?"

"Okay." He grinned at her as his father bundled him into his coat. "Will you have hot chocolate?"

"I'll make sure of it."

She walked them to the door, stood in the opening to watch them climb into the truck. Jack waved enthusiastically. Brody didn't look back at all.

A cautious man, she thought as they drove off. Well, she could hardly blame him. If she'd had something as precious as that little boy to worry about, she'd have been cautious, too.

But now that she'd met the son, she was even more interested in the man. He was a good father, one who obviously paid attention. Jack had been warmly dressed, healthy, friendly, happy.

It couldn't be easy, raising a child alone. But Brody O'Connell was doing it, and doing it well.

She respected that. Admired that. And, was attracted to that.

Maybe she'd been a little hasty, acting on pure chemistry. But she pressed her lips together, remembering the feel and taste of his and wondered who could blame her.

Still, it wouldn't hurt to take more time, to get to know him better.

After all, neither of them were going anywhere.

Chapter 4

"Earthquakes," Kate said.

"Ice storms," Brandon countered.

"Smog."

"Snow shovels."

She tossed back her hair. "The joy of the changing seasons."

He pulled her hair. "The beach."

They'd been having the debate for years—East Coast versus West. At the moment, Kate was using it to take her mind off the fact that Brandon was leaving in under an hour.

Just the post-Christmas blues, she assured herself. All that excitement and preparation, then the lovely warmth of a traditional Christmas at home had kept her so busy, and so involved.

The Kimballs had followed their Christmas Day celebrations with a two-day trip to New York, rounding everything off with all the chaos and confusion of their sprawling family.

Now it was nearly a new year. Freddie, her sister, was back in New York with her husband, Nick, and the kids. And Brandon was heading back to L.A.

She glanced out at the tidy, quiet main street as they walked. And smiled thinly. "Road rage."

"Hard-bodied blondes in convertibles."

"You are *so* shallow."

"Yeah." He hooked his arm around her neck. "You love that about me. Hey, check it out. You got men with trucks."

Still pouting, she looked down the street and saw the work trucks and laborers. Brody, she mused, didn't waste any time.

They circled around, picked their way over rubble and hillocks of winter dry grass to the rear of the building where the activity seemed to be centered. There was noise—someone was playing country music on a portable radio. There were scents—dirt, sweat and, oddly enough, mayonnaise.

Kate walked around a wheelbarrow, stepped cautiously down a ramp and peered into her basement.

Thick orange extension cords snaked to portable work lights that hung from beams or posts. Their bare-bulb glare made her basement resemble some archeological dig, still in its nasty stages.

She spotted Brody, in filthy jeans and boots, hammering a board into place on a form. Though his breath puffed out visibly as he worked, he'd stripped off his jacket. She could see the intriguing ripple of muscle under flannel.

She'd been right, Kate noted, he looked extremely good in a tool belt.

A laborer shoveled dirt into another wheelbarrow. And Jack was plopped down, digging with a small shovel and dumping his take—or most of it—into a bucket.

The boy spotted her first. Hopped up and danced. "I'm digging out the basement! I get a dollar. I get to help pour concrete. I got a truck for Christmas. You wanna see?"

"You bet."

She had taken another step down the ramp before Brody came over and blocked her. "You're not dressed to muck around down here."

She glanced down at his work boots, then her own suede sneakers. "Can't argue with that. Can you spare a minute?"

"All right. Jack, take a break."

Brody came up the ramp, squinting against the flash of winter sunlight, with his son scrambling behind him.

"This is my brother, Brandon. Brand, Brody O'Connell and Jack."

"Nice to meet you." Brody held up a grimy hand rather than offering to shake. "I've watched you play. It's a pleasure."

"Thanks. I've seen your work, same goes."

"Are you the baseball player?" Eyes huge, Jack stared up at Brandon.

"That's right." Brandon crouched down. "You like baseball?"

"Uh-huh. I saw your mitt. I've got one, too. And a bat and a ball and everything."

Knowing Brandon would keep Jack entertained, Kate moved a few steps away to give them room. "I didn't realize you were starting so soon," she said to Brody.

"Figured we'd take advantage of the break in the weather. Warm spell's supposed to last a few more days. We can get the basement dug out, formed up and poured before the next cold snap."

Warm was relative, she thought. It would be considerably chillier in the old stone walled basement, and considerably damper than out here in the sunlight. "I'm not complaining. How was your Christmas?"

"Great." He shifted so that his crew could muscle the next barrow of dirt up the ramp. "Yours?"

"Wonderful. I see you've expanded your crew. Was that dollar a day in my bid?"

"School's out," he said shortly. "I keep him with me. He knows the rules, and the men don't mind him."

She lifted her brows. "My, my. Sensitivo."

Brody hissed out a breath. "Sorry. Some clients don't like me having a kid on a job site."

"I'm not one of them."

"Hey, O'Connell, can you spare this guy for a bit?"

Brody glanced over, noted Jack's grimy hand was clasped in Brandon's. "Well…"

"We've got a little business up at the house," Brandon went on. "I'll drop him back down on my way to the airport. Half hour."

"*Please,* Dad. Can I?"

"I—"

"My brother's an idiot," Kate said with an easy smile. "But a responsible one."

No, Brody thought, *he* was the idiot, getting the jitters every time Jack went off with someone new. "Sure. Wash your hands off in the water bucket first, Jacks."

"Okay! Wait just a minute, okay? Just a minute." Jack raced off to splash some of the dirt away.

"I'll try to stop through on my way to spring training."

"Yeah. Okay." She wouldn't cry. She would *not* cry. "Stay away from those hard-bodied blondes."

"Not a chance." Brandon snatched her up, held tight. "Miss you," he murmured.

"Me, too." She pressed her face into the curve of his neck, then stepped back with a bright smile. "Take care of that leg, slugger."

"Hey, you're talking to Iron Man. Take care of your own. Let's go, Jack." He took the boy's marginally clean and wet hand, shot a salute to Brody, and started off.

"Bye, Dad! Bye. I'll be back."

"Your brother got a problem with his leg?"

"Pulled some tendons. Bad slide. Well, I'll let you get back to work." She kept the smile on her face until she'd rounded to the front of the house. Then she sat on the steps and had a nice little cry.

When Brody walked out to his truck ten minutes later,

she was still there. Tears had dried on her cheeks. A few more sparkled in her lashes.

"What? What's the matter?"

"Nothing."

"You've been crying."

She sniffled, shrugged. "So?"

He wanted to leave it at that. Really wanted to just get his…what the hell had he come out for? The problem was he'd never been able to walk away from tears. Resigned, he crossed the sidewalk and sat beside her.

"What's wrong?"

"I hate saying goodbye. I wouldn't have to say goodbye if he didn't insist on living three thousand miles away in stupid California. The dope."

Ah, her brother. "Well…" Because a fresh tear had spilled over, Brody yanked a bandanna from his pocket. "He works there."

"Excuse me, but I'm not feeling particularly logical." She took the bandanna. "Thanks."

"Don't mention it."

She dabbed at tears, then stared across the street. "Do you have any siblings?"

"No."

"Want one? I'll sell him cheap." She sighed, leaned back on the steps. "My sister's in New York. Brand's in L.A. I'm in West Virginia. I never thought we'd end up so scattered."

He remembered the way she and her brother had embraced, that natural flow of love. "You don't look scattered to me."

Kate looked back at him. In a moment, her eyes cleared. "You're right. You're absolutely right. That was exactly the right thing to say. So." She drew in a breath, handed him back his bandanna. "Take my mind off all this for a minute. What'd you do for Christmas? The big, noisy family thing?"

"Jack makes plenty of noise. He got me up at five." Remembering made Brody smile. "I think I peeled him off the ceiling around two that afternoon."

"Did he make it through Christmas dinner?"

Brody's smile faded. "Yeah, barely." He moved his shoulder. "We went over to his grandparents' for that. We live in the same town," he said. "But you could say we're scattered."

"I'm sorry."

"They dote on Jack. That's the important thing."

And why the hell did he bring it up? Maybe, he thought, maybe because it was stuck in his craw. Maybe because his father continued to dismiss everything he'd done with his life, everything he wanted to do.

"I'm having the dirt dumped around the other side of the house. You might want to have it spread there, start a garden or something in the spring."

"That's a good thought."

"Well." He got to his feet. "I've got to get back to work, before the boss docks my pay."

"Brody—" She wasn't sure what she meant to say, or how she meant to say it. Then the moment passed as Brandon pulled up to the curb in his spiffy rental car.

"Dad!" Jack was already fighting to free himself from

the seat belt. "Wait till you see! Brand gave me his mitt, and a baseball with his name wrote on it and everything."

"Written on it," Brody said automatically, then caught the bullet of his son as Jack shot toward him. "Let's have a look." He examined the mitt and ball, both warm from Jack's tight grip. "These are really special, and you'll have to take special care of them."

"I will. I promise. Thanks, Brand. Thanks! I'm going to keep them forever. Can we show the guys now, Dad?"

"You bet." Brody hitched Jack higher on his hip, looked down at Brandon. "Thanks."

"My pleasure. Remember, Jack. Keep your eye on the ball."

"I will! Bye."

"Safe trip," Brody added, and carted Jack around to show off his treasures to the crew.

Kate let out a little sigh, leaned down into Brandon's open window. "Maybe you're not such a jerk after all."

"Hell of a kid." He pinched Kate's chin. "You got an eye on the dad, I noticed."

"No. I've got both eyes on the dad." Laughing, she leaned in to give him a kiss. "You go ahead after those California girls, pal. I like country boys."

"Behave yourself."

"Not a chance."

He laughed, turned on the engine again. "See you, gorgeous."

She stepped back, waved. "Fly safe," she murmured.

* * *

It was traditional for Natasha to close the shop on New Year's Eve. She spent the day in the kitchen, preparing the myriad dishes she'd set out for the open house she held every New Year's Day. Family, friends, neighbors would crowd the house for hours.

"Brand should have stayed until after the party."

"I wish he could have." Natasha checked the apricots and water she was boiling for kissel, turned the mixture down to simmer. "Don't sulk, Katie. There were times your life and your work kept you away."

"I know." Kate continued to roll out pastry dough as she'd been taught. "I just need a little more sulk time. I miss the jerk, that's all."

"So do I."

On the stove, pots puffed steam. In the oven, an enormous ham was baking. Years ago, Natasha thought, she'd have had three children underfoot while she was juggling these chores. There would have been squabbling, giggling, spills to mop up. Her patience would have been sorely tried a dozen times.

It had been wonderful.

Now she only had her Kate, pouting over the pastry dough.

"You're restless." Natasha tapped a spoon on the side of a pot, set it on its holder. "You don't have enough to fill your time while the building is going on."

"I'm making plans."

"Yes, I know." She poured two cups of tea, brought them to the table. "Sit."

"Mama, I'm—"

"Sit. So, you're like me," Natasha continued as they both took seats at the crowded table. "Plans, details, goals. These are so important. We want to know what happens next, because if we know, we can have control."

"What's wrong with that?"

"Nothing. When I came here to open my store, it was very hard. Hard to leave the family. But I needed to. I didn't know I'd meet your father here. That wasn't planned."

"It was fate."

"Yes." Natasha smiled. "We plan, you and I, and we calculate. And still, we understand fate. So maybe fate, for all your plans, brought you back."

"Are you disappointed?" She blurted it out, and felt both relief and dread that it had finally been asked.

"In what? You? Why would you think so?"

"Mama." Searching for words, Kate turned her cup around and around. "I know how much you and Dad sacrificed—"

"Wait." Dark eyes kindling, Natasha tapped her fingers hard on the table. "Maybe, after all these years my English is failing. I don't understand the word *sacrifice* when it comes to my children. You have never been a sacrifice."

"I meant, you and Dad did so much, supported me in every way when I wanted to dance. Please, Mama," Kate said when Natasha started to speak. "Just let me finish this. It's been on my mind. All the lessons, all those years. The costumes, the shoes, the travel. Letting me go to New York when I know Dad would have preferred I'd gone to college. But you let me have what I needed most. I always knew that. I wanted you to be proud of me."

"Of course we were proud of you. What nonsense have you put in your head?"

"I know you were. I know. I could feel it, see it. When I was dancing and you were there, even when I couldn't see you through the footlights, I could *see*. And now I've tossed it away."

"No, you've set it aside. Kate, do you think we're only proud of you when you dance? Only proud of the artist, of that skill?"

Her eyes were brimming. She couldn't help it. "I worried that you might be disappointed that I gave it up to teach."

"Of all my children," Natasha said with a shake of her head, "you are the one forever searching in corners to see if there's a speck of dust. Even when there isn't, you can't help but poke in with the broom. Answer me this, do you want to be a good teacher?"

"Yes, very much."

"Then you will be, and we'll be proud of that. And between these times, between the dancer and the teacher, we're proud of you. Proud that you know what you want, and how to work for it. Proud that you're a lovely young woman with a kind heart and a strong mind. If you doubt that, Katie, you will disappoint me."

"I don't. I won't. Oh." She let out a long breath and

blinked at the tears. "I don't know what's wrong with me. I'm so weepy lately."

"You're changing your life. It's an emotional time. And you give yourself too much time to think and worry. Kate, why aren't you out with your friends? You have so many still in the area. Why aren't you going out to a party tonight, or with some handsome young man, instead of staying home on New Year's Eve to bake a ham with your mama?"

"I like baking hams with my mama."

"Kate."

"All right." But she got up to finish the pastry. She needed to keep her hands busy. "I thought about going to one of the parties tonight. But most of my friends are married, or at least coupled off. But I'm not a couple and I'm not really…shopping around. You know?"

"Mmm. And why aren't you…shopping around?"

"Because I've already seen something that appeals to me."

"Ah. Who?"

"Brody O'Connell."

"Ah," Natasha said again, and lifted her tea to sip and consider. "I see."

"I'm very attracted to him."

"He's a very attractive man." Natasha's eyes began to dance. "Yes, very attractive, and I like him very much."

"Mama—you didn't send him down to look at the job to throw us together, romantically?"

"No. But I would have if I'd thought of it. So, why

aren't you out with Brody O'Connell for New Year's Eve?"

"He's scared of me." Kate laughed when her mother made a dismissing noise. "Well, *uneasy* might be a better word. I might have come on a little strong, initially."

"You?" Natasha deliberately rounded her eyes. "My shy little Katie?"

"Okay, okay." Laughing now, Kate set aside the rolling pin. "I definitely came on too strong. But when I ran into him the first time in the toy store when he was getting a toy for Jack, and we were flirting, I thought we were on the same wavelength."

"In the toy store," Natasha murmured. She and Spence had met the first time in the toy store, when he had been picking out a doll for his daughter, Freddie.

Fate, she thought. You could never anticipate it.

"Yes, then when I realized he was buying that truck for his son, I assumed he was married. So I was annoyed he'd flirted back."

"Of course." Natasha was grinning now. It just got better and better.

"Then, of course, I found out he wasn't, and the field was open. He's interested, too," she muttered and banged the rolling pin. "Just stubborn about it."

"He's lonely."

Kate looked up, and the little spark of temper she'd hoped to fan into flame flickered out. "Yes, I know. But he keeps stepping back from me. Maybe he does that with everyone, but Jack."

"He's very warm and friendly with me. Yet when I

asked him to come by tomorrow, he made excuses. You should change his mind," Natasha decided. She rose to get back to work. "Yes, you should go by his house later, take him a dish of the black-eyed peas for luck in the new year, and change his mind about coming by tomorrow."

"It's pretty presumptuous, dropping by a man's house on New Year's Eve," Kate said, then grinned. "It's perfect. Thanks, Mama."

"Good." Natasha dipped a finger into the pastry filling, licked it off. "Then your father and I will have a little New Year's Eve party of our own."

Brody nursed a beer and wished he hadn't eaten that last slice of pizza. He was sprawled on the couch, with Jack, in the center of the disaster that had been their living room. Some B horror flick involving giant alien eyeballs was on TV.

He loved B movies—couldn't help himself.

In a couple of hours, he'd switch it over to the coverage of Time's Square. Jack wanted to see the ball drop—and had insisted he could stay awake until midnight.

He'd done everything but prop his eyelids open with toothpicks to make it, which explained the state of the house. He'd finally dropped, snuggled into the crook of Brody's arm.

Brody would hold the fort until five minutes before midnight, then wake Jack up to see the new year in.

Brody sipped his beer and watched the giant eye menace the humans.

And nearly jumped out of his skin when the knock sounded at his door.

Cursing, he slid Jack down onto the couch so he could lever himself off. The odds of someone coming to his door after ten at night, he figured, were about the same as giant alien eyeballs threatening the Earth.

He stepped over and around toys, shoes, socks, and headed for the door. Somebody lost or broken down, he decided. Everyone he knew was celebrating the new year, one way or the other.

Not everyone, he realized with a jolt as he opened the door to Kate.

"Hi. I took a chance you'd be home. My mother sends this."

He found the small covered bowl thrust into his hands. "Your mother?"

"Yes. You hurt her feelings saying you were too busy to come by tomorrow."

"I didn't say I was too busy, I…" What the hell had he said? He'd made it up on the spot, and for the life of him couldn't remember.

"The black-eyed peas are for luck," Kate told him. "Mama really hopes you'll change your mind and stop by. There'll be plenty of kids for Jack to hang out with. Is he up? I'll say hi."

She slipped past him into the house. He'd been too distracted to stop her. Or even try to. But he was already hurrying after her across the little foyer and into the big, messy living room where the TV blared.

Mortified, he snatched up toys and debris in her wake.

"Oh, don't start that." She waved a hand impatiently. "I know what houses with children look like. I grew up in one. What a great tree!"

Arms full, he stared at it. He'd seen the one in her parents' living room. Beautiful ornaments, placed with care. His and Jack's looked like it had been decorated by drunk elves.

"We had one that looked like this. Freddie, Brand and I nagged Mama until she agreed to let us do the tree one year. We made a hell of a mess. It was great."

There was a fire snapping in the hearth so she walked over to warm her hands. She'd spent over an hour dressing, so that she could look completely casual. The deep purple sweater was lightly tucked into gray trousers. Tiny gold hoops glinted at her ears. She'd left her hair loose after a heated self-debate, so that it streamed down to her waist.

She imagined he'd taken less than ten minutes to look fabulous in his jeans and sweatshirt. "Terrific house," she commented. "Native stone, right? Such a quiet spot. Must be great for Jack, all this running room. You'll need to get him a dog."

"Yeah, he's made noises in that area." What the hell was he supposed to do? Now? With her? "Thank your mother for the peas."

"Thank her yourself." Kate turned, then spotted Jack facedown on the couch, one arm dangling. "Conked out, did he?" she went to the boy, automatically lifting his arm back on the cushion, draping the ancient afghan over him. "Trying to stay awake till midnight?"

"Yeah."

He looked baffled, Kate thought. Baffled, rumpled and mouthwatering standing there with her mother's bowl and Jack's toys piled in his arms. "I love this movie," she said easily, glancing at the TV. "Especially the part where they open up that doorway and it's full of alien eyeballs and tentacles. Why don't you offer me a drink? It's traditional."

"Beer's it."

"Oh, major calories. Okay, I'll live dangerously." She walked over, took her mother's bowl. "Where's the kitchen?"

"It's…" She was wearing perfume—something just sliding toward hot. The room had never experienced that sort of seductive female scent before. He glanced to the left, dropped a toy car on his foot.

"I'll find it. Want a refill?"

"No, I've got—" For God's sake, he thought, dumping the toys and going after her again. "Look, Kate, you caught me at a bad time."

"Boy, look at these ceilings. Have you been doing the rehab yourself?"

"When I have some spare time. Listen—"

He broke off, swore, when she strolled into the kitchen. "Wow." She scanned the room. Granite countertops, slate floor, oak cupboards and a charming little stone hearth.

And every inch covered with dishes, pots, school papers, newspapers, discarded outerwear.

"Wow," she said again. "This took some real effort." She stepped over to the counter where what was left of the pizza had yet to be put away. Broke off a corner. Nibbled. "Good."

The drunk elves, he thought, had nothing on the war-crazed monkeys that had invaded his kitchen. "It's usually not this bad."

"You had a party with your son. Stop apologizing. Beer in the fridge?"

"Yeah, yeah." Hell with it. "Why aren't you at a party?"

"I am. I just came late." She handed him the beer. "Open that for me, will you?" She sniffed the air while he twisted off the cap. "I smell popcorn."

"We pretty much finished that off."

"Well, that's what I get for being late." She leaned back against the counter, took a sip of beer. "Want to go sit on the couch, watch the rest of the movie and make out?"

"Yeah. No."

"No to which, the movie or the making-out?"

She was laughing at him. He wanted to be enraged. But was only aroused. "You keep getting in my way."

"So what are you going to do about it?"

With his eyes on hers, he closed the distance between them. Took the bottle from her hand, set it aside.

New Year's Eve, he thought. Out with the old. In with the…who knew?

"Well." Pulses thrumming, she started to slide her hands up his chest, but he caught them in his.

"No. My turn."

He lowered his head, and his mouth began to whisper over hers.

"Dad?"

"Oh God." It came out on a low moan as Brody stepped back.

Jack stood in the doorway, rubbing sleepy eyes. "What are you doing, Dad?"

"Nothing." And the doing of nothing with Kate was very likely to kill him.

"Actually your dad was going to kiss me."

"Kate." He said it in precisely the same tone he'd used when Jack said something unfortunate.

"Nah." Jack, in his oldest Power Ranger pajamas, studied them owlishly. His hair stood up in pale spikes, and his cheeks were still flushed from sleep. "Dad doesn't kiss girls."

"Really?" Before Brody could back too far away, Kate simply grabbed ahold of his shirt. "Why not?"

"Because they're *girls*." To emphasize the point, Jack rolled his eyes. "Kissing girls is yuck."

"Oh, yeah." She bumped the father aside, crooked a finger to the son. "Come here, pal."

"How come?"

"So I can kiss you all over your face."

"Nuh-uh!" His eyes widened, and danced. "Yuck-o."

"Okay." She peeled off her coat, tossed it to Brody, then pushed up her sleeves. "That's it. You're doomed."

She made a grab, giving him enough time to yelp and run for cover. She played dodge and dart for a few minutes, surprising Brody at how easily she avoided trampling on toys. Jack squealed for help, obviously having a great time.

She caught him, wrestled him to the couch, pinned him while he laughed and screamed for mercy.

"Now...the ultimate punishment." She dashed kisses over his cheeks, punctuating them with loud smacks. "Say yummy," she ordered.

"Nuh-uh!" He was breathless and his belly was wild with laughter and delight.

"Say yummy, yummy, yummy or I'll never stop."

"Yummy!" he shouted, choking on giggles. "Yummy, yummy."

"There." She sat back, whistled out a breath. "My work is done."

Jack crawled right into her lap. She wasn't soft like Grandma, or hard like Dad. She was different, and her hair was soft and tickly. "Are you going to stay till midnight when it's new year?"

"I'd love to." She glanced over her shoulder at Brody. "If your dad says it's okay."

Some battles, he thought, were lost before they were waged. "I'll get your beer."

Chapter 5

"Now." Frederica Kimball LeBeck dragged her sister into Kate's bedroom, firmly closed the door. That would, she calculated, insure them approximately five minutes of quiet and privacy. "Tell me everything— from the beginning."

"Okay. According to scientific evidence, there was a great explosion in space."

"Ha-ha. About Brody O'Connell." Eight years Kate's senior—light where Kate was dark, petite where Kate was willowy, Freddie flopped on the bed. "Mama told me you've got him in your crosshairs."

"He's not a rabbit." Kate flopped on the bed in turn. "Gorgeous, though, huh?"

"Oh, yeah. Excellent shoulders. So what's the deal?"

"The deal is he's a widower, doing a bang up job raising a terrific boy. You saw Jack right?"

"Can't miss him. He's giving my Max a run for his money," she added, speaking of her own six-year-old son. "They're bonding over video games."

"Great, that'll push Brody into the social mix. I don't think he's given himself much chance to play."

"He's getting one now, whether he wants it or not. Grandpa and Uncle Mik shanghaied him. I saw them shoving him out the door so they could all go look at your building and make manly carpenter-guy noises over it."

"Perfect."

"So, is it just glands, or is it more?"

"Well, it started with glands. My glands are very susceptible to big, strong men—and their tool belts."

While Freddie snorted with laughter, Kate rolled over on her back, studied the ceiling. "Could be more. He seems like—I don't know, just a very nice man—solid, responsible, loving. The kind of man I haven't seen much of. Gun-shy, too, in a really sweet way, which makes him a wonderful challenge."

"And nobody likes a challenge more than you."

"True. Unless it's you. And I wouldn't mind pursuing the whole thing at that level. But every time I see him with Jack, there's this little…tug inside. You know?"

"Yeah." Freddie had started experiencing those tugs where her own husband, Nick, was concerned at approximately the age of thirteen. "Are you falling for him?"

"Too soon to know. But I really like him on all the important levels, which balances out nicely with all this wild lust."

She lifted her leg, pointed her toe at the ceiling. "I really want to get him alone somewhere and rip his clothes off. But I know I can also have a good conversation with him. Last night we watched the last part of that movie about the giant eye from space."

"Yeah. I love that movie."

"Me, too. That's what I mean. It was really comfortable and easy." And sweet, she thought with a long, lazy stretch. Absolutely sweet. "Even though he gives me that zing in the blood, it's nice to just sit on the couch and watch an old movie. Most of the guys I dated, it was either dancing, partying, dancing, art shows, dancing. There was never any let's just stay home for a night and relax. I'm really ready to do that."

"Small town, ballet school, a romance with a carpenter. It suits you, Katie."

"Yeah." Delighted Freddie could think so, she rolled over again. "It really does."

Yuri Stanislaski, a bull of a man with a fringe of stone-gray hair, stood in the center of the room destined to be a dance studio.

"So, this is good space. My granddaughter, she knows the value of space. Strong foundation." He walked over, gave the wall a punch with the side of his fist. "Good bones."

Mikhail, Yuri's oldest son, stood at the front windows. "She'll relive her childhood out here. It's good for her. And—" he turned, flashed a smile "—people look in, see the dancers. Advertisement. My niece is a clever girl."

There were pounding feet on the steps. Brody had no idea how many of the young people had come down with them. He thought most of them belonged to Mik, but it was impossible to keep track when there were so many of them, and all almost ridiculously good-looking.

He wasn't used to large families, all the byplay and interaction. And he had a feeling the Stanislaskis were about as big as a family could get without just bursting at the seams.

"Papa! Come on up. You gotta see this place. It's ancient. It's great!"

"My son, Griff," Mik said with a twinkle. "He likes old things."

"So, we go up." Yuri gave Brody a pat on the back that could have toppled an elephant. "We see what it is you do with this ancient great place to make my little girl safe and happy. She is a beauty, my Katie. Yes?"

"Yes," Brody said, cautiously.

"And strong."

"Ah." Unsure of his ground, he glanced toward Mikhail for help and got only that thousand-watt grin. "Sure."

"Also good bones." Yuri let out another hearty laugh, and twinkling at his son in what was an unmistakable inside joke, started up the stairs.

Brody didn't know how it happened. He'd meant to do no more than drop in on the Kimballs. To be polite, to thank Natasha for thinking of him and Jack.

He'd gotten swept in. Swallowed was more like it, he

decided. He wasn't sure he'd ever seen that many people in one place at one time before. And most of them were related in one way or the other.

Since his own family consisted of himself and Jack, his parents—with three aunts and uncles and six cousins scattered down south—the sheer number of Stanislaskis had been an eye-opener.

Frankly he didn't see how they kept track of each other.

They were loud, beautiful, boisterous, full of questions, stories and arguments. The house had been so full of people, food, drink, music, that although he'd ended staying until nearly eight, he'd had no more than a few snatches of conversation with Kate.

He'd been dragged off to the building, grilled over his plans—and he wasn't dim enough to have been fooled that the grilling had been exclusively on rehab.

Kate's family had been sizing him up. Connie's had done the same, he remembered. Certainly not with this good humor or affection or, well, sheer amusement, Brody decided. But the bottom line was identical.

Was this guy good enough for their princess? In Connie's case the answer had been an unqualified no. The resentment on both sides had tainted everything that had happened afterward with shadows.

His impression was the Stanislaski verdict was still pending. Nothing he'd done to tactfully demonstrate he wasn't looking to sweep the ballerina off her toe shoes had stopped them from cornering him—good-naturedly.

Asking questions—politely. Or giving him the old once-over—without the least bit of subtlety.

It was more than enough to make a man glad he was single, and intended to stay that way.

Now the party was over. The holidays were, thank the Lord, behind him. He could get back to work, remembering that Kate Kimball was a client. And not a lover.

He spent a week tearing out, cleaning out, prepping walls, checking pipes.

She never came by.

Every day when he arrived on the site, he imagined she'd stroll down at some point and check the progress. Every evening when he loaded his tools back into his truck he wondered what she was up to.

Obviously she was busy, had other things to deal with. Didn't care as much as she'd indicated about the job. Very obviously, she wasn't as interested in him as she'd pretended to be.

Which was why he'd been very smart to avoid getting tangled up with some sort of fling with her. She was probably staying out half the night living it up, and spending the other half with some slick New Yorker. He wouldn't be surprised at all. Not one bit. He wouldn't be surprised if she was already making plans to sell the property and shake the small-town dust off her dancing shoes.

But he was surprised to find himself striding up the steps to her front door and banging on it.

He paced the porch. She was the one who'd wanted to

nail down every detail, wasn't she? He strode back to the door, banged again. The least she could do was maintain some pretense of interest in the project for a lousy week.

He zigzagged back and forth across the porch again. What the hell was he doing? This was stupid. It was none of his business what she did or how she did it, as long as she paid the freight. He drew a deep breath, let it out slowly and had nearly calmed himself down when the door opened.

There she was, looking all heavy-eyed and sleepy, her face flushed, her hair just a little tumbled. Like a woman who'd just slid herself out of bed, and had plans to slide right back in again.

Damn it.

"Brody?"

"Yeah. Sorry to wake you up. After all it's only four in the afternoon."

Her brain was too fuzzy to register the insult, so she gave him a sleepy smile. "It's all right. If I go down for more than an hour in the afternoon, I don't sleep well at night. Come on in. I need coffee."

Assuming he'd follow, she turned and walked back toward the kitchen. She heard the door slam, but since it often did in this house, she didn't think anything of it. "I just got in a couple of hours ago." She started a fresh pot, willed it to hurry. To stretch out fatigued muscles, she automatically moved into the first position. "How are things going on my job?"

"Your interest in stuff always blow hot and cold?"

"Hmm? What?" Third position, rise to toes. Get coffee mugs from cupboard.

"You haven't been to the site in a week."

"I was out of town. You take it black, right? A little emergency in New York."

Instantly his annoyance shifted into concern. "Your family?"

"Oh, no. They're fine." She arched her back, twisted a little, winced. "Can you...I've got this spot right back..."

She curved her arm over her back, trying to reach a sore muscle between her shoulder blades. "Just press in there with your thumb for a minute. A little lower," she said when he complied. "Oh. Mmm, that's it. Harder." She let out a low, throaty groan, tipped her head back, closed her eyes. "Oh, yes. Yes. Don't stop."

"The hell with this." Viciously aroused, he spun her around, slammed her back against the counter and crushed his mouth to hers.

Heat flashed through her logy system, lights slashed through her sleep-dulled brain. Her lips parted on a gasp of surprise, and he took the kiss deep. Took her deep before she could find her balance. She lifted her hands, a helpless flutter, as she tried to catch up.

She was trapped between his body and the counter, two unyielding surfaces. All the fatigue, the vague aches, burned away in the sudden fireball of sensation.

Frustration, need, temper, lust. They'd all been bottled up inside him since the first moment he'd seen her. Now that the cork was popped, the passion poured out.

He took what he hadn't allowed himself to want, ravaging her mouth to feed the hunger.

And when she gripped his shoulders and began to tremble, he took more.

They were both breathless when he tore his mouth from hers. For a long moment they stayed as they were, staring at each other, with his hands fisted in her hair, and her fingers digging into his shoulders.

Then their mouths were locked again, a reckless war of lips and tongues and teeth. Her hands tugged at his shirt, his rushed under her sweater. Groping, gasping, they struggled to find more. His back rapped against the refrigerator; her teeth scraped along his neck. He circled around until they bumped the kitchen table. He molded her hips, was about to lift them onto that hard, flat surface.

"Katie, is that fresh coffee I…" Spencer Kimball stopped short in the doorway, slapped hard in the heart by the sight of his baby girl wrapped like a vine around his carpenter.

They broke apart, with the guilty jerk of a child caught with its hand in the cookie jar.

For an awkward, endless five seconds no one spoke nor moved.

"I, ah…" Dear God, was all Spencer could think. "I need to…hmm. In the music room."

He backed out, walked quickly away.

Brody dragged his hands through his hair, fisted them there. "Oh, God. Get me a gun. I'd like to shoot myself now and get it over with."

"We don't have one." She gripped the back of a ladder-back chair. The room was still spinning. "It's all right. My father knows I kiss men on occasion."

Brody dropped his hands. "I was about to do a hell of a lot more than kiss you, and on your mother's kitchen table."

"I know." Wasn't her pulse still banging like a kettle-drum? Couldn't she see the blind heat of desire in those wonderful eyes of his? "It's a damn shame Dad didn't have late classes today."

"This is not good." He hissed out a breath, turned on his heel and yanked a glass out of a cupboard. He filled it with cold water from the tap, considered splashing it in his face, then gulped it down instead. It didn't do much in the way of cooling him off, but it was a start. "This wouldn't have happened if you hadn't ticked me off."

"Ticked you off?" She wanted to smooth down all that streaky hair she'd mussed. Then she wanted to muss it all again. "About what?"

"Then you get me to touch you and you start making sex noises."

The hell with coffee, she decided, she wanted a drink. "Those weren't *sex* noises." She wrenched open the fridge, took out a bottle of white wine. "Those were muscle relief noises, which, I suppose, could amount to roughly the same thing. Get me down a damn wineglass, because now *I'm* ticked off."

"You?" He slammed open another cupboard, plucked out a simple stemmed glass, shoved it at her. "You go traipsing off to New York for a damn week. Don't tell anybody where you are."

"I beg your pardon." Her voice cut like ice. "Both my parents knew exactly where I was." She poured the wine, slammed the bottle down on the counter. "I was unaware I was required to check my schedule with you."

"You hired me to do a job, didn't you? A big, complicated job which you stated—clearly—you intended to be involved in, step by step. It so happens several steps have been taken during this week while you pulled your vanishing act."

"It couldn't be helped." She took a long sip of wine and tried to find the control button on her temper. "If you'd had any problems, any questions, either my mother or father could have put you in touch with me. Why didn't you ask them?"

"Because…" There had to be a reason. "My clients are usually old enough to leave me a contact number and not expect me to hunt them down through their parents."

"That's lame, O'Connell," she said, though the statement stung a bit. "However, in the future, you are directed to consult with either of my parents should you not be able to contact me. All right?"

"Fine." He jammed his hands into his pockets. "Dandy."

"And keen," she finished. It was a ridiculous argument, she decided. And though she didn't mind a good fight, she did object to being ridiculous. "Listen, I had to go to New York. When I left the company, I gave the director my word that should I be needed, and it was possible, I would fill in. I keep my word. Several of the dancers, including principals, were wiped out with the flu. We dance hurt, we dance sick, but sometimes you just can't pull it off. I gave him a week. Eight performances, while sick dancers recovered—and a couple more dropped."

She leaned back against the counter to take the weight off her legs. "My partner and I were unfamiliar with each other, which meant long, intense rehearsals. I haven't danced professionally in nearly three months. I was out of shape, so I took some extra morning classes. This didn't leave me a lot of time or energy to worry about a project I assumed was in capable hands. It didn't occur to me you'd need to reach me this early in the project, after we'd just spoken. I hope that clears things up for you."

"Yeah, that clears it up. Can I borrow a knife?"

"What?"

"You don't have a gun handy, but I can use a knife to slit my throat."

"Why don't you wait until you get home?" She sipped her wine again, watching him over the rim. "My mother hates blood on the kitchen floor."

"Your father probably doesn't like his daughter having sex on the kitchen table, either."

"I don't know. The subject's never come up before."

"I didn't mean to grab you that way."

"Really." She held out her glass. "Which way did you mean to grab me?"

"Not." With a shrug he took the wine from her hand,

sampled it. "You can see this is already getting complicated and jumbled up. The job, you, me. Sex."

"I'm very good at organizing and compartmentalizing. Some consider it one of my best—and most annoying—skills."

"Yeah, I bet." He handed her back the glass. "Kate."

She smiled. "Brody."

He laughed a little, and with his hands back in his pockets, roamed the room. "I've done a lot of screwing up in my life. With Connie—my wife—and Jack. I worked really hard to change that. Jack's only six. I'm all he's got. I can't put anything ahead of that."

"If you could, I'd think a great deal less of you. If you could, I wouldn't be attracted to you."

He turned back, studying her face. "I can't figure you."

"Maybe you should see if you can organize your schedule, so you can spend a little time on that problem?"

"Maybe we should just rent a motel room on Route 81 some afternoon and pretend there isn't a problem."

To his surprise, she laughed. "Well, that's another alternative. Personally, I'd like to do both. Why don't I leave it up to you, for the moment, as to which part of the solution we approach first?"

"Why don't we…" He glanced at the clock on the stove, swore. "I've got to go pick up Jack. Maybe you could come down to the job tomorrow at lunchtime. I'll buy you a sandwich and show you what we're doing."

"I'll do that." She tilted her head. "Want to kiss me goodbye?"

He glanced at the kitchen table, back at her. "Better not. Your father might have a weapon in the house you don't know about."

Spencer Kimball wasn't loading a shotgun. Kate found him in his studio going over his lesson plans for the current semester. He'd been going over the same page for the last ten minutes.

She crossed to where he sat at his desk looking out the window. She set a cup of coffee at his elbow, then wrapped her arms around him and propped her chin on his shoulder. "Hi."

"Hi. Thanks."

She rubbed her cheek against his and studied his view of their pretty backyard. She would ask her mother to help her plan the gardens for the school.

"Brody seems to be concerned you may shoot him."

"I don't have a gun."

"That's what I said. I also told him that my father knows I've kissed men. You do know that, don't you, Daddy?"

She only called him Daddy when she was trying to charm him. They both knew it. "What I know intellectually is a far cry from walking in on... He had his hands on your..." Spencer set his teeth. "He had his hands on my little girl."

"Your little girl had her hands on him, too." She scooted around, wiggled into her father's lap.

"I hardly think the kitchen is the proper place for you to..." What? Exactly what?

"You're right, of course." She made her voice very prim, very proper. "The kitchen is for cooking. I've certainly never seen you and Mama kissing in the kitchen. I'd have been horrified."

His lips wanted to twitch, but he overcame the urge. "Shut up."

"I always knew, if I happened to walk into the room and you and Mama *appeared* to be kissing, you were really practicing lifesaving techniques. Can't be too careful."

"You're going to need lifesaving techniques in a minute."

"Until then, let me ask you this. Do you like Brody, as a man?"

"Yes, of course, but that doesn't mean I'm going to do handsprings of joy when I walk into my kitchen and see…what I saw."

"Well, there's a possibility of a motel room on Route 81 in my future."

"Ah." Spencer dropped his forehead to hers. "Kate."

"You and Mom taught me I never had to hide anything from you. My feelings, my actions. I have feelings for Brody. I'm not completely sure what those feelings entail, but my actions are going to reflect them."

"Your actions have always reflected your feelings, with a stiff dose of logic tossed in."

"This won't be any different."

"What about his feelings?"

"He doesn't know. We'll figure it out."

"Doesn't know?" His eyes, so like hers, went to

smoky slits. "Well, the boy better make up his mind in a hurry, or—"

"*Oooh,* Daddy." Kate blinked rapidly, shivered. "Are you going to go beat him up for me? Can I watch?"

"*Really* going to need those lifesaving techniques," Spencer muttered.

"I love you." She pressed a kiss to his cheek. "You raised a child, on your own, for a number of years. You know what it means when you do that, when you love the child, when you're committed to the child."

His Freddie. His first baby, now with babies of her own. "Yes, I do."

"How could I not be attracted to that part of him, Daddy, that I love so much in you?"

"And how am I supposed to argue with that?" He cuddled her closer, sighed. "You can tell Brody I don't plan to buy a gun. Yet."

She went down for lunch the next day. Then made a habit of dropping by, taking pastries and coffee, subs or sandwiches, to Brody and his crew.

Some might have called it a bribe. In fact, Brody called it exactly that, as the offerings tended to make his men more cooperative when Kate skewered them with questions, or asked for changes to the original plan.

It didn't stop him from anticipating her visits, or gauging his time so he could spare twenty minutes or a half hour to walk with her around town, or share a cup of coffee with her in the little café up the street.

He knew his men were wiggling their eyebrows or

giving each other elbow nudges whenever he walked off with Kate. But since he'd gone to high school with most of them, he took it in the spirit it was meant.

And if he caught one of them, occasionally, checking out her butt or her legs, it only took one hard stare to have that individual getting busy elsewhere.

He still couldn't figure her. She sauntered down to the job looking, always, like something clipped from the glossy pages of a magazine. Perfect and female. But she poked around the dust and grime of the site as if she were one of the crew, asking pointed questions about things like the wiring.

He'd come across her having a heated debate with one of his men over baseball. And an hour later, he overheard her on her cell phone, chatting away in precise and fluent French.

No, after two weeks of this easy routine, he still couldn't figure her. But neither could he stop thinking about her.

Now, as she wandered the main studio, he couldn't stop looking at her.

She wore some soft sweater in deep blue over gray leggings. Her hair was bundled up in some fascinating way that left her nape bare and sexy.

The room was warm thanks to the new heating system. The plaster work was well underway, and he'd brought in the first samples of the woodwork he had molded himself to match the original.

His father had left only a short time before, after putting in six hours on plumbing. A difficult and tense six hours, Brody thought now. It was a pleasure to put that aside and look at Kate.

"The plasterer's doing a great job," she said after touring the walls. "I almost feel guilty that we're going to cover so much up with mirrors."

"Your glass is on order. It'll be in middle of February."

She picked up the sample of woodwork. "This is beautiful, Brody. You'll never be able to tell it from the original."

"That's the idea."

"Yes, it is." She set the wood down again. "You're moving along, right on schedule. Jobwise. But…" She started toward him. "In the personal department, you're lagging."

"Takes a while to lay the groundwork."

"Depends what you're planning on building, Brody." She laid her hands on his shoulder. "I want a date."

"We had lunch."

"A grown-up date. The sort reasonable, unattached adults indulge in from time to time. Dinner, O'Connell. Maybe a movie. You may not be aware, but many restaurants stay open after the lunch shift."

"I've heard that. Look, Kate." He backed up, but she moved forward with him. "There's Jack, and school nights, and complications."

"Yes, there's Jack. I enjoy spending time with him, but I'd like a little one-on-one with Jack's father. I don't think your son will be scarred for life if you go out one evening. In fact, here's what we're going to do. You, me, Friday night. Dinner. I'll make the arrangements.

Pick me up at seven. You, me, Jack, Saturday afternoon. Movies. My treat. I'll pick you both up at one. Settled."

"It's not that simple. There's the whole babysitter deal. I don't know who I'd—"

He turned, desperately relieved when the door jangled open.

"Dad!" And the man of the hour shot in like a bullet. "We saw your truck, so Mrs. Skully said we could stop. Hi, Kate." He dumped his Star Wars backpack on the floor, grinned. "Listen, it echoes. Hi, Kate!"

She had to laugh, and even before Brody could, scooped Jack off his feet. "Hi, Handsome Jack. Ready to kiss me?"

"Nah." But it was obvious he was half hoping she'd kiss him again.

"That's a real problem with the men in your family." She put him on his feet as a woman, a boy and a girl came through the door. The woman blew spiky bangs out of her eyes.

"Brody, saw your truck. I thought I'd drop Jack off, save you a trip. Unless you want me to take him home awhile yet."

"No, this is great, thanks. Ah, Beth Skully, Kate Kimball."

"Kate and I sort of know each other. Rod, no running in here. You probably don't remember me," she continued without missing a beat. "My sister JoBeth was friends with your sister, Freddie."

"JoBeth, of course. How is she?"

"She's great. She and her family live in Michigan.

She's a nurse-practitioner. I hope you don't mind me dropping in with the troops this way. I've been wondering what you're doing in this old place."

"Mom." The little girl, blonde and big-eyed tugged on sleeve.

"All right, Carrie, just a minute."

"I'll give you a tour," Kate offered. "If you can stand it."

"Actually, I'd love it, but we're still on the run. Having kids turns you into a bus driver. I guess you don't know, right yet, when you'll be opening your dance school?"

"I hope to start taking afternoon and evening students in April." She glanced down at Carrie, recognized the hope in those big eyes. "Are you interested in ballet, Carrie?"

"I want to be a ballerina."

"Ballerinas are sissies." Her brother sneered.

"Mom!" Carrie wailed.

"Rod, you just hush. I'm sorry about my little moron here, Kate."

"No, don't apologize. Sissies?" she said, turning to Rod, who looked pleased with himself.

"Yeah, uh-huh, 'cause they wear dopey clothes and go around like this." Rod boosted himself on tiptoe and took several small, rather mincing steps.

The result had his sister wailing for her mother yet again.

Before Beth could speak, Kate smiled and shook her head. "That's interesting. How many sissies do you know who can do this?"

Kate brought her leg up, braced a hand on her thigh and bringing her leg tight against the side of her body, pointed her toe at the ceiling.

Oh, my God, was the single thought that tumbled around in Brody's mind.

"Bet I can." Challenged, Rod grabbed his ankle, tried to pull his leg up, lost his balance and tumbled onto his butt.

"Rod, you'll snap yourself like a turkey wishbone," his mother warned, and with an arm around Carrie's shoulder smiled at Kate. "Doesn't that hurt?"

"Only if you think about it." She lowered her foot to the floor. "How old are you, Carrie?"

"I'm five. I can touch my toes."

Five, Kate thought. The bones were still soft. The body still able to learn to do the unnatural. "If you and your mama decide you should come to my school next spring, I'll teach you to dance. And you'll show your brother that ballet isn't for sissies."

She winked at Carrie, then let her body flow back into a smooth back-bend. She kicked her legs gracefully to the ceiling, held there a moment, then simply flowed upright again.

"Wow," Rod whispered to Jack. "She's cool."

Brody said nothing. Saliva had pooled in his mouth.

"Ballet is for athletes." Tossing back her hair, she angled her head at Rod. "A number of professional football players take rudimentary ballet, to help them move fast and smooth on the field."

"No way," Rod said.

"Way. Come with your sister a few times, Rod. I'll show you."

"Now, that's asking for a headache." With a laugh, Beth signaled her son. "Come on, trouble."

Brody slapped himself out of a particularly detailed fantasy that involved that stupendously flexible body. "Thanks for seeing to Jack, Beth."

"Oh, you know it's no bother. Happy to have old Jack anytime."

"Really?" Kate murmured, sending Brody a long look.

"Sure, he's..." Beth shifted her eyes between Brody and Kate, then bit down on a grin. Well, well, well. It was about damn time the man started looking past his nose. "He's a pure pleasure," Beth went on. "In fact, I was thinking about cooking up a big pot of spaghetti one night this week and seeing if Jack wanted to have dinner with Rod."

"Friday's a great night for spaghetti," Kate said sweetly. "Don't you think, Brody?"

"I don't know. I—"

"You know, Friday's just perfect." Thrilled to help Kate execute the squeeze play, Beth nudged her kids to the door. "We'll count on that then. Jack'll just come over after school, and stay for dinner. He and the kids can watch a video after. Maybe you should plan on him spending the night. That'll work out. Just send him to school Friday with a change of clothes. Nice to see you again, Kate."

"Very nice seeing you."

"I get to have a sleepover at Rod's." Thrilled, Jack plopped down to do some somersaults. "Thanks, Dad."

"Yeah." Kate trailed a finger down Brody's chest, chuckled at his shell-shocked expression. "Thanks, Dad."

Chapter 6

Friday was not turning out to be a terrific cap to the work week. One of his men called in sick, felled by the flu that was gleefully making the rounds. Brody sent another man home at noon who was too sick to be out of bed much less swinging a hammer.

Since the other half of his four-man crew was finishing up a trim job across the river in Maryland, that left Brody to deal with the plumbing inspector, to hang the drywall for the partition between Kate's office and the school's kitchen, and to finish stripping the woodwork in those two areas.

Most of all, and most stressful, was that it left him alone on the job with his father for the best part of the day.

Bob O'Connell was under the sink to his waist. His ancient work boots had had their soles glued back in place countless times. He'd staple them back on, Brody thought, before he'd spring for another pair.

Don't need what I don't need, the old man would say. About every damn thing.

His business, his way, Brody reminded himself and wished he could stop digging up reasons to be resentful.

They rubbed each other raw. Always had.

Bob clanged pipes. Brody measured drywall.

"Turn that damn noise off," Bob ordered. "How's a man supposed to work with that crap ringing in his ears?"

Saying nothing, Brody stepped over and snapped off the portable stereo. Whatever music he'd listened to was considered noise to his father's ear.

Bob swore and muttered while he worked. Which was, Brody thought, exactly why he'd had the music on.

"Damn stupid idea, cutting this kitchen up this-a-way. Waste of time and money. Office space, my ass. What's anybody need office space for to teach a buncha twinkle-toes?"

Brody had put off working on the kitchen side of the partition as long as possible. Now he hefted the drywall section he'd measured and cut, set it into place. "I've got the time," he said and plucked a drywall nail out of his pouch. "The client's got the money."

"Yeah, the Kimballs got plenty of money. No point in tossing it away, though, is there? You shoulda oughta told her she's making a mistake sectioning this kitchen off."

Brody hammered wall to stud. Told himself to keep his mouth shut. But the words just wouldn't stay down. "I don't think she's making a mistake. She doesn't need a kitchen this size down here. It was designed to cook up bar food. What's a dance school going to do with a small restaurant kitchen?"

"Dance school." Bob made a sound of disgust. "Open and close inside a month. Then how's she going to sell this place all cut up like this? Kid-height sinks in the bathrooms. Just have to pull them out again. Surprised the plumbing inspector didn't bust his gut laughing at the rough-in."

"When you teach kids, you have to have accommodations for kids."

"We got the elementary school for that, don't we?"

"Last I heard they weren't teaching ballet at the elementary school."

"Ought to tell you something," Bob muttered, rankled by his son's tone.

Bob told himself to keep his mouth shut, to mind his own business. But, like Brody, the words just wouldn't stay down. "You're supposed to do more than take a customer's money, boy. You're supposed to know enough to point them in the right direction."

"As long as it's your direction."

Bob wormed out from under the sink. His faded blue gimme cap sat askew on a head topped with short, grizzled gray hair. His face was square and lined deep. It had once been sternly handsome. His eyes were as green as his son's.

At times they seemed to be the only thing father and son shared.

"You want to watch that mouth of yours, boy."

"Ever think about watching yours?" Brody felt the band tightening around his head. A temper headache. A Bob O'Connell headache.

Bob tossed down his wrench, got to his feet. He was a big man, but had never run to fat. Even at sixty he was mostly muscle and grit. "When you got the years I got of living and working in the trade, you can say your piece as you please."

"Really." Brody muscled another sheet of drywall onto the sawhorses, marked his measuring cuts. "You've been saying the same damn thing to me since I was eight. I'd say I've got enough years behind me by now. This is my job—sited, designed, bid and contracted. It goes the way I say it goes."

He picked up his scoring knife, lifted his gaze to meet his father's. "The client gets what the client wants. And as long as she's satisfied there's nothing to discuss."

"From what I hear you're doing a lot more than satisfying your client on the job."

He hadn't meant to say that. Holy God, he hadn't meant to say that. But the words were out. Damn it, the boy always riled him so.

Brody's hand clenched on the knife. For a moment, too long a moment, he wanted to punch his fist into that hard, unyielding face. "What's between me and Kate Kimball is my business."

"I live in this town, too, and so does your ma. People talk about my blood, it washes over on me. You got a kid to raise, and no business running around with some fancy woman stirring gossip."

"Don't you bring Jack into this. Don't bring my son into this."

"Jack's my kin, too. Nothing's going to change that. You kept him down in the city all that time so you could do your running around and God knows, but you're here now. My home. I'm not having you shame me and that boy in my own front yard."

Running around, Brody thought. To doctors, hospitals, specialists. Then running around, trying to outrace your own grief and do what was right for a motherless two-year-old.

"You don't know anything about me. What I've done, what I do. What I am." Determined to hold his temper, he began to score the drywall along his mark. "But you've sure always managed to find the worst of it and rub it in my face."

"If I'd've rubbed it harder, maybe you wouldn't be raising a kid without his ma."

Brody's hand jerked on the knife, bore down and sliced it over his own hand.

Bob let out an oath over the bright gush of blood and grabbed for his bandanna. His shocked concern came out in hot disapproval. "Don't you know better'n to watch what you're doing with tools?"

"Get the hell away from me." Clamping a hand over the gash, Brody stepped back. He couldn't trust himself now. Wasn't sure what he might do. "Get your tools and get off my job."

"You get on out in my truck. You're gonna need stitches."

"I said get off my job. You're fired." The rapid beat of his own heart pumped blood through his fingers. "Pack up your tools and get out."

Shame warred with fury as Bob slammed his wrenches into his kit. "We got nothing to say to each other, from here on." He hauled up his tools and stalked out.

"We never did," Brody murmured.

Brody O'Connell was going to get an earful. If he ever showed up. He was going to learn, very shortly, that seven o'clock meant seven o'clock. Not seven-thirty.

She was sorry she'd convinced her parents to have an evening out. Now she had no one to complain to. She prowled the living room, glared at the phone.

No, she would not call him again. She'd called at seven-twenty and had gotten nothing but the annoyance of his answering machine.

She had a message for him, all right. But she was going to deliver it in person.

And when she thought of the trouble she'd gone to for tonight. Selecting just the right restaurant, the perfect dress. Now they'd be lucky to keep their reservation. No, she was canceling the reservation, and right this minute. If he thought she'd waltz out to dinner with a man who didn't have the common courtesy to be on time, he was very much mistaken.

She reached for the phone just as the doorbell rang. Kate squared her shoulders, lifted her chin to its haughtiest angle and took her sweet time going to the door.

"I'm late. I'm sorry. I got hung up, and should have called."

The icy words she'd planned went right out of her head. Not discourtesy, she realized after one look at his face. Upheaval. "Is something wrong with Jack?"

"No, no, he's fine. I just checked. I'm sorry, Kate." He lifted a hand in flustered apology. "Maybe we can do this another time."

"What did you do to your hand?" She grabbed it by the wrist. She could see the white gauze and bandage and the faint stain of antiseptic at the edges.

"Just stupidity. It's nothing really. A couple stitches. The ER was slow, and I got hung up."

"Are you in pain?"

"No, it's nothing," he insisted. "Nothing."

Oh, yes, she decided. It was something—and more than a physical injury. "Go home," she told him. "I'll be there in thirty minutes."

"What?"

"With dinner. We'll do the restaurant part some other time."

"Kate, you don't have to do this."

"Brody." She cupped his face in her hands. Oh, you poor thing, she thought. "Go home, and I'll be right along. Scram," she ordered when he still didn't move. And shut the door in his face.

She was, as always, precisely on time. When he opened the door, she breezed by him, hauling a huge hamper. "You're going to have a steak," she announced. "Lucky for you my parents had one thawing out in the fridge before I convinced them to go out for a romantic dinner."

She headed straight back to the kitchen as she spoke, and setting the hamper on the counter, shrugged out of her coat, then began to unpack. "Can you open the wine, or will your hand give you trouble?"

"I can handle it." He took the coat—it smelled of her—and hung it on one of the kitchen pegs. It didn't belong there, he thought, looking all female and smooth next to his ancient work jacket.

She didn't belong there, he decided, looking amazing in some little blue number that looked like it might have been painted on by some creative artist who'd been delightfully minimalist and stingy with the brush.

"Look, Kate—"

"Here."

He took the bottle, the corkscrew she held out. "Kate. Why? Why are you doing this?"

"Because I like you." She took two enormous potatoes to the sink to scrub. "And because you looked like you could use a steak dinner."

"How many men fall on their face in love with you?"

She smiled over her shoulder. "All of them. Open the wine, O'Connell."

"Yeah."

He put on music, fiddling with the radio dial until he found the classical he thought she'd like. He dug out the good dishes he hadn't seen in months and set them on

the trestle table in the formal dining room where he and
Jack had their celebratory meals.

He had candles—for emergency power outages. But
nothing fancy and slick. He debated just plunking them
down on the table anyway, then decided they'd just look
pitiful.

When he came back in the kitchen, she was putting
a salad together—and there were two white tapers in
simple glass holders on the counter.

She didn't miss a trick, he decided.

"You know you have a severe deficiency of fresh vegetables in your crisper."

"I buy those salad things that are all made up and
in a bag. Then you just, you know, dump it in a bowl."

"Lazy," she said and made him smile.

"Efficient." Because her hands were full, he picked
up her wine, lifted it to her lips.

"Thanks." She sipped, watching him. "Very nice."

He set the glass down, and after a moment's hesitation, lowered his head to touch his lips to hers.

"Mmm." She touched her tongue to her top lip. "Even
better. And, since you're injured, you're allowed to sit
down and relax while I finish this. You'll have time to
call and check on Jack one more time before dinner."

He winced. "Shows, huh."

"It looks good on you. Tell him I said hi, and I'll see
him tomorrow."

"You really want to do that? The movie thing?"

"I do things I don't want, but I never volunteer to do

them. Go call your boy. You're getting your steak medium rare in fifteen minutes."

She liked fussing with the meal. Liked fussing over him. Maybe it was because he so clearly didn't expect it, and was so appreciative of the little things other people tended to take for granted.

And though she'd never considered herself a nurturer, it made her feel good to be needed.

She waited until they were at the table, until he was well into his meal and on his second glass of wine. "Tell me what happened."

"Just a lousy day. What did you do with these potatoes? They're amazing."

"Secret Ukrainian recipe," she told him in a thick and exaggerated accent. "If I tell you, then I must kill you."

"I couldn't do it anyway. My kitchen wizardry with potatoes ends with my poking a few holes into one and tossing it into the mike. You speak Ukrainian? I heard you speaking French the other day."

"Yes, I speak Ukrainian, more or less. I also speak and understand English very well. So talk to me, Brody. What happened in your lousy day?"

"One thing, then the other." He moved his shoulders. "I got two guys out sick—your ballet flu's making an appearance in West Virginia. Since I had the rest of the crew on another job, it left me pretty shorthanded. Then I mistook my own hand for a sheet of drywall, bled all over the damn place, fired my father and spent a couple hours waiting to get sewn back together in the ER."

"You had a fight with your father." She laid a hand over his uninjured one. "I'm sorry."

"We don't get along—never have."

"But you hired him."

"He's a good plumber."

He slid his hand out from under hers, reached for his glass. "Brody."

"Yeah, I hired him. It was a mistake. It's tolerable when the other guys are around, but when it's just the two of us like it was today, it's asking for trouble. I'm a screwup, always was, always will be. The job's not being done right, my life isn't being done right. I'm chasing around after a fancy woman instead of seeing to my own."

"Now I'm a fancy woman?"

Brody pressed his fingers to his eyes. "I'm sorry. That was stupid, and typical. Once I start on him, I can't seem to stop."

"It's all right. I don't mind being a fancy woman." She stabbed a bite of steak. Her temper was on slow burn, but a rant wasn't what Brody needed right now. "He's probably as miserable and frustrated about what happened as you are. He doesn't know how to talk to you any more than you know how to talk to him. But that's not your fault. I hope you can make it up with him, in your own way."

"He doesn't see me."

Her heart broke for him. "Honey, that's not your fault, either. I wanted my parents to be proud of me, maybe wanted it too much, so I worked, sometimes brutally hard, to be sure they would. That wasn't their fault."

"My family's not like yours."

"Few are. But you're wrong. You and Jack—the family you've made—it's a lot like mine. Maybe, Brody, your father sees that, and wonders why he never made that connection with his own son."

"I was a screwup."

"No, you weren't. You were a work-in-progress."

"Really rough work. I couldn't wait to get through— to get through high school, to get through my eighteenth birthday. To get through so I could get out. That's what I did, on my eighteenth birthday. I packed up and headed down to D.C. Had about five hundred dollars, no job, no nothing. But I was out of there."

"And you made it work."

"I lived by the skin of my teeth for three years. Working construction, blowing my pay on beer and…fancy women," he said with a sudden grin. "Then I was twenty-one, broke, careless, stupid. And I met Connie. I was on the crew doing some work on her parents' guest house. I hit on her, and much to my surprise we started seeing each other."

"Why to your surprise?"

"She was a college girl—conservative daughter of a conservative family. She had money and class, education, style. I was the next step up from a bum."

She studied him. Strong face, she thought. Strong hands. Strong mind. "Obviously she didn't think so."

"No, she didn't. She was the first person who ever told

me I had potential. Who ever believed in me. She made me believe in myself, made me want to, so I could be what she saw when she looked at me. I stopped screwing up, and I started to grow up. You don't want to hear this."

"Yes, I do." To keep him talking, she topped off his wine. "Did she help you start your business?"

"That came later." He'd never talked about this with anyone, Brody realized. Not his parents, not his friends, not even Jack. "I was good with my hands, and I had a good eye for building. I had a strong back. I'd just never put them all to use at the same time. Then I figured out I liked myself a whole lot better when I did."

"Of course, because then you respected yourself."

"Yeah." Nail on the head, he thought. Did she ever miss? "Still, I was skilled labor, not a doctor or a lawyer or a business exec. Her parents objected to me—strongly."

She toyed with her potatoes, much more interested in what he told her than in the meal. "Then they were shortsighted. Connie wasn't."

"It wasn't easy for her to buck them, but she did. She was going to Georgetown, studying law. I was working full days and going to school at night, taking business classes. We started making plans. Couple of years down the road, we'd get married. She'd stay in school till she passed the bar, then I'd start my own business. Then she got pregnant."

He studied his wineglass, turned it around and around, but didn't lift it to drink. "We both wanted the baby. She more than me at first, because the whole thing didn't seem real to me. We got married. She kept up with her studies, and I took some extra jobs. Her parents were furious. This was what she got for throwing herself away on somebody like me. They cut her off, and that twisted her up pretty bad."

She could imagine it very well, because, she thought, she'd always had just the opposite in terms of a family that was there for her. "They didn't deserve her."

Brody lifted his eyes, met Kate's. "Damn right they didn't. The rougher it got, the more we dug in. We made it work. She made it work. A thousand times I panicked, and some of those thousand times I saw myself walking away. She'd go back to her parents, and everyone would be better off."

"But you didn't. You stuck."

"She loved me," he said simply. "The day Jack was born, I was in the delivery room, wanting to be pretty much anywhere else in the world. But she wanted me there, it was really important to her. So I pretended I wanted to be there, too. All I could think was get this over with, get this the hell over with because it's too hard. Nobody should have to do this. Then…there was Jack. This little, squirmy person. Everything changed. Everything clicked. I never knew you could love like that, in an instant, in a heartbeat, so it was everything. Every damn thing. I wanted, had to be, whatever he needed me to be. They made a man out of me, right there, in that moment. Connie and Jack made me."

Tears were flooding her cheeks, continued to spill over. She couldn't stop them, and didn't try.

"I'm sorry." He lifted his hands, let them fall again. "I don't know what got into me."

"No." She shook her head, could say nothing else quite yet. You stupid idiot, she thought. You've gone and made me fall in love with you. Now what? "That was lovely," she managed to say. "Just give me a minute." She got to her feet, and dashed off to the bathroom to compose herself.

As an alternative to banging his head on the table, Brody got up and paced. He'd come to the same conclusion as Kate—he was an idiot—but for different reasons. He'd taken her very nice gesture of a casual meal at home, one he imagined was supposed to be at least marginally romantic, and he'd turned it into a marathon on his troubles and his past.

He'd made her cry.

Great going, O'Connell, he thought in disgust. Maybe you can round on the evening by talking about how your dog died when you were ten. That would really jazz things up.

He imagined she'd want to take off as soon as possible, so began to clear the table to give her a way out.

"Sorry," he began when he heard the light click of her footsteps. "I'm an imbecile, dumping all that on you. I'll take care of this, and you can…"

He trailed off, froze, when her arms slid lightly around him and her head rested on his back.

"O'Connell, I come from strong Slavic blood. Strong and sentimental. We like to cry. Did you know my grandparents escaped from the Soviet Union when my mother was a child? My aunt Rachel is the only one who was born here in America. They went on foot, with three babies, over the mountains into Hungary."

"No, I didn't know that." He turned, cautiously, until he was facing her.

"They were cold and hungry and frightened. And when they came to America, a strange country with a strange language and strange customs, they were poor and they were alone. But they wanted something enough to fight for it, to make it work. I've heard the story dozens of times. It always makes me cry. It always makes me proud."

She turned away to stack dishes.

"Why are you telling me this?"

"Courage comes in different forms, Brody. There's strength—that's the muscle. But love's the heart. When you put them together, you can do anything. That's worth a few sentimental tears."

"You know, I figured this was the kind of day you just crossed off your list, but you've changed that."

"Well, thank you. Tell you what. We'll deal with these dishes, then you can dance with me." Time to lighten things up, she decided. "The way a man dances tells me a lot, and I haven't tested you out in that area yet."

He took the dishes out of her hands. "Let's dance now."

"Can't. Call it a character flaw, but if I don't tidy up first, I'll keep seeing unwashed dishes in my head."

He set them aside, took her hands to draw her out of the room. "That's anal."

"No, it's organized. Organized people get more done and have less headaches." She looked over her shoulder as he tugged her toward the living room. "Really, it'll only take a few minutes."

"It'll only take a few minutes later, too." Maybe he was rusty in the romance department, but he still remembered a few moves.

"Here's what we'll do. You pick out the music while I clear up the dishes."

He laughed and pulled her into the living room. "You really are compulsive." He switched the stereo to CD. "Funny, I was listening to this last night. And thinking about you."

"Oh?" The music flowed out, slow and sultry. A sexy little shuffle that spoke to the blood.

"Must've been fate," he said and slid her into his arms.

Her heart jerked once. "I'm a strong believer in fate." She ordered herself to relax, then realized she already was. Snugged up against him, moving with him, her heels making it easy—almost mandatory—to rest her cheek on his.

"Very smooth, O'Connell," she murmured. "Major points for smooth."

"Like you said, some things come back to you." He spun her out, made her laugh. Spun her back and had her breath catching.

"Nice move." Oh-oh. Oh-oh. It was getting hard to think. She'd come to the conclusion when she'd dealt with her tears that she really needed to do some serious thinking about Brody, and where this was all going.

She couldn't drive this train if she didn't have her wits about her.

She hadn't expected him to dance quite so well. If he'd fumbled a bit, she could have taken charge. Kept her balance. There were entirely too many things that were unexpected about him. And fascinating. And oh, it felt wonderful to glide around the room in his arms.

Her hair smelled fabulous. He'd nearly forgotten all the mysterious and alluring facets there were to a woman. The shape, the softness, the scents. Nearly forgotten the sensation of moving with one, slow and close. The images it had winding through a man's mind.

His lips brushed over her hair, trailed along her cheek, found hers.

She sighed into the kiss, wallowing in the sensation of her bones melting. So when the song ended and the next began, they just stood swaying together.

"That was perfect." Her mind was foggy, her heartbeat thick. And the needs she'd thought she had under control were tumbling in her belly. "I should go."

"Why?"

"Because." She lifted a hand to his cheek, eased away, just a little. "It's bad timing. Tonight you needed a friend."

"You're right." His hands slid down her arms until their fingers lightly linked. "The timing's probably off. The smart thing is to take this slow."

"I believe in doing the smart thing."

"Yeah." He walked her toward the doorway. "I've been

careful to try to do the smart thing for quite a while myself."

He paused, turned her back to face him. "I did need a friend tonight. Do need one," he added, drawing her a little closer. "And I need you, Kate. Stay with me."

He lowered his head, kept his eyes on hers when their lips brushed. "Be with me."

Chapter 7

The walls of his room were unfinished. A coil of electrical wire sat on a drywall compound bucket that stood in the corner. There were no curtains at his windows. He'd removed the closet doors, and they were currently in his shop waiting to be planed and refinished.

The floors were a wonderful random-width oak under years of dull, dark varnish. Sanding them down, sealing them clear, was down on the list of projects—far down.

The bed had been an impulse buy. The old iron headboard with its slim, straight bars had appealed to him. But he'd yet to think about linens, and habitually tossed a mismatched quilt over the sheets and considered the job done.

It wouldn't be what she was used to. Trying to see it through her eyes, Brody winced. "Not exactly the Taj Mahal."

"Another work in progress." She roamed the room, grateful to have a minute to settle the nerves she hadn't expected to feel. "It's a lovely space." She ran her fingers over the low windowsill he'd stripped down to its natural pine. "I know potential when I see it," she said, and turned back to him.

"I wanted to finish Jack's room first. Then it made more sense to work on the kitchen and the living areas. I don't do anything but sleep here. Up till now."

A quick thrill spurted through her. She was the first woman he'd brought to this room, to this bed. "It's going to be lovely." She walked to him as she spoke, every pulse point hammering. "Will you use the fireplace in here?"

"I use it now. It's a good heat source. I thought about putting in an insert, for efficiency, but…" What the hell was he doing? Talking about heat sources and inserts when he had the most beautiful woman in the world in his bedroom?

"It wouldn't be as charming," she finished, and with her eyes on his began unbuttoning his shirt.

"No. Do you want me to start a fire?"

"Later. Yes, I think that would be lovely, later. But for now, I have a feeling we can generate enough heat on our own."

"Kate." He curled his fingers around her wrists, and wondered that the need pumping through him didn't burn through the tips and singe her flesh. "If I fumble a little, blame it on this, okay?" He turned his injured hand.

He was nervous, too, she realized. Good. That put

them back on even ground. "I bet a man as clever with his hands as you can manage a zipper, no matter what the handicap." She turned, lifted her hair. "Why don't we see?"

"Yeah. Why don't we?"

He drew it down slowly, exposing pale gold skin inch by inch. The curve of her neck and shoulder enticed him, so he lowered his head, brushed his lips just there. When she shivered, arched, he indulged himself, nibbling along her spine, her shoulder blades.

When he turned her to face him, her breath had already quickened.

His mouth cruised over hers, a long, luxurious savoring that liquefied the bones. And while he savored, his hands roamed lightly over her face, into her hair, down her back as if she were some exotic delicacy to be enjoyed slowly. Thoroughly.

She'd expected a repeat of the blast of passion that had exploded between them in her mother's kitchen. And was undone by the tenderness.

"Tell me…" He nibbled his way across her jaw. "If there's something you don't like."

Her head fell back, inviting him to explore the exposed line of her throat. "I don't think that's going to be an issue."

His hands, strong, patient, skimmed up her sides to the shoulders of her dress. "I've imagined touching you. Driven myself crazy imagining it."

"You're doing a pretty good job of driving me crazy now." She pushed the flannel shirt aside, reached out to tug the thermal shirt he wore beneath it out of the waistband of his jeans, sliding over the hard muscles of his stomach.

But he eased her back. It had been a long time since he'd been with a woman. He had no intention of rushing it.

He brought her hands to his lips, kissed her fingers, her palms. And felt her pulse leap, then go thick.

"Let me do this," he murmured. He nudged the dress from her shoulders, watched it slide down her body to the floor.

She was so slender, so finely built a man could forget those tensile muscles beneath all that silky gold-dust skin. Her curves were subtle—a sleek female elegance that fascinated *and* demanded his touch.

Her breath snagged in her throat when he skimmed his fingertips along the curve of her breast, along the lace edging of her bra, then under it as if memorizing shape and texture. The hard pad of callus brushed her nipple and turned her knees to jelly.

Intrigued by her tremble, he shifted his gaze back to her face, watched her as his hands roamed down her torso, along her hips, stroked up her thighs.

"I think about your legs a lot," he told her, and flirted his fingertips along the top of her stocking. "Ballerina legs, you know?"

"Just don't pay any attention to my feet. Dancers have incredibly unattractive feet."

"Strong," he corrected. "Strong's really sexy to me. Maybe you can show me some of the things you can do later, like you did for Rod that day. I nearly swallowed my tongue."

Though she laughed, her hands were far from steady when she drew the shirt over his head, let her own fingers explore that tough wall of muscle.

"Sure. I can do even more interesting things."

They both quivered when he lifted her and laid her on the bed.

If it had been a dance, she'd have called it a waltz. Slow, circling steps in a match rhythm. The kiss was long and deep, warming the body from the inside out. She sighed into it, into him, and her arms encircled.

This, she thought, dreaming, this was something—someone—she wanted to hold. Love was a quiet miracle that bloomed in her like a rose. And loving, she would give.

Then his mouth was on the curve of her breast, rubbing along that edge of lace. Arousing, inciting, and bringing the first licks of heat toward the warmth. She moaned as his tongue slid over that swell of flesh, teasing the point then tugging on it through the thin barrier of lace. Her hips arched, and her fingers dug into his.

Waltz became tango, slow and hotly sexual.

His mind was full of her, the scents, the textures, the sounds. All of it, all of her seemed to whirl inside his brain, making him dizzy and drunk. She was carved clean as a statue, the long, hot length of her beautifully erotic. He wanted to touch, to taste everything. All of her.

Absorbed with her, he did as he pleased while she

rose and rolled and shuddered with him. And when he took her up the first time, when that lovely body tensed and her breath came and went on a sob, the thrill of it coursed through him like a drug.

More and still more. A little greedier, a little faster. He tugged away those barriers of lace. Now he wanted only flesh. Hot and wet and soft.

She matched him, step for step, rising to him, opening herself. Her mouth found his as they rolled over the quilt, diving heedlessly into the kiss while her hands pleased them both.

As desperation increased, she tugged open the button of his jeans, dragged them impatiently down his hips. "Oh, I love your body. I love what you do to mine. Hurry, hurry. I want—"

Her system erupted; her mind blanked. Even as she went limp, his fingers continued to stroke her. "I want to do more."

He used his mouth. Sliding down her, breast, torso, belly. She began to move again. And then to writhe while pleasure and need pounded together inside her. Her eyes were blind, her body quaking when he rose over her.

With his heart hammering, and his mind crowded with her, he filled her with one long stroke. With a low sound of pleasure he held himself there, sustaining the moment, letting the thrill of it batter his system.

Her hips lifted, then fell away to draw him with her. Beat for beat they moved together, eyes locked, breath tangled and ragged. Her hands groped for his, gripped.

The slide of flesh to flesh, slow and silky, the pulse of heart to heart, solid and real.

And when the wave rose up to swamp them both, he lowered his mouth to hers and completed the joining.

She lay limp as melted wax, eyes closed, lips curved and enjoyed the sensation of Brody collapsed on top of her. His heart continued to knock—hard, fast raps—that told her his system had been as delightfully assaulted as hers.

It had been a wonderful way to discover they were compatible in bed.

It was so fascinating to be in love. Really in love. Not like the couple of times she'd been enchanted with the *idea* of love. This was so unexpected. So intense.

She drew a long, satisfied breath and told herself she'd give the matter—and the consequences of it—a great deal of careful thought later. For the moment, she was going to enjoy it. And him.

No one had ever made her feel quite like this. No one had ever opened her up to so many *feelings*. Fate, she thought. He was hers. She'd known in some secret place inside her, the first instant she'd seen him.

And she was going to make certain he understood, when the time was right, that she was his.

She'd found him, she thought, utterly content as she stroked his back. And she was keeping him.

"For a man who claims to be out of practice, you certainly held your own."

He was trying to decide if he had any brain cells left,

and if so, when they would begin to work again. He managed a grunt. That response seemed to amuse her, as she laughed and locked her arms around him.

He managed to find the energy to turn his head, found his face buried in her hair and decided that was a fine place to be. "Want me to move?"

"No."

"Good. Just give me an elbow if I start to snore."

"O'Connell."

"Just kidding." He lifted his head, levered some of his weight off her and onto his elbows. The green of his eyes was blurry with satisfaction. "You're incredible to look at."

"So are you." She lifted a hand to play with his hair. Not really blond, she thought idly. Not really brown. But a wonderful mix of tones and textures. Like the man himself.

"You know, I wanted you here from the first time I saw you." She lifted her head just enough to bite lightly at his jaw. "Total lust at first sight—that's not usual for me."

"I had pretty much the same reaction. You jump-started parts of my system that had been on idle for a long time. Ticked me off."

"I know." She grinned. "I kind of liked it—the way you'd get all scowly and turned on at the same time. Very sexy. Very challenging."

"Well, you got me where you wanted." He lowered his head to give her a quick, nipping kiss. "Thanks."

"Oh, my pleasure."

"And since I'm here..." He moved his lips to the side of her throat, nuzzled.

Her laughing response turned to a gasp as she felt him harden inside her. Begin to move inside her.

"Hope you don't mind. I've got a lot of lost time to make up for."

"No." Her body woke, and pulsed. "Be my guest."

It wasn't easy, Brody discovered, to have a relation-ship—at least the physical part of it—with a woman when you had a child. Not that he'd change anything, but it took considerable ingenuity to juggle the demands of the man and the demands of the father.

He was grateful that Kate seemed to enjoy Jack, and didn't appear to resent spending time with him, or the time Brody devoted to him. The fact was, if she hadn't accepted the boundaries and responsibilities that went along with Jack, there wouldn't have been a relation-ship—physical or otherwise—to explore for long.

He guessed he was having an affair. That was a first. He'd never considered his relationship with Connie as an affair. Kids didn't have affairs at twenty-one. They had romances. He had to remind himself not to roman-ticize his situation with Kate.

They liked each other, they wanted each other, they enjoyed each other. Neither of them had indicated any-thing more than warm feelings, and lust. And that was for the best, he decided.

He was, first and last, a father. He didn't imagine most young women—career women with dozens of options ahead of them—generally chose to settle down with a man and his six-year-old son.

In any case, he wasn't looking for anything more than what there was. If he had been, he'd have to start tackling the problem of changes, adjustments and compromises for all three of them. That was bound to be messy.

Certainly a grown man was entitled to a simple affair with a like-minded woman without crowding it in with plans for a future.

Everybody was happy this way.

He stepped back, lowering his nail gun to examine the trim he'd just finished on Kate's office. It was a rich, elegant look, he decided. Classy. And it suited the woman.

He wondered where she was, what she was doing. And if they could manage to steal an hour alone before he had to go home and tackle the dinosaur poster Jack had to do for a school project.

Sex, carpentry and first grade, he thought as he moved over to start trimming the window. A man never knew what kind of mix was going to stir up his life.

"He'll love this." Kate examined the fierce, snapping jaws of the plastic predator.

"Dinosaurs are a no-fail choice." Annie rearranged toys that didn't need rearranging, and slid her gaze toward Kate. "That Jack O'Connell's as cute as they come."

"Mmm."

"His father's not shabby, either."

"No, they both ring the bell on the cute scale. And yes, we're still seeing each other."

"I didn't say a word." Annie folded her lips. "I never pry."

"No, you just poke." She tucked the dinosaur under her arm. "That's what I love about you. Now, I'm going to go back and say hi to Mama before I go."

"Want me to wrap that beast up for you?"

"No. Wrapped it's a gift. Unwrapped I can sneak it in as a research tool for his school project."

"You always were a smart one, Katie."

Smart enough, Katie thought, to know what she wanted and how to get it. It had been two weeks since she'd made love with Brody for the first time. Since then they'd had one other evening alone and a handful of hours here and there.

She wanted a lot more than that.

They'd taken Jack to the movies, shared a few meals as a trio, and had engaged in the mother of all snowball battles the previous Saturday when a solid foot of snow had fallen.

She wanted a lot more than that as far as Jack was concerned, too.

She knocked on her mother's office door, poked her head in.

Natasha was at her desk, her hair scooped up and the phone at her ear. She curved her finger in a come-ahead gesture. "Yes, thank you. I'll expect delivery next week."

She tapped a few keys at her computer, hung up and

sighed. "Perfect timing," she told Kate. "I need a cup of tea and a conversation that doesn't involve dolls."

"Happy to oblige. I'll even make the tea." Kate set the dinosaur on her mother's desk before turning to the teapot.

Natasha eyed the toy, then her daughter. "For Jack?"

"Mmm. He has a school project. I figured this might earn him some extra points, and be fun."

"He's a delightful little boy."

"Yes, I think so." Kate poured the hot water into cups. "Brody's done a wonderful job with him—though he had terrific material to work with."

"Yes, I agree. Still, it's never easy to raise a child alone."

"I don't intend for him to finish the job alone." Kate set her mother's cup on the desk, sat down with her own. "I'm in love with Brody, Mama, and I'm going to marry him."

"Oh, Kate!" Tears flooded Natasha's eyes even as she leaped up to embrace her daughter. "This is wonderful. I'm so happy for you. For all of us. My baby's getting married."

She crouched down to kiss both of Kate's cheeks. "You'll be the most beautiful bride. Have you set the date? We'll have so much planning to do. Wait until we tell your father."

"Wait, wait, wait." Laughing, Kate set her tea aside to grab Natasha's hand. "We haven't set a date, because I haven't convinced him to ask me yet."

"But—"

"I'm certain a man like Brody—he's really a traditional guy under it all—wants to do the asking. All I have to do is give him a nudge to the next stage so he'll ask, then we can get on with it."

As worry strangled the excitement, Natasha sat back on her heels. "Katie. Brody isn't a project that has stages."

"I didn't mean it exactly like that. But still, Mama, relationships have stages, don't they? And people in them work through those stages."

"Darling." Natasha straightened, sat on the corner of her desk. "I've always applauded your logic, your practicality and your sheer determination to earn a goal. But love, marriage, family—these things don't always run on logic. In fact, they rarely do."

"Mama, I love him," Katie said simply, and tears swam into her mother's eyes again.

"Yes, I know you do. I've seen it. And believe me, if you want him, I want him for you. But—"

"I want to be Jack's mother." Now Kate's voice thickened. "I didn't know I'd want that so much. At first he was just a delightful little boy, as you said. I enjoyed him, but I enjoy children. Mama, I'm falling in love with him. I'm just falling head over heels for that little boy."

Natasha picked up the dinosaur, smiled as she turned it in her hands. "I know what it is to fall in love with a child who didn't come from you. One who walks into your life already formed and makes such a difference in your life. I don't question that you would love him as your own, Katie."

"Then why are you worried?"

"Because you're my baby," Natasha said as she set the toy aside. "I don't want you to be hurt. You're ready to open your heart and your life. But that doesn't mean Brody is."

"He cares for me." She was sure of it. She couldn't be mistaken. But the worry niggled at her. "He's just cautious."

"He's a good man, and I have no doubt he cares for and about you. But, Katie, you don't say he loves you."

"I don't know if he does." Frustrated, Kate got to her feet. "Or if he loves me, if he knows it himself. That's why I'm trying to be patient. I'm trying to be practical. But, Mama, I ache."

"Baby." Murmuring, Natasha drew Kate into her arms, stroked her hair. "Love isn't tidy. It won't be, not even for you."

"I can be patient. For a little while," she added on a watery laugh. "I'm going to make it work." She closed her eyes tight. "I can make it work."

It was hard not to go over to the job site. She'd had to stop herself a half a dozen times from strolling over and seeing the progress. And seeing Brody. She made it easier on herself by spending part of the afternoon making and receiving calls in response to the ad she'd taken for her school.

The Kimball School of Dance would open in April, and she already had six potential students. There was an interview scheduled for the following week for an article in the local paper. That, she was sure, would generate more interest, more calls, more students.

A few more weeks, she thought as she pulled up behind Brody's truck in his driveway, and a new phase of her professional life would begin. She didn't intend for the next phase of her personal life to lag far behind.

He came to the door in his bare feet and smelling of crayons. The fact that she could find that both sexy and endearing in a grown man showed her just how far gone she was already.

"Hi. Sorry to drop by unannounced, but I have something for Jack."

"No, that's okay." He wiped at the magic marker staining his fingertips. "We're just in the middle… In the kitchen," he said, gesturing. "But it isn't pretty."

"The process of school projects rarely is."

It surprised him that she'd remembered the project. Had he talked about it too much? Brody wondered as he followed her back to the kitchen. He was pretty sure he'd only mentioned it—maybe moaned a little—in passing.

She stepped into the kitchen ahead of him. Surveyed the scene.

Jack was kneeling on a chair at the kitchen table, hunkered over a sheet of poster board and busily applying his crayon to the inside of an outline that resembled a large pig—as seen by Salvador Dalí.

Several picture books on dinosaurs were open on the table, along with illustrations probably printed off the computer. There was a scatter of plastic and rubber toys as well, and a forest of crayons, markers, pencils.

A pair of work boots and a pair of child's sneakers were kicked into a corner. A large pitcher half full of some violently red liquid sat on the counter. As Jack's mouth was liberally stained the same color, Kate assumed it was a beverage and not paint.

As she stepped in, her shoe stuck to the floor, then released with a little sucking sound.

"We just had a little accident with Kool-Aid," Brody explained when she glanced down. "I guess I missed a couple spots on the cleanup."

"Hi, Kate." Jack looked up and bounced. "I'm making dinosaurs."

"So I see. And what kind is this?"

"It's a Stag-e-o-saurus. See? Here he is in the book. Me and Dad, we don't draw very good."

"But you color really well," she said, admiring the bright green head on his current drawing.

"You gotta stay inside the lines. That's why we drew them really thick."

"Very sensible." She rested her chin on the top of his head and studied the poster.

She saw the light pencil marks where Brody had drawn straight lines for the lettering of the header. Jack had titled his piece A Parade Of Dinosaurs. She found it apt, as his drawings marched over the poster in a long squiggly dance.

"You're doing such a good job, I don't think you're going to need the tool I brought along for you."

"Is it a hammer?"

"Afraid not." She reached into her bag, pulled it out. "It's a deadly predator."

"It's a T-Rex! Look, Dad. They ate everybody."

"Very scary," Brody agreed and laid a hand on his son's shoulder.

"Can I take it into school? 'Cause look, its arms and legs move and everything. His mouth goes chomp. Can I?"

"I think it'd be a good visual aid to your project, don't you, Dad? And there's this little booklet here that talks about how he lived, and when, and how he ate everybody."

"Couldn't hurt. Jack, aren't you going to thank Kate?"

"Thanks, Kate." Jack marched the dinosaur across the poster. "Thanks a lot. He's really good."

"You're welcome a lot. How about a kiss?"

He grinned and covered his face with his hands. "Nuh-uh."

"Okay, I'll just kiss your dad." She turned her head before Brody could react and closed her mouth firmly over his.

He avoided kissing her, touching her, when Jack was around. That, Kate decided, deliberately sliding her arms around Brody's waist, would have to change.

Jack made gagging noises behind his hands. But he was watching carefully, and there was a funny fluttering in his stomach.

"A woman's got to take her kisses where she finds them," Kate stated, easing back while Brody stood flustered. "Now, my work is done, I have to go."

"Aw, can't you stay? You can help draw the dinosaurs. We're going to have sloppy burgers for dinner."

"As delightful as that is, I can't. I have an appointment in town." Which was true. But she thought the ambush— the drop-by, she corrected—would be more effective if she kept it brief and casual. "Maybe, this weekend if you're not busy, we can go to the movies again."

"All right!"

"I'll see you tomorrow, Brody. No, no," she said when he turned. "I know the way out. Get back to your dinosaurs."

"Thanks for coming by," he said, and said nothing else, not even when he heard her close the front door.

"Dad?"

"Hmm."

"Do you like kissing Kate?"

"Yeah. I mean…" Okay, Brody thought, here we go. Because Jack was watching him carefully, he sat. "It's kind of hard to explain, but when you get older… Most guys like kissing girls."

"Just the pretty ones?"

"No, well, no. But girls you like."

"And we like Kate, right?"

"Sure we do." Brody breathed a sigh of relief that the discussion hadn't deepened into some stickier area of sex education. Not yet, he thought. Not quite yet.

"Dad?"

"Yeah."

"Are you going to marry Kate?"

"Am I—" His shock was no less than if Jack had suddenly kicked his chair out from under him. "Jeez, Jack, where did that come from?"

"'Cause you like her, and you like kissing her, and you don't have a wife. Rod's mom and dad, sometimes they kiss each other in the kitchen, too."

"Not everybody…people kiss without getting married." Oh, man. "Marriage is a really important thing. You should know somebody really well, and understand them, and like them."

"You know Kate, and you like her."

Brody distinctly felt a single line of sweat dribble down his spine. "Sure I do. Yeah. But I know a lot of people, Jacks." Feeling trapped, Brody pushed away from the table and got down two clean glasses. "I don't marry them. You need to love someone to marry them."

"Don't you love Kate?"

He opened his mouth, closed it again. Funny, he thought, how much tougher it was to lie to your son than it was to lie to yourself. The simplest answer was that he didn't know. He wasn't sure what was building inside him when it came to Kate Kimball.

"It's complicated, Jack."

"How come?"

Questions about sex, Brody decided, would have been easier after all. He set the glasses down, came back to sit. "I loved your mother. You know that, right?"

"Uh-huh. She was pretty, too. And you took care of each other and me until she had to go to heaven. I wish she didn't have to go."

"I know. Me, too. The thing is, Jack, after she had

to go, it was really good for me to just concentrate on loving you. That worked really well for me. And we've done all right, haven't we?"

"Yeah. We're a team."

"You bet we are." Brody held out his hand so Jack could give him a high five. "Now let's see what this team can do with dinosaurs."

"Okay." Jack picked up his crayon. His eyes darted up to his father's face once. He liked that they were a team. But he liked to pretend that maybe Kate was part of the team, too.

Chapter 8

Brody set the first base cabinet in place, checked his level. He could hear, if he paid attention, the whirl of the drill from downstairs as one of his crew finished up the punch-out work on the main level. Up here there was the *whoosh* and *thunk* of nail guns and the whirl of saws, as other men worked in the bedroom of Kate's apartment.

It was going to be a hell of a nice space, Brody thought. The perfect apartment for a single, or a couple without children. It was a little too tight to offer a family a comfortable fit, he thought as he crouched to adjust his level.

Then he just stayed there, staring into space.

Are you going to marry her?

Why the devil had Jack put that idea into the air? Made everything sticky. He wasn't thinking about marriage. Couldn't afford to think about it. He had a kid to consider, and his business was just getting off the ground. He had a rambling, drafty old house that was barely half finished.

It simply wasn't the time to start thinking of adding someone else to the mix by getting married.

He'd jumped into that situation once before. He didn't regret it, not a minute of it. But he had to admit the timing had been lousy, the situation difficult for everyone involved. What was the point of heading back in that sort of direction when his life was still so much in flux?

Just asking for trouble, he decided.

Besides, Kate wouldn't be thinking about marriage. Would she? Of course not. She'd barely settled back into town herself. She had her school to think about. She had her freedom.

She spoke French, he thought irrelevantly. She'd *been to* France. And England and Russia. She might want to go back. Why wouldn't she want that? And he was anchored in West Virginia with a child.

Anyway, he and Connie had been stupid in love. Young and stupid, he thought with a gentle tug of sentiment. He and Kate were grown-ups. Sensible people who enjoyed each other's company.

Too sensible to get starry-eyed.

The hand that dropped on his shoulder had him jerking and nearly dropping the electric drill on his foot.

"Jeez, O'Connell, got the willies?"

Hissing out a breath, Brody got to his feet and turned to Jerry Skully. Rod's father had been a childhood pal.

Even though he was over thirty Jerry maintained his cheerfully youthful looks and goofy smile. It was spread over his face now.

"I didn't hear you."

"No kidding. I called you a couple of times. You were in the zone, man."

Jerry put his hands on his hips and strutted around the room. Put a suit and tie guy in a construction area, Brody thought, and they looked like strutters. "Need a job? I got an extra hammer."

"Ha-ha." It was an old joke. Jerry was a whiz with math, great in social situations and couldn't unscrew a light bulb without step-by-step written instructions.

"You ever get those shelves up in the laundry room?" Brody asked with his tongue in his cheek.

"They're up. Beth said elves put them in." He cocked his head. "You wouldn't know anything about that, would you?"

"I don't hire elves. Their union's a killer."

"Right. Too bad, because I'm really grateful to those elves for getting Beth off my back."

It was all the acknowledgment and thanks either of them required. "Downstairs is looking real good," Jerry went on. "Carrie's driving Beth and me crazy about starting up with this ballet stuff. I guess it's going to get going next month after all."

"No reason it can't. We'll be up here awhile longer, and there's some outside work yet, but she'll have the main level ready." Brody started to set the next cabinet.

"What're you doing hanging out in the middle of the afternoon? Banker's hours?"

"Banker's work a lot harder than you think, pal."

"Soft hands," Brody said, then sniffed. "Is that cologne I'm smelling?"

"Aftershave, you barbarian. Anyway, I had an outside meeting. Got done a little early, so I thought I'd come by to see what you're doing with this old place. My bank's money's getting hammered and nailed in here."

Brody tossed a grin over his shoulder. "That's why the client hired the best."

Jerry said something short and rude that symbolized the affection between two men. "So, I hear you and the ballerina are doing some pretty regular dancing."

"Small towns," Brody said. "Big noses."

"She's a looker." Jerry wandered closer, watched Brody finesse the angle of the cabinet. "You ever seen a real ballet?"

"Nope."

"I did. My little sister—you remember Tiffany? She took ballet for a few years when we were kids. Did the *Nutcracker.* My parents dragged me along. It had some moments," Jerry remembered. "Giant mice, sword fights, big-ass Christmas tree. The rest was just people jumping and twirling, if you ask me. Takes all kinds."

"Guess so."

"Anyway, Tiffany just came back home. She's been down in Kentucky the last couple of years. Finally divorced the jerk she married. Going to stay with the folks until she gets her feet back under her."

"Uh-huh." Brody laid his level across the top of the two cabinets, nodded.

"So, I was thinking maybe, since you're back in the dating swing, you could take her out sometime. Cheer her up a little. A movie, maybe dinner."

"Mmm." Brody moved the next cabinet to his mark where it would sit under the breakfast bar.

"That'd be great. She's had a tough time of it, you know? Be nice if she could spend some time with a guy who'd treat her decent."

"Yeah."

"She had a little crush on you when we were kids. So, you'll give her a call in the next couple of days?"

"Sure. What?" Surfacing, Brody glanced back. "Give who a call?"

"Jeez, Brody, Tiff. My sister. You're going to give her a call and ask her out."

"I am?"

"O'Connell, you just said—"

"Wait a minute. Just a minute." Brody set down the drill and tried to catch up. "Look, I don't think I can do that. I'm sort of seeing Kate."

"You're not married to her or living with her or anything. What's the big deal?"

He was pretty sure there was one. Being out of the stream for a few years didn't mean he didn't remember how it was supposed to work. Moreover, he didn't *want* to ask Tiffany, or anyone else out.

But he didn't think Jerry would appreciate him saying that. "The thing is, Jerry, I'm not into the dating scene."

"You're dating the ballerina."

"No, I'm not. That is… We're just—"

Perhaps it was best all around that while he was fumbling for an excuse, he looked away from Jerry. And saw Kate in the doorway.

"Ah. Kate. Hi."

"Hello." Her voice was cool; her eyes hot. "Sorry to interrupt."

Recognizing a potentially sticky situation, Jerry flashed his smile and prepared to desert his old friend on the battlefield. "Hey there, Kate. Good to see you again. Gosh, look at the time. I have to run. I'll get back to you on that, Brody. See you later."

He made tracks.

Brody picked up his drill again, passed it from hand to hand. "That was Jerry."

"Yes, I'm aware that was Jerry."

"Setting your cabinets today. I think you made the right choice with the natural cherry. We should have the bedroom closet framed in, and the drywall set with the first coat of mud by the end of the day."

"That's just dandy."

Her temper was a live thing, a nest of vipers curling and hissing in her gut. She had no intention of beating them back to keep them from sinking their fangs into Brody.

"So, we're not dating. We're just…" She came into the room on the pause. "Would that have been sleeping together? We're just sleeping together. Or do you have a simpler term for it?"

"Jerry put me on the spot."

"Really? Is that why you told him—so decisively—that you and I are 'sort of seeing each other'? I didn't realize that defining our relationship was such a dilemma for you, or that whatever that relationship might be causes you such embarrassment with your friends."

"Just hold on." He set the drill down again with an impatient snap of metal on wood. "If you were going to eavesdrop on a conversation, you should have listened to the whole thing. Jerry wanted me to take his sister out, and I was explaining why that wasn't a good idea."

"I see." She imagined she could chew every nail in his pouch, then spit them into his eye. "First, I wasn't eavesdropping. This is my place and I have every right to come into any room in it. Whenever I like. Second, in your explanation of why going out with Jerry's sister isn't a good idea, did the word *no* ever enter your head?"

"Yes. No," he corrected. "Because I wasn't paying—"

"Ah, there. You are capable of saying no. Let me tell you something, O'Connell." She punctuated the words by stabbing a finger into his chest. "I don't sleep around."

"Well, who the hell said you did?"

"When I'm with a man, I'm with *that* man. Period. If he is unable or unwilling to agree to do the same, I expect him to be honest enough to say so."

"I haven't—"

"*And,* I am not an excuse to be pulled out of the bag when you're scrambling to avoid a favor for a friend. So don't think you can *ever* use me that way, and with your pitiful, fumbling 'sort ofs.' And since it appears we aren't dating, you're perfectly free to call Jerry's sister or anyone else."

"Damn it, which is it? Are you going to be pissed off because I brush Jerry off, or pissed off because I don't?"

Her hands curled into fists. Punching him, she decided, would only give him delusions of grandeur. "Jerk." She bit the single word off, turned on her heel and, tossing something in Ukrainian over her shoulder, strode out of the room.

"Females," Brody muttered. He kicked his toolbox, and was only moderately satisfied by the clang.

An hour later, the cabinets were in place and Brody was at work on the pantry. He'd already run through the scene with Kate a half a dozen times, but with each play, he'd remembered things he should have said. Short, pithy statements that would have turned the tide in his favor. And the first chance he got, he was going to burn her ears with them.

He was not going to grovel, he told himself as he nailed in the brackets for a shelf. He had nothing to apologize for. Women, he decided, were just one of the many reasons a man was better off going through his life solo.

If he was such a jerk, why'd she bother to spend any time with him in the first place?

He backed out of the closet, turned and nearly ran right into Spencer Kimball.

"What *is* it with people?" Brody demanded.

"Sorry. I didn't think you could hear me with all the noise."

"I'm going to post signs." Brody stalked over to select one of the shelves he'd precut and sealed. "No suits, no ties, no females."

Spencer's eyebrows lifted. In all the months he'd known Brody, this was the first time he'd heard him anything but calm. "I take it I'm not the first interruption of the day."

"Not by a long shot." Brody tested the shelf. It slid smoothly into its slot. At least something was going right today, he thought. "If this is about the kitchen design for your place, once you approve it, I'll order materials. We'll be able to start in a couple of weeks."

"Actually, I'm staying out of that one. Tash has gotten very territorial over this kitchen deal. I just came by to see the progress here. The considerable progress."

"Yeah, moving right the hell along." Brody snatched up another shelf, then stopped, let out a breath. "Sorry. Bad day."

"Must be going around." And explained, Spencer decided, why his daughter was in a prickly mood. "Kate's downstairs setting up her office."

"Oh." Brody carted his shelves into the pantry, began to set them. Very deliberately. "I didn't realize she was still here."

"Furniture she ordered just came in. I didn't get much of a welcome from her, either. So, putting the evidence together, I conclude the two of you had an argument."

"It's not an argument when somebody jumps down somebody else's throat for no good reason. It's an attack."

"Mmm-hmm. At the risk of poking my nose in, I can tell you the women in my family always have what they consider a good reason for jumping down a man's throat. Of course, whether or not it actually *is* a good reason is debatable."

"Which is why women are just too much damn trouble."

"Tough doing without them, though, isn't it?"

"I was getting along. Jack and I were doing just fine." Frustration pumped off him as he turned back to Spencer. "What is it with women anyway, that they have to complicate things, then make you feel like an idiot?"

"Son, generations of men have pondered that question. There's only one answer. Because."

With a half laugh, Brody stepped back again, automatically eyeballing the shelves for level and fit. "I guess that's as good as it gets. Doesn't matter much at this point anyway. She dumped me."

"You don't strike me as a man who typically walks away from a problem."

"Nothing typical about your daughter." As soon as it was out, Brody winced. "Sorry."

"I took that as a compliment. My impression is the two of you bruised each other's feelings, maybe each other's pride. An insider tip? Kate's usual response to bruised feelings or pride is temper, followed by ice."

Brody dug out the hooks to be used in the pantry. He should leave that job for a laborer, he thought. But he needed to do something simple with his hands. "She made herself pretty clear. She called me a jerk—then something in Russian. Ukrainian. Whatever."

"She spit at you in Ukrainian?" Spence struggled to conceal his amusement. "She'd have to have been pretty worked up for that."

Brody's eyes narrowed as he hefted his screwdriver. "I don't know what it meant, but I didn't like the sound of it."

"It might have been something about you roasting on a spit over Hell fire. Her mother likes to use that one. Brody, do you have feelings for my daughter?"

Brody's palms went instantly damp. "Mr. Kimball—"

"Spence. I know it's not a simple question, or an easy one. But I'd like an answer."

"Would you mind stepping away from the toolbox first? There are a lot of sharp implements in there."

Spencer slid his hands into his pockets. "You have my word I won't challenge you to a duel with screwdrivers."

"Okay. I have feelings for Kate. They're kind of murky and unsettled, but I have them. I didn't intend to get involved with her. I'm not in a position to."

"Can I ask why?"

"That's pretty obvious—I'm a single father. I'm putting together a decent life for my son, but it's nothing like what Kate's used to, or what she can have."

Spencer rocked back on his heels. "They gave you a bad time, didn't they?"

"Excuse me?"

"Unlike some families, ours can be nosy, interfering, protective and irritating. But you'll also find we respect and support each other's choices and feelings. Brody, it's a mistake to judge one situation by the dynamics of another." Spencer paused for a moment, then continued, "But putting that aside for the moment, since you care about Kate, let me give you some unsolicited advice. Whether you want to take it or not is up to you. Deal with the problem. Deal with her. If you didn't matter to her, she'd have ended things gently, or worse, politely."

Deciding he'd given Brody enough to think about, Spencer turned to take a survey of the total construction chaos of the kitchen. "So this is what I've got to look forward to." He shot Brody a miserable look. "And you think you have problems."

When Spencer left him alone, Brody stood, tapping the screwdriver on his palm. The man was advising him to fight with his daughter. What kind of a screwy family was that?

His own parents never fought. Of course, that was because his father set the rules, and those rules were followed. Or at least it seemed that way.

He'd never fought with Connie. Not really. They'd had some disagreements, sure, but they'd just worked through them, or talked them out. Or ignored them, Brody admitted. Ignored them, he thought, because they'd both been cut off, isolated, and they only had each other to rely on.

Temper had never gotten him anywhere but in trouble. With his father, in school, in the early days on the job. He'd learned to rein it in, to use his head instead of his gut. Most of the time, he admitted, thinking about his last altercation with his father.

Still, maybe it was a mistake to compare what had been with what was. One thing was certain, he wasn't going to get rid of this nasty sensation in his gut until he spoke his mind.

He checked his men first, ran over some minor adjustments and the basic plan for the following day. It was nearly time to knock off, so he cut them loose. He didn't want an audience.

Kate hit the nail squarely on the head and bared her teeth in satisfaction. Brody O'Connell, the pig, wasn't the only one who could use a hammer.

She'd spent the last two hours meticulously setting up her office. Everything would be perfect when she was finished. She wouldn't settle for anything less.

Her desk was precisely where she wanted it, and its drawers already organized with the brochures she'd designed and ordered, her letterhead, the application forms for students.

Her filing cabinet was the same golden oak. In time, she expected the folders inside to be full.

She'd found the rug at an antique sale, and its faded pattern of cabbage roses set off the pale green walls, picked up the tone in the fabric of the accent chairs that now faced her desk.

Just because it was an office didn't mean it couldn't have style.

She hung yet another of the framed black-and-white

photos she'd chosen. Stood back and nodded with approval. Dancers at the *barre,* in rehearsal, onstage, backstage. Young students at recitals, lacing on toe shoes.

Sweating, sparkling, limp from exertion or flying. All the aspects of a dancer's world. They would remind her, on a daily basis, what she had done. And what she was doing.

She picked up another nail, set it neatly on her mark, slammed it. And what she wasn't doing, she thought, rapping it a second time, was wasting her time on Brody O'Connell.

The bastard.

Let him cozy up to Tiffany. Oh, she remembered Tiffany Skully. The busty bleached blonde had been a year ahead of her in high school. Lots of giggling. Lots of lipstick. Well, let the jerk take her out. What did she care?

She was done with him.

"If you'd told me you were going to cover the entire space with pictures," Brody commented, "I wouldn't have worked so hard on finishing the drywall. Nobody'd know the difference."

She jammed the photograph in place, picked up another nail. "One assumes you have a certain pride in your work, whether or not it can be admired. And since I paid for the wall, I'll do whatever the hell I like with it."

"Yeah, you want to riddle them with nail holes, it's your choice." The pictures looked great—not that he was going to say so. Not just the arrangement of them, which was cohesive without being rigid, but the theme.

He could see her in several of them, as a child, a

young girl, a woman. One of her sitting cross-legged on the floor, pounding shoes with a hammer, made him want to grin.

Instead he waved a finger toward it, casually. "I thought you were supposed to dance with those."

"For your information toe shoes need to be broken in. That's one method of doing so. Now, if you'll excuse me, I'd like to get my office finished. I have appointments here tomorrow afternoon."

"Then that gives you plenty of time." Particularly, he thought, since the office already looked perfect. He should have known she'd make it perfect.

"Let me put it this way." She pounded in another nail. "I'm busy, and I have no desire to talk to you. I'm not paying you to stand around and chat in any case."

"Don't pull that on me." He yanked the hammer out of her hand. "You writing checks for the job doesn't have anything to do with the rest of it. I'll be damned if you'll put it on that level."

He was right, of course, and it shamed her to have it pointed out. "True enough, but our personal business is done."

"The hell it is." He turned and shoved the pocket door closed.

"Just what do you think you're doing?"

"Getting some privacy. It doesn't seem to be in big supply around here."

"Open that door—then walk through it. And keep walking."

"Sit down and shut up."

Her eyes widened, more in shock than temper. "I beg your pardon?"

To solve the problem, he set the hammer aside—well out of her reach—walked over and pushed her into a chair. "Now listen."

She started to leap up, was pushed down firmly again. Temper heated, but it stayed at the bubble from the sheer surprise of seeing him so furious. "So, you've proved you're big and strong," she said derisively. "You don't have to prove you're stupid."

"And you don't have to prove you're spoiled and snotty. You try to get up again before I'm done, I'm going to tie you in that chair. I was minding my own business when Jerry came in. He's a friend. He and Beth have gone out of their way for me and Jack, so I owe him."

"So naturally you need to pay him back by dating his sister."

"Be quiet, Kate. I'm not dating his sister. I don't intend to date his sister. He was running off at the mouth, and I was shimming cabinets. I wasn't listening to him, and by the time I tuned back in…"

Brody raked a hand through his hair, took a restless turn around the room. "He caught me off guard, and I was trying to backtrack without stomping all over his feelings. He and Tiff have always been tight. He's worried about her, I guess, and he trusts me. What was I supposed to say? I'm not interested in your sister?"

Kate angled her chin. "Yes. But that's not really the point."

"Then what the hell is the point?"

"The point is you indicated, and obviously feel, there's nothing between us but sex. I require more than that in a relationship. I demand more than that. Loyalty, fidelity, affection, respect. I expect a man to be able to say— without tripping over his own clumsy tongue—that he and I are dating. That he cares about me."

"Damn it, it's been nearly ten years since I dated anyone. You'd think you could cut me some slack."

"Then you think wrong. Are we done here?"

"Man, you're a hard case. No, we're not done." He yanked her to her feet. "I haven't been with anyone else since you. I don't want to be. I'll make a point of making that crystal clear to Jerry or anyone else. I care about you, and I don't appreciate being made to feel like an idiot because I don't have a good handle on it."

"Fine. Now let go."

"If I could let go, I wouldn't be standing here wanting to strangle you."

"You insulted me. You insulted us. You're the one who should be strangled."

"I'm not going to apologize again." He dragged her toward the door.

"Apologize? I didn't hear any apology. What are you doing?"

"Just be quiet," he ordered as he shoved the door open, continued to pull her down the corridor.

"If you don't let go of me, this minute, I'm going to—"

The wind was knocked out of her when he simply hauled her up and over his shoulder. He clamped her legs still with one arm, yanked open the front door with his free hand.

"Have you lost your mind?" Too shocked to struggle, she shoved her hair up out of her face as he strode with her across the porch and down the front steps. "Have you completely lost your mind?"

"The minute I started thinking about you." He scanned the street, spotted a woman coming out of the apartment building. "Excuse me! Ma'am?"

She glanced over, blinked. "Ah...yes?"

"This is Kate. I'm Brody. I just wanted you to know that we're dating."

"Oh, my God," Kate whispered, and let her hair fall again.

"I see. Well..." The woman smiled, offered a little wave. "That's nice."

"Thanks." Brody shifted Kate, set her on her feet in front of him. "Would you like to keep going, or are you satisfied?"

She couldn't get the words out of her mouth. Simply couldn't shove them from where they seemed to be stuck in her throat. She solved the problem by rapping a fist against his chest and storming back into the building.

"Guess not," Brody decided, and strode in after her.

Chapter 9

He caught her an instant before she could slam her office door in his face. Not that it would have stopped him now that he was revved up.

"Not so fast, honey."

"Don't you call me honey. Don't you speak to me." She rounded on him. "You're nothing but a bully. Manhandling me that way. Embarrassing me on the street."

"Embarrassed?" He kept his eyes, every bit as hot as hers, level as he slid the door closed behind his back. "Why is that? I simply told a neighbor, without tripping over my—what was it—clumsy tongue, that we're dating. So what's the problem?"

"The problem is..." She retreated several steps as he advanced on her. That was another shocker—not just that he was backing her into a corner, but that she was letting him. She'd *never* backed down from a confrontation, and certainly never backed down from a man. "Just what do you think you're doing?"

"Being myself." Damned if it didn't feel good. "Been a while since I cut loose like this, but it's coming back to me. We may as well find out now if you have a problem with that."

"If you think you can—" She broke off as he grabbed her arms, pulled her up to her toes. "You'd just better calm down."

"You'd just better catch up." He crushed his mouth to hers and felt her instinctive jerk of protest. Ignored it.

"You got a problem with it?" he demanded lifting his head and meeting her eyes.

"Brody—" That was all she managed to say before he took her mouth over again.

"Yes or no."

"I don't—" His teeth scraped along her neck. "Oh God." She couldn't think. This had to be wrong. There had to be a dozen, two dozen, rational reasons why this was wrong.

She'd worry about them later.

"You want me to take my hands off you?" They moved over her, rough and possessive. "Yes or no. Pick now."

"No. Damn it." She fisted her hands in his hair and dragged his mouth back to hers.

She didn't know who pulled whom to the floor. It didn't seem to matter. She couldn't tell whose hands were more impatient as they tugged at clothing. She didn't care.

All she knew was she wanted this rough, angry man

every bit as much as she'd wanted the gentle, patient one. Her body was quaking for him, her heart bounding.

So much heat. She was amazed her system didn't simply implode from it. The sharp stabs of pain and pleasure fused together into one unbearable sensation.

Tangled together, they rolled over the floor. She set her teeth at his shoulder, craving that wild flavor of flesh.

He'd forgotten what it was to let himself want like this, to take like this. Without restriction or boundaries. To rush and plunder. His fingers tore at the triangle of lace that blocked her from him. And he drove her up, hard and high.

The bite of her nails on his back was a dark thrill, the blind shock in her eyes a violent triumph. Desperate for possession, he yanked up her hips and plunged.

She rose up, that agile body quivering, her fingers digging into the rug for stability as he pounded into her. An elemental mating that fed on hot blood. Even as she cried out, he dragged her up until her legs wrapped around his waist, her hands found slippery purchase on his sweat-slicked shoulders.

She held on, riding the razor-tipped edge of pleasure, clinging to it, to him. When the climax ripped through her, shredding her system to tatters, she bowed back and let him take his own.

She melted like candle wax onto the floor when he released her. Then simply lay there, weak and sated.

She'd been ravaged. She had allowed it. And she felt wonderful.

Though his vision was still a little blurry at the edges,

Brody studied her, then what was left of their clothes. "I ripped your shirt." When her eyes fluttered open, he recognized the lazy gleam of a satisfied woman. "And these things." He held up the tatters of her panties. "Well, I'm not going to apologize."

"I didn't ask for an apology."

"Good. Because if you had, I'd have been forced to haul you outside again—naked this time—to find another neighbor. Instead you can borrow my shirt. I've got a spare in the truck."

She sat up, took the offered shirt. The glow she'd felt was beginning to fade. "Are we still fighting?"

"I'm done, so I guess that's up to you."

She looked up. His eyes were clear now, and direct. This time it was she who fumbled—starting to speak, then shaking her head.

"No, go on. Say it. Let's make sure the air's completely clear."

"You hurt my feelings." It was lowering to admit it. Temper, she thought, was so much easier to handle than hurt.

"I get that." He took the shirt from her, draped it over her shoulders. "And that's something I will apologize for. If it helps any, you hurt mine right back."

"What are we doing, Brody?"

"Trying to figure each other out, I guess. I'm not embarrassed by what we've got going on, Kate. I don't want you to think that. But I don't have a handle on it yet."

"All right, that's fair enough." But it hurt a lot, she realized as she shrugged into the borrowed shirt. Hurt that she'd fallen in love, and he hadn't. Still, that didn't mean he wouldn't. She smiled a little, leaned over and up to kiss him. "You're not a jerk. I'm sorry I called you one."

He caught her chin. "You called me something worse than that, didn't you?"

Now the smile spread and was genuine. "Maybe."

"I'm going to buy a Ukrainian phrase book."

"Good luck. Besides they just don't have certain descriptive words and phrases in there."

"I'm getting one anyway." He got to his feet, drew her up to hers. "I've got to go pick up my kid."

His hair was a sexy mess, his eyes lazily satisfied. He was naked to the waist. And, she thought, he was a father who had to pick up his little boy from the school bus.

"That's part of it, isn't it? Part of your problem with getting a grip on our relationship? Trying to juggle the man and the father together."

"Maybe. Yes," he admitted. "Kate, there hasn't been anyone in…" He lifted a hand, smoothed it over his hair in some attempt to order it. "Connie was sick for a long time." He couldn't talk about that now, couldn't go back there. "Jack had a rough start. I guess we both did. All I can do is make up for it."

"You have. And you are. I know how to juggle, too, Brody. I think we can keep the balls in the air. As long as we both want to."

"I want to."

Her heart settled. "Then that's also fair enough. Go get Jack."

"Yeah." His gaze skimmed down. "Before I do, I'd just like to say you sure look good in flannel."

"Thanks."

"You want a lift home?"

"No. I really do have some things to finish up here."

"All right." He lowered his head, touched his mouth to hers. Ended up lingering. "Gotta go." But when he got to the door, he glanced back. "You want to go out Saturday night?"

Her eyebrow lifted. It was the first time he'd actually asked her out. It was, she supposed, some sort of progress. "I'd love to."

How it got to be spring break when it seemed they'd just gotten through Christmas vacation, Brody didn't know. School days had certainly not flown by when he'd been a kid.

Added to that, the Skullys had decided to take advantage of the time off to take the kids to Disney World. This had caused major problems with Jack who'd begged, pleaded and had fallen back on whining over the idea that they should go, too.

Brody had explained why it wasn't possible just now, patiently sympathized. Then had fallen back on the parental cop-out—because I said so—when the siege had shown no sign of ending.

As a result, he'd had a sulky kid on his hands for two days, and a raging case of the guilts. The combination made it very crowded in the small bathroom where he was trying to lay tile.

"You never let me go anywhere," Jack complained. He was thoroughly bored with the small pile of toys he'd been allowed to bring along.

Usually he liked coming to the job with his dad. But not when his best friend was in Disney World riding on Space Mountain. It was a gyp. A big fat gyp, he thought, relishing one of the words he'd picked up from the crew.

When his father ignored him and continued to lay tile, Jack stuck out his bottom lip. "How come I couldn't go to Grandma's?"

"I told you Grandma was busy this morning. She's going to come by and pick you up in a couple of hours. Then you can go over to her house." Thank God.

"I don't want to stay here. It's boring. It's not fair I gotta stay here and do nothing while everybody else has fun. I never get to do *anything*."

Brody shoved his trowel into the tray of adhesive. "Look. I've got a job to do. A job that sees to it you eat regular."

Damn it, how was his father's voice suddenly coming out of his mouth?

"I'm stuck with it," he added, "and so are you. Now keep it up, Jack. Just keep it up, and you won't be going anywhere."

"Grandpa gave me five dollars," Jack said, tearing up. "So you don't have to buy me any food."

"Great. Terrific. I'll retire tomorrow."

"Grandma and Grandpa can take me to Disney World, and you can't go."

"They're not taking you anywhere," Brody snapped,

cut to the bone by the childish slap. "You'll be lucky to go to Disney World by the time you're thirty. Now, cut it out."

"I want Grandma! I want to go home! I don't like you anymore."

Kate walked in on that, and the resulting angry, tired tears. She took one look at Brody's exhausted, frustrated face, the cranky little boy sprawled weeping on the floor, and stepped into the fray.

"What's all this, Handsome Jack?"

"I wanna go to Disney World."

He sobbed it out, between hiccups. Even as Brody got to his feet to deal with it, Kate crouched down between father and son. "Oh, boy, me, too. I bet we'd all like to go there more than anyplace."

"Dad doesn't."

"Sure he does. Dads like to go most of all. That's why it's harder for them, because they have to work."

"Kate, I can handle this."

"Who said you couldn't?" she muttered, but picked up the boy and got to her feet. "I bet you're tired of being cooped up, aren't you, baby? Why don't we go to my house awhile, and let Dad finish his work?"

"My mother's coming by to get him in a couple of hours. Just let me—" He reached for his son who only curled himself like a snake around Kate—and effectively cut his heart in two.

One look at the blank hurt on Brody's face made her want to sandwich Jack between them in a hard hug. But that, she thought wasn't the immediate answer. Distance was.

"I'm done for the day here, Brody. Why don't you let Jack come home with me, keep me company." *Take a nap,* she mouthed. "I'll call your mother and ask her to pick him up at my house instead."

"I want to go with Kate." Jack sobbed against her shoulder.

"Fine. Great." The miserable mix of temper and guilt had him snatching up his trowel again. Very much, Kate thought, like a cranky boy. "Thanks."

He sat down heavily on an overturned bucket as he heard Jack sniffle out, as Kate carried him off: "My daddy yelled at me."

"Yes, I know." She kissed Jack's hot, wet cheek as she walked downstairs. "You yelled at him, too. I bet he feels just as sad as you do."

"Nuh-uh." With a heavy, heavy sigh, Jack rested his head on Kate's shoulder. "He wouldn't take me to Disney World like Rod."

"I know. I guess that's my fault."

"How come?"

"Well, your dad's doing this job for me, and he promised me it would be done by a certain time. Because he promised, I made promises to other people who are depending on me now. If your dad broke his promise to me, then I broke mine to the other people, that wouldn't be right. Would it, Jack?"

"No, but, maybe just this one time."

"Does your dad break his promises to you?"

"No." Jack's head drooped.

"Don't be sad, Handsome Jack. When we get to my house, we're going to read a story about another Jack. The one with the beanstalk."

"Can I have a cookie?"

"Yes." In love, she gave him a hard squeeze.

He was asleep almost before Jack sold his cow for magic beans.

Poor little boy, she thought, tucking a light throw over him. Poor Brody.

She began to think she hadn't given the man enough credit. Parenthood wasn't all wrestling on the floor and ball games in the yard. It was also tears and tantrums, disappointments and discipline. It was saying no, having to say no, when your heart wanted to say yes.

"You're so well loved, Handsome Jack," she murmured and bent over to kiss the top of his head. "He needs you to know that."

And so is he, she thought with a sigh. "I wish the man would buy a clue. Because I'm not waiting much longer. I want both of you."

When the phone rang, she snatched it from the cradle. "Hello. Ah." Smiling now, she walked out of the room so as not to disturb Jack. "Davidov. What have I done to deserve a call from the master?"

Later, though she admitted it was foolish, Kate freshened her makeup and tidied her hair. It was the first time she would meet Brody's parents. Since she intended for them to be her in-laws, she wanted to make a good impression.

Jack had wakened from his nap energized. This had called for some running around the backyard, a fierce battle with action figures and a race with miniature cars that had resulted in a satisfying wreck of major proportions.

They finished the entertainment off with a snack in the kitchen.

"My dad's mad at me," Jack confided over slices of apple and cheese.

"I don't think so. I think he's a little upset because he couldn't give you what you wanted. Inside, parents want to give their children everything that would make them happy. But sometimes they can't."

She remembered throwing some impressive tantrums herself—snarls followed by sulks. And ending, she thought, like this in guilty unhappiness.

"Sometimes they can't because it's not the best thing, or the right thing just then. And sometimes because they just can't. When your little boy cries and yells and stomps his feet, it makes you mad for a while. But it also hurts your heart."

Jack lifted his face, all big eyes and trembling lips. "I didn't mean to."

"I know. And I bet if you tell him you're sorry, you'll both feel better."

"Did your dad ever yell at you?"

"Yes, he did. And it made me mad or unhappy. But after a while, I usually figured out I deserved it."

"Did I deserve it?"

"Yes, I'm afraid you did. There was this one thing I always knew, even when I was mad or unhappy. I knew my dad loved me. You know that about your dad, too."

"Yeah." Jack nodded solemnly. "We're a team."

"You're a great team."

Jack turned his apple slices around, making pictures and patterns. She was pretty, he thought. And she was nice. She could play games and read stories. He even liked when she kissed him, and the way she laughed when he pretended not to like it. Dad liked to kiss her, too. He said he did, and he didn't lie.

So she could maybe marry his dad—even though Dad said she wasn't going to—and then she could be Dad's wife and Jack's mother. They'd all live together in the big house.

And maybe, sometime, they could all go to Disney World.

"What are you thinking about so hard, Handsome Jack?"

"I was wondering if—"

"Oops." She smiled, rising as she heard the doorbell. "Hold that thought, okay? That must be your grandma."

She gave Jack's hair a quick rub and hurried out to answer. With her hand on the knob, she took a quick bracing breath. Silly to be nervous, she told herself. Then opened the door to Mr. and Mrs. O'Connell.

"Hi. It's good to see you." She stepped back in invitation. "Jack's just in the kitchen, having a snack."

"It's good of you to watch him for Brody." Mary

O'Connell stepped inside, tried not to make her quick scan of the entrance too obvious. She'd fussed with her makeup, too—much to her husband's disgust.

"I enjoy spending time with Jack. He's great company. Please come on back. Have some coffee."

"Don't want to put you out," Bob said. He'd been in the house plenty. When you fixed people's toilets, you weren't particularly impressed by their doodads and furniture.

"I've got a fresh pot. Please, come in—unless you're in a hurry."

"We've got to—"

Bob broke off as his wife gave him a subtle elbow nudge. "We'd love a cup of coffee. Thank you."

"Brody's going to be remodeling the kitchen for my mother," Kate began as they walked back. "My parents love the work he's done in the rest of the house."

"He always was good with his hands," Mary commented and gave her husband a quiet look when he folded his lips tight.

"He's certainly transformed the old house I bought. Hey, Jack, look who I've got."

"Hi!" Jack slurped his chocolate milk. "I've been playing with Kate."

Like father like son, Bob thought sourly, but his heart lifted as it always did at the sight of Jack's beaming face. "Where'd you get the chocolate cow, partner?"

"Oh, we keep her in the garden shed," Kate said as she got out cups and saucers. "And milk her twice a day."

"Kate's got toys. Her mom has a whole *store* of toys.

She said how on my birthday we can go there and I can pick one out."

"Isn't that nice?" Mary slid her gaze toward Kate, speculated. "How is your mother, Kate?"

"She's fine, thanks."

Mary approved of the way Kate set out the cups, the cream and sugar. Classy, but not fussy. And the ease with which she handed Jack a dishrag so he could wipe up a bit of spilled milk himself.

Good potential mother material, she decided. God knew her little lamb deserved one. As for potential wife material, well, she would see what she would see.

"Everyone's talking about your ballet school," she began, flushing slightly at her husband's soft snort. "You must be excited."

"I am. I've got several students lined up, and classes begin in just a few weeks. If you know anyone who might be interested, I'd appreciate it if you'd spread the word."

"Shepherdstown's some different from New York City," Bob said as he reached for the sugar.

"It certainly is." Kate's voice was smooth and easy—though she'd heard the snort. "I enjoyed living in New York, working there. Of course it helped considerably that I had family there as well. And I liked the traveling, seeing new places, having the opportunity to dance on the great stages. But this is home, and where I want to be. Do you think ballet is out of place here, Mr. O'Connell?"

He shrugged. "Don't know anything about it."

"It happens I do. And I think a good school of dance

will do very well here. We're a small town, of course," she added, sipping her coffee. "But we're also a college town. The university brings in a variety of people from a variety of places."

"Can I have a cookie?"

"Please," Jack's grandmother added.

"Can I please have a cookie?"

Kate started to rise, then let out a gasp as she saw Brody through the glass on the back door. With a shake of her head, she walked over to open it. "You gave me such a jolt."

"Sorry." He was a little out of breath, more from excitement than the quick jog around the house. "I tried to call you," he said, nodding in greeting to his parents. "To head you off. You must've been on the road."

"Said we were coming to pick the boy up at three," Bob said. "Got here at three."

"Yeah, well. I had a little change of plans." He looked at his son who sat with his eyes on his plate and his chin nearly on his chest. "Did you have a good time with Kate, Jack?"

Jack nodded his head, slowly looked up. His eyes were teary again. "I'm sorry I was bad. I'm sorry I hurt your heart."

Brody crouched down, cupped Jack's face. "I'm sorry I can't take you to Disney World. I'm sorry I yelled at you."

"You're not mad at me anymore?"

"No, I'm not mad at you."

The tears dried up. "Kate said you weren't."

"Kate was right." He picked Jack out of the chair for a hug before setting him on his feet.

"Can I go back to work with you? I won't be bad."

"Well, you could, except I'm not going back to work today."

"Man knocks off middle of the afternoon isn't putting in a good day's work."

Brody glanced over at his father, nodded. "True enough. And a man who doesn't take a few hours now and then to be with his son isn't working hard enough at being a father."

"You always had food in your belly," Bob shot back as he shoved away from the table.

"You're right. I want Jack to be able to say more than that about me. I've got something for you," he added, cupping Jack's chin as it had begun to wobble as it always did when Brody and his father exchanged words. "It isn't Disney World, but I think you'll like it even better than a ride on Space Mountain."

"Is it a new action figure?" Thrilled he began tugging at Brody's pockets.

"Nope."

"A car? A truck?"

"You are way off, and it's not in my pocket. It's outside on the porch."

"Can I see? Can I?" He was already running for the door, tugging the knob. And when he opened it, looked down, looked up again at his father, Brody had, in that wonderful moment of stupefied delight, everything that mattered.

"A puppy! A puppy!" Jack scooped up the black ball of fur that was trying to climb up his leg. "Is it mine? Can I keep him?"

"Looks like he wants to keep you," Brody commented as the pup wriggled in ecstasy, yipping and bathing Jack's face with his tongue.

"Look, Grandma, I got a puppy, and he's mine. And his name is Mike. Just like I always wanted."

"He sure is a pretty little thing. Oh, just look at those feet. Why he'll be bigger than you before long. You have to be real good to him, Jack."

"I will. I promise. Look, Kate. Look at Mike."

"He's great." Unable to resist, she got down and was treated to some puppy kisses. "So soft. So sweet." She turned her head, met Brody's eyes. "Very, very sweet."

"It's a good thing for a boy to have a dog." Still stinging from his son's comment, Bob gestured. "But who's going to tend to it when Jack's in school all day and you're working? Problem with you is you never think things through, just do what you want at the moment you want it, and don't consider."

"Bob." Mortified, Mary reached up to pat her husband's arm.

"I have a fenced yard," Brody said carefully. "And I've worked on plenty of jobs where dogs were around. He'll come with me till he's old enough to be on his own."

"You buy that dog for the boy, or to patch up your conscience because you can't give him a holiday like his friends?"

"I don't want to go to Disney World," Jack said in

a quavering voice. "I want to stay home with Dad and Mike."

"Why don't you take Mike outside, Jack?" Fixing a smile on her face, Kate walked to the door. "Puppies like to run around as much as boys do. And you need to get acquainted. Here, put on your jacket first."

Brody held it in until Kate nudged the boy out the door.

"It's none of your business if I get my son a dog, or why. But the fact is I had this one picked out from a litter three weeks ago for him, and was waiting until he was weaned. I was going to pick him up Sunday for Easter, but Jack needed a little cheering up today."

"You're not teaching him respect by giving him presents after he's sassed you."

"All you taught me was respect, and look where that got us."

"Please." Mary all but wrung her hands. "This isn't the place."

"Don't you tell me where I can speak my mind," Bob snapped. "My mistake was in not slapping you back harder and more often. You always did run your own way, as you pleased. Nothing but trouble, causing it and finding it and giving your mother heartache. Run off to the city before you're dry behind the ears, and pissing your life away."

"I didn't run off to the city. I ran away from you."

Bob's head jerked back at that, as if he'd been slapped. He went pale. "Now you're back, aren't you? Scrambling to make do, shuffling the boy off to neighbors so you can make a living. Stirring up gossip 'cause you're fooling around with women down the hall from where that boy sleeps, and teaching him to run wild as you did, and end up the same way."

"Just one minute." If her own temper hadn't hazed her vision, Kate would have realized she was stepping between two men very near to coming to blows. "It so happens Brody isn't fooling around with women, he's fooling around with me. And though that *is* none of your business, the fooling around has never gone on when Jack's asleep down the hall.

"And if you don't know that Brody would cut his own arm off rather than do anything, *anything* to hurt that child, then you're blind as well as stupid. You should be ashamed to speak to him as you did, to not have the guts to tell him you're proud of what he's making out of his life, and of the life he's making for his son."

"You're wasting your breath," Brody began, and she rounded on him.

"You shut up. You've plenty to answer for, too. You have no right to speak to your father as you did. No right whatsoever to show him disrespect. And in front of your own child. Don't you see that it frightens and hurts Jack to watch the two of you claw at each other this way?"

She spun back, searing both of them with one hot look. "The pair of you haven't got enough sense put together to equal the brains of a monkey. I'm going outside with Jack. As far as I'm concerned the two of you can pound each other into mush and be done with it."

She wrenched open the door and sailed outside.

She was still simmering when Brody joined her a few minutes later. Saying nothing he watched Jack wrestle with the puppy and try to get Mike to chase a small red ball.

"I want to apologize for bringing that into your house."

"My house has heard family arguments before, and I expect it will hear them again."

"You were right about it being wrong for us to start on each other in front of Jack." When she said nothing, he jammed his hands into his pockets. "Kate, that's just the way it is between me and my father. The way it's always been."

"And because it's been that way, it has to continue to be? If you can change one aspect of your life, Brody, you can change others. You just have to try harder."

"We grate each other, that's all. We're better when we keep our distance. I don't want Jack to feel that way about me. Maybe I overcompensate."

"Stop it." Impatient again, she turned to him. "Is that a happy, well-adjusted, healthy boy?"

"Yeah." Brody had to smile as Jack filled the air with belly laughs as he rolled over the grass with the puppy climbing all over him.

"You know you're a good father. It's taken work, and effort, but for the most part it's easy for you. Because you love him unconditionally. It's a lot more work, a lot more effort, Brody, for you to be a good son. Because there are a lot of conditions on the love you have for your father, and his for you."

"We don't love each other."

"Oh, you're wrong. If you didn't, you couldn't hurt each other."

Brody shrugged that off. She didn't understand, he thought. How could she? "First time I've ever seen him shocked speechless. I don't believe he's ever had a woman rip into him that way. Me, I'm getting used to it."

"Good. Now if you don't want me ripping into you again anytime soon, you'll apologize to your mother at the first opportunity. You embarrassed her."

"Man, you're strict. Mind if I play with my dog first?"

She arched a brow. "Whose dog?"

"Jack's. But Jack and I, we're—"

"A team," she finished. "Yes, I know."

Chapter 10

Kate made her plans, bided her time. And chose her moment.

She knew it was calculated. But really, what was wrong with that? Timing, approach, method—they were essential to any plan. So if she'd waited for that particular moment on a Friday night when Jack was enjoying a night over at his grandparents and Brody was relaxed after a particularly intense bout of lovemaking, it was simply rational planning.

"I've got something for you."

"Something else?" He was, as Jerry would have said, in the zone. "I get dinner, a bottle of wine and a night with a beautiful woman. I don't think there is anything else."

With a quiet laugh she slipped out of bed. "Oh, but there is."

He watched her—always he enjoyed watching the way she moved. He'd come to the conclusion there was more to this ballet business than he'd once thought.

It gave him a great deal of pleasure to see her here, in his room. The room, he thought, he'd been squeezing in hours late at night to finish. He was doing, thank you God, a lot more than sleeping there now.

The walls were finished and painted a strong, deep blue. Kate favored strong colors. The woodwork, stripped down to its natural tone and glossily sealed, was a good accent.

He hoped to get to the floors soon. Curtains and that kind of thing would be dealt with eventually.

But for now he just liked seeing her in here. The dusky skin against the smooth blue walls, and the way the shimmer of light from the low fire danced in shadows.

She'd left her earrings on his dresser once. It had given him a hell of a jolt to see them there the next morning. They'd looked so...female, he remembered.

Yet he'd been foolishly disappointed when she'd removed them.

What that had to say about him, about things, he'd just have to figure out.

She put on his shirt against the light chill of the room and walked over to her purse.

"I'm going to buy you a half dozen flannel shirts," Brody decided. "Just so I can see you walking around naked under them."

"I'll take them." She sat back on the bed, and dropped an envelope on his bare chest. "And these are for you."

"What?" Baffled, he sat up, tapped out the contents. The two airline tickets only increased his confusion. "What's this?"

"Two tickets on the shuttle to New York. Next Friday. One for you, one for Jack."

He eyed them, then eyed her. Cautiously. "Because?"

"Because I really want both of you to come. Have you ever been to New York?"

"No, but—"

"Even better. I get to introduce it to both of you. The director of my former company called me earlier in the week," she explained. "They're putting on a special performance—one show only, next Saturday night. It's for charity. There'll be several selections from several ballets performed by different artists. He'd asked me to participate some time ago, but I passed. So much going on, and it's all but running into the opening of my school."

"But now you decided not to pass."

"The dancer who was to perform the *pas de deux* from *The Red Rose*—that's a ballet Davidov first performed with his wife when they were partners—is out with an injury. It's not career-ending, thank God, but she can't dance for at least two weeks. That's put her out. He's asked me to fill in."

Simple, she thought. It was all very simple. And she wasn't going to give Brody any wiggle room.

"I've danced this part several times. Fact is, it's what he asked me to perform originally. So when he called, I didn't want to say no. Then, of course, he talked me into doing another segment from *Don Quixote*. I should leave Monday to get in shape for it, but I couldn't shuffle everything, so I'm leaving Tuesday."

He felt a little twinge in the gut at the thought of her leaving again. "You'll be great. But listen, Kate, I appreciate the gesture, but I just can't grab Jack and take off to New York like that."

"Why not?"

"Well, work, school, for starters. A new puppy for another. Your basics."

"You can leave after school on Friday, and be in New York before dinner. We can stay at my sister's. Saturday you can see some of the city, maybe take Jack to the top of the Empire State Building. Saturday night, you come to the ballet. Sunday, we see a little more of the city, go have dinner at my grandparents, catch the late shuttle back. Everyone's at school or work Monday."

She moved her shoulders. "Oh, and as for Mike, you bring him, of course."

"Bring a dog to New York?"

"Sure, my sister's kids will love it."

He felt as though he were sitting in a box and she was slowly closing the lid. "Kate, it's just not the kind of thing people like me do. Flying off to New York for the weekend."

"It's not a flight to Mars, O'Connell." Laughing she leaned over and kissed him. "It's a little adventure. Jack'll love it—and…" She'd saved the *coup de grâce,* as any good general. "He'll be able to give his pal Rod a little back for all the bragging about Disney World. Jack'll see where King Kong fell to his tragic death."

It hit the mark and had Brody struggling not to squirm. Forget the box, he thought. Now he felt like a fish with a hook firmly lodged in his mouth. "Don't take this the wrong way, okay? But I'm really not into ballet."

"Oh." She smiled, fluttered her lashes. "Which ones have you seen?"

"I haven't seen a public hanging, either, but I don't think I'd get much of a charge out of it."

"Think of it this way. You'll be able to give Jack his first look at New York. You'll have two days to enjoy yourself and only about two hours to be bored senseless. Not a bad deal. You've never seen me dance," she added, linking her fingers with his. "I'd like you to."

He frowned at the tickets, shook his head. "Hit all the angles, didn't you?"

"I don't think I missed any. Is it a deal?"

"Wait till Jack hears he's going to take his first plane trip. He'll flip."

He did more than flip. By the time they were shuffling onto the plane on Friday afternoon, he was all but turning himself inside out.

"Dad? Can't you ask if Mike can ride up with us? He's going to be scared in that box."

"Jack, I told you it's not allowed. He'll be fine, I promise. Remember he's got his toys, and now those other two dogs are riding in the dog seats with him."

"Yeah. I guess." Jack's eyes were huge with wonder, excitement and trepidation as they stepped through the doorway and onto the plane. "Look," he said in a desperate whisper. "There's the pilot guys."

The flight attendant clued in instantly. Jack was treated to a tour of the cockpit and given a pair of plastic wings. By the time they were preparing for takeoff, he'd decided to be an airline pilot.

For the next fifty minutes, he peppered his father with questions, often with his face pressed up to the window. Brody's ears were ringing by the time they touched down, but he had to admit, Jack was having the time of his life.

Now all he had to do was get through the next couple of days—outnumbered by Kate's family. If that wasn't enough to give a guy a headache, there was always the ballet.

What the hell are you doing here, O'Connell? he asked himself with a quick twinge of panic. A weekend in New York. The ballet. For God's sake, why aren't you home sanding drywall and thinking about making a Friday night pizza?

Because of Kate, he admitted, and the panic bumped up into his throat. Somehow she'd changed everything.

With the carry-on in one hand, and Jack's hand gripped firmly in the other, Brody came through the gate. He ordered himself to be calm—it was only a couple of days, after all—and looked for Kate. When a tall blond man waved, Brody flipped through his memory files and tried to put a name to Kate's brother-in-law.

"Nick LeBeck." Nick tugged Brody's bag free to take it himself. "You guys are bunking at our place. Kate wanted to pick you up herself, but she got hung up at rehearsal."

"We appreciate you coming out. We could've taken a cab."

"No problem. Any more luggage?"

"Just Mike."

"Right." Grinning, Nick leaned down to shake Jack's hand. "Good to see you. Max is pretty excited about you coming to visit. You met him on New Year's."

"Uh-huh, and Kate said we can have, like, a sleep-over for two nights."

"Yeah. We're having a big celebration dinner, too. You like fish-head soup?"

Jack's eyes went huge. Slowly he shook his head.

"Good, because we're not having any. Let's go spring Mike."

It wasn't as awkward as he'd expected it to be to find himself dumped in a strange city, in a strange house with people he barely knew. Jack dived right in, picking up his fledgling friendship with Max as if they'd just parted the day before. Mike was a huge hit, and in a buzz of excitement at the attention, peed on the rug.

"I'm really sorry. He's almost housebroken."

"So are my kids," Freddie told Brody, and handed him a damp rag. "We're used to spills around here—of all natures—so relax."

To Brody's surprise, he did. It was interesting, and entertaining to watch Jack interact with a family, to see how he slid into the mix with a brother and sister. It was cute the way he played with three-year-old Kelsey. Kind of like he was trying out his big brother muscles.

It wasn't always easy, Brody mused, being an only child.

"Want to escape?" Nick asked and jerked his head. As he walked out of the playroom he called out: "You break it, you buy it." Laughing moans followed them out.

He took Brody into the music room with its battered piano—one he'd kept more than a decade out of sentiment—and its wide, deep leather chairs. There were gleaming Tonys on a shelf and a clutter of sheet music on a bench.

Nick walked over to a clear-fronted minifridge. "Beer?"

"Oh," Brody said with feeling. "Yeah."

"Traveling with kids separates the men from the boys." Nick popped tops, offered a bottle. "Let's hear it for keeping them separate for ten blissful minutes."

"He never stopped talking, not from the minute I picked him up from school. I think he broke his own record."

"Wait till you try trans-Atlantic. Nine hours trapped on a plane with Max and Kelsey." He shuddered. "Do you know how many questions can be asked in nine uninterrupted hours? No, let's not think about it. It'll give us both nightmares."

At Nick's gesture, Brody sank gratefully into one of the chairs. "It's a great place you've got here. I guess when I think of New York, I think of little apartments where the windows all face a brick building, or big, sleek skyscrapers."

"We got all of that. When Freddie and I started writing together, I was living over my brother's bar. Lower East side. Great bar," Nick added, "and not a half bad apartment. But it's not the kind of place you want to try to raise a couple of kids."

He glanced up, grinned. "Ah, here's the prima now."

"Sorry I'm late." Kate rushed in, gave Nick a quick peck on the cheek, then turned, bent and gave Brody a much longer kiss. "And sorry I couldn't pick you up. Davidov's having one of his moments. The man can drive you to drink. Nick, my hero, if you get me a glass of wine, I'll be your slave."

"Sounds like a deal."

"Tell Freddie I'll be back in after I catch my breath."

"Sit," he ordered, and nudged her into the chair he vacated. "Rest those million-dollar feet."

"You bet I will." She groaned, and leaned over to slip off her shoes as Nick left the room.

Brody swore and was instantly on his knees in front of her, lifted her foot in his hand. "What the hell have you done?" Her feet were bandaged, and raw.

"I danced."

"Until your feet bleed?" he demanded.

"Why yes, when necessary. With Davidov, it's often necessary."

"He ought to be shot."

"Mmm." She leaned back, closed her eyes. "I considered it, a number of times over the last couple days.

Ballet isn't for wimps, O'Connell. And aching, bleeding feet are part of the job description."

"That's ridiculous."

"That's the life." She leaned over again, kissed his forehead. "Don't worry. They heal."

"How the hell are you supposed to dance on these tomorrow night?"

"Magnificently," she told him, then let out a huge sigh of gratitude when Nick came back. "My prince. Brody thinks Davidov should be shot."

"So you've said, plenty." Nick glanced down at her feet, winced. "God, what a mess. Want some ice?"

"No, thanks. I'll baby them later."

"You're going to take care of them right now." To settle the matter, Brody got up, plucked her out of the chair and into his arms.

"Oh, really, Brody, get a grip."

"Just be quiet," he ordered and carried her out of the room.

Nick tipped back his beer. "Man, he is *toast.*" He hurried off to find his wife and tell her.

"It was so romantic." Freddie's heart continued to sigh over it now, hours later, as she and Nick prepared for bed. "He just carried her right into the kitchen, with that wonderful scowl on his face, and demanded where he could find a basin and so on to soak Kate's poor feet."

"I told you." Absently Nick rapped a fist on the wall that adjoined their room with his son's. But he didn't really expect it to quiet the racket on the other side for long. "The man's a goner."

"And the way he looks at her—especially when he thinks no one, particularly Kate, is paying attention. Like he could just gobble her up in one big bite. It's great."

Nick stopped scratching his belly and frowned. "I look at you that way."

Freddie sniffed and started to turn down the bed. "Yeah, right."

"Hey." He walked over, turned her around by the shoulder. "Right here," he instructed, pointing at his own face, then attempting a smoldering look. "See?"

She snorted. "Yeah, that's it all right. I am a puddle."

"Are you insinuating that I'm not romantic? Are you saying the hammer-swinger's got me beat in that department?"

Enjoying herself, Freddie rolled her eyes. "Please," she said and wandered over to the dresser to run a brush through her hair.

The next thing she knew she was being swept off her feet. Her surprised yelp was muffled against his very determined mouth. "You want romance, pal? Boy, are you going to get it."

At the other end of the hall, as children finally fell into reluctant and exhausted sleep, Kate belted her robe. She'd put in several long, hard days—days that wore the body to a nub and left the mind fussy with fatigue.

But now, knowing Brody was just a few steps away, she was restless. And needy. She imagined he'd consider sneaking into her room rude. But that didn't mean she couldn't sneak into his.

She slipped from her room, walked quietly down the hall to peek in on the children. Even the dog, she noted, was sprawled out limply. Satisfied, she eased out again, and made her way to Brody's door.

No light shone under it. Well, if she had to wake him up, she had to wake him up. She opened it—a little creak of sound—and stepped in just as he turned from the window.

He'd been thinking of her—nothing new there, he admitted. And stood now, wearing only his jeans loosened at the waist. His mouth went dry as he saw her reach behind and flip the lock.

"Kate. The kids."

"Out for the count." She'd bought the robe only the day before, on an hour break. A ridiculous extravagance of peach-colored silk. But seeing the way his eyes darkened, hearing the way it whispered as she crossed the room, she considered it worth every penny.

"I just checked on them," she said, and ran her hands up his chest. "And if they wake up, one of the four of us will take care of it. Taking in the view?"

"It's pretty spectacular." He took her hands. "I was just thinking I'd never be able to sleep tonight, knowing you were so close, and not being able to touch you."

"Touch me now, and neither one of us will worry about sleep tonight."

He wondered how he had ever considered resisting her. She was every fantasy, every dream, every wish.

All silk and shadows. And she was real, as real as that warm yielding mouth, those long, sculpted arms.

With her, all the years of emptiness, all the lonely nights were locked away.

He slipped the silk from her shoulders, and found only Kate beneath.

Curves and muscle, sighs and trembles. He slid into the bed with her, and into that intimate world they created together. Perfumed flesh, soft, stroking hands. She was a wonder to him, a smoky-eyed seductress who could beckon with a look. A strong-minded woman who refused to back down from a fight. An openhearted friend with strong shoulders and a steady hand.

He could no longer imagine what his life would be like if she stepped back out of it.

Knowing it, finally admitting it to himself, he gathered her close, and just held.

"Brody?" Kate brushed her fingers through his hair. His arms had tightened around her so fiercely she wondered why she didn't simply snap in two. "What is it?"

"Nothing." He pressed his lips to the side of her neck and ordered himself not to think. For God's sake don't think now. "It's nothing. I want you. It's like starving the way I want you."

His mouth took hers now. Hot, ravenous, burning away all thoughts, all reason.

There was something different happening between them. Something more. But he was whipping her over the edge so fast, with a kind of quiet intensity that was kin to desperation. She could do nothing but feel, nothing but respond. Her heart, already lost to him, bounded like a deer.

City lights glanced against the dark windows. The sounds of traffic hummed on the street below. Whatever life pulsed there meant nothing in this tangle of sheets and needs.

She rose over him, slim and pale in the shadows. Her hair was a dark fall, tumbling down her back, then sliding forward to curtain them both as she leaned down to kiss him. The scent of it, of her, surrounded him. Drowned him.

Then she took him in, one fluid move that encased him in heat.

Twin moans merged. Eyes locked. He reached for her, his hands sliding, slippery, up her body, over her breasts. She covered them with her own, holding him to her. And then she began to move.

Slow. Painfully and gloriously slow so that each breath was a shudder. Pleasure slithered through the blood, and began to pulse. He watched her as she took both of them higher—that graceful arch of body, that delicate line of throat. Her eyes closed as she lost herself. Her arms lifted until her hands were buried in her own rich mass of hair.

A sound rippled in her throat of pleasure rising. She began to drive him, drive herself, her hips like lightning. It was all speed and power now. With a kind of greedy glee they dragged each other toward the edge. Held there, held until madness had them leaping recklessly over.

When she folded herself down to him, trembling still, his arms locked around her.

Love me, she thought. Her heart was raw with loving him. Tell me. Why won't you tell me?

He shifted her so that she could curl against him, so he could hold her there. "Will you stay?"

Kate closed her eyes. "Yes."

They lay quiet in each other's arms. But neither slept for a long time.

He woke reaching for her. Confusion came first as he struggled to remember where he was. He was alone in bed, in the dark. Groggy, he glanced over at a faint sound, and saw Kate, in the faint wash of light through the window, slipping into her robe.

"What is it?"

"Oh, I didn't mean to wake you." Whispering she stepped over to the side of the bed, bent down to kiss his cheek. "I have to go. Dance class."

"Huh? You're teaching class in the middle of the night?"

"I'm taking class—and it's not the middle of the night. It's nearly six."

He tried to clear his brain, but it objected to functioning on four hour's sleep. "You're taking class? I thought you knew how to dance."

"Smart aleck."

"No, wait." He grabbed for her hand before she could move away. "Why are you taking class? And why are you taking it at six in the morning?"

"I'm taking class because I'm a dancer, and dancers never really stop taking class—certainly not if they're performing. And I'm taking it at seven in the morning because I have a dress rehearsal at eleven. Now go back to sleep."

"Oh. Okay."

"Nick and Freddie are going to take you around later, wherever. Maybe you can drop by the theater."

She waited for a response, then leaned down. "Well," she muttered, "you didn't have any trouble taking that particular order."

She left him sleeping and went to prepare for a very long day.

"Are you sure it's okay?" Brody looked dubiously at the motley crew approaching the stage door. Three adults, three kids and a small, mixed-breed puppy.

"Absolutely," Freddie assured him. "Kate cleared it."

He still wasn't convinced, but he'd already discovered it was hard to argue with either Kimball sister.

Especially on five hour's sleep.

The kids had bounded awake by the time Kate was taking her class. And they'd created enough noise to wake the entire island of Manhattan. Anyone deaf enough to sleep through it, would have been jolted awake by Mike's high, ferociously joyful barking.

They'd had breakfast in a deli, which had delighted Jack, then had proceeded to walk their feet off. The Empire State Building, souvenir shops. Times Square, souvenir shops. Grand Central Station. God help him, souvenir shops.

Brody decided horning in on Kate's rehearsal wasn't such a bad idea after all. It was in a theater, and last time he checked a theater had chairs.

"Lips zipped," Nick warned. "Or they'll kick us out. That goes for you, too, furball," he added, scratching Mike behind the ears.

"Nothing like backstage." Freddie linked her hand with Nick as they entered.

A woman behind a high counter glanced up over wire-rim glasses, scanned, then nodded. "Nice to see you, Ms. Kimball, Mr. LeBeck. See you brought the crew."

"Kate clear the way?" Freddie asked.

"She did. Any of these kids understand Russian?"

"No."

"Good. Davidov's in rare form. You can leave the pup with me. I like dogs, and if he gets frisky out there, Davidov's liable to eat him."

"That kind of day, huh?" Nick grinned, and the woman rolled her eyes.

"You don't know the half of it. What's his name?"

"His name is Mike," Jack piped up. "He's mine."

"I'll take real good care of him."

"Okay." Biting his lip, Jack passed Mike up to her. "But if he cries, you have to come get me."

"That's a deal. Go on ahead, you know the way."

If they hadn't, after a short twist through backstage, they could have followed the bellows.

"Davidov." Freddie gave a mock shudder. "We'll just detour this way and go out front—where it's safe."

"Does he really eat dogs?" Jack asked in a hissing whisper.

"No." Brody took a firm hold of his son's hand. "She was just kidding." He hoped.

He didn't eat dogs, but at the moment, Davidov would have cheerfully dined on dancers.

He cut off the music again with a dramatic slice of his hand through the air. "You, you." He pointed at the couple currently panting and dripping sweat. "Go. Off my stage. Soak your heads. Maybe you'll come back in one hour, like dancers. Kimball!" he shouted. "Blackstone! Now!"

He paced back and forth, a slim man in dull gray sweats and a dramatic mane of gold-and-silver hair. His face was carved and cold.

"He's scary," Jack decided.

"Shh." Brody hitched Jack onto his lap after they'd slipped into a row of seats behind a lone woman.

Then Kate came onstage, and his mouth simply dropped.

"It's Kate. Look, Dad, she's all dressed up."

"Yeah, I see. Quiet now."

Her hair was loose, raining down the back of a flamboyant costume, boldly red with layers of skirt flowing out from a nipped waist. It stopped just below her knees and showed off long legs that ended in toe shoes.

She sauntered, hands on hips, until she was toe to

toe with Davidov. "You ordered me offstage. Don't do that again."

"I order you on, I order you off. That is what I do. What you do is dance. You." He flicked a finger at the tall, gilt haired man in white who'd come out with Kate. "Step back. Wait. *Red Rose,*" he told the orchestra. "Opening solo. Kimball. You are Carlotta," he said to Kate. "*Be* Carlotta. Lights!"

Kate sucked in a breath. Took her position. Left leg back, foot turned and straight as a ruler. Arms lifted, curved into fluid lines. Head up and defiant. When the music began, the strings, she felt the beats. The single spotlight hit her like a torch. She danced.

It was a viciously demanding solo. Fast, lightning fast and wildly flamboyant. Her muscles responded, her feet flew. She ended with a snap, in precisely the same spot and in the same position where she'd begun.

Heart pounding from the effort, she shot Davidov a defiant, and unscripted look, then pirouetted offstage as her partner leaped into his cue.

He'd never seen anything like it. Hadn't known there could be anything like it. She'd been…magic, Brody thought and was still trying to process this new aspect of her when she flew back onstage.

They danced together now, Kate and the man in white. He hadn't realized ballet could be…sexy. But this was, almost raw, certainly edgy, a kind of classic mating dance with arrogant male, defiant female.

He didn't see the small balancing steps, the sets, the releases. Didn't see how she helped her partner lift her by springing with her knees, or how the muscles in her legs trembled with the effort to keep them extended in midair.

He only saw the speed, the dazzle. The magic. And was jerked rudely out of the moment by the shout.

"Stop! Stop! Stop!" Davidov threw up his hands. "What is this, what is it? Do you have hot blood, do you have passion or are you strolling through the park on Sunday? Where is the fire?"

"I'll give you fire." Kate whirled on him.

"Good." He grabbed her at the waist. "With me. Show me." He hoisted her up even as she cursed him.

She came down like a thunderbolt, hearing the music only in her head now, soaring into a series of *jetés*. He caught her again, spun her into a triple pirouette, then lifted her, lowering her until her head nearly brushed the stage. Sharp moves, challenges, and she was back *en pointe,* her eyes firing darts into his.

"There, now. Do again. Stay angry."

"I hate you."

"Not me. Him." He flicked a hand and brought the music back.

"What the hell does he want?" Brody demanded, forgetting himself. "Blood?"

The woman in the row ahead turned, gave him a dazzling smile. "Yes. Exactly. He always has. A difficult man, Davidov."

"Daddy says he ought to be shot," Jack added, helpfully.

"Your father isn't alone in thinking that." She laughed,

turning farther in her seat as the dancing, and the cursing continued onstage. "He's harder, much harder, on the dancers who are the best. I used to dance with him myself, so I know."

"Did he yell at you?"

"Yes. And I yelled right back. But I was a better dancer for it, and for him. He still made me very, very angry, though."

"What did you do?" Jack's eyes were big as saucers. "Did you punch him in the nose?"

"No. I married him." She grinned at Brody. "I'm Ruth Bannion. You must be a friend of Kate's."

"Excuse me, I'd like to get my foot out of my mouth."

"No, no." She let out a low, delighted laugh. "Davidov brings out the best, and the worst. That's what makes him what he is. He adores Kate, and is still mourning she's left the company." Ruth glanced back toward the stage. "Look at her, and you can see why."

"All right, all right. Enough." Onstage, Davidov let out a windy sigh. "Go rest. Perhaps tonight you will find me some energy."

The blood was pounding in Kate's ears. Her feet were screaming. But she had enough energy, right now, for a short tirade.

When she was done, and simply panting, Davidov lifted his eyebrow. "You think because I'm Russian I don't know when a Ukrainian calls me a man with the heart of a pig?"

Her chin shot up. "I believe I said the *face* of a pig."
She stalked offstage and left him grinning after her.
"See?" Ruth smiled. "He adores her."

Chapter 11

Kate was busy kissing the Russian when Brody came to her dressing room door after the evening performance. She was wearing a robe—short and red—and full stage makeup. Her hair was still pinned up in some sleek and sophisticated knot, the way it had been during her second dance—the Spanish one, in the sexy little tutu.

The audience had gone wild for her, and so, Brody thought, had he.

Now, he'd come back to tell her only to find her wrapped around the Russian she'd cursed only that afternoon.

He wondered which one of them he should kill first.

"Sorry to interrupt."

Kate merely turned her head, eyes brilliant, and beamed at him. "Brody."

She held out a hand, but Davidov merely shifted his arm around her shoulders and eyed the intruder coolly.

"This is the carpenter? The one who wants to shoot me? Now, I think, he wants to shoot me more. He doesn't like that I kiss you."

"Oh, don't be silly."

Brody cut his eyes back to hers. "I don't like that he kisses you."

"That's absurd. This is Davidov."

"I know who it is." Brody shut the door behind him. He preferred spilling blood in relative privacy. "I met your wife today."

"Yes, she likes you, and your little boy. I have a son, and two daughters." Because he rarely resisted impulses, and it was delightful to watch the man's fury heat, Davidov kissed Kate's hair. "She knows, my wife, that I've come back to kiss this one. Who was," he continued drawing back, his hands sliding down her arms to link with hers, "magnificent. Who was perfect. Who I don't forgive for leaving me."

"I felt magnificent. I felt perfect." Still so perfect none of the aches could push through. "And I'm happy."

"Happy." He rolled his eyes to the ceiling. "As your director, what do I care if you're happy as long as you dance? As your friend." He heaved a sigh and kissed her hands. "I'm glad you have what you want."

"We'll all end up a lot happier if you step back," Brody commented.

Kate frowned. "Jealousy isn't attractive—and in this case certainly misplaced."

"Murder isn't attractive. But it really seems to fit."

"One minute," Davidov said, dismissively, to both of them. "You want to snarl at each other, wait until I finish. I wrote *The Red Rose* for my Ruth," he said to Kate. "My heart. There's no one but you who has been Carlotta as she was Carlotta."

"Oh." Tears swirled into her eyes, spilled out. "Damn it."

"You are missed. So I insist you be very, very happy, or I will come to your West Virginia and drag you back." Now he cupped her face, spoke quietly in Russian. "You want this man?"

She nodded. *"Da."*

"Well, then." He pressed his lips to her forehead, then turned to study Brody. "Me, I'm a man who loves his wife. You met her, so you should see that she is all I treasure. I kiss this one because she is also a treasure. If you had eyes in your head to watch her tonight, this you should also know."

His eyes gleamed now in amused challenge. "Still, if I find another man kissing what's mine, I break his legs. But I'm Russian."

"I usually start with the arms. I'm Irish."

Davidov's laugh was rich, and his face went brilliant. "I like him. Good." Satisfied, he slapped Brody on the shoulder on his way out the door.

"Isn't he wonderful?"

"A few hours ago, you hated him."

"Oh." She waved a hand and sat down to cream off

her makeup. "That was rehearsal. I always hate him during rehearsals."

"Do you always kiss him after a performance?"

"If it goes particularly well. He's a bully, a genius. He's Davidov," she said simply. "I wouldn't be the dancer I am, maybe not even the woman I am without having worked with him. We're intimate, Brody, but not sexually. Not ever. He adores his wife. All right?"

"You're saying it's an art thing."

"In a nutshell. Not that removed from ballplayers hugging each other and patting each other's butts after a really good game."

"I don't remember ever seeing your brother kiss his shortstop after a double play, but okay. I get it."

"Good. It went beautifully, didn't it?" She spun around on her stool. "Did you like it?"

"You were incredible. I've never seen anything like it. Never seen anything like you."

"Oh." She leaped off the stool, threw her arms around him. "I'm so glad! Oh." She laughed and rubbed at the smear she'd transferred to his cheek. "Sorry. I wanted it to be incredible. I got so nervous when I realized the family was here. Mama and Dad sneaking up from home, and Grandma and Grandpa. All the aunts and uncles and cousins. And Brandon sent flowers."

She grabbed more tissue, sniffling as she sat again. "I thought I might be sick, my stomach was churning so." She pressed a hand to it now. "But then all I felt was the music. When that happens you know. You just know."

He glanced around the room. It was crowded with

flowers, literally hundreds of roses. Bottles of champagne, her exotic costumes. All of those glamorous things filled it, and were pale next to her excitement.

How could she leave all this? he wondered. Why should she?

He started to ask, then her door burst open. Her family poured in and the moment was lost.

She seemed to be just as much in her element the next day in the house in Brooklyn where her grandparents lived. The exotic siren who'd flamed across the stage the night before had been replaced by a lovely woman comfortable in jeans and bare feet.

It was a puzzle, Brody decided, trying to fit the two of them together into a whole. He intended to take the time to do so.

But for now, the best he could do was experience. The house was crammed with people—so many of them, he wondered if there was enough oxygen to go around. The noise level was a wonder.

A piano stood against one wall and was played by various fingers at various times. Everything from rock to Bach. The scents of cooking wafted through the air. Wine was poured with generous hands, and nobody seemed to stay still for more than five minutes.

His son was wallowing in it. He could see him, if he angled his head through other bodies, sprawled on the worn rug with Max, bashing cars together. The last time he'd been able to spot Jack he'd been sitting on Yuri's lap having what appeared to have been a serious conversation that had involved a number of gumdrops.

And before that, he'd raced down the stairs in the wake of a couple of young teenagers. Since Brody hadn't seen him go up the stairs in the first place, he was trying to keep a closer eye on his son.

"He's fine." A woman with the trademark Stanislaski looks—wild, bold, beautiful—dropped onto the couch beside him. "Rachel," she said with a quick grin. "Kate's aunt. Hard to keep us straight, isn't it?"

"There are a lot of you." Rachel, he thought, trying desperately to remember the details. Kate's mother's sister. A judge. That's right. Married to…the guy who owned the bar. And the guy who owned the bar was Nick's stepbrother.

Was it any wonder a man couldn't keep them lined up?

"You'll get the hang of it. That's my guy there." She gestured toward a tall man who had his arm hooked around the throat of a gangly boy with dark hair. "Currently choking our son Gideon while he talks to Sydney—the exceptional redhead who's married to my brother Mik—and Laurel, Mik and Sydney's youngest. Mik's over there, arguing with my other brother Alex, while Alex's wife, Bess—the other exceptional redhead—appears to be discussing something of great importance with her daughter, Carmen, and Nick and Freddie's Kelsey. The tall, handsome young man just coming out of the kitchen is Mik's oldest, Griff, who seems to have charmed some food out of my mother, Nadia. Got that?"

"Ah…"

"You absorb that awhile." She laughed and patted his knee. "Because there are so many more of us. Meanwhile, your son's fine—and you don't have a drink. Wine?"

"Sure, why not?"

"No, I'll get it." She patted him again and dashed off. Almost immediately, Griff plopped down and began to talk carpentry.

That, at least, Brody had a handle on.

Kate wound her way through the bodies, sat on the arm of the couch and offered him one of two glasses of wine. "Okay over here?"

"Yeah, fine. I figure it's kind of like the Boy Scout rule—when you're lost sit down in one spot, and they'll find you. People drop down here, talk for a couple minutes, then move off. I'm starting to be able to keep them straight working it that way."

Even as he spoke, Alex settled on the couch, propped his feet on the coffee table. "So, Bess and I are thinking about adding a couple of rooms onto our weekend place."

"See," Brody said to Kate, then shifted. "What did you have in mind?"

Kate left him to it and wandered into the kitchen. Her mother was at the table, putting the finishing touches on an enormous salad. Nadia was at the stove, supervising as Mik's youngest son, Adam, stirred something in a pot. "Need some more hands?"

"Always too many hands in my kitchen," Nadia said. Her hair was snow-white now—a soft wave around a strong face lined with years. But her eyes danced with amusement as she patted Adam. "There, you have done well. Go."

"But we're going to eat soon, right? We're starving."

"Very soon. Tell your brothers and sisters, your cousins, my table must be set."

"All right!" He shot out of the room, shouting orders.

"He wants to be in charge, that one."

Natasha laughed. "Mama, they *all* want to be in charge. How's Brody holding up, Katie?"

"He's talking with Uncle Alex." Kate snitched a crouton then wandered to the stove to sniff at pots. "Isn't he adorable?"

"He has good eyes," Nadia said. "Strong, kind. And he raises his son well. You show good taste."

"I learned from the best." She leaned over to kiss Nadia's cheek. "Thank you for welcoming him."

Nadia felt her heart sigh. "Go, help set the table. Your young man and his little boy will think no one eats in this house."

"They'll soon find out differently." She snatched another crouton and kissed the top of her mother's head on the way out.

"Well." Nadia stared hard into a pot. "We'll be dancing at her wedding. You're pleased with him."

"Of course." Natasha could barely see as she prepared to dress the salad. "He's a good man. He makes her happy. And to be honest, I think if I could have chosen for her myself, it would have been Brody. Oh, Mama." Eyes drenched, Natasha looked over at the stove. "She's my baby."

"I know. I know." Nadia hurried over for the hug, then offered Natasha one corner of her apron while she used the other to dry her eyes.

By midweek, Kate was hard at work and anxious to open her doors for the first students. The studio itself was complete. The floors were smooth and gleaming, the walls glistening with mirrors. Her office was organized, the dressing areas outfitted.

And now the front window was finished.

Kimball School Of Dance

She stood out on the sidewalk, her palms together and pressed to her lips, reading it over and over again.

Dreams, she thought, came true. All you had to do was believe hard enough, and work long enough.

"Oh, miss?"

"Hmm?" Lost in her own joy, she turned, then blinked at the woman crossing the street. The woman, Kate remembered with a sinking stomach, who'd seen Brody cart her outside over his shoulder. "Oh. Yes. Hello."

"Hello. We didn't really meet before." The woman looked as uneasy as Kate and fiddled with the strap of her shoulder bag. "I'm Marjorie Rowan."

"Kate Kimball."

"Yes, I know. Actually, I sort of know your boyfriend, too. The landlord's hired him a couple of times to see to things in my building."

"Ah," Kate said. "Hmm."

"Anyway, I picked up one of your brochures the other day, from your mother's store. My little girl, she's eight, she's just been nagging me half to death about taking ballet classes."

Relief came first. It was not to be a conversation about creating public scenes on quiet streets. Then came the pleasure at the possibility of another student.

"I'd be happy to talk to you about it, and to her if you'd like. First classes start next week. Would you like to come in, see the school?"

"Truth is, we've peeked in the window a few times. I hope you don't mind."

"Of course not."

"I've been telling Audrey—that's my girl—that I'd think about it. I guess I have. I'd like her to be able to try it."

"Why don't you come inside, and tell me about Audrey."

"Thanks. She'll be home from school soon. This'll be a nice surprise." She started up the stairs, relaxing now. "You know I always wanted ballet lessons when I was a girl. We couldn't swing it."

"Why don't you take them now?"

"Now?" Marjorie laughed and stepped inside. "Oh, I'm too old for ballet lessons."

"They're wonderful exercise. It increases flexibility. And they're fun. No one's too old for that. You look to be in very good shape."

"I do what I can." Marjorie looked around, smiling a little dreamily at the *barres,* the mirrors, the framed posters. "I guess it would be fun. But I couldn't afford classes for both of us."

"We'll talk about that, too. Come on back to my office."

An hour later, Kate rushed upstairs. She wanted to share with someone, and Brody was elected. She had two new students—her first mother and daughter team. And the accomplishment had given her yet one more angle for her school.

Family plans.

She started to dash across the little living room and stopped in her tracks. Slowly she turned a circle. It was done. She hadn't been paying enough attention, she decided, and the progress had zipped right by her.

The floors and walls were finished. The woodwork glowed like silk.

Dazzled, she walked into her kitchen where everything gleamed. Cabinets waited only to be filled. The windowsill cried out for flowerpots.

She ran a fingertip along the countertop. Brody had been right about the breakfast bar, she thought. He had been right—no, *they* had been right, she corrected, about everything.

The apartment, just like the rest of the building, had been a team effort. And it was perfect.

She hurried into the bedroom where Brody was kneeling on the floor installing the lock sets on her closet doors. Jack sat crossed-legged, tongue caught in his teeth as he carefully tightened a screw in a brass plate on a wall plug.

Mike snored contentedly between them.

"There's nothing quite like watching men at work." They glanced up, and made her heart sing. "Hello, Handsome Jack."

"We're punching out," he told her. "I got to come help because Rod and Carrie had to go to the dentist. I went already and no cavities."

"Good for you. Brody, I've been so involved downstairs that I haven't taken in what you've done up here. It looks wonderful. It's exactly right."

"Still got a few details. Some outside work, too. But you're pretty much good to go." But he didn't have that lift of satisfaction he usually experienced toward the end of a job. He'd been depressed for days.

"I love it." She crouched down as Mike woke and gamboled over to greet her. "And I just signed two more students. Now, if I could just find a couple of handsome men who'd like to go out and celebrate, it would really round things off."

"We'll go!"

"Jack. It's a school night."

"I was thinking about an early dinner," Kate improvised as Jack's face fell. "Burgers and fries at Chez McDee."

"She means McDonald's," Jack explained, then fell on his father's back, hugging fiercely. "Please, can we?"

Cornered again, Brody thought. "Pretty tough for a guy to turn down a fancy meal like that."

"He means yes." Jack swung over to Kate and hugged her legs. "Can we go now?"

"I got some things to finish up here." Brody pushed his hair back. And just looked at her.

He'd been doing that quite a bit, Kate thought, since they'd come back from New York. Looking at her—and looking at her differently somehow.

Differently enough to have frogs leaping in her belly again.

"An hour okay with you?" he asked.

"Perfect. Do you mind if I steal your helper here? I want to go tell my mother. We can give Mike a little exercise on the way."

"Yeah, sure. Jack? No wheedling."

"He means I can't ask for toys. I'll get Mike's leash. Dad, can I—" He broke off then ran over to whisper in Brody's ear.

"Yeah, go ahead."

"We'll be back in an hour."

"Great." Brody waited until they'd chased Mike downstairs, then sat back on his heels.

He was going to have to make some decisions. And soon. It was bad enough he was stuck on Kate, but Jack was crazy about her.

A man could risk a few bumps and bruises on his own heart, but he couldn't risk his child's. The only thing to do was to sit down and have a talk with Kate. It was time they spelled out what was going on between them.

More, he was going to have to have a talk with Jack.

He had to know what the boy was thinking, what he was feeling.

Jack first, Brody decided. Could be, could very well be, his son looked at Kate as nothing more than a friend and would be upset at the idea of her being a more permanent, more important part of their lives. It had been the two of them as long as Jack could remember.

He looked over with a little jolt as a movement caught the corner of his eye.

"You turn that noise down," Bob O'Connell said, "you wouldn't get taken by surprise."

"I like music on the job." But Brody rose, shut off the radio. "Something you need?"

They hadn't spoken since the scene in the Kimball kitchen. Both men eyed each other warily.

"I got something to say," Bob stated.

"Then say it."

"I did my best by you. It ain't right for you to say different, when I did my best by you. Maybe I was hard on you, but you had a wild streak and you needed hard. I had a family to support, and I did it the only way I knew how. Maybe you think I didn't spend enough time with you—" Bob broke off, jammed his hands into his pockets. "Maybe I didn't. I don't have the knack for it, not the way you do with your boy. Fact is, you weren't the same pleasure to be around Jack is. He's a credit to you. Maybe I should've said so before, but I'm saying so now."

Brody said nothing for a long moment, adjusting to the shock even as his father glared at him. "You know,

I'm pretty sure that's about the longest speech you ever aimed in my direction."

Bob's face hardened. "I'm done with it," he said and turned.

"Dad." Brody set his drill aside. "I appreciate it."

Bob let out a breath, the way a man might as the trap-door opened under his feet. "Well." He turned back, fought with the words in his head. "Might as well finish it off then. Probably I shouldn't have jumped on you the other day, not in front of your boy and your...the Kimball girl. Your mother lit into me over it."

Brody could only stare. "Mom?"

"Yeah." With a look of frustrated disgust, Bob kicked lightly at the doorjamb. "She don't do it often, but when she does, she can peel the skin off your ass. Hardly speaking to me yet. Says I embarrassed her."

"I got the same line from Kate—she did some peeling of her own."

"Didn't much care having her claw at me the way she did. But I gotta say, she's got spine. Keep you straight."

"It's my job to keep myself straight."

Bob nodded. The weight that had been pressing on his chest for days eased. "Guess I figure you've been doing your job there. You do good work. For a carpenter."

For the first time in a long while, Brody was able to smile at his father and mean it. "You do good work. For a plumber."

"Didn't have any problem firing me."

"You pissed me off."

"Hell, boy, you fire every man who pisses you off,

how are you going to put a crew together? How's the hand?"

Brody lifted it, flexed his fingers. "Good enough."

"Since you've got no permanent damage, maybe you can use that hand to dial the phone. Call your ma and let her know we cleared the air some. She might not take my word on it, given her current state of mind."

"I'll do that. I know I was a disappointment to you."

"Now, hold on—"

"I was," Brody continued. "Maybe I was a disappointment to myself, too. But I think I made up for it. I did it for Connie, and for Jack. For myself, too. And I did it, partly anyway, for you. So I could show you I was worth something."

"You showed me." Bob wasn't good at taking first steps, but he took this one. He crossed the room, held out his hand. "I guess I'm proud of how you turned out."

"Thanks." He took his father's hand in a firm grip. "I've a kitchen remodel coming up. Needs some plumbing work. Interested?"

Bob's lips twitched. "Could be."

Chapter 12

While father and son were closing a gap, Kate strolled with the third generation of O'Connell male.

"I didn't wheedle, right?"

"Wheedle?" She sent him a shocked stare. "Why Handsome Jack, Mama and I had to practically force that plane on you. We had to *beg* you to accept it."

Jack grinned up at her. "You'll tell Dad?"

"Of course. He's going to want to play with it, you know. It's a very cool plane."

Jack swirled it through the air. "It's like the one I got to fly on, all the way to New York and back again. It was fun. I told everybody thanks in the cards I sent. Did you like your card? I did it almost all by myself."

"I loved my card." Kate patted her pocket where the thank-you note, painstakingly printed, resided. "It was very polite and gentlemanly of you to write one to me, and to Freddie and Nick and to my grandparents."

"They said I could come back. Papa Yuri said I could sometime spend the night at his house."

"You'd like that?"

"Yeah. He can wiggle his ears."

"I know."

"Kate?"

"Hmm." She bent to untangle Mike from his leash, then glanced up to see Jack studying her. So serious, she thought, so intent. Just like his father. "What is it, Handsome Jack?"

"Can we…can we sit on the wall so we can talk about stuff?"

"Sure." Very serious, Kate realized as she boosted him up on the wall in front of the college. She passed Mike up to him, then hopped up beside them. "What kind of stuff?"

"I was wondering…" He trailed off again while Mike scrambled off to sniff at the grass behind them.

He'd talked it all over with his best friends. Max in New York, and then Rod at school. It was a secret. They'd spit on their palms to seal it. "You like my dad, don't you?"

"Of course I do. I like him very much."

"And you like kids. Like me?"

"I like kids. I especially like you." She draped an arm around him, rubbed his shoulder. "We're friends."

"Dad and I like you, too. A whole lot. So I was wondering…" He looked up at her, his eyes so young, so earnest. "Will you marry us?"

"Oh." Her heart stumbled, then fell with a splat. "Oh, Jack."

"If you did, you could come live in our house. Dad's fixing it up good. And we have a yard and everything, and we're going to plant a garden soon. In the mornings you could have breakfast with us, then drive to your school and teach people how to dance. Then you could drive home. It's not real far."

Staggered, she laid her cheek on the top of his head. "Oh, boy."

"Dad's really nice," Jack rushed on. "He hardly ever yells. He doesn't have a wife anymore, because she had to go to heaven. I wish she didn't, but she did."

"I know. Oh, baby."

"Maybe Dad's afraid to ask you in case you go to heaven, too. That's what Rod thinks. Maybe. But you won't, will you?"

"Jack." She fought back tears and cupped his face. "I plan to stay here for a very long time. Have you talked to your father about this?"

"Nuh-uh, 'cause you're supposed to ask the girl. That's what Max said. The boy has to ask the girl. Me and Dad'll buy you a ring, 'cause girls need to have one. I won't mind if you kiss me, and I'll be really good. You and Dad can make babies like people do when they get married. I'd rather have a brother, but if it's a sister, that's okay. We'll love each other and everything. So will you please marry us?"

In all her dreams and fantasies, she'd never imagined being proposed to by a six-year-old boy, while sitting on a wall on an afternoon in early spring. Nothing could have been more touching, she thought. More lovely.

"Jack, I'm going to tell you a secret. I already love you."

"You do?"

"Yes, I do. I already love your dad, too. I'm going to think really hard about everything you said. Really hard. That way, if I say yes, you're going to know, absolutely, that it's what I want more than anything else in the whole world. If I say yes you wouldn't just be your dad's little boy anymore. You'd be mine, too. Do you understand that?"

He nodded, all eyes. "You'd be my mom, right?"

"Yes, I'd be your mom."

"Okay. Would you?"

"I'm going to think about it." She pressed her lips to his forehead, then hopped down.

"Will it take a long time to think?"

She reached up for him. "Not this time." She held him close before she set him on his feet. "But let's keep this a secret, a little while longer, while I do."

She gave it almost twenty-four hours. After all she was a woman who knew her own mind. Maybe the timing wasn't quite perfect, but it couldn't be helped.

Certainly the way things were tumbling weren't in the nice, neat logical row she'd have preferred. But she could be flexible. When she wanted something badly enough, she could be very flexible.

She considered asking Brody out for a romantic dinner for two. Rejected it. A proposal in a public restaurant would make it too difficult to pin him down, should it become necessary.

She toyed with the idea of waiting for the weekend, planning that romantic dinner for two at Brody's house. Candlelight, wine, seductive music.

That was her next rejection. If Jack hadn't spilled the beans by then, she very likely would herself.

It wouldn't be exactly the way she'd pictured it. There wouldn't be moonlight and music, with Brody looking deep into her eyes as he told her he loved her, asked her to spend her life loving him.

Maybe it wouldn't be perfect, but it would be right. Atmosphere didn't matter at this point, she told herself. Results did. So why wait?

She started upstairs. It was good timing after all, she realized. He was just finishing the job that had brought them together. Why not propose marriage in the space they had, in a very real way, made together? It was perfect.

Convinced of it, Kate was very displeased to find the rooms over the school empty.

"Well, where the hell did you go?" She fisted her hands on her hips and paced.

School bus, she remembered, spinning for the door. It was one of his days to pick up Jack. She glanced at her watch as she sprinted down the stairs. He couldn't have been gone more than a few minutes.

"Hey! Where's the fire." Spence caught her as she leaped down the last steps.

"Dad. Sorry. Gotta run. I need to catch Brody."

"Something wrong?"

"No, no." She gave him a quick kiss on the cheek and wiggled free. "I need to ask him to marry me."

"Oh, well…whoa." She was younger, faster, but parental shock shot him to the door in time to snag her. "What did you say?"

"I'm going to ask Brody to marry me. I've got it all worked out."

"Katie."

"I love him. I love Jack. Dad, I don't have time to explain it all, but I've thought it through. Trust me."

"Just catch your breath and let me…" But he looked at her face, into her eyes. Stars, he thought. His little girl had stars in her eyes. "He hasn't got a prayer."

"Thanks." She threw her arms around her father's neck. "Wish me luck anyway."

"Good luck." He let her go, then watched her run. "Bye, baby," he murmured.

Brody made a stop for milk, bread and eggs. Jack had developed an obsession with French Toast. As he turned into his lane, he checked his watch. A good ten minutes before the bus, he noted. He'd mistimed it a bit.

Resigned to the wait, he climbed out, let Mike race up the hill and back. Spring was coming on fine, he thought.

Greening the leaves, teasing the early flowers into tight buds. It brought something into the air, he mused.

Maybe it was hope.

The house, the ramble of it, was looking like a home. Soon he'd stick a hammock in the yard, maybe a rocker on the porch. Maybe a porch swing. He'd get Jack a little splash pool.

Jack and Mike could play in the yard, roll around on the grass on those long, hot summer evenings. He'd sit on the porch swing and watch. Sit on the swing with Kate.

Funny, he couldn't put a real picture into his head anymore, unless Kate was in it.

And didn't want to.

He'd have to take his time, Brody mused. Get a sense of where Jack stood in all of it. After that, it would be a matter of seeing if Kate was willing to take everything to the next level.

Maybe it was time to give her a little nudge in that direction. Nothing was ever perfect, was it? Everything in life was a work in progress.

It was like building a house. He figured they had a good, solid foundation. He had the design in his head— him, Kate, Jack and the kids who came along after. A house needed kids. So it was time to start putting up the frame, making it solid.

Maybe she wouldn't be ready for marriage yet—with her school just getting off the ground. She might need some time to adjust to the idea of being a mother to a six-year-old. He could give her some time.

He stood, looking over his land, studying the house on the hill that just seemed to be waiting.

Not a lot of time, he decided. Once he started building, he liked to keep right on building. And he wanted Kate working on this, the most important project of his life, with him.

The first thing to do, he decided as he walked to the mailbox, was to talk to Jack about it. His son had to feel secure, comfortable and happy. Jack was crazy about Kate. Maybe Jack would be a little worried about the changes marrying her would bring, but Brody could reassure his son.

They'd talk about it tonight, he decided, after dinner.

He just couldn't wait any longer than that to start things moving.

When he and Jack were square, he'd figure out what to say to Kate, what to do, to move everybody along to the next stage of the floor plan.

He got the mail out of the box, and was sifting through it on the way back to the truck when Kate pulled in beside him.

"Hey." Surprised, he tossed the mail into the cab of his truck. "Didn't expect to see you out this way today."

After she got out of the car, she picked up the mangled hunk of rope Mike spit at her feet, engaged him in a brief bout of tug-of-war, then threw it—she had a damn good arm—far enough to keep him busy awhile.

Watching her playing with the dog, all Brody could think about was that he couldn't wait very long.

"I just missed you at the school," she told him.

"Problem there?"

"No, not at all. No problem anywhere." She walked to him and slid her hands up his chest, a habit that never failed to pump up his heart rate. "You didn't kiss me goodbye."

"Your office door was closed. I figured you were busy."

"Kiss me goodbye now." She brushed her lips over his, arched a brow when he kept it light and started to ease back. "Do better."

"Kate, the bus is going to come along in a couple minutes."

"Do better," she murmured, and melting against him shifted the mood.

He fisted a hand in the back of her shirt, another in her hair. And indulged both of them.

"Mmmm. That's more like it. It's spring," she added, tipping back so that she could see his face. "Do you know what a young man's fancy turns to in spring? Besides baseball."

He grinned at her. "Plowing?"

She laughed, linking her fingers behind his neck. Yeah, the frogs were still jumping. But she liked it. "All right, do you know what a young woman's fancy turns to? What this young woman's fancy turns to?"

"Is that what you came out here to tell me?"

"Yes. More or less. Brody…" She nibbled her bottom lip, then just blurted it out, "I want you to marry me."

He jerked, froze. There was a buzzing in his ears—a hive of wild bees. He had to be hearing things, he decided. Had to. She couldn't have just asked him to marry her when he'd spent the last five minutes trying to figure out how and when to ask her.

To get his bearings, he retreated a step.

"It's not very flattering for you to gape at me as though I'd just hit you over the head with a two-by-four."

"Where did this come from?" Maybe he was just dreaming. But she looked real. She'd tasted real. And the thundering of his own heart wasn't the least bit dreamlike. Besides, in his dreams, he asked her. Damn it. "A woman doesn't just walk up to a man in the middle of the day and ask him to marry her."

"Why not?"

"Because…" How was he supposed to think of reasons with all those bees in his head? "Because she doesn't."

"Well, I just did." She felt her temper sizzle into her throat and managed to swallow it. Her fingers shook slightly as she lifted them to begin ticking off points. "We've been seeing each other exclusively for months. We're not children. We enjoy each other, we respect each other. It's a natural and perfectly logical progression to consider marriage."

He needed to take control back, he realized. Right here, right now. "You didn't say let's consider marriage, did you? You didn't say let's discuss it." Which had been his plan if she'd given him the chance. "There are a lot of factors here besides two people who enjoy and respect each other."

And love each other, he thought. God, he loved her. But he needed to know what they wanted for the future—

separately, together, as a family. There were things they were just going to have to set straight, once and for all.

"Of course there are," she began. "But—"

"Let's start with you. Right now, you're free to pick up your dance career anytime you want. There's nothing stopping you from going back to New York, back on stage."

"My school is stopping me. I made that decision before I met you."

"Kate, I saw you. I watched you up there, and you were a miracle. Teaching's never going to give you what that gave you."

"No, it's not. It's going to give me something else, the something else I want now. I'm not a person who makes decisions lightly, Brody. When I left the company to come back here, I knew what I was doing. What I was leaving behind, what I was moving toward. If you don't trust me to make a commitment, then stand by it, you don't know me."

"It's not a matter of trust. But I wanted to hear you say it, to me, just like that. You say you mean to stay, you mean to stay. I've never known anybody as focused on a goal as you."

He'd thought, moments before, he'd known how he would handle this. The steps he'd take toward asking her to share his life. Building on that foundation. Now the woman had finished nailing on the trim and wanted a wreath for the door.

She was going to have to back up a few steps, because he built to last. "I've got something more than a career decision to consider. I've got Jack. Everything I do or don't do involves Jack."

"Brody, I'm perfectly aware of that. You know I am."

"I know he likes you, but he's secure the way things are, and he needs to be sure of me. Kate…God, he's only ever had me. Connie, she got sick when he was only a few months old. Between doctors and the treatments and the hospitals…"

"Oh, Brody." She could imagine it too well. The panic, the upheaval. The grief.

"She couldn't really be there for him, and I was just trying to hold it all together. The world was falling apart on us, and I had nothing extra to give Jack. The first two years of his life were a nightmare."

"And you've done everything you can to give him a happy and normal life. Don't you see how much I admire that? How much I respect it?"

Flustered, he stared at her. He'd never thought of parenting as admirable. "It's what I'm supposed to do. Thinking of him first, that's how it has to be. It's not just you and me, Kate. If it were…but it's not. A change like this—a life-altering one—he has to be in on it."

"And who's saying differently?" she demanded.

"Well, damn it. I can't just go tell him I'm getting married, just like that. I need to talk to him about it, prepare him. So do you. That's the kind of thing you'd be taking on. He needs to be as sure of you as he is of me."

"For heaven's sake, O'Connell, don't you think I've taken all of that into account? You've known me for months now. You ought to be able to give me more credit."

"It's not a matter of—"

"It was Jack who asked me to marry you in the first place."

Brody stared into her flushed and furious face, then held up his hands. "I have to sit down." He backed up, dropped down on a flattened stump. Because the dog was shoving the rope into his lap, Brody tossed it. "What did you just say?"

"Am I speaking English?" she demanded. "Jack proposed to me yesterday. Apparently he doesn't have as much trouble making up his mind as his father. He asked me to marry you, both of you. And I've never had a lovelier offer. Obviously, I'm not going to get one from you."

"You would have if you'd waited a couple of days," he muttered under his breath. "So are you doing this to make Jack happy?"

"Listen up. However much I love that child, I wouldn't marry his bone-headed father unless I wanted to. He happens to think we'd all be good for each other. I happen to agree with him. But you can just sit there like a—like a bump on that log."

Not only had Kate beat him to the punch, Brody thought, his six-year-old son had crossed the finish line ahead of him. He wasn't sure if he was annoyed or delighted. "Maybe I wouldn't be if you hadn't snuck up on me with this."

"Snuck up on you? How could you not *see?* I've done everything but paint a heart on my sleeve. Why haven't I moved my things out of storage and into that apartment, Brody? An organized, practical woman like me doesn't ignore something like that unless she has no intention of ever living there."

He got to his feet. "I figured you just wanted...I don't know."

"Why have I squeezed every minute I could manage out of the last few months to spend with you, or with you and Jack? Why would I come here like this, toss away my pride and ask you to marry me? Why would I do any of those things unless I loved you? You idiot."

She whipped around and stomped off toward her car while tears of hurt and fury sparkled in her eyes.

There was a fist squeezing his heart. Brutally. "Kate, if you get in that car, I'm just going to have to drag you out again. We're not finished."

She stopped with her hand on the door. "I'm too angry to talk to you now."

"You won't have to do that much talking. Sit," he said, and gestured to the stump.

"I don't want to sit."

"Kate."

She threw up her hands, stalked over and sat. "There. Happy?"

"First, I don't intend to marry anyone just to give Jack a mother. And I don't intend to marry anyone who can't be a mother to him. Now let's put that aside and deal with you and me. I know you're mad, but don't cry."

"I wouldn't waste a single tear over you."

He pulled out his bandanna and dropped it in her lap. "Get rid of them, okay? I'm having a hard enough time."

She left his bandanna where it was and dashed tears away with her fingers.

"Okay, this is a box." He pointed at the ground. "Everything we've just said is going into this box, and I'm closing the lid. We can open it later on, but we start fresh right here and right now."

"As far as I'm concerned you can nail the lid on it and throw the entire thing into a pit."

"I was going to talk to Jack tonight," he began. "See how he felt about some changes. I figured he'd have liked the idea. I know my kid pretty well. Not as well as I assumed since he's going around proposing to my woman behind my back."

"Your woman?"

"Quiet," he said mildly. "If you'd been quiet a little while longer, we'd have started out this particular area of discussion more like this."

He moved closer, took her lifted chin in his hand. "Kate, I'm in love with you. No, you just sit there," he told her as she started to rise. "I was trying to work out how I'd do this right before you drove up."

"Before I…" She let out a long breath. "Oh." As her heart began to thud she shifted her gaze to the ground. "Is the lid on that box really tight?"

"Yeah, it's really tight."

"Okay." She had to close her eyes a moment, try to clear her head. But the thrill racing through her refused to let her think straight. And that, she decided, was perfect. Just perfect.

"Would you mind starting again?" she asked him. "With the I love you part?"

"Sure. I love you. I started sliding the first minute I saw you. Kept thinking I'd get my balance back, that you couldn't be for me. Every once in a while I'd start sliding fast, I had to pull myself back. I had lots of reasons to. I can't think of a single one of them right now, but I had them."

"I was for you, Brody. Just like you were for me."

"That night in your sister's house, I couldn't pull myself back anymore. I just dropped off the edge in love with you, I'm still staggering the next day when I see you dance. Not like I saw you that day in your school where it was pretty, and like a dream. But strong and powerful. That messed me up some again."

He crouched down in front of her. "Kate, a few minutes ago I was standing here, putting a picture in my mind. I do that sometimes. You and me, sitting on a porch swing I still have to buy."

Tears wanted to come again, but she held them back. "I like that picture."

"Me, too. See, I was figuring we were building a house—not the kind up the hill there. A kind of relationship house. I take my time building things because it's important to build them right—to build them to last."

"And I rushed you."

"Yeah, you rushed me. Something else I figured out.

Two people don't always have to move at the same pace for them to end up at the same place. The right place."

A tear escaped. "This is the right place for me." She framed his face with her hands. "I love you, Brody. I want—"

"No, you don't. I'm making the moves here." He drew her to her feet. "See that house up there on the hill?"

"Yes."

"Needs work, but it's got potential. That dog chasing his tail in the yard's just about housebroken. I've got a son who's coming home from school on a bus that's running late. He's a good boy. I want to share all that with you. And I want to come to your school sometimes, just to watch you dance. I want to make babies with you. I think I'm good with them."

"Oh, Brody."

"Quiet. I'm not finished. Come summer, I want to sit out in the garden we'll plant together. You're the only one I want to have all that with."

"Oh, God, just ask me before I fall apart and can't even answer you."

"You're pushy. I like that about you. Marry me, Kate." He touched his lips to hers. "Marry me."

She couldn't answer, could only lock her arms around him. Her heart poured into the kiss and gave him more than words. The dog began to yip and race in desperate circles around them. Clinging to Brody, Kate began to laugh.

"I'm so happy."

"I still wouldn't mind hearing you say yes."

She tipped her head back, started to speak. And the rude blast of the school bus's air brakes drowned out her words.

She turned, sliding her arm around Brody's waist and watched Jack burst out the door. The pup took a running leap into Jack's arms.

"Let me," Kate murmured. "Please. Hey, handsome."

"Hi." He looked at the tears on her cheeks and sent a worried look at his father. "Did you get hurt?"

"No, I didn't. Sometimes people cry when they're so happy everything bursts inside them. That's what I am right now. Remember what you asked me yesterday, Jack?"

He bit his lip, glanced warily at his father again. "Uh-huh."

"Well, here's the answer for both of you." With one hand still caught in Brody's, she touched Jack's cheek. "Yes."

His eyes went huge. "Really?"

"Really."

"Dad! Guess what?"

"What?"

"Kate's going to marry us. That's okay, right?"

"That's absolutely okay. Let's go home."

They left the truck and car parked where they were, and started walking toward the house together. Jack raced ahead, the dog at his heels. At the edge of the lawn, Brody stopped, turned, kissed her.

No, it wasn't okay, Kate thought.

It was perfect.

Epilogue

"Dad? How much longer?"

"Just a few minutes. Here, let me fix this thing." He hauled Jack up on a chair and straightened his fancy black tie. Fiddled with the red rosebud on his lapel. "My hands are sweaty," Brody said with a little laugh.

"Do you got cold feet? Grandpa said how sometimes guys get cold feet on their wedding day."

"No, I don't have cold feet. I love Kate. I want to marry her."

"Me, too. You get to be the groom, and I get to be the best man."

"That's it." He stepped back, surveyed his son. A six-year-old in a tux, he thought. "You sure look slick, Jacks."

"We look handsome. Grandma said so. And she

cried. Girls cry at weddings, that's what Max said. How come?"

"I don't know. Afterward, we'll find a girl and you can ask her."

He turned Jack so they could look in the mirror together. "It's a big day. Today, the three of us become a family."

"I get a mom and more grandparents and aunts and uncles and cousins and *everything.* After you kiss the bride, we get to go have a party and lots of cake. Nana said so." Kate's mother had said he could call her Nana. Jack liked saying it.

"That's right."

"Then you go on your honeymoon so you can do lots more kissing."

"That's the plan. We're going to call, Jack, and send you postcards," he added, trying not to fret about going away without his boy.

"Uh-huh, and when you come back, we'll all live together. Rod said you and Kate are going to make a baby on your honeymoon. Are you?"

Oh, boy. "Kate and I will have to talk about that."

"I can call her Mom now, can't I?"

Brody shifted his gaze back to Jack's in the mirror. "Yeah. She loves you, Jack."

"I know." Jack rolled his eyes. "That's why she's marrying us."

Brandon opened the door to see the groom and his best man grinning at each other. "You guys ready?"

"Yeah! Come on, Dad. Come on. Let's get married."

* * *

Kate stepped out of the bride's room, held out a hand to her father.

"You're so beautiful." He lifted her hand to his lips. "My baby."

"Don't make me cry again. I've just put myself back together from Mom." She brushed fussily at his lapel. "I'm so happy, Daddy. But I am *not* going to walk down the aisle with wet cheeks and red eyes."

"Frogs in your stomach?"

"I think they're doing the polka. I love you."

"I love you, Katie."

"Okay. We're okay." She heard the music, nodded. "That's our cue."

She waited, her arm tucked in her father's while her sister and her cousins who were her attendants walked down the aisle. While her little niece sprinkled rose petals on the long white runner.

Then she stepped into the doorway, in the billowing white dress and sparkling veil. All the nerves faded into sheer joy.

"Look at them, Daddy. Aren't they wonderful?"

She walked to them, feeling the music. And when her father put her hand in Brody's, it was steady and sure.

"Kate." As her father had, Brody lifted her hand to his lips. "I'll make her happy," he said to Spence, then looked into Kate's eyes. "You make me happy."

"You look pretty." Forgetting himself Jack bounced in his new shoes. His voice carried through the church. "You look really pretty. Mom."

Her heart, already full, overflowed. She bent to him, kissed his cheek. "I love you, Jack. You're mine now," she told him, then straightened, met Brody's eyes. "And so are you."

She passed her bouquet to her sister, took Jack's hand in her free one.

And married them both.

* * * * *

MILLS & BOON®

Why shop at millsandboon.co.uk?

Each year, thousands of romance readers find their perfect read at millsandboon.co.uk. That's because we're passionate about bringing you the very best romantic fiction. Here are some of the advantages of shopping at www.millsandboon.co.uk:

* **Get new books first**—you'll be able to buy your favourite books one month before they hit the shops

* **Get exclusive discounts**—you'll also be able to buy our specially created monthly collections, with up to 50% off the RRP

* **Find your favourite authors**—latest news, interviews and new releases for all your favourite authors and series on our website, plus ideas for what to try next

* **Join in**—once you've bought your favourite books, don't forget to register with us to rate, review and join in the discussions

Visit **www.millsandboon.co.uk**
for all this and more today!